Caiseal Mór was ⬛⬛⬛⬛⬛⬛⬛ storytelling and ⬛⬛⬛⬛⬛ the brass-strung ⬛⬛⬛⬛⬛⬛ tradition. He spent several ⬛⬛⬛⬛⬛⬛⬛⬛ music of the Celtic lands ⬛⬛⬛⬛⬛⬛⬛⬛⬛⬛⬛⬛, Scotland and Brittany. He ⬛⬛⬛⬛⬛⬛⬛⬛⬛ performing arts from the University of Western Sydney and has worked as an actor, a teacher and a musician.

Also By Caiseal Mór

The Watchers series:
The Meeting of the Waters

The Wanderers series:
The Circle and the Cross
The Song of the Earth
The Water of Life

The Tilecutter's Penny
Scratches in the Margin
The Moon on the Lake
Carolan's Concerto

For children:
The Harp at Midnight

the
KING
of
SLEEP

BOOK TWO OF THE WATCHERS TRILOGY

CAISEAL MÓR

EARTHLIGHT

SIMON & SCHUSTER

London • New York • Sydney • Tokyo • Singapore • Toronto • Dublin

A VIACOM COMPANY

First published in Australia by Earthlight, an imprint of
Simon & Schuster Australia Pty Limited, 2001
First published in Great Britain by Earthlight, 2003
An imprint of Simon & Schuster UK Ltd
A Viacom company

1 3 5 7 9 10 8 6 4 2

Simon & Schuster UK Ltd
Africa House
64–78 kingsway
London WC2B 6AH

www.simonsays.co.uk

Simon & Schuster ustralia
Sydney

A CIP catalogue record for this book is available from
the British Library

ISBN 0-7434-6854-6

Printed and bound in Great Britain by
Bookmarque Ltd, Croydon, Surrey

For my Guardian Angel

Acknowledgements

I am extremely grateful to several people who gave such encouragement to me to write this novel. Selwa Anthony, my literary agent, has always been a believer in these novels and the tales I write. Without here support and friendship I would never have put a word down on paper in the first place. Thank you, Selwa, for changing my life.

Julia Stiles has edited all my novels, beginning with *The Circle and the Cross*. I thank you, Julia, for your magnificent patience in dealing with my often wild rambles.

I would like to thank all at Simon & Schuster Australia, but especially Angelo Loukakis, who recognised the potential of the Watchers series and set about getting them published.

Finally I must thank all the readers who continue to write to me through e-mail and snail mail. These many letters convinced me to continue with this cycle of stories and reminded me constantly what a joy it is to share a tale with others. If you would like to write to me to share your opinions on my novels, I may be contacted through my publisher or by e-mail at *harp@caiseal.net* or by following the links from my web page. The URL is: *www.caiseal.net*

Author's Note

I n the gentle glow of firelight an old man, his hands hardened from a lifetime tilling the soil, warmed himself against the winter. His eyes brightened as I opened a bottle and found a seat opposite him. He told me no one listened to his stories these days. By the time that bottle of whiskey was gone I had heard one or two of his tales, but I'm certain he kept the best stories to himself.

Music and storytelling have been a part of my life since childhood. My grandmother was a talented tale-weaver who had a gift for meshing different stories together. Her style was to overlap her tales into one long legend that explained the origins of the Irish people. In the early 1980s I travelled to Ireland and there was privileged to meet some very fine storytellers. The legends and anecdotes I heard inspired me to record as much as possible. In my enthusiasm I filled notebooks with wise and humorous sayings I picked up, as well as the general gist of some fascinating tales.

When I returned to Australia I put the notes away and got on with earning a degree in the arts. It was ten years before I looked at those scribblings again. By that time I had a much better knowledge of folklore and the storyteller's craft.

Then, by a remarkable chance, almost as if it had happened in one of those old stories, I met a mentor who would become my literary agent: Selwa Anthony. She suggested I write a story based on some of the tales I had collected. At first I envisaged a much broader storyline which incorporated the origins of the mystical Tuatha-De-Danaan and their traditional rivals the Fir-Bolg. I even planned to end the tale in the time of the Viking incursions into Ireland.

But as I had no idea whether the first book would ever be taken up or even prove popular, I decided to focus on just one small section of the story. So it was I started the long tale in the middle with the arrival in Eirinn of Bishop Palladius, the first Roman missionary, in the fifth century after Christ. *The Circle and The Cross* was so well received I soon had an offer to complete a trilogy. By the time *The Song of the Earth* was published my first novel was already a bestseller and the last in the Wanderers series, *The Water of Life,* was in preparation.

Now I'm getting on with the rest of the story.

PROLOGUE

sword, a spade and a good story are three things that should never be allowed to rust. So hush your foolish chatter and let me have the floor so I can get my tale done with, eat some of your fine smoked meats and go home before the sun rises.

There's no sense in shuddering. I'm no ghost. I'm no dark spirit of the night. I'm made of flesh and blood just as you are. So don't get it into your head that you're any better than me or you'll taste my talons on your soft pink skin.

I may not be able to lift a pen with these claws but you'll never read a tale such as the one I'll tell. Ravens have no need for pens and ink. Our folk are blessed with clear memories, though I admit my kindred are too often selective in their recollections. I don't entirely blame them.

Your breed are untrustworthy, dishonourable and greedy. Your kind have brought woe to this world too many times in your selfish quest for wealth and power. Even the best among you are always rushing about in a frenzy of confusion.

Stupid creatures, the whole lot of you. And of all the tribes born of the sons and daughters of man, you Gaedhals are more foolish than most.

And I should know. I was yet young when your folk first made their landfall on this shore. Who would've thought the coming of your forebears would signal such terrible changes? Who could have dreamed, even in their darkest nightmare, that the Gaedhals were capable of so much evil?

They cut down the forests and turned the bogs into wastelands. They turned up the turf to fuel fireside and forge without a thought for the future. Wherever they settled, lough and stream were fished out. Wherever they wandered they left their mark on the sacred stones, the hillsides and every stretch of coast.

Your ancestors hunted out the creatures of the woodland until there wasn't a badger could leave its burrow without the taint of fear in its heart. The stag no longer ruled the mountain passes. The hare was forced to leave off journeying in daylight and nowadays they're only seen abroad at night. The great bear and the wolf were viciously pursued until not one was left alive on the whole island of Innisfail. Terrible was the bloodshed when the Gaedhals set out to battle with their own kindred, but wolf and bear suffered a worse fate. So complete was their slaughter that in time your folk forgot they had ever dwelt upon these shores.

Through all these troubles it was the Raven kind who were most affronted by the coming of your race. My people were driven to despair by your ill-mannered ancestors. No respect for anything, that's the trouble with you lot. No care for the countryside or thought for the future.

Don't shake your head as if it isn't true. I was there. I saw what the warriors did. I watched your kindred pillage the land for food. They ignored the age-old prohibitions on cutting down trees. They didn't heed the warnings about upsetting the eternal cycles of the Earth's precious bounty.

They took whatever stone they desired to build their fortresses, showing no regard for how long the rocks might have rested where they lay. And with the ancient foundations stripped away, many hillsides washed into the sea within a generation.

The Forest of the Burren, an aged stand of venerable trees, was fashioned into ships which brought more Gaedhals over from the Iberian lands. With no roots to hold down the soil, the life-giving earth simply picked up on the wind and blew away. To this day nothing grows upon the rocky plain of the Burren. The scars can still be plainly seen after a hundred generations. And no Gaedhal among you will ever be able to put it right. The dead, stony Burren is the only enduring monument your people ever left behind them.

When your fine houses, halls and harbours are no more than memory in the minds of storytellers, the wind will still wail over the grey Burren lamenting the day your kindred came to Innisfail.

Of course your teachers never taught you all this when you were children, did they? I'll wager they filled your heads full of heroic nonsense about the brave King Eber and his brother Éremon who sailed their ships across the heaving oceans and defeated the mysterious treacherous Danaan wizards in open battle.

I've heard the foolish songs your lot sing about Amergin the Bard and his fine poems. Well the truth is, his skill was nothing compared to that of any Danaan Druid or Fir-Bolg Brehon. His music was no match for any of the Old Ones.

You probably believe all that rubbish about the warrior bands of the Fian who roamed the country round, seeking out any who dared threaten the sovereignty of the Gaedhal. And how they bent the Faerie folk to their will even when faced with their powerful and frightening sorcery.

I know quite a different story to be true. And you'd better heed it well, for the wheel of the seasons has turned and now your folk in turn have come under threat from invaders. The Danaans are but a memory. The Fir-Bolg are no more than a dim legend. But the Raven kind have not disappeared. We're still watching.

So take a careful note of what I have to say. Follow my advice and perhaps the Ancient Ones will lend you a hand in these trying times. Brush off my tales as pure invention and you will pay the price for your foolishness.

But don't get it into your head that I care one jot about you, your tall stone churches or the cursed unceasing ringing of bells you all seem so fond of. I come because I was commanded to do so by my queen. I am but a representative of my kindred come to offer you my wisdom and a comfort no book can give you. I bring you peace in my storytelling. If you can learn from what I have to tell you, you will live a happy life and go to your death with gladness and never a thought of Lochlann Vikings to trouble your dreams.

I've already told you the story of the arrival of Eber and Éremon, how the Danaan Druids tried to raise a tempest against these invaders but were not strong enough, and how at last they resorted to a terrible enchantment in the hope of saving their people from slaughter.

If by some unlikely chance you've listened well, you'll know about the Quicken Brew which conferred a state of perfect health and unending life upon all who tasted it. And you'll recall the manner in which the wise sages of the Tuatha-De-Danaan opened the doorway to the Otherworld so that their people might find refuge in that place.

Now I'll bring to mind the next part of the story. So sit still and listen while the mood is on me. If you value your tongues don't ask me questions and don't interrupt. Give me your silence and I'll begin.

Two lighten the road. So I've heard tell. There was a road. I knew it well. Lengthy some folk might call it. But it was long enough for me by any measure. Even though my wings are wasted and my breath comes hard, I'm still a traveller

4

upon that wearisome path.

May the road rise to meet you, a man once said to me. I didn't understand his meaning then.

I do now.

He meant to say, follow the road. Don't concern yourself with where it's going. Don't idly daydream of your destination. You'll recognise the place you've been making for when you get there. The road will unfold itself with each dusty bend or lonely river crossing.

Be patient.

The road has many branches, some no more than well-worn tracks. But each arm of it, from the wide highway to the rambling path, is paved with joy and lined with bliss. And every cobblestone is heavy with enchantment.

This is the only thing that matters. To deny the delight of one's own private journey through life is a perilous folly. Only the wilful arrogance of a stubborn spirit dares to shun the purpose for which it was embodied on this Earth. But perhaps I am expecting too much of you to imagine you understand anything I say.

If you let the road light your soul, then you'll know the essence of trust and the absence of fear. You'll hear your inner voices, as frightening or as soothing as they might be. And you'll also learn to pay attention to muffled whispers from beyond.

This is your challenge. For what is there really to be afraid of?

Death?

Embrace it. While you live, listen with your spirit so you will be well guided on your voyage.

That's the one thing about you Gaedhals I never understood. You are fascinated with the quest for immortality, for riches and perfect health. Foolish dreaming brought you to desire such empty pleasures.

Without the hardships of life there is no learning. Without a rest from all the cares of life there can be no renewing. Without some illness there can be no true healing. Unless there is adversity, friendship is never tested and so remains forever shallow.

Value well your travelling companions, your soul friends. And don't for a moment think of squandering your time among folk you don't deeply appreciate and respect. The enticing glimmer of a soft eye on a cold night won't always warm you against the winter.

Look deeper.

I've always said the greatest test of a friendship is a long journey. That's certainly proved true for me time and again. My dearest companions were the ones with whom I shared each burden cheerfully. Pain had no power over us when we walked together side by side and shared a laugh.

So it must be true after all that two shorten the road.

Every one of us is being tested. With every breath we take, with each passing moment. There's no respite until the end. Consider my words and you'll understand my meaning.

You may think me nothing more than a bitter old bird but I have more than a thousand winters behind me. You may think I preach too much at times, but indulge me and perhaps you'll learn something.

I'll say only one more thing then I'll go on with my story.

The many paths that make up the road of which I speak can be as hard as they are enlightening. But of all these roads the best is the road taken by the willing pilgrim. Enjoy your pilgrimage while you may. There'll be time enough for resting at the end.

Savour every footstep, every mile. Seek out that which makes your heart sing. That's what you're here for. And each night before you go to sleep say a little prayer for the quiet repose of Lom-Dubh the Raven who once walked the Earth as a man.

Chapter One

No cloud showed a face in the darkening sky. The old fisherman looked up as he gathered the nets from his leather curragh at the seashore. The western horizon glowed red-gold and he knew from experience there would be no rain tomorrow.

He ventured a silent prayer to the Goddess Danu that she would see fit to gift him with a storm. Not a full-fledged tempest, just a squall with water on its fingertips to wash the land clean and entice the fish closer to shore.

He turned his attention to the handful of sea creatures he'd dragged from their watery home. His nimble fingers sorted the catch and he counted under his breath as each one fell into his basket.

The fisherman had tucked them all away for the journey back to his family when a strange scent wafted in on the faint breeze. It was not salt, nor the briny rotting seaweed that had washed up on the shore. This was something familiar yet out of place.

In the same instant he felt a soft thudding on the sand beneath his toes and he glanced over his shoulder at the rocks above. But there was no sign of anyone so he turned back to his nets.

But a sailor's instincts are impeccable. And this old man had been going to sea longer than anyone he knew. A nagging urgency tugged at his attention and he looked up again. Almost immediately he spotted a group of strangers running barefoot along the beach toward him. Their clothes were strange, their faces fierce and they all carried long silver swords.

'Gaedhals!' the fisherman gasped.

Without a thought for his own safety the old man drew a leaf-shaped bronze knife from his belt and stood up straight, waiting for the strangers to come on him. There was no doubt in his mind from their jeering laughter and yelping cries that they meant to take his precious catch.

A warrior with long golden hair flowing freely behind him sprinted out ahead of the others. He called out that he'd settle with the fisherman and his comrades could just sit back and watch.

But this old fisherman had not always farmed the sea. He'd been a warrior in his youth before he took to boats and nets. And he was a proud Fir-Bolg determined not to submit to some boastful foreigner.

The stranger ran directly at him but the fisherman dodged aside, tripped him up and slashed his knife across the warrior's face. The man cried out in agony, dropped his sword and crawled around in the sand until he found the sea water. Then he sat washing his wound while his comrades came running over.

The fisherman counted a dozen well-armed Gaedhals and knew he didn't stand a chance against them. He began to regret his hasty attack.

The warriors laughed heartily at the old man's misfortune as they swiftly surrounded him, but only one among them dared to come within reach of his knife. This Gaedhal was broadly built but no more than thirty summers old. His long brown hair was carefully combed so it looked perfectly clean, an unusual style for a warrior.

8

'Throw down your weapon,' he commanded. 'We're going to feast on your fish tonight and there's nothing you can do about it. So you might as well stand away and save yourself a beating.'

The golden-haired warrior who'd led the pack recovered himself at these words and stood up, picking up his blade in a rage. With blood streaming down his face he charged through the circle of his comrades, pushing them out of the way.

'Stay where you are, Conan,' the warrior with the brushed hair bellowed. 'I don't want it said my brother wasted his foolish life for a boatload of fishes.'

'Half a boatload,' the old man corrected him defiantly.

The warrior caught the fisherman's eye and couldn't help feeling some degree of admiration for the old man. 'Half a boatload,' he smiled.

'He's right,' a woman pleaded, grasping Conan by the shoulder. 'Listen to your elder brother.'

'Shut up, Mughain,' Conan shouted, blind with rage. 'There'll be a bitter brew in the mead barrel before I'm bested by a bloody boatman.'

But he'd no sooner bellowed these few words than the old man lunged at him with his long knife and slashed the warrior's hand. Conan dropped his sword and screamed an unintelligible phrase. Before anyone could intervene he had knocked the fisherman down with the back of his good hand. Then he brutally kicked the defenceless old man in the face and began laying into him with both fists.

By the time Mughain and the others had dragged him away the fisherman was curled up senseless in the sand.

The warrior with the finely kept hair grabbed his brother by the tunic and dragged him to the water, where he unceremoniously dumped him into the sea.

'Cool off!' he ordered. Then he turned to Mughain. 'See to the fish. My belly's empty.'

The warriors dispersed to sit on the beach and wait as the woman sorted through the basket. Just as she stood up to report there was barely half a boatful of edible seafood she was knocked off balance and sent sprawling face first in the sand.

The next thing she heard was her war-leader's voice.

'Conan! No!'

But by the time she rolled over the blond warrior had struck the fisherman in the side of the head with his sword. Such was the force of the blow that Mughain's face was spattered with the old man's blood. She had to turn away, struggling to keep down what little she had in her stomach.

She was so shocked she didn't hear the other warriors jump on Conan to disarm him. Nor did she hear the stream of abuse his brother heaped on him for the cowardly act. And she didn't notice the last strained breath of the Fir-Bolg fisherman.

It wasn't until she felt the gentle touch of a hand on her shoulder that she became aware she was lying face down in the sand with her hands over her head.

'He's mad,' the war-leader told her. 'My brother's lost all his senses.'

Mughain rolled over to look at him and he wiped the sand, tears and blood from her cheeks as she hugged him close.

'He can't help himself, Goll,' she whimpered. 'Don't punish him.'

The war-leader growled under his breath so that only she could hear. 'I can't let this sort of thing go on unchecked.'

Mughain got to her knees and held his hands in hers, silently begging his forbearance. Goll calmly pushed her away and stood up. He looked across at his brother being restrained by four of the strongest warriors in his band.

Then he gave his orders. 'Burn the boat and the body.'

'What about the fish?' someone asked bitterly.

'A brave man gave his life in defence of that catch,' the war-leader stated. 'We'll honour his memory with a feast.'

In the silent depths of the Aillwee caves, on the north coast of the Burren, Brocan, King of the Fir-Bolg of that country, lowered his torch. Then, just to experience the comforting sound of a voice in this dark world, he spoke a few quiet words to himself.

'Very well, Brocan, you've come a thousand paces now.'

The rolling confident tones immediately eased his apprehension. The mysterious winding passages of this bottomless cave seemed to resent the sound of Fir-Bolg speech, but Brocan didn't care.

'I am lord of this place now,' he asserted, challenging the cold spirits of the cave. 'I'll show my warriors there's nothing to fear down here. I'll prove to the chieftains that our people can live securely here and one day call these caves home.'

The Fir-Bolg king lifted his rush light high above his head again, then moved on. But before he had passed another thirty paces two things happened. First he felt fine sand beneath his feet where before there had only been rock. Then he realised he had run out of the tiny white pebbles he dropped to mark his passage. The path he'd laid down was his only hope of finding his way back to the cave entrance through this confusing maze.

Brocan held the rush light as still as he possibly could and peered ahead into the darkness. Before him stretched a vast cavern with a high roof. The floor was covered in the finest white sand he'd ever seen. Far off in the distance he thought he heard the gentle lapping of waves upon a shore, but he believed his ears must be playing tricks on him.

Tempted to set out across the sand, the king took a few short steps. But commonsense prevailed. He had no idea how far it was to the water, if indeed that was what he could hear. He had no more pebbles and could so easily become lost.

Disappointed, Brocan retreated into the passage which led back to the surface. When he felt hard stone under his feet again he propped the rush light into a crack in a monstrous boulder embedded in the cave wall. Then he settled down beside the massive rock to rest.

The king stretched his legs out and gently massaged his right thigh. The air was cold and damp and he felt a twinge of pain from an old battle wound. The irritation soon passed and Brocan began rummaging through his pouch for something to eat.

When he found a honey oatcake he hummed with delight. Then he unhooked the leather bottle from his belt and removed the stopper. In moments he was enjoying an underground feast and feeling much refreshed.

His mind drifted to the problems of the world above and the dilemma his daughter posed for him. A messenger had come from Eber Finn that very morning with the offer of a close alliance between his southern Gaedhals and the Fir-Bolg of the Burren. To that end the King of the South had invited Brocan and all his court to a feast at Dun Gur to celebrate the midsummer.

Brocan had sent the messenger back to his king with an expression of interest but no firm answer for the moment. He had to have time to think about the offer. And to ask himself why Eber would want to bring their peoples closer together.

'He's planning a war,' Brocan hissed, slapping his hand against his thigh for not having understood that from the outset. There could be no other reason for a war-leader to seek alliance.

12

This meant Brocan would have to make a speedy decision as to which side to take. It was obvious Eber was not arming his people against the Danaans for they no longer posed a threat to anyone. Cecht and his folk had withdrawn behind the veil of the Otherworld and rarely left the safety of their retreat. The only other enemy King Eber could have in mind was the Gaedhals of the north, ruled by Éremon, Eber's brother.

In a flash Brocan realised the habitual rivalry between the two leaders was more than brotherly sport. And it was quite likely that Éremon was planning his own excursion into the south. By all reports his warriors would easily outnumber Eber's on the battlefield.

Now Brocan was becoming concerned. If he chose to join with Eber he would likely be siding with the weaker brother. But if he chose Éremon, the northern king might prove to be a tyrant.

'Better the foeman you know than the enemy you don't,' he whispered, making up his mind to support Eber and respond with all haste to his offer of alliance.

Yet Brocan sighed heavily at the prospect of another war. His whole life had been nothing but one fight after another. Some he had managed to win easily; others had resulted in devastating casualties for friend and foe alike.

His heart was full of sadness for all the deaths he had caused, all in the name of protecting his people. He rebuked himself for having thought that battles could ever solve any dispute. So many times he could have chosen to sit down and talk with his enemies and yet he had always decided to fight.

However, he'd been war-leader and king over his kinfolk for too long to let his own sentiment mask the truth of this situation. Alliance was the only option. It would probably lead to war but that would come anyway if the Gaedhals were set on bickering among themselves. There was nothing he could do to stave it off. And his people were few, too few to stand alone.

Brocan spoke to the cold stone wall opposite him.

'The only question is what price I'll put on the lives of my people.'

Then his heart jumped as it occurred to him he was faced with a unique opportunity. The Gaedhals knew the secret of smelting iron. Their weapons, ploughs and cooking utensils were fashioned from the black metal, far superior to Fir-Bolg bronze.

That would be the price of his people's loyalty. He'd demand the mystery of iron be revealed to the craftspeople of the Fir-Bolg.

But Brocan knew Eber would demand something of equal value in return to bind the treaty. He dismissed the idea of offering cattle or horses. Livestock would not be enough. Gold and grain were likewise of little consequence in this kind of situation. Only kinship would ensure both parties kept their agreement sacred. A bond of blood would forever tie the southern Gaedhals to the Fir-Bolg and ensure King Eber didn't turn on his allies once the victory was complete.

Brocan rubbed the thick stubble at his chin as he searched for a solution. Then in a flash of inspiration the answer came to him. Eber Finn had no wife. If among the Fir-Bolg a woman of sufficient status and suitable intelligence could be found, a royal marriage might be possible. Such a bond was the only way to secure the future of his folk.

However, no eligible females came to mind. He resolved to consider the whole matter later and to ask Dalan the Brehon judge his advice. So, with a feeling that he had gone some way to solving one of the many problems pressing upon his kingship, he made a move to rise and return to the mouth of the caves.

As he was getting to his knees he noticed something

strange on the floor against the opposite wall. It was so unexpected a sight in this forsaken place that at first he didn't recognise it for what it was.

Three large flat stones lay one upon the other hard against the rock face. Brocan had noticed rocks strewn haphazardly about the passageways throughout the caves, but this neat arrangement was unusual.

Then the meaning of the arrangement hit him and his heart began to race with excitement. These stones formed a crude stairway. They must have been deliberately placed here. He struggled to his feet, his torch raised high again.

And then he saw why someone had positioned these rocks just so. High across the wall vibrant pictures of bears, boar and hunters bearing spears stretched out before his disbelieving eyes. The paintings were in brilliant hues of red and yellow, with outlines and subtle shadings in black. And all around these lifelike studies were crafted dazzling decorations so that spirals, wavy lines and dotted circles framed the scene.

Suddenly Brocan ran back to stare intensely at the white expanse of sand. When he could not make out any footprints other than his own he began to breathe more easily, but still a shudder quivered down his spine.

Ever since he was a boy he'd heard tales of the Sen Erainn, the mysterious folk who were cousins of the Fir-Bolg but who'd disavowed war for a peaceful existence in the quiet places — the forests, valleys and caves. They were reputedly very protective of their secret homes, and some stories portrayed them as extremely hostile toward any outsider who trespassed on their ground.

Brocan's grandfather had told a tale of a chance meeting with these strange folk. The old man had been but a lad himself when a stranger, a woman, came to Dun Burren seeking shelter from a wild storm. She was as small as any child of

15

nine years though her body was perfectly proportioned and covered in spiral designs pricked into her skin with blue dye. Her complexion had been dark and her eyes like black pools of still water. Brocan's grandfather said she was a Druid who had strayed away from her people. Out of kindness the woman was given a place to sleep by the fire and food to fill her belly.

The next morning when the storm cleared two fierce-looking warriors came and stood at the walls of the fortress waiting until she joined them, leaving without a word of thanks. Brocan's grandfather had called them savages though he never explained why he'd come to that conclusion.

In ancient times the Sen Erainn were kinfolk to Brocan's own people. But a bitter war broke out between the two brothers of King Ómor of the Fir-Bolg. To silence their quarrel the king gave one brother sovereignty over the islands of Arainn and to the other he granted kingship over the western coast of Innisfail.

Those folk who went to Arainn called themselves the Sen Erainn. In time their language and customs diverged from their cousins on the mainland. And after many generations they had become a story told to frighten children. Though they had been confined to Arainn the tales told how they returned to inhabit the forests and caves of the Burren. It was said they were waiting for the day when their king would seize the lands of the west for his own people again.

Believing his grandfather's story proof enough that the Sen Erainn had not stayed on the isles of Arainn, Brocan shuddered to think he may have stumbled upon one of their dwelling places. The king stopped breathing to listen more intently to the sounds within the cave. He heard nothing but the thudding of his own heart though he sensed he had no need to fear the Sen Erainn. Nevertheless, he knew it was time to leave.

So Brocan made his way back to the mouth of the cave,

glancing over his shoulder every once in a while to make sure he wasn't being followed. The rest of the time his eyes darted between the floor, where his pebbles marked the route, and the ceiling, where he searched for further paintings.

He found no more evidence of the underground artisans so he decided only to mention the paintings to a few trusted advisers. After all, he was trying to encourage a deeper exploration of the caves. He didn't want to give his warriors an excuse not to venture into the depths.

At length King Brocan emerged from the dark cavern to find Fineen the Healer waiting patiently inside the cave mouth. He was seated on a stone with his forest-green breacan cloak wrapped about his shoulders. When he heard the king's footsteps the Druid rose to greet him, bowing his head in reverence.

The king acknowledged Fineen with a sharp nod as he pushed the end of his torch into the ground to extinguish it. Then the two of them walked out together from the chill of the cave into the afternoon sunshine.

'It seems you didn't encounter any dangers in the depths,' the healer commented.

'What did you expect? A bear? Or the ghost of a bear? There haven't been any bears in that place since my great-grandsire's time.'

'Your warriors seem convinced there is some danger lurking down there.'

'If that is so,' Brocan stated confidently, 'then it stayed well clear of me while I wandered around its home. There's enough room in those chambers to house all the Fir-Bolg folk who were forced to leave their homes in Dun Burren. And there is fresh air further down as well.'

'So there must be hidden passages which help ventilate the lower chambers,' Fineen enthused. 'That's a good sign.'

'Did you send for my son?' Brocan asked.

'I sent his twin brother,' the healer stated, referring to his student, Sárán.

Brocan grunted gruffly in reply then looked to the sky. It wasn't his intention to appear abrupt or sullen but this was his way when faced with difficult dilemmas. 'They'll be back before sunset. We'd better go to the hall and await them. I want young Lom to hear your news. The more experience my son gets in these matters, the better equipped he'll be for kingship in later life.'

'Does he wish to be king?' Fineen asked.

'My grandfather was elected king,' Brocan snorted. 'And my father also. It's in Lom's blood to rule. He'll be a good king to our people one day if I teach him well.'

'But surely you will rule for many seasons yet,' the healer remarked with surprise.

'Perhaps.'

'I hope so,' Fineen said with warmth. After a pause he added, 'You know I've just returned from Dun Gur where I've spent time with Máel Máedóc, counsellor to King Eber Finn.'

'Were you commissioned to carry any message from the king?'

'No,' Fineen replied. 'But I can tell you what I saw.'

Brocan grabbed the healer's sleeve, urging him to continue.

'Eber Finn is amassing an arsenal of weapons. He's building war-carts and has a store of new swords fresh from the forge.'

'Who is he intending to fight?' the king pressed.

Fineen shrugged. 'He's been telling his folk that the Danaans are still a threat.'

Brocan touched the healer on the shoulder and bit his bottom lip. 'But we both know that's not very likely.'

'Eber knows it too, I think,' Fineen confirmed. 'Máel Máedóc fears there may be trouble brewing with King

18

Éremon, though Eber Finn has not spoken openly of any falling-out with his brother.'

'I knew it!' Brocan hissed, picking up his pace so that Fineen had to struggle to catch him. 'These bloody Gaedhals aren't happy unless they're fighting, are they?'

Near the caves of Aillwee the Fir-Bolg had constructed a temporary settlement, housing craftsmen, stone-builders, warriors and displaced Fir-Bolg in an irregular gathering of round wattle-houses and long, rectangular halls.

Fortifications were still being laid out around the cave mouth according to Brocan's instructions. Once complete these defences would be almost impossible to breach. And if necessary his people would be able to retreat into the depths of the cavern and survive a long siege. The caves in the upper levels were cold and dry, ideal for storing large quantities of food.

The destruction of Dun Burren was a dishonourable act conducted by the Gaedhals under cover of darkness. The disaster had taught Brocan a valuable lesson and he was determined his people would never fall victim to such an attack again. That was why the Aillwee caves were chosen for the new fortress.

At the first house Fergus the veteran was seated on a wooden bench by the door, waiting patiently for his king.

'All went well in the caves?' the warrior asked expectantly as he stood to greet his old friend.

'Of course it did,' Brocan snapped, handing the smouldering torch to the veteran. 'What did you expect?'

Fergus looked away. He had been as a brother to Brocan since they were both small boys and he could tell when something was troubling the king.

'Now that you have proved there's nothing to fear, the warriors will surely take to exploring deeper into the caves,' he assured Brocan.

'They've all become like frightened children,' the king spat.

'Some of them recall the fight in the Fomor forest,' Fergus reminded him with a shudder.

'Owls,' Brocan sighed in exasperation. 'We were attacked by flocks of owls. Not demons or bears or Sen Erainn.'

'Sen Erainn?' Fineen breathed.

'They're nothing more than an old tale told to children to keep them from straying at night,' Brocan dismissed, cursing himself for even mentioning them. 'What has become of everyone? Are there no stout hearts left among my kinfolk?'

The veteran saw no point in pressing the matter. 'I've had news from Rath Carriaghe,' he announced. 'I must return home to my own close kindred as soon as possible.'

'What's this?' Brocan protested. 'You know I can't build the stronghold without your help.'

'My mother is ill. She may already have passed on to the Halls of Waiting. I have a duty to visit her if I can before death takes her.'

'How long will you be gone?'

'A few days at the most. If I leave round midnight I'll have an easy walk under the stars and will reach the rath by sunrise.'

'Hurry back,' Brocan ordered. 'There is much to be done.'

'Have you no words for my mother?'

Brocan blushed, realising he had been brash and unfeeling toward his old friend in his time of sorrow. 'Give her my blessing and tell her my fondest thoughts go with her on her journey.'

Fergus nodded. He was accustomed to Brocan's manner. The veteran touched his friend on the sleeve. 'What's the matter?'

'I found something strange in the caves,' the king blurted.

The healer raised his eyebrows. Brocan had not mentioned anything to him about an unusual discovery.

The king sensed Fineen's interest and turned to include him

in the conversation. 'I didn't say anything at first because I wanted to wait until Dalan had returned to us,' he explained. 'He knows more about these things than any Druid alive.'

'Dalan will be here in a day or two,' Fineen told him. 'He has gone to the eastern hills to search for a colleague of mine who may be able to help him in his work.'

'We'll talk about this matter then,' the king sighed. 'I'm sure it can wait until we're all assembled in the one place again.'

Brocan took Fergus by the hand. 'I'm sorry I was so abrupt with you,' he offered. 'I have so much on my mind at present. My thoughts go with you. May your journey be safe. May you return to us in good health.'

Fergus nodded, accepting the apology.

'Come to my hall and take some food with me before you leave,' the king added. 'We'll open a new barrel of mead together and you'll take one of my finest bottles with you to your mother's home for the wake.'

'Thank you, my lord,' Fergus replied with a weary smile, then disappeared inside his hut.

Brocan walked away, his head down. 'I've noticed how old he is becoming,' he confided to the healer after some moments silence.

'That is the way with all mortals,' answered Fineen. 'Only three winters have passed since the Battle of Sliabh Mis, yet they have been hard times and his body is showing the strain.'

The king stopped abruptly and faced Fineen. 'You tricked me into taking the Quicken Brew,' he stated bitterly.

'I saved your life,' the healer replied in consternation. 'If I had not administered the brew you would have bled to death by that foreign arrow.

'Now I find I cannot do without a sup of it each Samhain,' Brocan signed ruefully. 'If I fail to take my annual cup I am laid up with unbearable pain until the brew passes my lips.'

'And none can say what might happen if you did not share the brew at all,' Fineen shrugged apologetically. 'But think on this; if you had died on the field of Sliabh Mis, who would have negotiated a treaty with the Gaedhals? Who would have led your kinfolk here and been able to envision a stronghold in this place?'

Brocan grunted. 'My best friend is aging fast. I don't want to see him die. I can't lead my people all alone. I need his help.'

'Then speak with him when he returns,' Fineen shrugged. 'Perhaps he will see the wisdom of taking the Quicken Brew for the good of his people.'

'I could try,' Brocan told him, 'but I doubt old Fergus would consent. His spirit is looking forward to a well-earned rest in the Halls of Waiting. I too was looking forward to the long sleep before I was forced to drink the brew. So I'll find it difficult to convince him to relinquish his soul-rest.'

'Your people need your wisdom if they are going to rise to the challenges of the future.'

Brocan looked away thoughtfully. When he spoke again there was bitter resentment in his voice. 'Long ages before the Danaans and their Quicken Brew, the Fir-Bolg held sovereignty over Innisfail. Since ancient days folk of my bloodline were the guardians of this land and its people. From generation to generation wisdom learned was passed down through the stewardship of our kings and Druids.'

He caught Fineen's eye in a wild stare that caused the healer to take a step back in surprise.

'I have earned my respite from the trials of life,' Brocan went on, barely keeping his anger in check, 'yet I have no chance of claiming any rest. My wife and queen left me for the Danaan king. My children have disappointed me at every turn. I thought to bring an end to war and fighting. I thought to bring peace and security to my kinfolk. But I have failed and I am tired. My spirit has no fire left for kingly duties.

Your Danaan potions may cure the body and ensure eternal life, but they cannot heal the maladies of the soul.'

Fineen looked down to the ground in silent acknowledgment of the truth. Brocan was calmer now, but the anguish he was suffering was still discernible.

'Fergus is going to farewell his mother,' the king went on solemnly. 'His only hope of meeting her again is in the Halls of Waiting or in the next life into which his spirit is reborn. How can I ask him to abandon the chance of ever crossing paths with her again?'

Brocan took a deep breath. 'Too many of my loved ones passed away without tasting the Quicken Brew. I have no hope of encountering their souls again. That's a bitter grief to me. And I wouldn't wish such a fate on anyone.'

'They'll be reborn into the world,' Fineen soothed. 'You'll meet them and recognise them when they appear in your life. The brew offers other gifts if you would but open your eyes and your mind to them.'

Brocan glanced at the healer in frustration. 'You haven't heard a word I've said. But one day you'll know what I'm talking about. One day you'll understand why I respect the wishes of my old friend Fergus. He has chosen to retain his mortality. I wish I had that choice.'

Then the king put a hand on Fineen's shoulder. 'I'll rule my people alone if I must, though there was never a greater burden placed on any king.'

Fineen shrugged. 'If you are determined to leave Fergus to grow old and die, then I certainly won't be able to convince you otherwise.'

'It is well that you and I will live forever,' Brocan stated coldly. 'Because it will take many seasons for me to understand what prompted you to bring me back from the brink of death. And many more before I find it in my heart to forgive you.'

'I saved your life,' the healer protested.

'It's my soul I'm concerned about.' And without another word Brocan walked off, leaving Fineen to reflect on all his king had said. And so touched was the healer by what he'd heard that it was a long while before he continued on his way.

At last, with a heavy heart, he sought out the poets' house where all Druids lodged whenever they stayed at the Aillwee. Within that hall he knew he'd find a barrel of mead. And he knew the honey brew would ease his troubled thoughts, if only for a while.

Chapter Two

I obhar the Gaedhal halted in the middle of the steep well-worn path which led to the summit of an abandoned stone hill fort. His chest heaved as he tried to catch his breath. Surely it would be no dishonour to him if he turned around now and abandoned the chase.

A hundred paces up the slope ran a young Fir-Bolg woman, a sword strapped to her back. Her shining copper hair flew wild in the wind. She was quick, sure-footed and determined. And she didn't once turn around to look back at him.

A wave of determination came over proud young Iobhar. In the next second he was hurrying up the steep incline again, eyes fixed on his quarry.

'Just wait till I catch you, my girl,' he hissed under his breath.

In moments she had climbed a rocky outcrop and disappeared completely from view. Iobhar gritted his teeth, trying to ignore the terrible aching in his legs. But before long the warrior stopped in his tracks again, overwhelmed by exhaustion. The chase had lasted all morning. His spirit was flagging. He placed a hand on the hilt of his sword to reassure himself it was still there, then wiped the sweat from his brow with the back of his hand.

The beautiful young woman was well out of reach now.

There wasn't a warrior alive who could make up the ground between them before she reached the safety of the summit.

But even as his heart was mourning her loss, something happened to inspire him to take up the pursuit once more. As the woman reappeared on the rough hillside track she slipped on the wet grass, tumbled over backwards and rolled down the hill toward him. By the time she managed to arrest her haphazard descent, she had lost at least fifty paces.

She glanced back down at her pursuer as she righted herself. Iobhar felt a rush of energy surge through his tired limbs. But the woman's face showed a mix of fear and self-reproach. That soon passed and in a flash she was up again, retracing her steps as nimbly as an anxious mountain goat.

Iobhar touched the hilt of his blade again in thankful blessing and laughed out loud. All thoughts of giving up the chase departed with the heady scent of victory. A simple turn of fortune had granted him another chance to capture this Fir-Bolg woman. And he was not going to squander that opportunity.

In the next instant the Gaedhal let out a triumphant call and his voice was spiced with mischievous delight. When the Fir-Bolg woman heard it she stopped in her tracks to face him down, holding her hands up above her head to give a show of bold defiance to this arrogant foreigner.

'Do you guess you've caught me?' she taunted. 'You're a bloody fool of a Gaedhal if that's what you're thinking. I've a wee bit of fight left in me yet and I guarantee this won't be easy for you.'

Iobhar stared up at her, roused to anger by her contemptuous tone. She was no more than a girl, yet she'd led him a fine chase all morning. And now, just as she was about to taste defeat, she was insulting him. The Gaedhal resolved to teach her a lesson in respect.

He raised his eyes to the woman again and yelled across the distance between them. 'Your feet are swift and for a while luck has run with you today. But when I lay hands on you, my girl, we'll see who's the fool.'

The woman grasped the hilt of her sword and drew it from the leather scabbard secured across her back. 'Would you battle with me, foreigner?' she challenged. 'I promise you'll not come away from the fight unscathed.'

'My people are not foreigners in this land,' he snapped back. 'We won the sovereignty of this island in open combat. This is our country now and your folk made a treaty to withdraw behind the veil of enchantment. You're trespassing in the country of Eirinn, ruled over by King Eber Finn, son of Queen Scota.'

She gave no reply. All her attention was suddenly focused on a point further down the hillside. The Gaedhal frowned as he turned to look behind him but he couldn't discern what had distracted her.

'I am Aoife, daughter of Brocan, King of the Fir-Bolg of the Burren,' she cried, Iobhar still squinting to follow her gaze. 'My father made no treaty with the Gaedhal. If you don't believe me, you can ask my brother and my betrothed. They'll be here shortly.'

All Iobhar's jubilation departed as he beheld two armed warriors sprinting over a field toward the foot of the hill. A third man followed some twenty paces or so behind them. The Gaedhal would soon be outnumbered.

He took a full draught of air into his lungs, shook the long brown wisps of hair from his face, then let out another battle cry. His voice echoed down the hillside, passing from boulder to boulder like a hurled rock bouncing down the slope.

No sooner had the call left his mouth than Iobhar took up the chase again. By the time Aoife had disappeared over the lip of the ruined walls he had gained much valuable ground. Only twenty paces lay between them.

Near a jumble of stones that had once been a stout

defensive wall, Iobhar felt his own foot slip on the grass. He fell hard on his elbows, nearly losing a grip on his blade as he did so. Then he realised how stupid he was. Aoife would likely be waiting for him to emerge at the same spot where she had clambered over the wall. It would then be a simple matter for her to strike him down. Iobhar thought a moment then decided to surprise her instead.

In the next second he was scurrying quietly around to the far side of the wall where the stones were not as high and the climb into the hill fort not quite so treacherous. His hands were cut and grazed from the strenuous pursuit up the hill; his legs ached for rest. Below were two well-armed warriors making good speed on the steep ground. Yet Iobhar knew he still had a slim chance of victory, provided he was swift about it. To tarry too long would be disastrous.

'Aoife!' one of the young warriors called out from below. 'Don't try to take him on by yourself.'

She did not reply.

Alone on the flat expanse of grass where her forefathers had constructed a great defensive work the young woman gazed steadily at the section of wall before her, awaiting the Gaedhal. The light breeze teased her red ringlets.

Aoife stilled her breath to listen but she could hear no sound of the enemy's approach. She gripped her sword in readiness for the first swing the very moment he showed his head above the stones.

Around her stood the blackened shells of ruined buildings, silent ghosts with empty eyes and lonely spirits. All this destruction had been wrought by the Gaedhals, by Eber Finn who called himself the King of the South. He and his kinfolk had brought this misfortune on her people.

Aoife felt righteous anger rise in her. And for the first time in three winters her heart desired nothing but vengeance. She cast her mind back to the night when this hill fort had been attacked and saw again the leaping flames devouring timber and thatch. It was a cowardly, skulking assault on her home. And these empty walls were testimony to the treacherous ways of the foreigners. That night had changed her life and those of all her people forever.

'You won't catch me!' she hissed at her assailant, though she still couldn't see him. 'I'd gladly die before I'd fall into the hands of a Gaedhal.'

The wind picked up and whipped at her tunic with cold fingertips. Aoife calmly raised her blade above her, set her feet firmly apart and bent her knees, ready to spring forward to the fight. She had taken no more than three breaths when a rock dislodged from its place in the wall behind her and tumbled down the hill. The young woman turned sharply just in time to see Iobhar leap over the ruined defence and stand with his blade pointed directly toward her throat.

'Throw down your weapon,' he demanded, 'and I promise you'll not be harmed.'

Aoife's answer was short, sharp and direct. The sword above her head swung down as she retreated one short pace. Her bronze blade sang as it struck the strong foreign steel. Then, with all the grace of a dancer, the young woman spun around on her heel, dragging her weapon whistling through the air.

The Gaedhal hadn't expected her to offer this much resistance. After the long chase he thought she'd be exhausted and unwilling to face him down alone.

He raised his sword instinctively to block her blow. Their weapons met with a heavy clang that echoed around the deserted hill fort.

The young woman sidestepped as she slashed her blade again at her opponent. The point of it tore at the sleeve of his saffron shirt, leaving a gaping gash in the fine linen. No blood was spilled but the young Gaedhal grasped the damaged garment as if the cut had torn into muscle.

Now red rage gripped him.

In a practised move, Iobhar pivoted on one foot and swung his sword wide. As he did so he crouched low to avoid Aoife's blade. Then, with the flat of his weapon, he slammed the young woman behind the knees. He lacked her grace but the manoeuvre was nevertheless effective.

The weight of the Gaedhal's sword shocked the breath out of Aoife. But she used the momentum of her fall to carry her out of harm's way so that by the time Iobhar had taken up the distance she was already standing at her defence again.

'That was an admirable recovery,' the Gaedhal gasped.

Her reply was another slash with her blade which caught and tore his sleeve again. Iobhar's admiration instantly turned to outrage.

'You savage!' he screamed, thrusting forward in vain with the point of his sword. Aoife easily parried the attack, pushing his blade to one side with the flat of her own weapon. But this manoeuvre brought them close enough for Iobhar to make a grab at her.

As she was stepping back to regain her balance, the young Gaedhal caught Aoife by the shoulder of her tunic. His strong hand twisted the linen around at her throat to restrict her breathing. In this position Aoife could not bring her sword to bear upon the warrior. His blade arm, however, was free, and he was able to lift the point of his weapon to her slender neck.

For several moments the two of them stood breathing hard, staring each other down as Iobhar pressed his blade into Aoife's flesh near the collarbone. Aoife stubbornly gritted her teeth but gave no sign that she would surrender.

The Gaedhal pushed harder until the sharp point made her gasp. In the next breath she dropped her sword to the ground and held up both her hands to indicate she would offer no further resistance.

Iobhar was overjoyed. He released the pressure of his weapon against her chest, though he still kept a hand on her tunic.

'Do you submit?' he panted.

'My rescuers will be here soon. How will you fight them off? They are two seasoned warriors who fought at the Battle of Sliabh Mis.'

'I fought at Sliabh Mis among the host of Gaedhals. And we were victorious. As I recall, your people fled the battlefield then came crawling back with their tails between their legs to seek a treaty. I have no fear of your people.'

'Your folk won that fight because we let you,' Aoife laughed. 'It suited our purposes.'

'I've heard of many battle tactics employed to confuse an enemy,' Iobhar chortled, 'but I've never heard of a war-leader inviting a crushing defeat in order to win what he wanted. You must think I'm stupid.'

'Aren't you?'

Iobhar grasped her tunic tighter. 'Do you submit?' he hissed.

Aoife leaned in close to his ear to reply. 'No,' she answered softly.

The word had hardly left her mouth before she managed to place her hands firmly on his shoulders. Iobhar tried to lift his blade but it was too late — a blinding agony pierced his guts as Aoife's knee connected with his groin.

He slumped down to the ground on his knees, clutching at the bruised flesh between his legs and struggling not to vomit with the intense pain. Through tear-filled eyes he saw his sword lying in the grass beside him but he was powerless to pick it up. All his thoughts were on this wrenching agony.

By the time Iobhar had recovered his senses Aoife was standing over him with her weapon point placed lightly but strategically on the nape of his neck.

'Do you submit?' she asked.

'Never,' he gasped.

'I would advise you to give yourself up,' a male voice interrupted. 'My sister is a ruthless fighter and now you have three of us to contend with.'

Iobhar rolled over. Two warriors, one with golden hair, the other with jet black, stood watching him with mirthful grins on their faces.

'Come on, lad,' the black-haired man laughed. 'It would be wise to admit defeat if only to save yourself further bruising.'

'Admit it,' Aoife teased. 'I outwitted you.'

'You cheated,' Iobhar snapped back. 'No warrior with any honour would have done what you did.'

'Did you hear that, Mahon?' the young woman laughed. 'He says I didn't play fair.'

'He shouldn't have challenged you in the first place,' the fair-haired warrior replied. 'But I have to agree with him. You don't fight honourably.' Mahon turned to Aoife's brother. 'Lom, do you remember that time she lured us into that little valley, slipped by us in the shadows and left us searching for her the rest of the afternoon?'

'It rained heavily,' Lom recalled.

'We were soaked through,' Mahon agreed.

'I caught a chill that day which I carried around for weeks,' Lom mumbled, beginning to sympathise with the Gaedhal. 'She shouldn't be playing warrior games anyway.' He turned to his sister. 'You're a Druid. Your kind is forbidden to take up the sword. What would your teacher say if he knew you were out on the Burren making sport with three warriors?'

'Dalan doesn't mind how I spend my days,' she snapped. 'He's too busy with business of his own. And in any case, I am not a very adept student of the Draoi craft. I'm more suited to the Warrior Circle.'

'Your path was decided for you,' Lom reminded her.

'Dalan was merciful to you in his judgement and you should be grateful. It's not for you or I to say what our future will be. It's time you accepted that and started making the best of your lot in life.'

With that he stepped forward, grasped Iobhar by the hand and dragged the Gaedhal to his feet. 'You should be glad there's peace between our peoples now,' Lom noted, brushing the grass from the other man's clothes. 'If a half-trained Druid girl could bring you down in a mock skirmish, I fear for your life in a real battle.'

Iobhar ran his hands over the tears in his shirt, holding the tatters between his fingers. 'This shirt was a gift from King Eber Finn,' he moaned.

'A fine gift too,' Mahon cut in. 'But if you'll accept a better one from me then I'll know you're not offended.'

'You're a hospitable man,' Iobhar conceded. 'And you're calm in a crisis. You deserve a woman with an even temper and a quiet disposition.'

'I'm level-headed!' Aoife snapped.

All three men passed knowing glances between them.

The young woman noticed their reaction and shrugged her shoulders. 'I was caught up in the excitement of the chase,' she admitted. 'The way he taunted me was infuriating.'

'Maybe you'll calm down when you're wed to Mahon,' Iobhar suggested.

Before he had a chance to regret his words the young woman dropped her sword, took two steps forward and punched the Gaedhal square in the jaw. He fell to the ground senseless.

'Aoife!' Mahon protested.

'It's time he learned to be polite. I won't have a Gaedhal insulting me.'

Mahon tenderly placed a hand on her shoulder to calm her. 'Go easy on the lad. He didn't mean to insult you. Try to remember he's a guest at your father's court. You can't go round beating visitors into submission just because they suffer a momentary lapse of good sense. I told you this wager was a stupid idea.'

Aoife grudgingly apologised. 'I hope you're not too badly hurt,' she offered. 'Don't forget you promised to teach me how to use a bow in the style of your people.'

But Iobhar didn't respond. He was utterly senseless, or at least smart enough to appear that way.

'I don't like the idea of you being given lessons in the arrows of the Gaedhal,' Mahon protested.

'I don't much care whether you like it or not. Besides, Iobhar gave me his word,' the woman insisted.

As she spoke a figure cloaked from head to foot in a dark green mantle climbed over the wall and dropped onto the grass nearby. Lom drew his sword instinctively and Mahon spun round to challenge this unexpected intruder.

Of all of them only Aoife remained calm. She had glimpsed him earlier and had guessed who this hooded stranger might be. 'Put your swords away, boys,' she gently rebuked her brother and her lover. 'Don't you recognise this fellow? He was following you all the way up the hill.'

Mahon looked at Lom with a frown, then turned back to the intruder.

'Who are you?' Lom demanded.

The stranger slowly pulled back the hooded breacan cloak from his eyes and as he did so Lom's expression transformed from concern into recognition. There before him was a man whose face was exactly the same in every detail as his own. The long black hair tied at the back of the neck was his. The smooth clear skin and the dark eyes were also his. Even the way this fellow curled his lip on one side as he grinned was the very way Lom himself smiled.

'Sárán!' Lom cried out as he ran forward to take his twin

brother in a warm embrace. 'I haven't looked on your features for two winters.'

'Except in the cold reflection of a still pool,' Sárán noted dryly.

'What are you doing here?' Aoife begged as she ran to her brother's side. 'We thought you were away in the east with your teacher, Fineen.'

'We returned this morning,' Sárán replied as he bowed politely to Mahon.

It was then he noticed the unconscious form of Iobhar sprawled out upon the grass. He raised his eyebrows at the scene before he went on. 'Father ordered I be sent out to search for you. He had a notion you might come up here to the ruins of Dun Burren to waste time play-fighting.'

'Brocan was informed that we intend to spend the night here,' Mahon cut in. 'We'll return tomorrow.'

'You are to come back to the caves with me before sunset,' Sárán announced sharply. 'You all have duties to fulfil and Fineen has brought news which concerns all the people of the Fir-Bolg.'

'Surely it can wait till first light,' Aoife protested. 'Even if we left straightaway it would be dark before we arrived home.'

'Your king, your father, has commanded it,' Sárán asserted.

'We'll come then,' Lom conceded, taking his brother by the arm to shake him affectionately. 'It does my heart good to see you again.'

'I'm glad,' Sárán answered in a restrained tone, and for the first time Aoife realised that a great distance had come between the twins since they had taken up their separate vocations. They so resembled each other physically it would be hard for most folk to tell them apart. But Sárán had developed an air of seriousness, while Lom had retained the carefree demeanour of a warrior youth.

'Let's go then,' she reluctantly agreed. 'I'm disappointed we couldn't spend a night under the stars in our old home. Iobhar was going to instruct me in the bow.'

'What about the Gaedhal?' Lom laughed, pointing at the unconscious youth.

'I suppose I'd better carry him home,' Mahon sighed. 'We can't leave the emissary of King Eber out on the hills at night. He might imagine we don't think highly of him.'

'Where would he have got that impression?' Lom asked in mock horror. 'Would it be the manner in which our sister has welcomed the poor lad to her bosom?'

'Be quiet, the both of you,' Aoife snapped, 'or you'll feel the back of my hand!'

'It's the knob of your kneecap I'm fearful of,' Mahon grunted as he carefully lifted the limp body over his shoulder.

'You did this?' Sárán sneered at his sister. 'You brought this warrior down?'

Aoife shrugged and did her best to look as if it had all been a mishap. 'We had a wager. He reckoned he could run me down before noon. I knew it would take a better man than he.'

'You're a Druid!' her brother gasped, stepping closer to look her in the eye. 'You're forbidden to engage in such sport. Does your teacher know of this?'

Aoife gritted her teeth, picked up her sword and sheathed it. 'I've already had this discussion once today,' she hissed, tired of being rebuked. 'It's time we were heading back to Aillwee.'

Her brother watched the way she handled her blade with confidence and familiarity. He could hardly believe his eyes.

'You have no right to bear such a weapon!' Sárán whispered in stunned shock. 'What has become of you? Have you strayed from the path?'

'My teacher holds no objection to me bearing arms,' she told him. 'He understands that I was born to the blade, not the Bard craft. I've never made a secret of the fact that I would be happier following the ways of the Warrior Circle.'

'Your life has been chosen for you! There's no turning back. We must pay the price for our misdeeds. Devotion to the Druid Circle will annul our sins. It is the only hope we have of washing our souls clean.'

Mahon and Lom both looked away, embarrassed by Sárán's outburst.

'Hush! That's enough,' Aoife appealed. 'I'll not talk of this with you now. This isn't the time for such things.' The young woman glanced nervously at Mahon, who had propped Iobhar beside the ruined wall that overlooked the bay.

'Have you forgiven us?' Sárán asked the blond warrior.

'I know what happened to my brother Fearna on that night long ago,' the warrior replied without turning to face Sárán. 'I'm aware that you and Aoife led him into the winter's night and abandoned him to his death. But I believe the judgement that was brought down on the pair of you was just. So I can't bear a grudge against either you or your sister.'

Sárán screwed his face up into a sneer of contempt. 'You are blinded by your love for Aoife in the same way young Fearna was.'

'That was long ago,' Aoife protested. 'I'm older and wiser. I have learned from my misdeeds.'

'My brother passed away a long time ago,' Mahon cut in. 'I miss him and I mourn for him. But nothing will bring him back to me.'

'You must have hay between your ears to follow her around the way you do,' Sárán scoffed.

'Then you'd have a barnful yourself,' Mahon replied. 'How many times has she led you into trouble?'

'How dare you speak to me like that? I'm a member of the Druid Circle! And so is my sister. If you had any respect for our standing you'd dare not utter a sound in our presence.

37

That's the trouble with you warriors. You lack any real discipline in your lives. Anyone can learn to throw a blade about. But let's hear you speak on tradition and tales of old.'

'The Druid Circle is a fine vocation for one who enjoys a life of the mind,' Aoife interrupted. 'I'm not such a one. Endless chanting, learning songs I'll never have the chance to sing before an appreciative audience. It drives me to despair. And what do I care for all those law-tracts from days gone by?'

'You are a gifted harper,' Sárán reminded her. 'Would you abandon your talent for the way of the sword?'

'A warrior is not forbidden to take up the harp for their own entertainment,' she pointed out. 'And I don't want to just sing songs about the valorous deeds of others. I want to live to hear songs sung about me.'

'No one has ever been permitted to leave the Druid Circle to take up the blade,' her brother told her flatly. 'You are wasting your time wishing for such a thing.'

'Many a seasoned fighter has left the Warrior Circle for the Draoi path,' she countered.

'That is a natural progression,' Sárán explained loftily. 'It's a sign of maturity and wisdom for a warrior to move into the Druid Circle and abandon the foolishness of fighting.'

'Let's go,' Mahon interceded, tired of their bickering. 'It'll be dark by the time we reach the caves. We can talk about this on the way.'

Sárán turned to the Danaan and his eyes narrowed to slits. 'Be silent!' he stormed. 'You are not worthy of this discussion. You are neither a Druid nor of the Fir-Bolg blood. You will not interrupt the conversation of your betters.'

'Don't rebuke Mahon!' Aoife protested angrily. 'He's done nothing to offend you!'

'He's the one who's led you to this foolish behaviour,' Sárán shot back. 'If you hadn't lost your silly heart to him you would not have fallen under his influence. I can see now your teacher has been too lenient with you. I will speak to Dalan when we return to the settlement. I'm sure he'll willingly remedy that situation.'

'Dalan's away in the east looking for some Draoi master,' Aoife jeered. 'Why don't you go off after him?'

Sárán didn't dignify this with a reply. He turned up his lip in a sneer then turned his back on his sister to climb over the wall.

'Brother,' Lom called, touching his twin on the shoulder, 'will you not wait and journey with us?'

Sárán spun around and looked his twin coldly in the eye. 'You should have been taking more care of her. She is not a child any longer who can roam the hills to her heart's desire. It may be fine for you lads to spend your days playing at mock fights, but she is a Druid in training. Druid song-makers keep the traditions of our people alive. She should be at home tending to her duties and studying the law-tracts.'

He turned his face to Aoife to make sure his words touched her.

'We are the guardians of our people's memory. We make the songs that praise or ridicule those of the Warrior Circle. It is clear which is the nobler profession.'

He turned back to his twin brother and began climbing over the wall, all the while speaking. 'You will not interfere with her education any more. Do you understand?'

Lom nodded, even though he did not understand his brother's anger. In the next instant Sárán had leapt the wall and was gone, leaving behind him an uncomfortable silence.

Mahon, Aoife and Lom stood for a while watching him make his steady way down the hill. At length his green cloak passed out of sight behind the bushes near the spring.

'We'd best be going,' Lom suggested.

'My head hurts,' Iobhar moaned as he began to regain his wits.

'Then we'd better get you home,' Mahon laughed. He hauled Iobhar to his feet and threw him over his shoulder. Then he patted the Gaedhal on the backside, swung his feet over the wall and was off down the hill.

On that same warm summer morning upon another hill top just two days journey away, a man stood with his arms raised to the heavens in praise. His clothes were of a simple dark brown cloth with a checked pattern in a lighter colour highlighting the weft and weave. His sun-bleached breeches were tightly bound with leather about the calf, and on his feet were short boots of soft doeskin.

His saffron-coloured tunic was clean and fresh. And his breacan, a long cloak that could be worn in a variety of styles depending on the weather, looked as if it had leapt off the loom onto his shoulders. The brown of the dye was fresh and bright and of the same reddish hue as a chestnut.

About his waist the dark-haired man wore a wide belt holding in place a large leather pouch under his breacan. He bore no sword nor weapon of any kind, though he had the strong body and broad shoulders of a warrior.

But this fellow had an unearthly air about him. His swiftly darting eyes were just a little too intense, his long fingernails too strong and well maintained to belong to any mortal man. Perhaps if you had met him on a midnight stroll his presence might have raised your hair on end.

When his meditations were done he cast a critical eye over the treetops of the forest that surrounded the hill. He leaned against the ruined wall of the once mighty fortress, his fingers lovingly caressing the stones.

Suddenly the wind picked up, tossing his hair about his

face and lifting the edge of his breacan cloak so that it tangled against his body. In an effort to straighten it out he turned around to face the breeze, but the wind grabbed his cloak again and whipped it up over his forehead.

In frustration the man snatched the breacan away from his eyes and at that moment the breeze dropped. A cloud passed briefly away from the sun, momentarily blinding him. He held a hand up to shade his eyes.

And then he saw her. At first she was just a dark outline in the glare. But in a few breaths the sunlight was swallowed up by a cloud again and he could make out the features of her face. The man lowered his hand and bowed politely.

'You're late,' he informed her.

'I had business to attend to,' she replied curtly.

'King Eber of the Gaedhals is his name, I've heard. And it's said he's quite taken with you.'

'Charming as ever, my dear Lochie,' the woman replied in a sarcastic tone. Then, to show she was thoroughly displeased by his remark, she abruptly changed the subject. 'Those are fine clothes you're wearing. I don't believe I've ever seen you dressed so well. Is this an attempt to impress me?'

'Isleen, my darling, I'm wearing the latest fashion. These colours are much admired among the young warriors of the Gaedhal. Surely you must have recognised the style.' A mischievous smile played across his face, then he added, 'Or perhaps you only have eyes for the king.'

'I'm not tempted to take the bait from your hook,' she shrugged. 'Now, let me have a look at you.'

Lochie held his arms out as if he were about to embrace her. Then he slowly turned around on the spot.

'Very nice,' she conceded. 'But how vain of you to take the appearance of a young warrior.'

'A younger man's body has many advantages, not the least of which is the attention it draws from lovely young women.

But you know what I'm talking about. After all, you've taken a rather exquisite form yourself.' His bright green eyes sparkled with admiration.

'This is the guise of my Seer,' she reminded him. 'You know her well enough.'

'But I haven't looked on her lovely red hair and her milk-white skin since just after the Battle of Sliabh Mis ... That was nearly three winters ago. Have you spent all your time since then with Eber of the Southern Gaedhals?'

'I am his trusted adviser,' Isleen answered proudly. 'The king makes no move or decision without consulting me.'

'There's no better place from which to rule a kingdom than the bedchamber,' Lochie laughed, 'or so I've heard tell.'

Isleen frowned deeply but she could never remain upset with Lochie for long. Her mouth curled into a little smile and her face relaxed as she echoed her old companion's laughter. Her eyes twinkled with merriment as she admitted, 'I've missed you.'

'You didn't miss me enough to seek me out and speak with me.'

'I've told you I was distracted.'

'He must be quite a man, this king of yours.'

'Do I detect a hint of jealousy in your voice?' Isleen smiled.

'No.' He turned away and gazed out over the treetops again.

'What have you been doing these last three winters?' she inquired. 'You could have sought me out. Has Lochie found himself a distracting woman?'

'I've spent all my time wandering this land from one end to the other,' he replied sharply. 'I've been waiting patiently for the right moment to bring the next part of our strategy into play. I'm a watcher of the patterns of life and do not engage in empty pursuits.' His expression was suddenly quite serious.

'What troubles you so?'

Lachie put a hand to the stubble at his chin and rubbed it with his thumb. 'The days are passing swiftly by. Time is no longer our friend as it once was. With every sunrise we squander another opportunity to regain our freedom.'

'You spend too much time out here alone,' she advised. 'There's no sense in trying to conjure up the past. The old days are gone.'

'Don't you realise what is happening to us? Aren't you concerned for the fate of your soul?'

'Of course I am,' Isleen countered.

'Have you forgotten that we made a pact together? Are you so enamoured of Eber Finn that you could cast away our only hope of salvation?'

'Is that what you think I've been doing all this while?' she seethed, insulted again. 'Do you imagine I've spent three hard winters in mortal form because I'm in love with the King of the Gaedhals?'

'What have you been doing all this time then?' he shot back.

'I've been working away slowly to win Eber's confidence. I've been leading him along the path to war. Don't you know that another conflict is building? That's what you wanted, wasn't it?'

'Yes.'

'I've convinced King Eber that I'm in love with him. And I know he's smitten with me. The first part of your strategy is in place.'

'How long before the fighting begins?' Lochie inquired.

'It's now midsummer,' Isleen replied. 'Before this moon turns a half cycle there will be blood spilled on the earth. And we'll be able to survey at least one battlefield where the dead outnumber the living.'

'You've done well,' her companion nodded, acknowledging her efforts. 'I'm sorry I rebuked you. It was unjust.'

Isleen took a step closer and placed a comforting hand on his shoulder. 'If you and I indulge ourselves in petty quarrels, we will be defeated,' she reminded him firmly. 'Whatever challenges arise, we must always stand together.'

Lochie reached up to touch the hand that rested on his shoulder. 'And there will be plenty of challenges ahead,' he nodded. 'Since the road to war is well paved, it's time for us to seek out our learned Druid and let him know the troubles we are brewing for his people. He's knowledgable in the ways of enchantment and wise enough to put his fears and prejudices aside to help us. Among the Draoi kind Dalan is the only one I would put my faith in.'

'I seem to remember he held some animosity for you when last you met at Sliabh Mis,' Isleen quipped sarcastically. 'Will this prodigy of yours aid us willingly?'

'I'm certain he will,' Lochie enthused. 'He has a compassionate heart. And he has a rare talent. He's able to listen to both sides of any argument and see the merit in each. Besides, I've convinced him of the urgency of our quest. I know he is doing his best to find an answer to our problem, though I must say he is taking longer than I'd hoped.'

'Then I think we should stir this fellow up a little,' Isleen decided. 'It's time we lit a hot hearth-fire under him. If you want to get a man moving, roast his backside, as they say.'

'It wouldn't hurt to help him acquire a burning inspiration to act on our behalf,' Lochie agreed.

'If this war goes the way I've planned there'll be plenty of good reasons for him to want us out of the way,' Isleen agreed. 'If he's as wise as you say, he'll soon realise we're behind the coming conflict. If that doesn't move him to action, nothing will.'

Lochie exhaled in satisfaction, savouring the sensation of the breath passing out through his mouth. 'We'll stir up some intrigue, a little implied threat, and add an enchantment or two where necessary. But I'll have to rid the land of a few folk who might stand in our way.'

'Do as you see fit. These people mean nothing to us.' Isleen let her hand drop away from Lochie's shoulder and stared dreamily at the far-off forest.

Lochie watched her solemnly. 'I visited our brothers and sisters a short while ago.'

'Why do you torture yourself with what might have been?' Isleen chided, her eyes never leaving the distant trees.

'Because I feel I owe it to the seven others of our kind to ease the distress of their fate,' he shot back.

'How can you be so sure they are distressed to be resting within the standing stones?'

'Would you be at peace?'

Isleen shook her head without hesitation.

'Balor turned a terrible treachery on us by his enchantment,' she confirmed. 'If he had been victorious over the Danaans and the Fir-Bolg we would have outlived our usefulness. Perhaps if he had prevailed we would have been destroyed by some other means. I can't say. All I know for certain is that the patterns of the Earth must move on.'

Lochie did not answer. He simply gazed into the distance considering her words.

'Even we who are eternal must change,' she reasoned. 'We were created through Draoi craft. Death has been taken away from us. The only alternative is sleep. Our brothers and sisters are asleep.'

'I wish I could awaken them,' he whispered.

'There's nothing we can do for the others now. They're entombed in the heart of the stones and beyond our help. If we are to save ourselves from sharing their terrible fate, we must concentrate all our energies on the next turning of the seasons. Before this coming Samhain our future will be reckoned.'

Lochie went to the edge of the hilltop and closed his eyes, reassured by her words. He stood there for a long while before he spoke again. 'I remember there was a time when I had to struggle to convince you we had any chance of steering our own fate. You seem very confident now that liberty from this bond of immortality is within our grasp.'

'I took your advice. I've kept myself busy. After all, it was world-weariness and boredom that made our brothers and sisters lose heart. And in my idle hours I've been working away on that wager we made in the days before the coming of the Gaedhals.'

'You still believe you can win that bet?' Lochie chortled, shaking his head in mockery at her confidence.

'Aoife will never marry Mahon, the son of Cecht,' she stated definitely. 'And I have so woven her fate into the means of our freedom that you will gasp at the intricacy of my plan. I will win the wager and break our bonds in one stroke.'

'Why does Aoife interest you so much? She's no more than the daughter of a king whose people are in decline. In three or four generations they will call themselves Gaedhals and have forgotten all about their heritage.'

'It amuses me to dabble in the lives of these folk,' Isleen answered with a shrug. 'I've learned that maintaining an active mind keeps me alert. It staves off the sleep of stone. And I find I enjoy exerting influence over the affairs of others.'

With a mischievous smile Isleen sauntered up to Lochie and with each pace her long cloak slipped away inch by inch from her shoulders. Beneath this garment she wore a pair of black travelling breeches and a leather tunic that accentuated the contours of her body.

'I have you to thank for inspiring me again,' she said as she laid a gentle hand upon Lochie's chest.

She searched his eyes and he returned her smile. 'I'm feeling much more like my old self. It's as if I've woken from a long, dismal dream. I've rediscovered the pleasure and the pain of mortalkind. I've nurtured the spark of passion in my soul and it has warmed my spirit. I'm sure that's what has saved me from the terrible fate of our seven companions.'

'May their souls find peace,' Lochie added solemnly.

'They are beyond our help,' she rebuked him gently. 'There is nothing we can do for them. Our duty is to ourselves. Are you willing to keep working with me toward our goal?'

'I am.'

Isleen put a hand under Lochie's chin, lifted his head and, with their eyes still locked, leaned forward to kiss him gently on the lips.

'I've grown accustomed to my mortal form,' she admitted as she stroked her fingers through his hair. 'I will be sad indeed when the time comes to abandon it forever.'

'One day our souls will soar free from the prison of our enchantment,' Lochie assured her. 'When our spirits quit this Earth and go to rest among our kindred in the Halls of Waiting, we'll have a reason to rejoice for the first time in many generations.'

Isleen closed her eyes and nodded slowly in agreement. 'I will share the quest for death with you, my friend. But for now let's enjoy these forms of flesh, the world of texture, of flavour and aroma. If we should fail and our dreams come to nothing, we'll find ourselves trapped within the cold stones alongside our companions. And if that should come to pass I will need some sweet memories to dull the edge of eternal imprisonment.'

Lochie touched her face with his fingers, stroking the soft skin of her cheek. His eyes were full of wonder as if the experience were completely new to him.

'We will not fail,' he assured her in a deep, confident tone.

Then Isleen and Lochie, the last two Watchers of the nine, locked in an embrace. And for a while put away all their cares.

Chapter Three

A finely wrought two-wheeled chariot rolled smoothly along behind the proud black mare. The warhorse neighed as she shook her head nervously. She hadn't worn a harness for nearly four cycles of the seasons. She constantly turned her noble head, striving to catch a glimpse of King Eber Finn at the reins. He had raised her from a foal and his presence reassured her greatly.

The black mare was the king's favourite warhorse. A special ship had been sent back to the homeland to fetch her once the warriors had been landed. She was a powerful animal and more than up to the task of pulling this flimsy vehicle

By the time they had nearly reached the line of trees at the far edge of the field, the mare was much more relaxed. The king decided to let her have her head to test the strength and manoeuvrability of his new vehicle.

With all the caution of a seasoned charioteer, Eber slowly let out some slack upon the right rein while pulling back gently on the left. His warhorse understood immediately the meaning of this almost imperceptible change in pressure on the bit. And she knew that if she ignored the request it could suddenly turn to cruel command.

Eber hummed with satisfaction as his chariot wheeled to the left in a great arc. In the first joyous throes of a new acquisition he laughed out loud and then began whistling through his teeth with an ear-piercing intensity. With both reins securely held in his left hand, he lifted the whip in his right. The handle of this instrument was adorned with bright red feathers taken from a bird native to the homeland of his people. In triumph he waved the whip high in the air.

Far away on the brow of a hill, three figures waited for his return. The lame blacksmith sat securely in a leather harness strapped to the back of his old friend and constant companion, the blind wheelwright and chariot maker. Beside them stood an old man with grey hair and a long beard. He was dressed in the dark blue robes of a Druid counsellor and he held a finely carved staff of honey-gold hazelwood in his thin bony hands.

None of them had the slightest notion what was on the mind of their king. To them he seemed to be enjoying himself immensely. But in truth, Eber Finn was also taking this opportunity to give expression to his frustration.

That morning he'd received a messenger from his brother Éremon, King of the North. The warrior had addressed him as Eber of the Leth Moga, the province of the servant. This was the name the northerners gave to the southern kingdom of the Gaedhals. The messenger had referred to his own king as ruler of Leth Cuinn, the province of the chieftain. The inference was clear. Éremon considered himself of a higher status than his brother. If this were not bad enough, the northern king had also demanded taxes from the people over whom Eber ruled. The king raised his whip again and the red feathers fluttered above his head.

'The king is signalling to us,' Méaraigh the blacksmith whispered into his friend Tuargain's ear. 'He's turning the chariot round with remarkable skill. Surely he's a sight to behold dressed in his scarlet tunic and his dark green cloak. There never was a king like him. Not even in the legends of the ancient days.'

'He's already surpassed his father,' the wheelwright declared. 'And Míl was certainly the greatest warrior who ever lived. Do you think the king is happy with our work?'

But Eber was too far off for the blacksmith to observe whether the king was calling out in ecstasy or bellowing in anger. Méaraigh squinted to see better but didn't answer.

'How are the wheels holding up?' Tuargain demanded to know. 'Is the king taking it easy? I warned him not to drive too fast until he has a feel for the balance of it.'

'He's driving like a fool,' the Druid answered solemnly. 'Tuargain, you shouldn't have allowed him to take it out before it was properly tested. If he should fall and break his neck there'll be trouble to pay.'

'He won't falter, Máel Máedóc,' the blacksmith cut in. 'Eber Finn is the greatest warrior alive. It would take more than a fall from a chariot to change his fortunes.'

'A small wedge cut from the oak tree can be used to split it,' the Druid answered. 'In just such a manner a man can be the cause of his own ruination.'

Even as the old counsellor spoke, both sighted men saw the vehicle kick up the dirt. Together they gasped as the chariot jumped into the air only to land again with the king still firmly standing in his place at the reins.

'What's happened?' Tuargain asked urgently. 'Has there been some mishap?'

'All's well,' Máel Máedóc reassured him. 'But I fear young Eber is taking far too many risks.'

At that the Druid bit his tongue. He knew that most of the southern Gaedhals thought very highly of their war-leader. Eber had led them at the Battle of Sliabh Mis and successfully negotiated an extremely favourable treaty with the mystical Danaans, the native inhabitants of this island. The Danaans had agreed to withdraw behind the veil of the Otherworld, leaving all their lands to the Gaedhals. Only a few of their kind had remained living in scattered pockets among the Fir-Bolg of the Burren.

But even if he had not been victorious, Eber Finn would have been well respected. He was the youngest son of King Míl and Queen Scota who had ruled their people in the lands of Iber before the tribes had elected to make a journey northwards in search of new territory.

Máel Máedóc did not wish anyone to know he had reservations about the young war-leader. Nevertheless he could not hide a frown, and his expression was full of concern. Before long the Druid realised that Méaraigh was glancing at him suspiciously, so he pulled the cowl of his breacan cloak over his face and hugged his hazelwood staff close to his body.

'It's a fine chariot,' the blacksmith told Tuargain. 'I wish you could see it. You'd be mighty proud.'

'You are my eyes as much as I am your legs,' the wheelwright reminded his friend. 'I have a clear picture of the scene in my imagination. But tell me what you see.'

As Méaraigh the blacksmith began his poetic description of the war-cart, Máel Máedóc closed his eyes and tried to shut out all that was being said. He had a difficult decision to make and these two craftsmen were distracting him from his thoughts.

The old Druid sincerely wished he had not sanctioned the building of these new chariots at the last meeting of the Council of Chieftains.

At the opening of the meeting, the gathering of advisers, counsellors and elders had expressed unprecedented gratitude to their young war-leader for his role in making a treaty with the Danaans. As a sign of their respect the council had conferred upon him a cap of bright gold to wear with honour and granted him the title of Finn, the Bright-Headed One. Then the leaders of the Fian, the warrior bands who roamed the countryside outside the protection and influence of the king, declared their allegiance to him. They named him Eber Finn of the Fianna and promised he would hold the title for life whether he remained King of the Southern Gaedhals or not.

With such an open show of support young Eber had confidently argued that to arm for war was a necessity his people could not afford to neglect. He called for the building of a fleet of war-carts and easily won over the majority of elders to his cause. They all remembered the Battle of Sliabh Mis and believed that the Danaan treaty had to be guarded with weapons that could not be challenged by a people who seemed impervious to swords and arrows.

Máel Máedóc had not stood up then to voice his concerns, having no good reason for his misgivings. It was only his intuition which led him to question the wisdom of building these chariots, for he knew no king ever equipped his warriors unless he meant them to fight.

The Druid was suddenly woken from his meditations by the sound of yelling and shouts of delight. He lifted his steely blue eyes and drew back his cowl to watch the young king put his war-cart through its paces.

Even though he suspected Eber's motives, he had to admit the king was gifted at the storyteller's art. His words at the council had stirred the chieftains, and by the last evening of the gathering they were all calling for chariots like as many dogs baying at the moon. And the king had granted their demands after a short consideration, as if he were bowing to popular acclaim.

'He's a fine charioteer,' Méaraigh observed once more, his voice full of admiration as Eber charged ecstatically around the oat field in his war-cart like a child chasing dandelion feathers on the breeze.

'He's a clever man,' Máel Máedóc countered, and the blacksmith frowned.

The Druid lifted his eyebrows so that deep ruts formed across his brow, and reminded himself to keep his opinions to himself. He knew that if he spoke out about his fears it would mean denouncing Eber to his kinfolk. And tradition dictated that the denunciation of a king must be in the form of a special poem addressed to everyone of importance in the king's household. Such a verse had to be specifically composed to ridicule the recipient. It was known as a satire.

Kings, queens and war-leaders all through the generations had been kept in check by the power of poetry. But a satire was not something to be undertaken lightly. Máel Máedóc quickly determined to try to reason with Eber just one more time.

If the king refused to see sense, then and only then would he create a satire to shake the chieftains and the elders from their complacency. Eber did not mean to use his weaponry to defend his people, he meant to use it to go to war.

'There has been too much war already,' the Druid told himself under his breath.

But his voice was loud enough for both the blacksmith and the wheelwright to hear him. The pair of them coughed uncomfortably but the Druid didn't notice. He was rattling through his mind, searching for a way out of this dilemma that would preserve King Eber's dignity and diminish the threat of war. Deep in his heart Máel Máedóc knew Eber would easily win any debate in the Council of Chieftains. The king had gained their ears with flattery and fine deeds. And there were not enough Brehon judges among the Gaedhal folk to enforce a judgement by consensus of the Great Council of Druidry. Because warriors were given priority, only a dozen trained Druids had set sail from Iber with the invasion force. Originally it had been proposed that more would set out once the new land was firmly held, but only a handful had made the journey since the treaty was agreed upon.

Máel Máedóc knew Amergin the Bard would not support any criticism of his brother Eber, and as the most learned judge in the land he had the last word on any matters brought to trial. So there was nothing to be gained by bringing any charge of unjustified war-making against Eber. It would simply be dismissed out of hand.

The old counsellor briefly considered trying to win over each chieftain in turn, but there was no time for protracted negotiations. Eber's war plans were far advanced. Twenty war-carts had been delivered. The harvest would soon be in, and the warriors would be freed from all other work.

'I would speak with our king alone,' the old man stated out loud.

'You'll have your chance in a moment,' the blacksmith replied. 'Eber Finn has turned his chariot around.'

Máel Máedóc shaded his eyes from the sun and watched as Eber brought his war-cart back to where the three men were waiting for him. The chariot jumped at every uneven patch of ground. The king whooped with excitement and drove the horse on at a reckless pace.

The Druid tried to read the expressions on the faces of the smith and the wheelwright. But it was impossible to tell whether either man had any reservations about their king. Máel Máedóc wondered how they would respond to his satire. He didn't want to make any enemies amongst the craftspeople. He would have to rely on their support if the chieftains decided to ignore him.

As these thoughts and doubts filled the Druid's head, Eber Finn drew his chariot into a tight circle. The mare frothed at the mouth, wild-eyed and sweaty. The oat field was torn in a great sweeping arc where the cart's wheels ripped into the soil. Eber Finn pulled the chariot in dangerously close to the three observers, chewing up earth, grain and stalks. Then, with a few words of encouragement to his beloved mare, he brought the vehicle to a harness-jangling halt.

The wheels had no sooner stopped turning than the king leapt out from behind the reins, gasping with the thrill of the ride. He walked a few steps on unsteady feet then turned around to admire his new possession, to marvel at its craftsmanship. And to enjoy the powerful rush of excitement that still pumped hot blood through his veins.

Eber whistled through his teeth as he imagined the effect a hundred of these war-carts would have upon an enemy. Then he turned to the wheelwright and nodded with satisfaction.

'That is the finest chariot I have ever had the good fortune to drive,' the king enthused. 'You are truly a master craftsman, Tuargain of the Skilled Hand. And I pass my compliments to those who work with you. You have some talented apprentices under your guidance.'

'Thank you, my lord,' Tuargain replied as he attempted a flattered bow, so overcome by the comment that he forgot the blacksmith was strapped into his harness and nearly lost his balance.

Méaraigh held on tight until his knuckles whitened. He narrowed his eyes and gritted his teeth. He was clearly affronted at such high praise for the chariot-maker without any mention of the ironwork that had gone into building the vehicle.

'Truly your reputation is well deserved,' the king added.

Méaraigh coughed. The veins on his thick neck stood out and his great round face began to redden with indignation. Then he reached down with one hand to move one of his withered legs in the harness. It was a simple enough gesture but in the abrupt movement there was a hint that the blacksmith was about to withdraw his labour from this project in protest.

Máel Máedóc held his breath, hoping the man would find

the strength to resist Eber. He knew such a move would be inspired by pride and nothing less. But he didn't care. Méaraigh and Tuargain were the only two people capable of constructing the war-carts. If one of them withdrew his participation, that would be an end to any threat of war.

The blacksmith drew a breath and opened his mouth to speak.

But Eber held up his hand to silence the man. He knew the value of flattery as well as he knew the damage any omission might do to his cause.

'The chariot harness is both a work of beauty and a sturdy companion I can trust. You are to be congratulated, Méaraigh. You've done a remarkable job with it. Surely you are the most renowned blacksmith in the whole island of Eirinn and unequalled among the people of the Gaedhal.'

Méaraigh bowed his head in acceptance of this praise as he rested once again on his friend's back.

'The Druids will sing songs about these war-carts, expounding on the fearsome appearance, the courage of their drivers, the skill of the makers and the swiftness of the conquest.'

'The conquest?' Máel Máedóc cut in with a gasp. 'What conquest?'

Eber Finn turned to the Druid sharply and squinted. He had rightly expected some opposition from the old man. His kind were masters of words, music and law. They rarely condoned the practice of war.

'What do you think of this chariot, Máel Máedóc?' the king demanded before the Druid could repeat his question. 'Have I not spoken the truth? Is it not magnificent?'

The old Druid smiled when he realised the trap Eber had set for him. If he spoke out against this scheme now he risked offending both Méaraigh the blacksmith and Tuargain the chariot-builder.

'I have never seen the likes of such a war-cart,' Máel

Máedóc nodded. 'Truly there will be songs sung about this first chariot and the deeds performed in it. I am certain all folk will remember the glorious battles fought in its name.'

There was something in his tone that caught the two craftsmen by surprise. Both men frowned, catching the hint of a deeper message in the Druid's words.

'In the generations to come all the people of the Gaedhal will tell the tale of King Eber's new war-cart,' Máel Máedóc went on, realising he had their full attention. 'The Bards will speak of the destruction which spread under its wheels fashioned of strong iron-bound oak. With honour they will list the enemies who fled before it on the battlefield. With respect they will recite the names of the brave fallen who perished in battles yet to come.'

The craftsmen both showed a measure of unease as they considered these words.

'There will be much joy and also weeping over this weapon, the first of many to be made,' Máel Máedóc concluded. 'And above all the folk of future generations will remember the names Tuargain and Méaraigh, the craftsmen who constructed Eber's chariot. You will be known as the two men without whom no battles could have been contemplated.'

The king turned his lips up in a strained smile. There was a hint of admiration for the old Druid's wordcraft in the gesture. But Eber wasn't about to let such a biting criticism go unchecked. The king turned slowly to his adviser and his smile deepened.

'Do you have an objection to the building of these chariots?' he demanded gently, his soft, firm voice indicating that he wouldn't tolerate dissension. 'Why didn't you speak up at the Council of Chieftains when you had the chance?'

'I had no pressing reservations at that time,' Máel Máedóc replied, mirroring the king's tone.

'And now?'

The old Druid glanced toward the two waiting craftsmen, then caught Eber's gaze. The king immediately understood his counsellor's silent suggestion that this was a matter best discussed in private.

Eber nodded. Then with smooth confidence he took Tuargain by the shoulder and put his arm about Méaraigh the blacksmith. 'You've both done very well,' he told them with a laugh. 'So I wish to gift you each with a cow chosen by my husbandman from the royal herd. You shall each have a fine healthy beast recently arrived from our homeland. They are strong animals and will bear many offspring.'

Both men hummed in appreciation and took Eber by the hand in gratitude. A cow was of immeasurable value as a source of milk, and animals from the royal herd were much prized as breeding stock. This was a gift which carried great honour that would pass down the generations with each new calf.

'Go now to the house of my husbandman. He has your beasts waiting to be delivered into your hands.'

The craftsmen thanked the king together and then Tuargain, guided by the blacksmith's keen eyes, set off for Dun Gur. They travelled with surprising speed considering one was blind and the other lame, and it wasn't long before they had disappeared around the edge of the hill on their way to the fortress.

Eber waited a few moments after the blacksmith and the wheelwright had gone, then turned with fire in his eyes to face his counsellor.

'How dare you?' the king bellowed. Then, realising his voice was too loud, he lowered it to a hoarse whisper before going on, but the anger in it had not diminished. 'What makes you think you can criticise me in front of two trusted servants?'

'Tuargain and Méaraigh are not servants indentured to you by debt,' Máel Máedóc reminded his lord. 'They are freemen and Masters of the Crafts. They owe allegiance to their trades, not to you.'

'I am King of the Southern Gaedhals!'

'You rule at the whim of the chieftains. The council may replace you as war-leader at any time if you step beyond the bounds of your office. You are not above reproach.'

'Why are you speaking out in this manner?' the king hissed.

'I cannot see the sense in arming the young warriors any further.'

'We must make ready to defend ourselves.'

'The Danaans are not preparing for war.'

'How do you know?' Eber asked, his voice wavering.

'I have spoken with Fineen the Healer,' Máel Máedóc told him. 'He is a Danaan Druid who has been instructing me in their laws.'

'You can't be certain this Fineen is telling the truth,' the king countered.

Máel Máedóc sighed. It would be a waste of breath to remind Eber that the word of a Druid could always be trusted. The king would simply reply that the word of a Danaan could never under any circumstances be relied upon. So the old counsellor decided to tackle the argument from a different direction. Exercising the mental agility for which he was renowned, he instantly changed his approach.

'The younger warriors have been behaving very badly of late,' he stated. 'A Fir-Bolg fisherman went missing on the western coast of their country a week ago. There were many footprints in the sand and his boat was found burned on the beach.'

'Who's to say it was the Fian bands who were responsible?'

'Fir-Bolg folk do not need to steal fish to feed their

families,' the counsellor pointed out. 'The Fian, on the other hand, are forced to fend for themselves. They often make do on short rations. If they were hungry enough and disgruntled enough, there's no telling what they might do. It would only take a few to influence their comrades.'

'It is a tradition among our people that the Fianna receive only token aid from their king or chieftain. Once they graduate into their inheritances and their responsibilities they are welcomed into the clan and can share the bounty of the people. How can anyone without a broad experience of the world take part in councils and the decision-making of their kinfolk?'

'That was true,' the Druid conceded. 'In the days when our folk dwelt in the lands of Iber the young warriors were sent out to fend for themselves. It meant they learned self-reliance and their youthful exuberance was directed at each other, not at their kinfolk. It was appropriate that after a period among the Fian a warrior was considered trustworthy and well trained.'

'It is essential the young warriors learn for themselves,' Eber insisted. 'It's a time-honoured tradition. Never give a sword to a man who cannot dance, is the old saying. Never grant responsibility in the clanhold to a warrior who hasn't proved they are capable of restraint. Restraint can only be learned through discipline and hardship. The value of life can only be appreciated when one has been close to death. It teaches them to value the hard work of their ancestors so they do not squander the inheritance they receive from their family. And it encourages them to pass on a healthy, secure legacy to their own children.'

'We're in a new land,' the Druid reasoned. 'They've fought a bitter war. They should be compensated for their efforts. Perhaps tradition might be relaxed to some degree in this instance.'

Eber grunted in grudging agreement. Máel Máedóc narrowed his eyes, certain his concerns were not being taken seriously. He coughed to gain the king's attention before he went on to his next piece of news.

'A band of ten Fian made a raid on a herd from a Fir-Bolg settlement some days ago. They dragged one of the poor herdsman home with them.'

'I am aware of the incident,' Eber answered sharply. 'The farmer was compensated.'

'Yet no one was punished for this breach of treaty and honour,' the Druid pressed. 'I understand there was little you could do about the fisherman's disappearance, but there were witnesses on this occasion.'

'I have spoken with the warriors who were responsible. I am convinced it was merely a case of youthful high spirits which got out of control, nothing more. We have all been guilty of that at some time in our lives.'

'It wasn't just the hot blood of youth that inspired this outrageous raid,' Máel Máedóc protested.

'Then what was it?' Eber snapped, clearly losing patience. 'What's the point you're trying to make?'

'Unrest is spreading through the ranks of the warriors like a fire through dry thatch. They must be brought to heel before they turn their frustration on their own folk.'

'Some among their ranks are restless,' Eber admitted. 'Clearly they perceive the mounting threat to our claim over this land. The warriors suspect, just as I do, that the Danaans are lulling us into a false sense of security in the hope we will relax our watchfulness. The youngest and least experienced of the Fianna can see the danger, even if the wisest of the Druids cannot.'

'The Fianna are bored,' Máel Máedóc countered flatly. 'They have had nothing to do for three winters since our victory at the Battle of Sliabh Mis. Give them work. Set them to patrolling the coasts or exploring the forests. Give purpose to their lives, for without that they have nothing. Mark my words, they will resent a king who steals their dignity by letting them roam the land looting and burning for entertainment.'

Eber dropped his eyes as he considered the counsellor's comments. For a long while he was silent and the Druid waited patiently by his side. At last Eber Finn nodded his head.

'You're right,' he admitted. 'I will assign the warriors some labour to occupy their time. Work on the chariots will be suspended for now. There's no sense in giving them new weapons if they are going to turn them on the innocent. Twenty war-carts are more than enough for my purpose.'

'Which is?'

'The defence of Dun Gur.'

'My lord,' the Druid sighed, 'I am your counsellor. It is my duty to advise you on all matters. It's your obligation to share your concerns with me. Kings have relied on Druid knowledge in this manner since our people first called themselves Gaedhals. But I can't help you in your work if you don't tell me of your worries.'

For a moment Eber considered telling the old counsellor all that had happened in the last few days. He would have been happy to unburden his soul and share the threats Éremon had sent with his messenger. War, his brother had warned, would be the result of Eber's failure to pay a tribute to the Kingdom of the North.

But the king could not bring himself to trust the old Druid. As wise and as respected as he was, Máel Máedóc was a compatriot of Amergin. They were contemporaries and often consulted one another. Amergin had decided to take Éremon's part in this disagreement. So Eber dared not trust his own counsellor.

'I have told everything there is to tell,' the king declared, but his tone was not convincing. 'I promise I'll keep you informed of any developments with the Danaans.'

Although Máel Máedóc suspected Eber was not being entirely truthful, the old man did not want to be rushed into presenting his satire. So for the moment he was content to accept what Eber told him.

'I have another matter I wish to discuss with you, my lord,' the Druid went on, neatly changing the subject.

'What's that?' Eber frowned.

'The level of the lough around Dun Gur is falling daily. Within a single turning of the moon there may be no water left in it all.'

'How do you account for this?' the king asked with a frown.

'There has been no rain for two moon cycles,' Máel Máedóc explained. 'The Danaan Druids say this has been known to happen before, though rarely.'

'Is it the result of their sorcery?'

Máel Máedóc looked deep into the king's eyes. He was a little surprised at the question. 'I would simply put it down to nature running its course,' the old Druid replied. 'The learned Danaans say it is a sure sign of a hard winter ahead. In any case the lough has never completely drained. The Danaan Druids say —'

'I am sick to the stomach of all this talk of the Danaan Druids!' Eber cried, interrupting the old man. 'If I hear them mentioned again, I won't be held responsible for the measure of my rage.'

The king turned his whole body in open confrontation with the counsellor. 'Can't you do anything about the falling level of the lough?' he mocked. 'I thought your kind were masters of the subtle arts.'

Máel Máedóc let no emotion show on his face; instead he

carefully concealed his disgust at this blatant show of disrespect. 'I have no learning in such matters,' he replied, carefully controlling his voice.

Eber laughed. 'It's difficult for me to take you seriously sometimes, old man,' the king spat. 'You were an adviser to my father so I have always had a certain respect for you. But perhaps it's time you considered stepping aside to allow a younger man to take up your duties. It seems you've begun to lose your good judgement. Why haven't you set about seeking a solution to this problem?'

Máel Máedóc took a deep breath, determined not to be roused by the young king's provocative manner. 'Don't break a shin on a stool that's not in your way,' he advised. 'I thought it my duty to inform you of the problem first.'

'Must I deal personally with every little trouble that besets our folk?' Eber countered. 'If you can't cope with the responsibilities of your office, I suggest you step aside before the Council of Chieftains replaces you. I wouldn't wish to see you suffer any such dishonour, but I fear you're not the man you once were.'

The old counsellor closed his eyes. He now had no choice but to act quickly if he was to have a chance of halting Eber Finn's plans. 'I am not quite ready for retirement,' he answered.

'You're an old man. You've served your people well in the past. But you're becoming a liability. I will speak with the council and we'll decide on your replacement as soon as possible.'

'There is none who could take my place. There are no Druids younger than myself among the people of the south.'

'Then send a message to my brother Amergin to ask his advice.' Eber waved his hand to signal the discussion was ended.

The Druid took two paces back, his eyes to the ground as

a mark of respect to his king. He was relieved the audience was over and was eager to find himself a quiet corner where he could begin to compose his satire.

With a sharp turn on his heel, Máel Máedóc spun around and hurried away. But he had not gone more than five steps when the king shouted out to him.

'If you interfere with the duties of my kingship, you had better have good reason. I am the duly elected war-leader of my people. And I am carrying out legitimate and justifiable preparations to defend our homes and pastures. No Brehon judge would question my right to take this action.'

Máel Máedóc faced the king again. 'Take care you don't misuse the authority granted by the Council of Chieftains.'

Eber pretended he didn't hear the warning as he strode off toward his chariot. He patted his mare on the nose, leapt into the cart and in moments was charging off over the fields, whistling and whooping as he had earlier.

The old Druid sighed heavily and the first line of his satire came clearly to his mind.

'I saw a child playing at being a warrior,' he whispered to himself. 'In the field he trampled down the oat stalks, leaving a terrible trail of their dead and wounded in his wake.'

Chapter Four

Ollamh Dalan mac Math, Brehon judge and nominee for the office of High Druid, leaned against the oak tree and coughed. As he rested he gathered the long, finely matted locks of his dark brown hair that were falling about his face and tied them together at the back of his head.

Then he stared down toward the bubbling spring at the bottom of the little valley while he caught his breath. As he did so he again thought about whether he should accept the acclamation of his peers and take up the highest appointment a Druid could aspire to — Dagda. Many of his friends had pledged their support. More had expressed their confidence in his judgement and experience. But Dalan was not sure if he was ready for such a commitment. He had other, more pressing matters to attend to before he chose the future path of his vocation.

In the three winters since the Battle of Sliabh Mis he'd tracked down every scrap of knowledge, every whispered rumour, every tradition, song, poem and legend of the Watchers. And yet he seemed no closer to his goal.

After the battle he'd lost track of the Watchers entirely, though he'd heard they'd appeared in the north and were occasionally spotted at the court of King Eber. He hadn't made any attempts to follow them — to travel such distances just to speak with them would have availed him nothing.

The Watchers were unpredictable, dangerous, ruthless and vengeful. They wielded an ancient, powerful enchantment yet were imprisoned by that same spell. They were a force to be feared and Dalan was as determined as ever to rid the world of them, though he was still at a loss to know how this was to be done.

These three winters past he'd been trudging the country-side in search of all those Druid folk who had preserved tiny snippets of the Watchers' legend. Many knew the same stories, but once in a while he came across someone who knew more.

And that's how he came to be here on a narrow muddy path which led deep into a shaded forest. If Fineen the Healer was right, the Druid woman who made this glen her home held the final pieces of the mystery that had plagued him for so long.

With nimble fingers the Brehon rubbed his calf muscles. He'd been walking all day and his feet were rubbed raw in places from the wear of his new boots. It would take many more journeys before the leather softened. Once his massage had soothed the soreness Dalan put his pack on the ground and listened carefully to the sounds of the woods. He heard the cries of many birds in the distance and the wind rushing through the leafy trees. Then his attention was drawn to the relentless voice of the water as it joyfully erupted from the dark earth into the sunlight at the spring.

An unexpected noise caught his attention so he cocked his head to one side like a fox listening for the hunter. Then his jaw dropped open in surprise and his hands stopped rubbing his calf muscles.

Dalan was certain he could hear a song on the air. The words were foreign to him but the voice was haunting. He strained to capture every note that came to him on the breeze.

And it was a delightful tune that serenaded his senses. The kind of melody that has you tapping your toes in time one second and stomping your feet the next.

The light-hearted song reminded Dalan of a warm sunny morning after a cold rainy night. The Brehon couldn't help grinning broadly in appreciation and twitching his fingers to the beat. The smile spread across his face as his head began to nod in time with the music.

This was like no tune he had ever heard. One moment the melody was dancing over flower-strewn fields. The next it was full of passion that threatened to engulf the listener in a flooding torrent of rising emotion.

The Druid felt his heart begin to race as his imagination invented countermelodies and harmonies. His eyes closed briefly but he knew this was not a dream vision that would become clearer if he shut the rest of the world out. A bird fluttered out of a tree nearby, distracting him from his reverie. In the next breath he sensed a large black shadow pass by at the furthest edge of his vision. He turned swiftly to catch sight of it before it disappeared into the cover of the woods.

But he was too late. The bird had gone.

A cold chill passed over Dalan. The shape he'd glimpsed seemed much bigger than any bird he'd ever seen. He shook his head to clear his senses. Then he realised he couldn't hear the tuneful song any more.

'You bloody fool!' he berated himself. 'You should know better than to let down your guard in the forest. Who knows what spirits inhabit this place.'

His mind was full of memories of a night three summers earlier when he, Aoife and Mahon had fought off an attack from a horde of Otherworldly owls in the great woods to the south.

The memory made him very uneasy. With a long harper's fingernail he drew a quick gesture of banishment in the air directly in front of his face. Then he shouldered his pack and gathered up his black Druid cloak of Raven feathers so it would not drag along in the mud. For once he was glad not to be lugging a heavy leather instrument case around with him on his travels. This was one journey he was unlikely to be needing a harp.

Dalan sniffed the air and listened once more but he couldn't sense any challenge or hostility. Hoping the inhabitants of this forest would tolerate his presence, he set off to follow the path which led down to the spring.

It was not far to the bottom of the little glen but with such sore feet Dalan thought he'd never reach the pond which formed around the bubbling waters. But soon enough he stood by the boiling trickle of water that spilled over the rocks through a narrow crevice. When he had offered up a silent little prayer of thanks, he turned around to listen again. A long while passed before he cupped his hands to his mouth and called out a cautious greeting.

There was no answer save an echo from the rocks above and the murmuring of the spring as it filled the pool beneath it. There was no hint of a melody in its voice now, just a monotonous gurgling without any disciplined rhythm.

'Where is she?' the Brehon muttered to himself in frustration as he sat down on a flat stone at the edge of the pond.

In a few moments he'd pulled off his boots and was soaking his feet in the cool swirling flood. Soothed by the spring water he inwardly called down a heartfelt blessing on this place as cool healing ripples swirled about his ankles.

The day had been unusually hot. There had been no rain nor hint of it since the dark of the last moon. Dalan frowned deeply as he realised the silver orb of night had almost returned to the dark part of its cycle again.

He searched the skies but there were only a few white puffs of cloud on the horizon and no sign of relief for the land. The reading of the weather was not his special skill. He only knew a few little tricks to tell whether the next day would be wet or rainless. The sky in the west was shaded pink as the sun came closer to crossing the horizon. Dalan understood that meant the following day would be dry. He sighed deeply, resigned to the fact that there was nothing he could do about it. Then he slipped the cloak off his shoulders and lay down among the feathers to wait and rest by the pool.

Since the woman he was seeking was nowhere to be seen he decided to take advantage of this precious time alone. It wasn't often he was given a chance to relax completely.

He glanced at the rocks surrounding the pool. There was a bundle of dry twigs nearby and a stack of split timber. Fineen had told him that the Druid woman came back here at sunset every evening to perform her devotions. If that was true it would be only a short while before she arrived.

The water round his legs was so refreshing, tranquil and lulling he soon forgot about the strange song he'd heard earlier, or any thoughts of danger. His body was aching with exhaustion. His clothes stank of sweat.

The Brehon untied the thin leather strap that held his tightly matted locks in place at the back of his neck. Then he scooped up two handfuls of water and threw them over his head. The locks fell about his face and he gently squeezed them until the water oozed out, carrying the dust of the road with it.

This style of hair was reserved for the most ascetic among the Druid kind. Each strand was twisted about into locks almost as thick as a harper's little finger. Dalan had decided to take on this style until he solved the puzzle of the Watchers, but only he knew the secret vow he'd made to himself. He would cut his hair on the day he freed them from their bonds and released them from this world. After three winters his hair was already shoulder length and had earned him the respect and awe of his fellow Druids.

He lay back on the cushion his locks provided for him. As Dalan the Brehon closed his eyes he didn't give another thought to the black shadow that had crossed his path. Nor did he think to keep his wits about him and stay on guard lest the spirits of the forest assail him. He was suddenly exhausted and all he desired was rest. His only thought was that this was the most beautiful, restful place on the whole island of Innisfail. His feet dangled listlessly in the pool. His eyelids grew heavy and the Brehon nodded off to sleep.

After a long while in the water Dalan's toes got cold. So he lifted his legs up onto the Raven feather cloak and lapsed into a deeper state of relaxation.

Perhaps he should have been more careful. Perhaps it would have served him better to have stayed awake, at the ready for any sign of trouble. But even Druids and Brehons of great learning are capable of foolish mistakes.

The unintelligible muttering of the spring water dancing over the rocks put all care from the Brehon and he could feel himself gradually slipping into a dream trance.

Once in a while his conscious mind struggled to rally itself into readiness again. But there was a blackness that engulfed his senses. He had no fight left in him. His body was too weary from the journey. His spirit was free to drift up toward the treetops.

Just as his heart settled into a slow, steady, sleepy rhythm, Dalan crossed the mysterious threshold into trance. His spirit was free of the flesh and a bright strange world opened to his imagination. The next thing the Brehon knew he was wandering down roads at once familiar and frightening. And with every step he swore to himself he would not travel unprepared to this place again.

Led by nagging curiosity and wonder that his exhaustion had dropped away, he moved on through the Otherworldly landscape. In dreams such as this, time runs differently. Seasons may seem to pass in the span it takes the dreamer to draw a single breath.

At length Dalan's meandering soul came to the summit of a little rounded hill and there on the other side was an astounding sight. Before him was the most amazing and unusual tree he'd ever seen, either in this world or the other. The wonder of it snatched his breath away. A gorgeous green luminescence lit the air all about its branches, creating a thin, shimmering cloak of dull light. All the grass about its feet lay bathed in this enticing glow.

Dalan sensed a strong spirit in the tree, an old wise soul sharply aware of everything and surely mindful of his incursion into its sanctuary.

As the Brehon moved cautiously closer to the bottom of the hill his eyes widened in awe at what was revealed to him. The trunk of this tree was enormous, larger than anything he could have imagined. The whole surface was covered in a thick, scaly brown skin.

Dalan walked around it, counting out his paces as he went. He put his foot down at fifty and shook his head in disbelief. He'd never known a tree to grow so large.

In the next second he found his attention entirely captured by the elegant shape of the leaves, the little red fruit and the white flowers. The whole tree gently moved in time with the fluttering breeze.

The Brehon frowned when he realised he couldn't name the tree. He would have said this was a rowan but it was too high and wide. Its branches twisted about in a contorted shape he had never seen before in that species.

With a trembling hand Dalan reached out, plucked a flower and held it to his face to feel the softness of the petals against his skin. He smelled the scent of rowan stronger than he could ever recall. Then he took a berry between his fingers and, with great reverence for the wonder contained within, broke it open with his fingernails. Inside was hidden a star shape with six points. This was confirmation enough for him.

'Rowan,' Dalan declared.

'Indeed it is a rowan,' a woman replied, and the Brehon wasn't in the least startled to hear another voice.

He turned his head in a slow, dreamy movement to look for her. But all he saw, all that filled his field of vision, were two dark, wet enticing eyes beckoning to him.

Dalan felt the stirring of a passion deep within his being. A craving came over him such as he hadn't felt since he was a younger man. And for all his learning, for all his mastery of the poet's art and the musician's craft, he could find no word to describe this sensation.

The woman's smile was immediately comforting. Her face recalled to him all the folk he truly loved in this life. Her hand beckoned him closer with a gentle, calming gesture. The Brehon took a step toward the woman. The shadows began to lengthen, heralding the approach of night. And above in the darkening sky a bright star shone out.

The first star. The Evening Star. She who watches over all on Earth.

'Who are you?' Dalan asked, his mouth dry with anticipation.

The woman laughed. It wasn't a mocking sound but one of mirthful, childlike teasing. And there was such an innocence and purity in it that the Brehon could not help but join her chorus of joy.

So together they stood laughing with each other long after tears had filled the Brehon's eyes. In those moments Dalan could have believed all the cares of the world had dropped away from his spirit. He forgot fear. His consciousness was filled with only light, warmth and hope for the future. Nothing else mattered but the delight which overwhelmed his senses.

When the laughter passed, Dalan's heart still thumped cheerfully in his breast. His skin tingled with pleasure. The subtle green glow around the tree intensified, demanding the Brehon take notice of it. But he could look only on the form of the most beautiful woman he had ever met.

Her long, dark green cloak flowed over her body like the water running over the rocks from the spring into the pool. Her hair was as white as her skin, contrasting sharply with the deep dark blue wells of her eyes.

Dalan frowned as he struggled to recognise her. He was certain he had met her many times in this fantastic vision-world. But he had unaccustomed difficulty recalling her name.

'Curse my feeble memory,' he muttered to himself.

She smiled at him as if she were indulging a little child who was trying to learn a new skill. 'You have no need of recollections here,' she told him in a voice that was like a sweet humming sigh. 'We are beyond the realm of thoughts, actions and deeds. Don't be surprised if some things you hold in your memory refuse to come to mind.'

Dalan grunted. His forehead wrinkled as he listened to her familiar tones.

'I am Cuimhne,' she told him. 'I brought you once to the Stones of the Watchers.'

'The Watchers?' Dalan repeated in a daze of confused concern. 'Are they here?'

'No.'

'Then why have you brought me to this place?'

'You came of your own free will. No one summoned you. No one expected you. I've been sent to watch over you while you are here and to see to your wellbeing.'

The mention of the Watchers reminded Dalan that he had a duty to perform. They were the reason he had travelled to this spring in the forest.

'I'd like to return to where my body lies resting,' the Brehon told her. 'There's someone I should meet there. Can you show me the way?'

Cuimhne nodded and took Dalan by the hand. Her strong reassuring presence enveloped him in love and care and he was overwhelmed with gratitude. Suddenly he was a child again and this woman was a doting parent.

'Do not fear,' she whispered. 'I am with you.'

Then together they rose up in the air like steam rising from a bubbling cauldron. To Dalan's delight they flew straight up into the sky and soon he was looking down on the magnificent rowan tree. It was no less awesome from high above.

In less time than it takes to draw ten breaths they covered the vast distance Dalan had walked in his dream state. On the way they passed high mountains, sweeping valleys edged with more strange trees, and far-off silvery rivers. Below them they could see stone settlements and drifting herds of cattle grazing contentedly in the fields.

At length Cuimhne led the Brehon back down through the treetops toward the Earth. Dalan clearly observed his own body far below, lying upon his black cloak of Raven feathers by the pond.

'You mustn't travel to the dream land lightly,' Cuimhne warned him as she set him down. 'You must learn to know when is the best time for such a journey and when it is safer to stay at home. The Faidh is a terrible gift when it can't be reined in.'

But Dalan wasn't listening. He remembered he had a question for her. 'You told me the story of the Watchers once,' he began urgently.

'I did.'

'But you didn't tell me how I should rid the land of their evil.'

Cuimhne laughed and hovered closer. 'They're not evil!' she cried in amusement. 'They're the Watchers.'

'But you warned me they were dangerous!'

'So they are,' Cuimhne nodded, suddenly serious. 'But they will not take matters into their own hands unless the situation is desperate. Their power derives from the evil they inspire in others. They have certain skills of enchantment which they use to great effect but the most perilous art they practise is that of persuasion. Through the use of subtle argument they spread havoc among their enemies.'

'And are they still abroad in the land?'

'Of course they are. The one who should be chasing them down is sleeping by the side of a pool. They won't be captured while he dallies and indulges himself in the Faidh.'

Dalan looked to the ground in shame. 'I have not been able to discover a way to deal with the Watchers,' he admitted.

'Then you had better commence a wider search for the answer to your riddle. It's no use wasting the hours with fruitless rest. There'll be time enough for that later. One day you will be free to sleep your life away, but not until you find a way to deal with the Watchers. If you falter, great changes will come upon this land and Innisfail may go the same way as the Islands of the West.'

'Where will I find the answers I seek?'

'Ask the right person and they will be able to tell you,' she chided. 'How will you ever find anything out if you don't ask the right questions?'

As she finished speaking she began to float slowly skyward out of his sight. The Brehon watched, still awe-struck by her beauty. Her cloak was no more than a tiny dot of green high above when a thought struck him.

'Do you know what can be done about the Watchers?'

But Cuimhne was already beyond his hearing. His voice fell empty back to Earth.

Just then the Brehon heard a noise nearby that startled him. It was the spitting crackle of a fire. All around him was an orange glow, and on the rocky outcrop which jutted out above the spring there was a dark shape he had not noticed before.

A stranger.

In a rushing dizzying spin Dalan felt his spirit drawn back into his body. In another moment his lungs filled with air and he sat bolt upright on his cloak of feathers. The heavy sensation which accompanied his return to his cold body sobered him a little.

For a moment the Brehon was bewildered but then he was on his knees, head jutted forward, eyes squinted down to tiny slits in their effort to focus. Despite the darkness Dalan was certain he saw the dark shape move slightly.

'Who's there?' he ventured cautiously.

His voice echoed back to him as before but there was no reply. The figure edged into the shadows. Dalan listened for any sound that might identify this stranger but the constant trickle of the spring frustrated him. He couldn't hear anything but its senseless babble.

The Brehon leaned forward, straining all his senses. He asked himself why anyone would hide themselves in such a manner. The only answer he could think of did not reassure him.

All the while the stranger sat above and across from him on the rock Dalan could feel eyes staring back down at him. He felt his hair shiver on end with fear and he shuddered.

'Am I still in the dream state?' he asked himself aloud.

Suddenly the stranger leaned forward into the light so that he could see her face. Dalan recognised the young woman instantly. Her skin was no longer pale and the wisps of hair

that framed her dark eyes were changed to jet black. But he
would have recognised her features anywhere.

'Cuimhne?' he stuttered. 'Is that you?'

The woman raised an eyebrow. Then she leaned
against her staff and with a gentle grace used it to help herself
stand up.

'I am called Sorcha,' she told him once she was on her
feet. 'This is my spring. You must be Dalan. I've been
expecting you.'

Goll mac Morna, chief warrior of the southern Gaedhals and
leader of the Fianna, sat on the green windswept ridge and
looked out toward the rounded hilltop a thousand paces
away. Wattle and mud walls surrounded the summit and the
circular houses clustered closely together. The style of building clearly marked this as a Fir-Bolg settlement.

Seven small huts lay within the walls atop the man-made
hill which bulged out of the surrounding fields like a half-
buried river stone. The Fir-Bolg word for these isolated little
communities was rath.

With quiet excitement Goll surveyed the far-off hill,
determined to discover the purpose each building served. He
decided there were four main households, each with their
own low round cottage. That left three buildings, any of
which could be a grain store or a shelter for the cattle. Cows
were cared for well by the Fir-Bolg. Often their shelters were
as fine as the houses meant for the tribespeople.

As he watched for signs of life Goll reached out through
the swaying grasses until his fingers touched the rough
surface of his fine leather shield. It was a wondrous piece of
workmanship and his constant companion. He caressed the

black, hardened hide, silently invoking the spirit of the bull that had provided it.

Then his hand moved on to search out another friend who lay nearby. When his fingers felt a cold smooth flat surface, the warrior felt greatly reassured. He sighed as he gently stroked the long polished steel sword which lay in the grass naked, free of its sheath.

This blade had hung from his waist for nine summers and served three generations of his family. No blacksmith made such swords any more. It was hefty, pitted and capable of cutting through a heavy bale of hay with three strokes. The younger warriors wouldn't touch such a weapon. The wielding of it required great skill and constant practice. Only the older Fian bothered to turn their discipline to this style of blade.

Goll, son of Morna, pronounced his own name to himself under his breath, then he added the new titles he had just been granted by his war-leader Eber. The honours still sounded strange to his ears.

Fer-Gniae, Aire-Échta. Gearbha Sliabh Mis.

King's Champion, Lord of Slaughter and Guardian of the Mountain of Mis.

His fingers searched for a piece of dried beef in the pouch at his belt. When the warrior found a narrow slice of it he put it in his mouth and chewed slowly, considering what these accolades might mean under the surface.

The salty flavour of the leathery meat burned his tastebuds. He was tired of winter rations. Dried beef and travellers' biscuits were all the king would give to the roving bands of Fian who patrolled the kingdom. A warrior's lot was not always a comfortable one.

This meat was lean and easily stored. It was light and took up only a little space in a fighter's pack. Well-salted beef was filling, nourishing and if boiled up with some wild onions and herbs made a hearty broth. But, in time, such a monotonous diet left the bowels loosened and the warrior craving the food of a farmer.

Smoke seeped through the thatches on the houses in the rath. Goll knew there was food cooking at each hearth. He imagined the honeyed oatcakes, herbs, butter, cheeses and vegetables placed around the fire in their pots or laid out ready to be eaten.

'It'd suit me to have a fine hot meal right now,' Goll grumbled to himself.

He spat out the fibrous residue of dry beef, lay back on the soft grass and stared into the blue afternoon sky. This season marked the thirtieth summer since Goll had been born into the world. By the standards of some he was as yet inexperienced, but the younger warriors in his band thought of him as a battle-hardened veteran. They looked up to him as teacher, mentor and guardian brother.

Goll laughed half-heartedly to himself. He often felt he was just an old man in a youthful body. His spirit was tired of fighting, of training for war, of playing out the strategies of the battlefield until they came to him as easily as his own name. Yet what else was he to do?

War, as his father had always said, was the only honourable pursuit for a strong youth lacking a talent for poetry. The Druids taught through their stories that each person must accept their place in the world. The duty of every able-bodied soul was to live out a life full of passion for the talents they had been gifted with at birth.

'I was granted the skills of a warrior,' he said aloud, as if to reassure himself that he was following the right path. 'So I must make war or live without purpose, passion and satisfaction.'

The King of the Southern Gaedhals had bestowed on him a great honour in these pretty titles, he reasoned. It was his obligation to live up to the accolades. Yet Goll mac Morna still could not entirely understand how he had earned such praise. Suspicion turned his lip into a sneer of distrust as he considered Eber's motives in bestowing such flattery.

Goll flicked his long brown hair from his face, then tied it back with a strip of fine leather cord. When that was done he searched in the pouch attached to his belt until he found a small drinking flask. Soon every corner of his mouth was tingling with warming honey-brewed mead. He swallowed the measure and, satisfied for the moment, carefully replaced the stopper in the top of the bottle.

Goll shook his head to clear his thoughts. He could not see the worth of a king's champion when there was no fighting to be done. There wasn't any work for a hardened warrior like himself now the conquest of the country was complete. Peace was no comfort to him. And yet he was tired of fighting.

He reached down to caress his sword again, touching it as tenderly as he might a lover. This sword was made for one purpose only — killing.

The warrior-champion turned away from the weapon and his eyes fell on the magnificent shield which, like the sword, his father had also once carried. This thick round shield was an awe-inspiring piece of leather craftsmanship. According to his father it had taken three seasons for the master shieldmaker to create this marvel.

In the first season the cowhide was soaked in water steeped with oak bark. In the second season the cleaned skin was hammered into shape upon a wooden mould-board carved with ridges and runnels. The leather was pounded day after day until every contour was perfectly formed. In the third season the shield was carefully dried in a house specially constructed for the purpose. By the end of the process it was a toughened board of sturdy workmanship that would withstand the blow of any weapon. It would not split under a sharpened blade nor crack from the thrust of a spear point. And Goll knew that as long as he kept the shield well rubbed with beeswax it would never let him down in a fight.

Then a realisation came to him like the sun peeping from behind a cloud to light a path for him.

He must try to be more like his sword and his shield. He would not weaken. He would do his duty as a warrior.

The champion sat forward again and scanned the lands around the Fir-Bolg settlement for any sign of life. A few farmers were out in the fields preparing to harvest their barley.

Further off toward the river some laughing women were driving their cows to fresh pasture. They were followed by a group of noisy playful children. Goll counted the cattle. There were twelve cows, a healthy number for so small a community. Elsewhere he noticed goats and long-horned sheep. A leather curragh was leaning up against the outer wall of the settlement. Clearly these people had fisherfolk among them.

Just then Goll's attention was drawn to two men who appeared from behind a hill. They were carrying a curragh triumphantly above their heads. And they had their catch hanging between them. Goll's mouth watered at the thought of all that fresh fish baking by the fires in the warm houses. The fishermen put the curragh down by one house then went into a smaller building, which Goll guessed was their smoke house.

The warrior squinted as he tried to discern which building was the grain store. In the end he made a guess, then lay back down among the grasses to stare at the sky once more.

As his mind drifted off with the clouds Goll wondered what it would have been like to have been born into a farming family. His father, Morna the Fighter, was a legendary warrior in his day and a companion of old King Míl, father of Eber Finn.

If life had given him other chances, he told himself, he might have been content to work hard for his food and live among folk whose only care was for their children, their cattle and the coming winter. Perhaps instead of swordplay and spearcraft he might have learned to fish with a net.

Just then, Goll mac Morna heard the muffled whisper of his name not far away. The sound plucked him swiftly from his daydream.

'I'm over here!' he answered gruffly, not bothering to lower his voice. The Fir-Bolg were a long way off. They weren't going to hear him.

A woman dressed in warrior clothes of brown deerskin ran toward the champion in a crouch, trying to remain as close to the ground as possible. Her black hair was knotted in long, winding, unwashed tresses which were gathered behind her head and fell lankly over her left shoulder. Her tunic was belted close about her waist, her breeches weather-worn and tight-fitting underneath. A short sword in a red leather scabbard hung at her side and a plain breacan cloak was wrapped up under her arm. She moved with all the steady discipline of a warrior, her right hand ever ready to draw a blade for battle.

Goll mac Morna looked up at her with impatience, annoyed at being disturbed. But before he could reprimand her the young woman drew her sword so she would be able to stretch out beside him on the hillside. Then she rolled down into the grass and slid closer. Without taking her eyes off the rath for a second she spoke lowly to make her report.

'There is a Fir-Bolg warrior travelling in this direction from the coast.'

'He is alone?' Goll demanded, raising his eyebrows in interest.

'Yes.'

The king's champion laughed. 'Just a travelling messenger.'

83

He turned his head. 'Mughain,' he began, speaking slowly so she would catch the tone of a teacher in his voice, 'we are twenty. Twenty Fian of the King of the Southern Gaedhals. One Fir-Bolg with his brittle bronze axe is no challenge to us. In any case he's likely only a messenger. Let him pass.'

'The Fir-Bolg have the force of enchantment on their side,' the warrior woman countered nervously.

'Who says so?'

'Your brother was just speaking of it when we saw the Fir-Bolg warrior,' Mughain stuttered, a little taken aback at being challenged.

'Conan has become too familiar with the ale cup,' the champion snapped. 'His imagination has been given too much freedom of late.'

'It isn't his imagination, nor ale that makes him speak so. Everyone's talking about the magic powers of the dark people.'

'My brother missed his calling,' Goll replied sharply. 'The field where he nurtures his idle thoughts is a fertile one. Perhaps Conan should have been a storyteller or a Bard. His aspirations to the warrior path were certainly misguided. I'm certain I could call the spirit of a certain old fisherman to attest to that fact.'

'Your brother might be misguided and at times a little confused, but I and many of the Fian believe he may be right. He is so much like you many respects. Perhaps that's why you shun him.'

Goll rolled his eyes dismissively. 'You're as mad as he is. I should have punished him more severely for the death of that fisherman. He hasn't been the same since Sliabh Mis.'

'I was also at the Battle of Sliabh Mis,' the young woman answered defensively. 'I saw the wounded heroes of the Danaan rise up from where they had fallen. And they were healed of all their injuries by the time they stood on their feet again.'

'The Danaans are a different matter,' Goll conceded. 'The

Fir-Bolg have no such enchantment skills. Have you forgotten our first fight with them? You were with me in the raiding party that burned Dun Burren, the home of the King of the Fir-Bolg.'

The king's champion turned his head to look her in the eyes before he went on. 'Their houses smoulder and their cattle may be raided the same as any other people. Their grain can be taken and their smoked fish make a fine feast. Fir-Bolg mead is the best I've ever tasted, and I'll wager their children make hard-working slaves.'

'Slaves?'

Goll caught the surprise in the woman's voice but he was expecting it. 'In my father's day raiders came from the hot countries over the sea and made incursions on the lands of Iber. Any captives taken in battle were treated as a source of indentured labour. With hard work and loyal service these captives could earn their freedom and were allowed to return to their own kindred.'

He noticed the young warrior woman frowning but he continued to present his argument with a calm firmness. 'The punishment for taking up arms against the tribes of the Gaedhal has always been to pay a fine. It doesn't matter whether the penalty is paid in cattle, gold or, for those who have no wealth, in service. The warrior class are entitled to claim the best of these hostages because we risk our lives each day in the defence of all our kindred.'

'Have you forgotten that a treaty was agreed with the Fir-Bolg and the Danaan?' Mughain gasped.

'That agreement was not presented to the warriors for their approval. Our losses on the battlefield were not recompensed. Eber Finn overlooked the debt he owes us when he negotiated his treaty with the enemy.'

Mughain was clearly dismayed. It was an affront to tradition to talk of a king being indebted to the Fianna.

85

Goll mac Morna leaned over and grabbed Mughain's sleeve lightly, dragging her close to him. Then he looked his trembling comrade fiercely in the eye.

'Remember all our friends who fell at Sliabh Mis?' he hissed. 'Did any of them rise from the battlefield healed of their wounds?' He didn't give her a chance to reply. 'No, they did not. They're seated now in the Halls of Waiting with their ancestors. They died to secure this island as a new homeland for our people. Did they die in vain? Will you defile their memory by accepting the dishonourable treaty of Dun Gur?'

'Eber Finn gave his word as our king,' the woman replied with a deep frown of concern. 'He's our war-leader. We must abide by his decisions and respect his wisdom.'

'Do you think Eber ever really intended to keep his word?'

Mughain pulled away and Goll did not try to stop her. He let go his hold on her tunic, rested on one elbow and spoke sternly.

'There is no room in this land for Fir-Bolg and Gaedhal to live together unless the Fir-Bolg submit to the will of our leadership. Let them offer tribute to Eber Finn and dwell under the protection of our warriors. Let them abide by our laws and our customs. Why should we be dictated to by their Brehon Druids? Have we not enough good judges among our own kindred?'

Mughain didn't answer.

'Eber's treaty sealed our conquest,' Goll nodded. 'But what king would trade the traditions of his people for peace? What value the victory if our people cannot govern themselves by their own long-established laws?'

'The Danaans gave us Dun Gur in settlement of the treaty,' she countered. 'And they've offered us the wisdom of the Druids since so few of our own folk tread the sacred path. In return our king has pledged peace. Unless the Fir-Bolg or the Danaan break faith with us, we must abide by Eber's commitment.'

'They'll break it. There's nothing more certain. It's only a matter of when and how. So we must strike first to let them know who holds this island now.'

The young woman glared sharply at the champion as the true meaning of his speech dawned on her. 'Have you brought us here to make war on that rath?' she demanded, pointing in the direction of the Fir-Bolg settlement.

Goll nodded. 'We are warriors. It's what we were born to do.'

'Does this action have the sanction of King Eber?'

'The king knows nothing of my intentions,' Goll admitted. 'Nor should he. If he had any inkling of my plans, his integrity could be called into question later. And he will need to appear honourable when the time comes to settle this whole question once and for all. Even the Druid judges of the Gaedhal would find against him if they thought he had a hand in this.'

'There is peace between our peoples,' Mughain protested. 'You have no sanction from the chieftains or the king to breach it.'

'I am the leader of the Fian bands. The methods I employ to train my warriors are my own affair. It has been three summers since any among us lifted a sword in battle. That is far too long. The older fighters are becoming complacent. The younger ones are itching for a scrap. If we don't focus our aggression on a common target, we risk the disintegration of the Fianna into a splintered, ineffectual rabble.'

The warrior lay back and looked at the sky again. 'Aren't you becoming tired of eating dried beef for every meal?'

'It's the food of a warrior.'

'Only in midwinter when there is no game!' he cried. 'At any other time it's fit only for the elderly and the infirm. It's not good enough for men and women who risk their lives for the protection of their clans.'

'Why are we not permitted to hunt for game?' the warrior woman asked.

'The treaty forbids all hunting except in the immediate vicinity of Dun Gur.'

Mughain looked to the ground as she spoke.

'The nearby forests are empty of game,' she noted, 'and have been since last winter.'

'Something must be done,' Goll urged. 'The warriors will not silently bear their burdens much longer. Their stomachs rumble in the night for want of a decent meal. How long before that rumbling becomes an outcry?'

'Have you spoken with the king about the unrest among the Fianna?'

Goll gave a mocking laugh. 'Eber is still full of himself after the victory of Sliabh Mis.'

'We mustn't do anything that might bring dishonour on our people,' Mughain offered cautiously.

'Would you like to see our people end up fighting amongst themselves?' Goll snapped back. 'Do you think the Danaans and the Fir-Bolg would have any scruples about making war against us if they perceived the slightest weakness in our ranks?'

The warrior woman leaned back on her elbow but her eyes did not stray from the king's champion for a moment. It was true enough that the other fighters in their band had turned to complaining about their lot in life. As if to add weight to Goll's assertions, her stomach growled loudly.

Mughain had to admit she was less than happy. Several times in the last week she had dreamt she was basting a fine roast pig on the spit. She and her comrades ate poorly and slept in the open countryside while the king feasted each night on the finest of meats safe in the fortress of Dun Gur.

'You may be right,' the young warrior woman agreed at last.

'I know I'm right,' the champion told her as he reached into his pouch for a piece of dried beef.

Goll pulled out the strip of meat and offered it to Mughain. The woman winced a little when she realised what it was, but she took it to stave off her hunger. A small section came away in her teeth and she handed what was left back to the champion. He popped it in his mouth, chewed for a few moments and then went on to issue his orders.

'We will attack four hours after dawn, just after the fishermen go out. No Fir-Bolg lives are to be taken. We've come to raid cattle, grain and fish to feed our warriors. No innocent people are to be harmed in any manner. They are to be treated with respect.'

'Is it not some measure of disrespect to be stealing their cattle?' Mughain shot back.

Goll chose to ignore this comment.

'We won't be taking slaves. I don't see any sense in stirring up too much trouble. Our grievance isn't with these poor farming folk. Our message is for Eber Finn and the Fir-Bolg king.'

Goll looked down as he deftly wove a little ring of green from a few grass stalks he'd picked. When he'd finished he reached out to Mughain and gently stroked her forearm.

'Tell the others there'll be no fires tonight. They can make do with dried beef for one more meal. There is to be no talking, no noise whatsoever. I want every man and woman to rest well. And only two sentries will guard the camp. I doubt the Fir-Bolg even suspect there are Fian in the hills, so we need not keep too close a watch.'

Mughain acknowledged the orders with a nod.

'Let Conan know he is free to leave my company if he won't stand by me,' Goll concluded.

The young woman opened her mouth to protest, but before she could make a sound Goll reached out to her again.

He looked into her eyes, put a finger lightly to her lips and hushed her. Then, in the next instant, he slipped the little ring of grass into her hand.

'When you've passed the word around I want you to come back to me,' the champion whispered. 'It's a fine day and I have other sport on my mind than the taking of cattle.'

Mughain was a little taken aback but she slipped the ring over one of her fingers. Goll's smile widened and suddenly all her doubts deserted her. She was completely disarmed by his mischievous and flattering way. With a laugh the young woman slapped the back of his wrist playfully. Then she held her hand up before her eyes to admire the ring.

'And what makes you think I'd want to play at your sport?' she teased.

Goll shrugged, looked down at the ground and for a moment seemed to her like an awkward little boy. She had to remind herself that he was only thirty summers old. He always seemed to have an air of wisdom about him, such as his father had possessed.

An unexpected yearning gripped Mughain's heart, an urgent desire such as she hadn't experienced in a long while. It was the hunger for excitement. The thrilling rush which always coursed through her body before a battle. It was a knife-edge trepidation that aroused her most deep-rooted instincts.

'Eber Finn was never much of a warrior,' she remarked dismissively.

'Indeed he has no stomach for the rigorous training it takes to become a Fian fighter,' Goll agreed.

'Have you ever thought of making a bid for the kingship yourself?'

The champion allowed no expression to show on his face. The thought had indeed occurred to him on more than one occasion, but no one had ever suggested it openly to him before. Suddenly what had once seemed a wild dream appeared possible merely because someone else had given voice to it.

'Go now and do as I bid you,' he said softly, barely controlling a tremor of excitement.

'I'll be back soon enough,' she breathed.

Without another word Mughain was off to find the rest of the warrior band. In her haste she left her own sword lying in the grass beside Goll's. He noticed it immediately but did not call after her. She wouldn't need her weapon till the morning.

As soon as the young woman was gone the king's champion spat out a mouthful of leathery salt beef. Then he rolled over again onto his back.

He plucked another blade of grass and held the long stem of it in his teeth to drive off the salty taste of the meat.

'King Goll mac Morna, War-Leader of the Southern Gaedhals,' he whispered. 'That's a title I understand.'

Then he closed his eyes in the warm sunlight to rest a little before Mughain returned.

Chapter Five

Dalan wasted no time climbing across to the rock where the Druid woman called Sorcha was waiting for him. A rough staircase had been cut into the side of the boulder, allowing for a good foothold.

'I'll come down to you,' Sorcha called to him. 'Just wait at the foot of the rock until I've finished packing my things.'

'Don't worry,' Dalan replied. 'I'll be up in a minute to give you some help.'

Sorcha said nothing more until the Brehon had reached the top. Just before he stepped onto the flat rock platform she held up the palm of her hand.

'You must come no further!' she warned. 'This place is only for those who have been initiated into its secrets.'

Dalan frowned in confusion but made no attempt to come closer. 'I am a member of the inner circle of the Druid Assembly,' he informed her. 'I have the personal sanction of the Dagda himself to visit all the holy places in the land. You have no authority to stop me.'

'This is a sacred precinct. You must not enter.'

Sorcha took two steps forward and the Brehon noticed she was standing in the centre of a perfect circle of countless red-topped mushrooms. Each one had a sprinkling of white about the crown.

'Redcaps!' Dalan gasped. 'I've never seen so many growing in summer.'

He could hardly believe his eyes. There were many stories circulating the college of Druids about the followers of the redcaps, but few folk ever took the tales seriously. Yet there was little doubt about it. This Druid woman must have been engaged in venerating the tiny mushrooms.

It was at that point Dalan noticed there were flames leaping from a strange copper cauldron in the centre of the ring. Then he realised the air had turned chill and he had left his cloak down by the pool.

But Dalan's curiosity was aroused so he easily shrugged off the cold. He'd never seen a sight like this before. Here was a cooking fire built within the walls of a cauldron instead of around the vessel. As a scholar of ritual he knew that to reverse the purpose of such an everyday item was a potent symbol, one that might be considered unethical by many learned Druids. There could be only one purpose to such a ritual — the conjuring of powerful spirits from the Otherworld.

Dalan shook himself to drive away a nagging intuition that he was in danger.

'Why were you seated in the centre of this circle?' he inquired, choosing his words carefully.

Sorcha stood absolutely motionless. No sound passed her lips. Her dark brown breacan cloak obscured her shape and the hood now covered her head completely. There seemed to be no form to her at all. But Dalan noticed her hand move to her belt.

'Is that a knife you have there?' he stuttered, stunned at the possibility that he might be threatened by one of his own kind. All the most disturbing stories he had heard about this notorious cult of the redcaps were coming to mind. Some folk said these renegade Druids soaked the ground in blood to feed their sacred mushrooms and imbue them with their deep red hue.

Sorcha threw back her cloak to reveal a hand firmly placed upon the handle of a long bronze half-moon sickle which was thrust through her belt. 'Don't come any closer,' she warned. 'Until you can give me some proof of who you are.'

The Brehon frowned. 'I thought you recognised me from Fineen's description. I am called Dalan. I'm a Brehon judge.'

'How do I know you're telling the truth?'

'I'm a Druid. I'm sworn to truth.'

'But if you are merely posing as a Druid, the truth would not be important to you.'

'What are you taking about? Who on the whole island of Innisfail would want to impersonate me? And to what end?'

'The real Dalan has dangerous interests,' Sorcha noted. 'I wouldn't want to upset the folk he's chasing.'

Suddenly he began to understand her concern. 'You mean the Watchers?' he asked.

'Do I?'

Dalan thought now that she was wise to be so careful. 'How can I prove to you that I am who I say I am?'

'That's your problem.'

'I have my cloak,' he offered.

'What cloak?'

'It's made of Raven feathers. No one else has one like it. I'm famous for it.'

'I've never heard anyone mention that Dalan owned a Raven-feather cloak,' she replied with suspicion in her voice.

'I'll show it to you,' he told her. 'Just wait here while I fetch it.'

In the next breath he'd disappeared back down the side of the rock. He jumped to the ground and ran to the pool to grab his cloak. In a flash he was clambering back up the rock face.

'Here it is,' he told Sorcha and wrapped the beautiful black garment around his shoulders.

'It suits you well,' she observed dryly. 'But it doesn't in any measure establish your identity.' She stepped closer to the edge of the circle of mushrooms to have a closer look. 'It's a very fine cloak. I've never seen anything like it. Where did you get it?'

'Cuimhne gave it to me,' he replied.

'You've met Cuimhne?'

'She's been my guide in the spirit world since before the Battle of Sliabh Mis. I've travelled with her many times.'

'Then I will trust you,' Sorcha declared. 'I also have journeyed with Cuimhne. Though he chose to present himself to me as a man.'

'But the Cuimhne I know looks almost exactly like you!' the Brehon protested.

'Then I believe you truly are Dalan the Brehon,' she sighed with relief. 'For when I met with Cuimhne he took a form which closely resembled you. He must have known we would need to recognise one another.'

Sorcha's hand dropped away from the sickle at her belt and she bowed her head. 'Forgive me,' she whispered. 'I hope I didn't cause any offence to your rank and experience.'

'There's nothing to forgive,' the Brehon assured her. 'It was right for you to be so careful. These are dangerous times. But tell me, how did you know I was coming to visit you?'

'I am a practitioner of the Frith. I learned that you were involved with the Watchers and sent word to Fineen the Healer asking him to track you down. He is well known to you, I believe.'

'Indeed he is.'

Dalan raised an eyebrow, impressed at this woman's vocation. He could name barely a dozen Druids such as himself for whom the gift of future-seeing came unbidden. In this form the Sight was known as Faidh. But he knew of only a few who had mastered the craft of Frith. It took a brave and confident soul to summon such visions at will.

The method of summoning visions varied from one practitioner to the next. Some would partake of a medicinal concoction. Others would chant or dance their way into a trance state and there experience the world of the Frith.

The most common method in former days had been the eating of the mushrooms specially prepared so that they did no harm to the body. But this practice had been largely abandoned as it took great discipline and self-awareness to ply the craft of Frith this way. Misjudge the amount or the lateness of the season and the result could be death or madness.

'Well, Fineen passed this way with his apprentice Sárán before the onset of winter. The healer told me of your suspicions about the Watchers and Sárán told the tale of his experience with Isleen.'

'The poor foolish boy was led on by her,' Dalan nodded. 'He was very fortunate to come away from the experience unscathed.'

'You're certain this Isleen was a Watcher?'

'Absolutely.'

'I told Fineen the part of their tale I know. He said you would be excited by what I had to say. So I had an inkling you'd seek me out at the first opportunity.'

Dalan frowned, still a little unsure whether this meeting was merely a strange extension of his dream. Try as he might he could only see the face of his spirit guide, Cuimhne. In fact, now that Sorcha was closer, the resemblance was even more disturbing.

She drew the hood of her breacan cloak away from her head and Dalan was surprised to see that she was growing her hair in the same fashion as he'd adopted. Her hair was matted in thin, tangled masses of brown that were longer and much more unruly than his own.

'Why did you choose to wear the Druid-locks?' he asked.

'I'm awaiting advancement,' she replied. 'My teacher suggested I abandon my attachment to outward appearances. I will cut my hair when my instruction is completed.'

She paused, obviously feeling more comfortable in Dalan's presence. 'And why do you wear the matted hair?'

'I have told no one else of this, but I vowed not to cut my hair until I had solved the mystery of the Watchers,' he told her. 'Do you live in the forest?'

A broad smile lightened Sorcha's face. 'Of course.'

'How long have you lived here by the spring?' he ventured, intrigued by her solitary lifestyle.

'I don't live here,' she replied, stifling a giggle as if the idea were ridiculous. 'I have a house on the other side of the hill. It is my duty to light the morning and evening fires at this spring and pay homage to the sun.'

'You keep the Ritual of the Sun?' Dalan asked.

'I do.'

'Few practise that rite in these times. And fewer still dare to cultivate the mushrooms.'

'Few understand the true meaning behind much of what I do,' she countered defensively. 'Many among the learned Druid Assembly look on the Ritual of the Sun as archaic nonsense beneath their dignity. Some among the wise believe this rite involves the drawing of blood from sacrificial victims. And others only see it as a practice which does no harm but does not bring any good either.'

Dalan avoided her eyes.

'Which are you?' she asked him.

The Brehon coughed uncomfortably. 'I long ago decided not to take sides in such matters,' he replied diplomatically. 'I believe each person has the right to their own beliefs and to the veneration of their own gods and goddesses. I only asked because I've never seen the rite performed, nor met a Druid who really knew anything about it.'

Sorcha laughed again. 'You've known plenty of Druids who practise the Ritual of the Sun, they just didn't reveal their knowledge to you. The rite is very ancient. It harks back to the Empire of the West in the days long before the destruction of the Blessed Isles.'

'Why wouldn't my colleagues tell me if they were involved in such a rite? What have they to be afraid of?'

'There were those among the Druid Assembly in the ancient days who used their wisdom poorly,' Sorcha explained. 'According to tradition a dozen dissenters deserted their kinfolk to make alliance with Balor of the Evil Eye, he who brought the Watchers into being. From these treacherous Druids Balor learned the Ritual of the Sun. He instituted it among his own folk so he could invoke the elements to perform his enchantments.'

'So that was the source of Balor's strength!' Dalan exclaimed, beginning to see the whole tale in a new light. 'He used this ritual to create the terrible weapon known as the Evil Eye. I've often wondered where he learned his craft.'

'He gained it from the twelve Fir-Bolg Druids who offered him their knowledge,' the woman explained. 'And when the Druid Assembly learned what these renegades had done, they outlawed them. The twelve were banished beyond the help or hearth of all their kindred forever more. And the Ritual of the Sun was discarded by our people.'

'Discarded?'

'The Ritual of the Sun opens the mind of the celebrant to the wonders of creation,' Sorcha explained. 'Through the deep meditative trance one enters when conducting the Ritual one may glimpse the unity of all things. Some among the wise call this awareness Oneness. Once a practitioner understands they are merely part of everything that exists, it is possible to exert some influence over the world about them.'

'I was taught the principle of Oneness when I was an apprentice Druid,' Dalan noted. 'Yet I don't have the ability to alter my surroundings at will.'

'Knowing it in your head is one thing.'

She tapped her forehead with a finger then moved it down to point at her heart.

'But experiencing it with every fibre of your being is another matter altogether. Stories may explain the world but experience is the only teacher worth listening to.'

'So the Evil Eye of Balor was created this way?' the Brehon asked.

'Balor was not very adept. He created a crude enchantment which burned his enemies to ash with his gaze. If he had truly understood the force of the Ritual he would not have used such a clumsy method of defeating his foes.'

'You were performing the rite when I arrived?'

Sorcha nodded.

'Do you have this ability? Can you change the world about you to your will?'

'And what would be the sense in that?'

Dalan frowned when he realised she hadn't answered his question. But he thought it best not to press her on this point.

'I don't recall learning that it was forbidden to perform the ritual,' the Brehon commented.

'It was outlawed on pain of banishment.'

'Yet it's merely frowned upon now,' Dalan asserted. 'Times have changed. The assembly is more tolerant nowadays.'

'The redcaps are another matter though,' Sorcha added quickly.

The Brehon cast an uneasy eye over the circle. 'There are those among the College of Druids who would condemn you for this practice,' he agreed.

'Only because they are afraid of it,' Sorcha countered. 'Yet in truth there are many who keep this ritual.'

'Many?'

'Oh yes, but those among us who have the knowledge prefer to keep it to ourselves,' the young woman confided. 'We all fear the same fate as those twelve Druids of old.'

'You seem to know a lot of tales I've never heard,' the Brehon observed. 'What became of those dissenting Fir-Bolg?'

Sorcha raised her eyebrows, surprised at the question. 'I thought you would have understood that by now,' she told him. 'I was under the impression you had researched this story thoroughly.'

Dalan frowned deeply and searched her eyes for an answer. It was clear he had no idea what she meant. So Sorcha explained it to him.

'The twelve who deserted their kindred were adopted by the Fomor at the insistence of Balor. They lived among those people, married and passed on their knowledge, and when Balor asked their help they gave it willingly. He had become like a father to them. So when he needed nine skilled Druids for a task that would bring down a terrible fate on the Fir-Bolg and the Danaans, he knew he could rely on their support.'

'Who were these traitors?' Dalan whispered, for he had begun to draw a terrible conclusion and he was half afraid Sorcha would confirm it.

'The three who remained were initiates of the Ritual of the Sun. They helped heal the Fomor of the many maladies which afflicted their race. Until this time they were a misshapen people who hated every beautiful thing on Earth. Their ability to manipulate the realm of the material world ensured their acceptance among the Fomorians. These three were also given stewardship over the Evil Eye.'

'And what of the nine whom Balor had chosen?' the Brehon pressed, though he had already guessed the terrible truth.

'The names they were given at birth are lost and long forgotten,' she informed him. 'No one can guess to which clans they all belonged. But nine of the twelve became known to all, at length, as the Watchers.'

'The Watchers were of the Fir-Bolg?' the Brehon asked, stunned that such a thing might be possible. 'What else do you know about them?'

'I know the tale of their enchantment and the method. I know about the seven sleepers in stone. And when I was a Druid in training I was told the manner in which they might be released from that bond, but I only ever heard that Draoi song once in my whole life.'

'You must try to remember it!' the Brehon cried. 'If you set the Watchers free from their enchantment, many others will be saved from further suffering.'

'I was very young and I had many more important matters on my mind when I heard that song.'

'You must recall it!' Dalan insisted. 'The future of all the peoples of Innisfail is in your hands.'

Sorcha put up her hands to calm him. 'I have tried many times to recall the song — it slips from my memory each time.' She paused a moment, then said, 'I am but a humble student of the Draoi craft, yet I think I may be able to compose a song myself. I have already collected three melodies which I hope will embody the required elements.'

'You'll make a song yourself?' Dalan asked in amazement.

'I know of no other way. Balor guarded the secret of his enchantment jealously to the last and only one Danaan Druid in each lifetime since has known the true nature of it. Besides, I'm fairly certain the actual song itself wasn't passed down through the generations, merely echoes of it.'

'If you intend to compose a new melody, how long will that task take?'

Sorcha shrugged her shoulders. 'It will take as long as it

must. The more I concentrate on the problem the more likely I am to find a solution to it.'

'Will you come back with me to the new settlement at Aillwee?' Dalan asked.

Sorcha raised her eyebrows. 'Is the situation really that desperate? Do the Watchers pose such an immediate threat?'

'I've spoken with them,' the Brehon told her grimly. 'They warned me they would bring all their talents to bear against the peoples of this land unless I find a way to free them.'

The words had no sooner left his mouth than Sorcha leapt over the ring of mushrooms and grabbed his sleeve. As she pulled him close she whispered urgently in his ear.

'Say nothing more of this till we're safe within my house. The night may carry your words a distance on the evening breeze. I had no idea that events had come this far. There are other bitter wandering spirits who would be cheered no end if they knew the Watchers were intending to spread havoc.'

'Others?'

'This is a discussion for around the fire. We'll be safe there. None come to my hearth but those I've invited.'

Dalan nodded and Sorcha let go of his sleeve. Then she quickly doused her fire, swept the hearthstone and gathered her gear.

The shadows were already deep by the time they climbed down the face of the rock to the pool.

'Follow me,' Sorcha told Dalan, and then, without waiting for him to shoulder his pack, she marched purposefully off into the shadows, the darkness retreating before her rush light.

The Brehon watched the evening shadows swell around her body as she passed through them like a seal swimming through a calm sea. Then he ran to catch up with the Druid woman as she made her way out of the little valley into the night.

Chapter Six

Eber Finn rode his chariot around the field until he was sure old Máel Máedóc had gone and would not return. Then he pulled his warhorse to a halt at a respectable distance from the ancient ritual ground not far from the fortress of Dun Gur.

He quickly dismounted the war-cart and walked a few paces to stretch his legs. He knew his mare would not stray with the heavy chariot while there was green grass to be nibbled at.

When he'd loosened up the muscles in his legs he worked on his arms and hands as he would do before a battle, preparing himself to move quickly without straining. Once he was satisfied that he was ready to begin blade practice the king unsheathed his sword and briefly drew his thumb along the edge. Satisfied the weapon was not too dull he swung it around a few times in the air. Then in a sudden burst of battle fury he slashed at three invisible opponents one by one, revelling in the exalting rush of blood that resulted from these exercises.

Eber was a disciplined man who knew the value of slow steady practice. So he abandoned the pointless slashing and prepared himself for the ritual. He spent a few moments resting his sword in his hand, weighing it up before launching into the rehearsed moves of a swordsman.

Every warrior in training had to learn the weapon dance before they were allowed to so much as touch a blade or challenge another to a test of skill. Some fighters were so dedicated to their craft that they played the whole sequence out a dozen times a day in order to remain at the peak of their strength, flexibility and readiness for battle.

Eber Finn, on the other hand, did not consider the exercises that important. He knew them off by heart and though he started the dance each morning before breakfast he rarely ever made his way through all the motions. To him, true discipline was the ability to call on his battle instincts whenever the need arose.

The dance, however, was an important way of focusing his mind, but once he gained a heightened state of consciousness he abandoned it.

And the more experience the king gained, the more convinced he became that luck had as much to do with survival on the battlefield as any oft-repeated skill. He'd already performed the dance that morning so he had no other intention but to distract himself from Máel Máedóc's interference.

He raised the blade above his head and pointed it parallel with the ground, raising the tip above his left shoulder. With knees slightly bent and feet apart, he slowly moved the blade in a wide low arc, balancing his body in a countermovement with his left arm, finishing the sword cycle with the tip pointed at the ground. Eber breathed out forcefully with a loud grunt. This move was immediately followed by a step to the rear which incorporated a parry.

But Eber Finn was already bored. He came to the end of a short sequence of parries and attacks by letting the blade drop to his side with the impetus of its own weight. He gently exhaled a breath, let his body relax and his mind drift on to other matters.

In the perfect stillness the king swallowed hard and cast a careful eye over the scene before him. He was searching for enemies or any sign of danger among the scattered stones and venerable trees which guarded the circle.

This archaic holy place had fascinated him ever since he'd taken possession of Dun Gur. All around these fields the ancient awe-inspiring Danaan folk had built their sacred sanctuaries of old. But this was the largest stone circle of all and it was to this place he was always drawn.

The people Eber had supplanted when he'd gained the field at Sliabh Mis were gone from Dun Gur now. The Danaans had submitted to him, retreated beyond the veil into the Otherworld and given their island fortress in the middle of the lough into his keeping as a pledge of their treaty.

But the king had never been convinced of the victory. All those Danaans wounded, maimed or killed at Sliabh Mis had by some miracle walked away unscathed. Not even the wisest of Gaedhal Druids could tell him how this had come to be. Máel Máedóc's only explanation was that the Danaans were descended from a race of enchanters who had mastered the healing arts. The old man further claimed that these folk could choose the hour and place of their death if they so desired. But if they ever grew sick or suffered any wound, even though it seemed they were in fact dead, they could be brought back to health again.

The Danaan Druids had defeated death, which made their people the ideal warrior race. For any folk who conquer mortality fear no one. They go to the fight cheerfully, knowing they will live no matter what.

The king knew these mystical folk could have easily defeated his people if they'd wished to do so, simply by employing their healing craft to their advantage. Why then, he wondered, had the Danaans submitted to him and called for a treaty which was so generous to the Gaedhals?

At first he had suspected treachery. The Danaans had tried to trick him once before, so it wasn't impossible they would try again. But as the moons had passed on to the third winter after Sliabh Mis, Eber Finn had come to a different conclusion. The Danaan Druids had done all they could to help his people settle into their new home.

Their Brehon judges had been placed at his disposal in order to quell any disputes between his victorious chieftains. The Danaans had opened up their storehouses during the first hard winter and shared whatever they had with the newcomers. King Cecht, their overlord, often sent gifts of gold and grain to Eber. And Brocan, ruler of the Fir-Bolg, had sent hostages to live at Eber's court to learn the ways of his people.

Eber Finn now believed the Danaan plan was to gradually bring the two peoples closer together through mutual dependence. This tactic, played out over generations, would probably culminate in total reliance on the Danaans for everything, from music to medicine.

The king glanced around uneasily. His eyes told him he was alone but all his other instincts were on tense alert.

I've been living like a hunted fox for so long I've forgotten how to really rest, he upbraided himself. Still he could not shake off his nervousness. There was something about this place, about the sacred enclosure, that both frightened and attracted him.

The stone circle was encompassed by tall and ancient trees of every clan. The oak was there, low and heavy with summer foliage. The birch, yew, hazel and rowan were all nearby as if one representative of each tree kindred had been assigned the task of standing sentry.

At one point in the circle there was a gap in the trees which led to a large grey boulder. The king was determined to overcome his fear but still he had no desire to pass under the branches of any of these trees, so he approached the low ring of standing stones through this gap.

He was soon facing the most impressive part of the Danaan stone circle — what seemed to be an entrance between the large grey boulder and a smaller stone. On either side the rocks were piled up like steps.

Even in the bright summer sunshine this place had a disturbing aura of mystery about it. His head ached with the pounding in his ears. Every sense felt on edge. Eber raised his sword and moved a little closer to the ring. A strange unearthly silence engulfed him. His heart began to beat hard against his rib cage and the sweat poured down his chin. His mouth was dry, his breath strained.

White-knuckled fingers gripped the hilt of his sword as he struggled to move his trembling legs. The air was thick with an invisible threat for which Eber could find no name. His feet seemed to move reluctantly until he stood but one step away from the ring of solid stone.

In that instant a small cloud passed over the sun. Eber looked up to the sky. In a flash it had moved on and the king found himself squinting into the orb, the origin of all daylight.

As he exhaled his next breath he felt the tension in his body float away.

Defences relaxed. Fears dissolved. Eber Finn was overcome by an urge to drop his sword in the grass and simply leave it. The weapon slipped from his fingers and landed with a thud upon the ground. He heard it fall and the sound was strangely reassuring.

'There is no danger here,' Eber whispered, feeling completely safe for the first time since he had come to this strange land. 'I should have visited this holy place long ago.'

The words had barely passed his lips when he laid a foot firmly on one low stepping stone and, leaning against the large grey boulder, entered the circle.

No sooner had his foot touched the earth on the other side than Eber Finn found himself drawn directly to the centre of the smooth open grassy patch within. He had no idea of the ceremonies that had been practised here in times gone by. But now he had experienced this mysterious place he was certain the stone circle was the source of some powerful enchantment.

The air within the ring was fresh and cool in the afternoon sun. There was a soothing serenity to the place which settled the soul. For the first time in many seasons he sensed the stillness within himself. His heart was light. All his kingly troubles seemed mere petty trifles to be easily dealt with.

Eber had not felt so safe since he was a boy. Indeed it was as if he'd suddenly become a lad again without any worry or responsibility to disturb his sleep. His mind raced through all the experiences of his childhood and youth as if his whole existence from cradle to this moment were being played out in his memory.

Tears welled up in his eyes as he was overcome with gratitude for having been granted such a rich life. Fond faces came to him, folk he hadn't thought of since he was very young. Intense waves of emotion began to wash over the king. His knees felt weak. They quivered beneath him as if all strength had suddenly been sapped from his legs. He turned on his heel, feeling light-headed and drowsy.

It was then Eber Finn noticed hordes of tiny mushrooms all around the inside perimeter of the circle. They were gathered close to the stones as if they were keeping the grey rocks from falling over. Each had a long cap and a stem of milky white.

Fried in fresh butter, mushrooms were the king's favourite delicacy. But these were a species of fungus he had never seen before. The temptation to pick a few to take home over-whelmed him and he took ten steps toward the edge of the circle.

But then he realised how strange it was to see mushrooms so abundant at this time of year. He had seen none in the fields beyond. This multitude of little fungi was growing here under the protection of the spirits of the stone circle. They were not being cultivated for food but for the secret seeing rituals of the Druids. To eat them unprepared would be to tempt either madness or death.

Eber swallowed hard, realising that he was feeling absolutely no fear at all. This wasn't natural, he told himself. He was obviously falling under some enchantment and beginning to feel as if the world in which he usually dwelt was slipping away from him.

It was then he noticed the bright sunlight being quickly blotted out by a muffled foggy haze. The haze soon spread into a mist which brought a deep drowsiness down upon him like a great weight. Still no fear disturbed his heart, only wonder at the transformation. The green of the grass darkened before his astounded gaze. The grey of the stones turned to a tone that was cold and yet intensely beautiful.

The mist grew thicker with every moment until Eber could perceive nothing beyond the enclosing circle of roughly hewn stones. Even the bodies and branches of the guardian trees were no longer visible to him.

The king felt an overwhelming urge to remain here in this place forever. Some unfamiliar voice whispered to him that he would be welcome to stay, to take refuge from the troubles of the world and rest his weary soul.

Eber was not disturbed to hear this disembodied voice. Indeed he felt privileged the spirits of this circle had given a sign of welcome. But his head ached with a numbing intensity now. His throat was dry and he felt he could sleep forever.

The voice spoke up again and told him to stretch out upon the grass and sleep away until his soul was refreshed and ready for the world again. He would be watched over and safe no matter what befell the world beyond the stones.

He was so tired. The lawn in the centre of the circle looked so soft and inviting.

'Sleep,' the strange voice beckoned. 'Sleep away your cares and we will watch over you.'

With bowed head the King of the Gaedhals began to succumb. But first he decided it was important he express his gratitude to the unseen guardians of this place. So he made his dreamy way back toward a flattened swirl of grass in the centre of the lawn. There he knelt to offer up a prayer of thanks. And before he knew what he was saying he was addressing the inexplicable powers that had shaped his life. He couldn't name them because he'd never acknowledged their existence before.

'Thank you for the hunger which set my heart to searching,' he offered. 'Thank you for the ocean wave which carried me through storm and tempest to this shore. Thank you for the wind that tore my sails and tried to send me home. Thank you for every misfortune great and small that has held me back and frustrated me.'

In that instant he knew there was really no such thing as hardship. Every trial was just a strengthening process which enhanced his life with the wisdom it imparted.

'And thank you for the lessons I have learned along the way.'

Eber raised his arms and the mist departed before his unbelieving eyes. Suddenly he felt the sun on his skin once more. He closed his eyes and turned his face toward its warmth.

'I thank you,' he went on, 'whose face is too terrible to look upon, whose light brings life unto the world. My thanks to you, the source of all things, who brought fire into the darkness, who created every living thing and grants new life each day.'

Then Eber got to his feet. The air vibrated with an ecstatic enlivening energy but he felt the opportunity to remain in this place had passed. He bowed reverently to the four corners of the Earth.

When this was done he quickly made his way to the edge of the circle. The feeling of peace and serenity did not leave him when he stepped over the stones, so he decided to indulge himself and enjoy the elation he was experiencing. In the shade of a young oak tree which grew within a stone's throw of the sacred enclosure Eber Finn lay down and stared at the circle with awe. After a while he closed his eyes, still experiencing the intense peace within his soul.

His thoughts were buzzing with pleasant memories and warm recollections. He hummed a little childhood song to himself and smiled. And above all he felt refreshed, as if he had slept for a week and woken to a new world.

Gradually, however, the mood began to pass and Eber's worldly concerns began to press in on him. His brother's demands filled his thoughts.

In the first few seasons after the treaty with the Danaans was settled Eber Finn had not dared to defy his brother. He had been working hard to secure his own position as King of the South. Too many of the southern chieftains had close friends or kinfolk in the north, and Eber depended on the support of those chieftains to retain his office. However, he had continued to push for the chieftains to build the war-chariots, presenting the Danaans as the real threat. And all the while he had been hoping to foster good relations with the Danaan court.

He wondered what the chieftains would say when they discovered he had been quietly planning to forge an alliance with the very people he had told them were untrustworthy enemies.

The king grinned. What would old Máel Máedóc say when

he found out? He congratulated himself on his wily deception, the fruits of which would soon come to maturity.

'What better ally could the Southern Gaedhals have,' Eber reasoned proudly under his breath, rehearsing his speech to the council, 'than a people who possess the secret of immortality? The kinfolk of Danu will help us defeat the threats from my brother in the north.'

By the end of the coming winter Eber incorrectly reckoned he would have perhaps thirty of the war-carts at his disposal. The kingship of the whole island would soon be within his grasp.

Now it was time to put the next part of his plan into action. It was time to announce his intentions and forge a stronger alliance with the Danaans, an alliance based on mutual obligation in time of war. But Eber was aware he had to be careful to retain the loyalty of his chieftains.

Of course Eber had no way of knowing that his task was hopeless. He had no true understanding of what had really taken place when the Danaans had retreated into the Otherworld. The People of Danu would not stand beside him because they had travelled to a place beyond the cares of this material realm.

The king looked up to the sky as he imagined himself as the first Gaedhal elected High-King of all Eirinn.

'I will father a clan of leaders,' he muttered to himself, 'who will honour my name forever. I will be the first High-King of the Gaedhals.'

'You have grand expectations of yourself,' a woman's voice cut in mockingly.

Eber was snapped out of his daydream as surely as if a cauldron of cold water had been thrown over him. In a second he was on his feet and scanning the area. He shuddered with fright when he could see no one else around. It was then he missed his sword.

'Are you looking for this?'

The tall, red-haired woman seemed to step out of nowhere as if a door to the Otherworld were concealed nearby. Now she was standing in front of Eber, smiling sweetly as she offered him his blade.

The king knew her immediately and quickly calmed himself. He was shaken by her unexpected arrival but he didn't want her to think he was unsettled by her strange ways.

'Isleen? Where did you spring from?'

'I'm visiting the holy stones,' she explained. 'This ground was not given to your people. Why are you trespassing here?'

'Why must you always sneak around like that?' he countered. 'Can't you announce yourself like everyone else? It's usually considered the polite thing to do!'

'I'm sorry if I surprised you,' she soothed. 'I noticed you were meditating. I didn't mean to startle you.'

She took a step closer to hand him his weapon and Eber snatched the hilt out of her grasp.

'You didn't startle me!' he hissed.

'What are you doing here?' she asked again. 'This is Danaan holy ground. You have no rights here. That is the agreement you made with our folk.'

'I was curious.'

'Don't be. There are spirits dwelling in this place which you can never safely approach. Not even if you were to undergo initiation into the mysteries. Your curiosity will serve you better if employed to more worldly tasks. There is still a lot of work to be done if your dreams are ever to come true.'

'I have had a strange experience,' he admitted. 'I feel so much closer to my goal.'

'You have been lulled by the spirits of the circle,' Isleen countered coldly. 'Only a fool would carry the elation felt within the safety of the stones into the outer world where greed reigns and mortals chase ambition.'

'I know I'll be High-King.'

'If you listen to my advice and do not question me, you will have whatever you desire,' she assured him. 'I've told you that many times before.'

'Why are you helping me?' Eber asked suspiciously. 'Why are you betraying your people to aid my cause?'

Isleen smiled but she didn't answer.

'Why are you afraid that Fineen the Danaan Druid will find out you are dwelling with me? Why don't you want my own people to know that you have been acting as my adviser?'

'You have a suspicious mind,' she chided. 'That's a good thing for a king. Especially an ambitious one. As a matter of fact I don't see my collusion with you to be an act of betrayal at all. As for Fineen, he has his reasons for mistrusting me. Well-founded reasons, I might add.'

She stepped closer to the king, close enough to run a finger down his cheek. 'You see, my dear king, one day I intend to marry you. One day I will be your queen. What do you think of that?'

The Gaedhal breathed in a deep draught of her sweet scent. It reminded him of lavender mixed with a delicate touch of early morning dew in the springtime.

'I like the idea,' Eber grinned, as intoxicated as if he'd swallowed a measure of mead. The soulful sparkle in her deep green eyes always enthralled him and he silently surrendered his spirit.

'You must realise that I've gained a few enemies during my life,' Isleen went on. 'Folk like Fineen would rather see me banished than wed to a king.'

Eber frowned, wondering what crimes she had committed that would inspire such hatred from her own folk. Isleen saw the concern on his face and spoke before he had an opportunity to give voice to his doubts.

'I don't want to wed a weak ruler,' she warned. 'I want a

king who truly is the lord of all the land. I want to live in luxury. I want to feast until I'm full, and sleep sound in the knowledge that no man would dare attempt to take this life away from me.'

'You shall have that assurance.'

'But how?' Isleen shrugged. 'How can you promise me such security while your brother is arming for war? As we speak he's planning to come here and take your hard-won kingdom away from you.'

'If Éremon marches into my kingdom I'll be ready for him,' Eber stated.

'Will you? And will you rely on your own young warriors to defend the south?'

'It was always our plan to bring your people in to help me,' the king reminded her. 'I've already invited Brocan to the midsummer feast. I plan to win his confidence then and gain his aid.'

'There's only one way to ensure an alliance with the Fir-Bolg,' Isleen countered. 'And that is by bond of marriage.'

'I'll gladly marry you to forge that bond.'

The woman laughed out loud, laying the palm of her hand against his chest to steady herself. Eber relished her touch and smiled back, utterly captivated by everything about her.

'I am nothing to my people but a wandering Druid,' she explained. 'Marriages of alliance are not forged with the daughter of a homeless poet. The woman you wed must be of noble blood, preferably the offspring of a war-leader or a king.'

'I thought you said you wanted to marry me?' Eber frowned.

'And so I will one day when your first wife has served her purpose. For a while we will have to continue to conceal our feelings for one another. Do you think you can do that?'

Eber nodded. Isleen smiled. That is what they had been doing for the last three winters.

'I very much doubt you will be able to keep your intentions to yourself indefinitely,' she scoffed mischievously. 'But we'll worry about that problem when it arises.'

She ran her fingers through his brown hair and cupped his head in her hands. 'I've arranged for a suitable candidate,' she told him softly. 'You'll meet her soon enough if all goes to plan.'

Then she kissed the king lightly on the lips.

'She's the daughter of King Brocan of the Fir-Bolg whose people live on the Burren. Her folk once held an ancient enmity against the Danaans but she has spent much time among those folk. She is a Druid in training who is not attentive to her studies. She would rather have been chosen to the warrior class. Her discontent will make it easy for us to persuade her father that marriage would be better suited to her.'

Eber opened his mouth to ask a question but she kissed his lips lightly again to silence him. 'She is under punishment for a misdeed committed against the Danaan king, Cecht.'

'Cecht is the king I should be seeking alliance with,' the king cut in. 'The Fir-Bolg are too few to swing the balance in my favour.'

'The Danaans will not come to your aid. And even if they cared about your trifling concerns Cecht still bears a grudge against you.'

'I suppose he doesn't think that kindly of me,' Eber admitted.

'You didn't treat him with much honour,' Isleen reminded him. 'He was your prisoner before the Battle of Sliabh Mis. You should have taken care of him and offered him your best food and mead. You could have given him a decent bed at least.'

'He was rude to me.'

'You captured him in the dead of night and dragged him

away with the wife of the Fir-Bolg king, with whom I suspect he was engaged in a recreation best played out by moonlight. Not only did you break the Brehon laws governing war, you also announced to the world that King Cecht and Queen Riona were out alone together beyond the confines of Dun Burren at midnight. It was very embarrassing for everyone concerned.'

Eber dropped his eyes to the ground, trying to shrug off the reprimand. 'I might have done a better job if you had stayed by my side,' he noted. 'But you decided to abandon me in my hour of need.'

'You were being stubborn and tiresome,' Isleen dismissed. 'What was I to do?

'Fortunately everything has worked out for the best,' she went on. 'Riona decided to divorce her husband King Brocan of the Fir-Bolg and I believe all parties are well pleased with the way things turned out. I've heard her bless the chance that brought you to capture her with Cecht because afterwards she was forced to make a choice between her husband and her lover.'

Isleen stopped for a moment to admire the golden torc around the king's neck, that ornament which marked his office and his standing with his people. She continued.

'Riona couldn't go back to her husband after that. She chose to act before old Brocan had the chance to accuse her of infidelity. If he'd brought such a charge against her she could have lost all her worldly goods and gone to Cecht without any possessions or dowry.'

Isleen took a breath while she waited to see if Eber was following her tale.

'So because her secret tryst with Cecht was exposed to the world, Riona left her husband?' the king asked.

'Indeed she did,' Isleen smiled. 'I think I can safely say you have her on your side. Riona is a formidable woman who may be relied on to remember those who have served her well. But don't expect her to do anything more than remember your service.'

'She is the mother of this woman you'd have me wed?'

'Your future wife is every bit her mother's daughter. She has the same red hair, the same cold green eyes and the same self-serving nature.'

'What's her name, this woman?'

'She's called Aoife,' Isleen told him. 'I've been watching her for a long time. She is perfectly suited to our purposes.'

'How long will it be before my brother loses patience with me and marches his warriors south?'

'You haven't given in to his demand for taxes and tribute, have you?'

'Of course not!'

'He won't come this summer,' Isleen assured him. 'He still has the harvest to bring in. But we can expect him at snow-melt for certain.'

'That doesn't give us much time.'

'At the feast of Samhain, the Danaans who have not crossed over to the Otherworld and the Fir-Bolg will send their representatives to you for the ceremonial planting of the sacred Quicken Tree. By then you must win over young Aoife if you are to have any hope of gaining an alliance with those folk.'

'Win her over?' Eber frowned. 'I don't understand you.'

'Aoife is young and inexperienced,' Isleen explained. 'Encourage her love and she will go to the Danaan court in your name to present your plea for help. They will listen to one of their own.'

'And what will become of this girl when my brother has been defeated?'

'I have set aside a place where no man will ever find her, though they search for a thousand winters. For although she is a Fir-Bolg she has been gifted with Danaan immortality so

118

she cannot be eliminated completely. But she must be kept apart from her kind forever.'

'I'll be High-King?'

'Without question.'

'When?' Eber pressed.

'I'll tell you all in good time, my dear,' Isleen laughed.

Then she leaned forward to kiss Eber once more. This time she flooded him with her passion and he closed his eyes to savour her scent and touch. Soft fingers stroked the back of his neck and Eber Finn groaned with pleasure.

Then Isleen suddenly pushed him away with the palm of her hand, turned and strode purposefully toward the chariot.

'So, Eber Finn of the Twenty War-carts,' she taunted, 'High-King of all Eirinn and Master of the Warrior Circle, I think it's time you took me for a ride on the back of your chariot.'

The king laughed, sheathed his sword and brushed the dirt from his backside. Then he sauntered after her with half-closed eyes. And not for the first time he blessed the day he'd met Isleen of the Teasing Fingertips.

Dalan followed the Druid woman a short distance until they came to a densely wooded grove. They picked their way through the trees for no more than sixty paces before Sorcha halted and turned to face her guest.

'Say nothing,' she whispered in an urgent hiss. 'No matter what you see ahead of you, don't let a sound pass your lips. If you do you will offend my guardians. And I will not be responsible for what happens to you afterwards.'

Dalan nodded, pressing his tongue hard against his teeth so he wouldn't be able to utter a sound.

Sorcha looked him sternly in the eye, then turned on her heel and marched down the narrow track which cut its winding way between the trees.

Dalan tried hard to stay a few steps behind her, but he began to feel an unnatural fear descend upon him. It was as if the trees themselves were alive with a menace so all-pervasive it stifled every little noise within the woods. The air was thick as if no breeze had passed through the forest in many seasons.

The Brehon's throat was dry; his hands sweated profusely. Dalan tried to calm down, telling himself Sorcha's house could not be too much further. But with each pace he felt his heart falter as fear gave way to unspeakable terror. He began to question the wisdom of placing himself so entirely in this woman's hands.

At length they came to an arched gateway formed by the intertwined branches of two mighty oak trees. Sorcha stopped again to put a finger emphatically to her lips. The Brehon asked himself what possible force could be so malign as to be stirred by the voice of a stranger.

The perspiration rolled down his forehead and his breath came in short shallow draughts. He thought his body would collapse with the overwhelming sense of threat that seeped up through the ground into the soles of his feet with every step as they passed under the arched gate.

He glimpsed a shape ahead of him to one side of the path and at first he thought it was a small child waiting. But as they got closer he noticed the shape was perfectly still.

In seconds he could make out the detail of a crudely carved face. The features were long and drawn like those of a carrion bird. The body was hunched and twisted, half Raven, half human.

But it was the eyes that turned the Brehon's blood to ice. Orbs of fluid blackness they were. And though carved out of a dead tree trunk they gave this sculpture life, and an air of deadly hatred.

Panic gripped poor Dalan's heart. Sorcha might have warned him not to speak but the Brehon was so profoundly frightened he was incapable of speech.

As he drew level with the statue he stopped in his tracks. As much as he wanted to be away from this terrifying sculpture he could not step beyond it. Frozen to the spot as if held by an invisible hand, Dalan began to shake, the spasms spreading through every muscle in his body.

Sorcha didn't notice his predicament. She was soon gone beyond his sight and he was left entirely alone on the path.

The Brehon stood there in almost utter darkness for what seemed hours. He was unable to move his feet forward and unwilling to try. But the Raven was no less frightening in the shadows; indeed it was more so. And Dalan swore he saw the eyes twinkle once or twice as they coldly regarded him.

Just as the Brehon thought his legs would give way under him, Sorcha returned, searching for her guest along the path. She walked straight up to him, took his hand and half dragged him past the statue. The moment he was beyond the reach of those dark eyes his journey became a little easier. Until the next sculpture loomed ahead and Sorcha had to coax him gently on again. Ten more Ravens stood as sentinels to her home. And even when Dalan came to the last one he was still as frightened as he had been when he'd encountered the first.

'We're here,' the Druid woman whispered. 'You've done well to keep silent.'

Dalan still didn't dare answer nor make any sound. But he frowned when he noticed nothing before him but a bare grassy hill.

Sorcha smiled, pleased her illusion had taken him in.

'I live under the ground,' she explained with a wink.

And with that simple phrase she banished all Dalan's fears. There was something in the sparkle of her eyes and her patient manner that reminded him of Cuimhne. As he looked at Sorcha now he was all the more convinced he'd met her in another place, perhaps while he was under the influence of the Faidh.

The young woman strode forward, knelt down and fumbled for something in the grass. When she stood up again she dragged on a heavy object and to Dalan's surprise an opening appeared in the hillside. The Druid woman removed a perfect circle of grass, laid it down on the ground, then motioned for him to follow her.

The soft glow of candlelight spilled forth from this opening in the earth. The honey-golden luminescence spoke of safety and welcome. Dalan bowed low as he followed the Druid woman into her hall, then the door slid down upon its hinges behind him and shut out the woodland spirits.

The first thing the Brehon noticed was a tinge of fragrant smoke and the aroma of a hot meal bubbling gently by a fire. He took a deep draught of this sweet air and felt the homeliness of it seep into his bones. This house was a sanctuary from the terrors waiting outside the door.

Sorcha took off her brown breacan cloak as Dalan surveyed the interior of the dwelling. The building was perfectly circular, exactly the same as any Fir-Bolg home. Nine thick posts of oak supported the roof. There was plenty of room but the air was unusually smoky. The Brehon soon understood why.

As he peered toward the roof timbers he realised there was no chimney hole in the ceiling. So the smoke from the fire in the centre of the chamber had to filter out through the layers of turf and sod above. This design was more primitive than he was accustomed to but Dalan didn't mind the slight discomfort.

Sorcha had everything she needed here. Cooking pots and herbs hung from the rafters. A huge barrel of what he guessed was water stood beside the door. Skins and furs were curing all about the place, aided by the smoky air. And an empty butter churn stood near a beautifully carved low-set Brandubh table.

'Take off that cloak!' Sorcha demanded tersely. 'And put it out of sight.'

Taken aback by her gruff tone, Dalan did as she told him without a word, obediently hanging his cloak up by the door and covering it over with her plain breacan. He must have offended her in some way, though he did not know how. He turned to offer her an apology but what he saw rendered him speechless. High in the rafters a dark shape moved slightly, just enough to draw attention to its presence.

Dalan couldn't breathe. Once more he was paralysed with the same fear he had known in the woods. There was another movement in the dark rafters.

Then, in a sudden flurry of black wings, a Raven dived down from its perch and landed on the Brandubh table, scattering pieces this way and that.

And never for a moment did the carrion bird take her gaze from the Brehon.

Sorcha busied herself filling two wooden bowls with broth from a small cauldron which hung over the fire. She didn't seem to notice the sudden appearance of this disturbing black shadow.

'Will you take some food with me?' she asked.

The Brehon nodded. But the Druid woman wasn't watching.

'What's that?' Sorcha asked again when she heard no reply.

'I will take some food. Yes please.'

'It's good to hear you've not lost your voice in the evening air.'

'I didn't expect to journey through such a grove after sunset,' he ventured. 'It has been an unnerving experience.'

'You kept your head remarkably well.'

The Raven clicked her beak, making the Brehon jump.

'Is something wrong?' Sorcha inquired.

'What's the bird's name?' Dalan stuttered, gesturing in the Raven's direction.

The great black carrion creature set about preening herself, but the Brehon was sure she was taking careful note of everything he said and each tiny move he made.

'I've never asked her,' Sorcha shrugged as she placed a steaming bowl in Dalan's hand. 'Would you like some oatcakes?'

He nodded.

'They'll be a little while yet. I've just laid them out to bake among the coals.'

The Raven stretched her wings out, opened her mouth wide and yawned.

'I've never seen a bird do that before,' the Brehon commented. 'I've seen dogs yawn, and cats, but never a Raven.'

'When you were a child, weren't you taught that it's rude to stare?' Sorcha snapped. 'That bird lives with me. She's my companion. If I knew her name I probably wouldn't be able to pronounce it to her satisfaction. It doesn't interest me. Only our kind are concerned with naming things. All the other inhabitants of this Earth use other means to identify each other.'

'Yours is an unusual name,' the Brehon ventured, trying to make up for his rudeness. 'I've never heard it before.'

'It's an ancient name. It has been in my family for generations.'

'Do you live here alone?' he asked, his curiosity running unchecked.

'I just told you. That bird lives here with me. Are you deaf? This is her house as much as it is mine.'

There was frustration in the young woman's voice so Dalan did not pursue the conversation. And he promised himself he would not bring the matter up with her again. Everyone, he reasoned, is entitled to their privacy. A good guest doesn't see or hear everything in the house of his host.

The Brehon put the rim of the bowl to his lips and gently sipped the broth. It was warming and thick. And the flavouring of earthy herbs cooked into the soup reminded him of the home he had been born to and the life he'd led before he took the Druid vows.

Sorcha finished her meal quickly then ran her fingers round the bowl and licked them clean. When she had eaten every last tiny morsel she went to the water barrel, dunked the vessel in and drew it out again brimming. The bowl was drained in a few moments and she belched loudly. Dalan was a little disconcerted by this, accustomed as he was to the polite manners of King Brocan's court.

'The cakes won't be long,' Sorcha told him. 'But I'm too tired to eat any more. I'm off to bed. I must be up before the dawn to attend to the rituals at the spring. Then I'll come with you wherever you go in search of the Watchers.'

'Will you not share more of your knowledge with me?' the Brehon begged.

'Bye and bye,' she yawned. 'But I'll do it in the bright light of morning as we share the road. I've no mind to upsetting the restless spirits of this wood with such talk. I ask that you honour my wishes and ask no more of me while we are under the protection of the trees.'

She pointed to a pile of furs near to where he sat. 'You sleep over there. I make it a rule never to share my bed with strangers. So if you get cold in the night you'll have to blow up the fire.'

Dalan nodded.

'Rest well,' she said finally, then lay down on her own furs, wrapped herself tightly and rolled away from the fire to sleep.

Dalan put down his bowl and stopped eating, compelled by the many thoughts buzzing around in his head. For a long while he stared blankly into the fire. At length he looked up and stared at the shapeless form of Sorcha breathing deeply under her furs.

Of all the wonders he had witnessed that evening none struck him so much as this woman's resemblance to his spirit guide. Her face, her eyes, her voice, even her turn of phrase were identical to Cuimhne's.

Suddenly the Druid woman stirred and rolled over. She raised herself on one elbow and said, 'Do you know how difficult it is to sleep with someone watching you?'

'I'm sorry,' muttered Dalan.

'What were you thinking?'

The Brehon coughed with embarrassment. 'It's so strange that I recognise your face.'

'I find it unnerving too, especially as Cuimhne chose to present himself to me in your form,' she agreed. 'But we've surely never crossed paths before.'

'Other than in my dreams,' he replied wistfully.

Sorcha sat up and looked him directly in the eye, unsure whether he was serious. And then she burst out laughing.

'You'll have to do better than that, gentle Brehon, if you want to get into bed with me,' she spluttered in unrestrained amusement. 'It's times such as this I'm glad I was never struck with the Faidh. It weakens the mind, to be sure. I feel much safer under the sway of the Frith. At least I know I am in control. When I call on the Frith I am the master of my own fate.'

Then, still giggling, she turned over without hearing his stuttered protests. When the laughter passed she pulled

126

the furs about her head, wiped the tears of mirth from her cheeks and in muffled tones wished her guest a pleasant, restful sleep.

Dalan felt his cheeks flushing with shame. She had mistaken his meaning, he told himself as he took the cakes from the fire. But his appetite was gone. No one had laughed at something he'd said for a long time. Everyone took him so seriously. But a voice within whispered, 'Perhaps it is you who take yourself too seriously, Dalan mac Math.'

Unsettled by this possibility, the Brehon wrapped his furs about him and huddled close beside the fire. The bird was still looking down at him with a hard, hateful glare. So he rolled over to face the wall. With his eyes turned away from the Raven he relaxed a little, though sleep evaded him for a long time.

At length, exhausted by the struggle not to think of Cuimhne or the Druid woman, he closed his eyes. But Dalan couldn't rest. All he could think of was the forest round about. And when he remembered that the woods were peopled with savage idols carved of oaken wood, he shuddered to his bones.

Chapter Seven

fter sunset Fineen the Healer rose from the fireside and went outside to greet the evening star. His thoughts were somewhat clouded by the mead cup so he stood for a few moments at the door of his lodgings and tried to clear his head.

Whenever he and Sárán stayed at Aillwee, the poets' house was given to them to share with any other Druids who chanced to be visiting the Fir-Bolg. It was one of the better shelters in the settlement, certainly finer than King Brocan's own hall.

At length the healer cast his eyes to the ground and sighed. He was born of Danaan blood and now more than ever he felt like a stranger among the Fir-Bolg folk. He thought on the circumstances that had brought him to Aillwee while the rest of his kinfolk had retreated into the Otherworld.

Fineen had been a young man studying the healing arts when he had met a young Fir-Bolg woman who had ignited a passion deep in his soul. Sadly, his affections were never returned but his broken heart was soothed by the hospitality and kindness of her kinfolk, and he found himself fascinated by this strange race.

As he thought back now he was surprised to find he could not even recall the young woman's name. He had to laugh.

After a lifetime's experience he understood he had been led to her so that he would one day fulfil his destiny with the Fir-Bolg.

Few of his kindred had ever bothered to study these people, but Fineen had devoted his life to learning all he could about their ways. He spent his winters among the Fir-Bolg, delving into their legends, examining their laws and customs. He built up a great assortment of herbs, tinctures and natural oils derived from Fir-Bolg tradition. Before the time of the Quicken Brew his Danaan colleagues had often drawn on his collection when searching for some new remedy in times of famine or disease.

Fineen had even gone so far as to learn old Fir-Bolg songs that had fallen out of fashion. But for all his learning, for all his ardent study and patient service to their people, he had to admit something to himself. He didn't understand any of them. Least of all their king, Brocan. He was just shaking his head in amusement at this when the king strode past him headed toward the caves.

The healer was quite surprised to see Brocan again so soon. The evening shadows were lengthening and it would soon be dark.

'Are you going back into the Aillwee?' Fineen asked, and Brocan shrugged his shoulders at the question.

'I am.'

'I'll walk with you if you like,' the healer offered.

'I'd be happy to have you along,' he assured Fineen with a sudden change of tone. 'Indeed, I was going to invite you.'

'Did you leave something at the caves this afternoon?' the Druid asked, taking step by the old war-leader's side.

Brocan turned his head and frowned as if he didn't understand. Then the healer's meaning seemed to dawn on him and he laughed. 'No. I'm going back to take another look at something.'

'What might that be?' Fineen inquired.

'A chamber I stumbled on in the dark,' Brocan explained.

There was a hesitation in his words the healer had never heard before, even in times of great excitement. The voice almost didn't fit the king at all. Fineen decided he must have witnessed something quite remarkable.

'What's so special about this chamber?'

King Brocan stopped dead in his tracks, seemingly trying to cobble words together to describe his experience. The healer had never seen Brocan so distracted and upset. It was almost as if he were looking on the face of a stranger.

Finally the Fir-Bolg king put a hand to Fineen's blue tunic, grasped the linen garment and pulled him close so no one else would hear. 'You'll have to wait until I show you.'

'Very well,' the healer nodded, trying to conceal his concern for Brocan.

Before Fineen had straightened his tunic the king set off again toward the caves. Even for someone of such an unpredictable nature, Brocan was behaving in a very odd manner.

'I've thought about all you said earlier,' the healer offered.

Brocan grunted in reply.

'You may be right,' Fineen added. 'I hope you'll accept my apology.'

The king stopped in his tracks and turned to face the Danaan Druid, an uncharacteristic light in his expression.

'Good,' he nodded. 'Splendid. I accept your apology and we'll say nothing more about the matter.'

'As you wish,' the healer frowned. 'Shouldn't you be resting?' he asked, concerned by the obvious state of tension Brocan was in. 'Surely you can show me this chamber in the morning.'

'It's always dark in the depths of the Earth,' the king replied, striding off once more.

'I'm rather tired myself,' the healer protested, struggling to keep up.

'Come with me,' Brocan barked.

'Are you certain it's safe to go into the caves so soon after sunset?'

'Who knows? Perhaps it is. Perhaps it isn't,' the king snapped, hurrying ahead.

'I don't think we should go in,' Fineen called after him. 'Surely it would be better to wait for the new light of day.'

Brocan halted again by the entrance to the Aillwee. He picked up a few rocks, seemingly to examine them while waiting for the healer to catch up. As Fineen approached, catching his breath, the king turned around and threw a stone at him.

The missile flew wide, never really having any hope of hitting him, but the Druid was shocked nonetheless.

'My lord? What are you doing?' he stammered.

'Are you coming with me or not?' Brocan bellowed.

'Is it wise for you to be entering the caves again without sufficient rest?' the healer tried.

'I'll rest when my spirit is free,' the king sighed.

The Druid thought he'd never heard such sadness in any voice. Surely, he told himself, a great change had come over Brocan of the Fir-Bolg.

'You have a short memory,' the king went on. 'I've taken the Quicken Brew. What harm will come to me?'

'No one can be certain whether the Quicken Brew will protect us from all ills,' Fineen argued. 'Do not tempt fate, my lord.'

'Healer, are you going to accompany me or not?'

Without waiting for an answer the king took a rush light, lit it on the sentry fire and nodded to the two warriors standing guard. Then, his light burning brightly, he made his way purposefully into the entrance.

'Very well then,' the king called back over his shoulder. 'I'm not afraid to go alone. There is no danger I won't face for my people.' And with those words he disappeared within the cave.

Fineen ran to the entrance, calling for the guards to help him.

'The caves aren't safe,' the first one told him with a gesture that clearly indicated he should calm down.

'You must do something!' the healer pleaded.

The other guard spoke up. 'Most of us Fir-Bolg didn't take the Quicken Brew. I'm not going to risk my life by following him into danger. Our king drank the Danaan potion of health and life. He'll come to no harm.'

But Fineen was not convinced. The king's behaviour had been very disturbing. As a healer he simply could not let Brocan go alone into the depths in such a state. In a flash Fineen grabbed another rush light and was off after the king, following the flickering light which reflected off the walls from Brocan's light.

'Wait for me!' the healer called out.

But there was no reply. Fineen came breathlessly to a sharp bend in the passageway and suddenly there was an explosion of lights. Sparks flew in every direction. The shock nearly knocked him over.

Then out jumped Brocan with a war cry, still brandishing the rush light he had thumped against the wall.

'What is wrong with you?' Fineen cried in horror.

Brocan smiled, pointed down the passageway. 'I'll show you what's wrong.'

The healer thought for a moment the king must be playing some strange game with him. Surely Brocan wasn't being serious. Fineen hardly had time for these thoughts to enter his head when old Brocan was off again, storming down the passageway with his torch held aloft.

'Wait!' the Druid called out, but to no avail. He had no choice but to do the best he could to keep up with the king. And hope he didn't lose himself in this maze of underground tunnels.

It wasn't long before they passed beyond the part of the caves which had been excavated by the ancestors of the Fir-Bolg. The passages were becoming steadily narrower and the floor was very rough. Unrelenting in his pace, the Fir-Bolg king rushed on ever deeper into the bowels of the Earth. Soon he started taking abrupt turns and Fineen was sorely challenged to keep up.

Brocan climbed through a tiny opening in the rock wall, out into a wider gallery where he scaled a pile of silted sand and entered a chamber in the ceiling. This time he waited till Fineen had caught up before he moved on.

They struggled through a knee-deep torrent of a stream which tumbled out of one side of the cave, crossed the cavern's breadth and disappeared down a thundering shaft at the lower end. Then they began to descend down a wide shaft cut into the wall to form an entrance resembling the stone gate on the surface. Brocan didn't slow his pace at all, climbing many walls and slithering down escarpments.

Fineen was sure they'd have to stop soon to rest. He was becoming convinced Brocan must be lost. They'd spent too much time underground — they must have walked more than a thousand paces by now.

As if he had heard the thought, Brocan turned around to the healer. 'I'm not lost. I know exactly where I am. The place I'm taking you to is not much further. Try to keep up.'

Fineen nodded and put his reservations aside for the moment. At least he'd soon discover what old Brocan was making such a fuss about.

At last the king climbed up on a large boulder and disappeared from view.

'Where are you?' Fineen called out.

'Up here. Climb up, dear Druid. Join me. You'll think your eyes are lying to you. I give you my word, there's a wonder here which will certainly confound you. I'm sure of it.'

Fineen raised an eyebrow. He was keen to learn the answer to this mystery but he found it hard to be as enthusiastic as the king. He dragged himself up to where he could swing his leg onto a narrow ledge. Then he hauled his body up the rest of the way, out of one cave passage into the great hall of a shimmering cavern. Ten paces away Brocan stood facing the inner depths of the chamber.

A small trickle of water from an insignificant spring had formed a pool across the floor. Brocan's rush light was reflecting off the ceiling in a spectacular display.

The sight was beautiful, Fineen conceded, but it hardly warranted the king's strange behaviour, nor his hurry to return. The healer scanned the gallery, thinking he might have missed some other wonder.

But there was nothing else remarkable about the chamber at all.

'My lord,' he began, 'I don't see any sights that would confound my senses. Am I missing something?'

'Indeed you are.'

'Then show me the wonders you speak of and let me judge with my own eyes. Old as they are, they have never lied to me.'

Brocan laughed. As he did so he slowly turned to confront the healer, gliding around in a graceful sweeping motion. With alarming speed a mist gathered its long fingers around the king, completely concealing him from view. Fineen gasped and took several steps back until he was pressed to the wall.

Then, just as suddenly as it had appeared, the mist lifted. The healer frowned, astounded at what he saw. Before him, where Brocan should have been, stood a tall, muscular man who somehow seemed familiar.

The features were known to him, though he could not place a name with the face. The stranger smiled as if he understood the Druid's struggle. Then he began to stare at Fineen, as if observing him for the first time. Such was the intensity of his scrutiny that the healer felt as if his inner being was under examination.

'You'll do nicely,' the stranger stated with some satisfaction. 'You don't seem too intelligent. I always find it easier to play down to the expectations of others.'

Fineen was so outraged at the insult he couldn't even mouth a response.

'I know your face!' Fineen stuttered finally. 'You called yourself Lochie. You claimed to be a Druid from the north.'

The stranger nodded and politely bowed in affirmation.

'But you aren't a Druid, are you?'

Lochie held his palms up to the ceiling and rolled his eyes. It was gesture which conveyed both admission of the truth and delight that the game was going so well.

There was no other reply. And Fineen needed no further confirmation.

'You merely posed as one of the Druid kind. You're one of the Watchers.'

'You've guessed right,' Lochie nodded. 'But you'll never guess why I've brought you all the way down here beneath the Earth.'

Fineen took a quick glance over his shoulder in the direction he had come. There was only one way out of this cavern and that was down the opening he had just climbed through. But where only moments ago there had been an opening, there was now only a grey limestone wall. He touched his forehead, realising he was feeling very disoriented and confused.

'Have you taken the Quicken Brew?' Lochie asked.

'I was the brewer,' Fineen told him.

The Watcher smiled. This healer was the key he'd been searching for. Now there was a hope of disposing of Brocan as he had planned. 'I am going to enjoy this,' he sniggered. 'If only all those who cooked up remedies were also forced to take them. We're going to put your recipe to the test. I want to know to what extent the Quicken Brew will preserve life and limb. It must have its limitations.'

'If I tell you what you want to know, will you release me?'

Lochie could hardly believe his luck. He had intended to conduct a few tests of his own on this Druid. Now it seemed Fineen was willing to save him the bother and tell him everything he knew about the Quicken Brew.

'You're willing to divulge such information? I would've thought you'd want to guard it with your life.'

'You'd find some way to learn the secret anyway,' Fineen noted. 'You're a shape-shifter. It would be no trouble for you to find out anything you wished to know. So I might as well tell you and save us both a lot of bother.'

'You are wise,' Lochie conceded. 'I'll allow you to leave when I have the information I am seeking.'

'Very well. I'll tell you all there is to know about the Quicken Brew.'

Lochie bowed in a gesture of thanks. He caught his captive's eye as he straightened up. Suddenly flames erupted and a small fire appeared between them. It was set in a fireplace constructed just like any central hearth.

Fineen was still gasping when he stumbled sideways onto a sturdy three-legged stool. He almost fell but caught himself and was left leaning heavily on it for support. His eyes were unbelieving.

'Take a seat and tell me your tale,' Lochie hummed as he squatted by the fire.

Hesitating a moment, the healer drew the stool up to the fire. Then he sat down to face the Watcher, ready to relate the story.

Of the many legends, tales, songs and epic poems, none were so ancient, so shrouded by the mists of time, as the story of the Quicken. Arcane motifs had been added to the telling of it and it was only a skilled tale-weaver who could discern their meaning.

When the empire of the Islands of the West was entering decline the Druid herbalists of that time stumbled on one of nature's great secrets. Afraid of the ramifications of their find the Druids jealously guarded the discovery. However, it was generally agreed by scholars of the histories that they'd hit upon some hidden key to the mystery of procreation. Whatever the truth, within twelve seasons there were new grains being cultivated that could withstand high rainfall or dry spells.

Elated by their success the Druids applied to their assembly to continue investigations along this path. The Druid Assembly attested to the value of the work but expressed concern at such tampering with nature's ways. The herbalists were challenged to find an unquestionable advantage to justify the continuation of this study.

The wisest of the Druid healers were called in to help. And within nine summers the Quicken Tree was planted as a sapling.

It was claimed that a berry from this tree could cure all ills in man and beast alike. And what is more, whoever consumed its broth would live forever without blemish of time or mark of age.

The Druid Assembly were unanimously appalled at such a prospect and they outlawed the Druid herbalist who was custodian of the tree, banishing him beyond the waves. And for good measure they ordered all his work be censured indefinitely. The Druid healer left the Islands of the West and came to Innisfail. With him he brought some berries from the Quicken.

In time he was accepted by the Danaan folk for he had great skill as a healer and herbalist. In secret he cultivated his own Quicken, never speaking of its mysteries to anyone except his apprentice. That young woman guarded the tree throughout her lifetime and passed the secrets on to her student.

And that was how, Fineen explained, he had come to be the latest in the line of healers whose knowledge descended from that first outlawed Druid. That was how he came to be the Guardian of the Tree, Keeper of the Quicken Berries. And only one other Druid alive knew the recipe for the healing brew.

Lochie listened to Fineen's account with rapt attention. When the healer had finished the Watcher asked the question that was at the forefront of his thoughts.

'Is there any way the effects of the Quicken Brew may be annulled?'

'If anyone who has tasted the brew should fail to take it at least once in every turning of the seasons, they may suffer some malady,' Fineen asserted. 'But no one knows exactly what form that might take. The knowledge has been lost down the generations.'

'And any sickness may be cured by the brew?'

'If one who has taken the brew falls ill, the effects of the sickness will last but a short while, perhaps no longer than the time it takes for a small cauldron of water to boil.'

'And wounds are healed completely?'

'In a much shorter time,' Fineen confirmed with a nod.

'But does the brew keep hunger at bay?'

'No. In fact I find my appetite much improved since taking the brew.'

'And if, for instance, no food were available?'

'Do you mean what would happen if there was famine in the land?'

Lochie nodded.

The healer held a hand to his chin to consider the question. 'I have no idea,' he admitted at last. 'All I can say is that there have been a few occasions where I've been observing a fast as part of my duties and at each time I've felt incredibly sleepy. Not merely tired but totally exhausted to the point where I had to be helped out of bed on the third morning of the fast.'

'Have others attested to this?'

'Yes,' Fineen answered. 'Dalan and I were joking about it the other day.'

The healer stopped short. 'I've told you what I know,' he said. 'Now set me free.'

Lochie stood up and shrugged. Then he smiled and there was an unusual warmth in his expression.

'Fineen,' the Watcher began, 'you've been most helpful. I'd be happy to release you.'

He paused, held out a hand to the fire and the flames dropped down.

'But the truth is, I can't afford to,' he went on. 'I need to do some work among the Fir-Bolg and you have provided me with the perfect disguise. To that end I've decided I will keep you here for a while.'

'No,' Fineen whispered.

'I can't leave you any food but I can assure you the fire won't go out,' Lochie continued. 'So you'll be warm and dry at least. The water from the springs in these caves is drinkable so you won't thirst.'

'How long do you intend to leave me here?'

'A few moons, no more.'

'I'll be missed.'

'No you won't. I'll be taking your place.'

With these words Lochie's face transformed before the

healer's eyes. And for the first time in his life Fineen saw himself as others saw him. This was no mirror image glimpsed in a clear pool. This was how he appeared to the world.

His fascination overcame his panic. 'What do you hope to achieve by this?'

'I don't want to let on just yet,' Lochie said, and his voice was Fineen's own. 'All will become clear with time. Do not fear, I won't let any harm come to you.'

'Abandoning me here in this cave will hardly be good for my health!' the healer added sarcastically.

The Watcher came a little closer then and spoke in a sympathetic tone. 'You may not believe me, but I would not wish anything to happen to you.'

'I'll be missed.'

Lochie shook his head. 'No one will even guess that you are biding your time in the depths of these caves. Why would they when they will see you going about your normal daily business as if nothing was wrong? I must admit you could have posed me quite a problem. I mean to say, I can't kill you, can I? The best I can hope is to store you somewhere for a while.'

The Watcher looked around the chamber mockingly, his arms held wide. He smiled but managed to restrain his laughter. When he spoke again his tone was threatening.

'There's no sense trying to escape. I've sealed the entrance to this cavern. None of Brocan's folk have ever come this deep so they won't notice the changes I've made. Go where you will within this domain. But you should understand you are beyond aid. No one can hear your cries nor witness your tears.'

'But what will become of me? I may drift into an unending sleep if there's no food for me to eat. No one really knows enough about the Quicken brew to state confidently whether there may be some adverse result.'

Fineen looked away in anguish.

'Well, my friend, we shall just have to wait and see.'

Lochie placed a hand lightly on Fineen's shoulder.

The captive turned to face his tormentor, but though Fineen could still feel the pressure of a hand upon his shoulder, the Watcher was already gone. The fire blew up, warming the healer but not cheering him.

It was much later that the shock of all that had happened finally hit the forsaken Danaan Druid. But it was long after that he sat down upon the stool in defeat, placed his head in his hands and sobbed.

At the same moment Lochie was revealing his impersonation of the Fir-Bolg king to the healer, Brocan himself was shut away with his closest adviser. Fergus the Veteran, friend and confidant of the king, lay down by the fire, carefully considering a strategy for the Brandubh contest.

The gaming board was a short-legged table no higher than a baby's knee on which was carved the signs which marked its purpose. Seven squares measured each of the four sides, with a central place for the white warlord High-King. The white pieces had been turned from the teeth of a walrus. And the twelve dark Ravens were gouged out of the hearts of rare black stones.

This table had been crafted in the days of long ago when the Fir-Bolg were fighting off the Danaans. In those times the white pieces on the board, the kings, represented the four tribes of their people. And the fifth piece, the warlord, symbolised their chosen king, their saviour in time of mutual threat.

Now only two tribes of the Fir-Bolg remained after having gradually absorbed the other two. In the west and south of Innisfail the Cairaighe held sway. Brocan and the Burren folk were of this kindred. In the north and east the Cruitne were predominant. Many of those folk had moved on to the eastern land of Alban since the coming of the Danaans.

So this gaming board had seen the fortunes of the Fir-Bolg fall and rise throughout the generations. And now once more, as many times before, the floor of the king's house was laid with furs and the board had been set by the fire for competition.

The king lay stretched out opposite his chief counsellor, the two challenging each other with strategies while they tried to put to rest the problems of their people.

Fergus laid a large hand on one of the dark pieces and shifted it along the board. Then he sighed and rolled on his back to stare aimlessly at the ceiling. Brocan frowned, leaning his arm on the corner of the table as he sat up. He picked up his wooden cup and drained the last drops of mead. He reached over for a doeskin bag, removed its stopper, poured himself a cupful and then offered the skin to his friend.

Fergus considered the offer for a few seconds then shook his head. He didn't want to arrive at his mother's house smelling of mead. Brocan sighed with frustration. 'Where are they?' he fumed. 'Lom and Aoife should have been back by now.'

The veteran didn't even bother to reply. He'd heard this question twenty times since the game began.

'Try to relax,' Fergus advised. 'Even if Aoife and Lom were here right now you would be no closer to finding a solution or making a decision.'

'I would be if you could offer some advice! But all you do is move your pieces and lie upon your back. You haven't said a word since I told you about the message from King Eber and his suggestion of alliance.'

'I've been considering all that you've said,' Fergus protested. 'I want to be sure I have explored all the possibilities in my mind before I utter any word that might be interpreted as advice.'

'Do you think you'll be ready to comment before dawn tomorrow?' Brocan snapped.

'It's just passing sunset now,' the veteran assured him. 'It's very generous of you to give me so much time to think about it.'

This comment stopped the king. He couldn't be sure whether Fergus was joking. And he never found out for at that moment the leather flap over the doorway lifted and a warrior poked his head through.

'My lord, your son wishes to speak with you.'

'He's arrived at last!' Brocan huffed. 'Send Lom in to me immediately.'

The sentry coughed nervously. 'It isn't Lom, my lord, it's Sárán.'

The king sighed as he stretched out by the Brandubh table again. 'That bloody misfit! Very well, let him in. But bring Lom and Aoife to me the very instant they return.'

'Yes, my lord.'

Immediately Sárán opened the flap and entered. It was clear by the dour expression on his face he'd heard the whole exchange. Brocan made no move to greet his son so the young man came no further into the house.

Fergus lay still, staring at the ceiling, unwilling to say a word lest it be read by the king as lending support to Sárán.

'Don't bother to rise,' the young man began, seeing they weren't about to anyway. 'I've come to tell you I delivered your message. Aoife, Lom and the others were at Dun Burren playing warriors. When I arrived your daughter, ever the gentle Druid, had just rendered Iobhar of the Gaedhals unconscious with a knee applied enthusiastically to his groin.'

'What?' cried the king.

'When I departed, Mahon was preparing to carry the poor

foreigner back here upon his shoulders. I expect that is why they're so far behind me.'

'She was playing at warriors again?' Brocan snarled.

'With her lover, Mahon, son of Cecht, spurring her on,' Sárán added, relishing the pain his words were causing. 'She is certainly in violation of the Druid prohibition against such behaviour. I will be bringing this matter up with her tutor.'

'Be quiet!' the king bellowed. 'This is none of your affair. I forbid you to interfere.'

Brocan sat up and looked at Sárán for the first time. 'Get out of my sight. Go back to your master Fineen. I have no further use for you.'

Sárán bowed low as he lifted the leather flap and left the house.

'You shouldn't be so hard on the lad,' Fergus advised. 'One day you'll regret your sour treatment of him.'

'I only regret the day he was born,' Brocan grunted. 'He's never been anything but trouble.'

'He's just a lad.'

'He betrayed me by stealing the Cauldron of Plenty which was awarded to me by the Druid Assembly. He handed my honour over to my enemies. Prior to that he affronted the Warrior Circle with an unprovoked attack under the very mantle of a truce. He is trouble and I bless the day when Fineen took him away from me once and for all.'

'You've since forgiven your enemies,' the veteran noted.

'I expect my foes to take advantage of my weaknesses. I expect betrayal at their hand. I don't expect it from my son.'

'I have a suggestion,' the veteran cut in.

'I've heard enough of Sárán for one day!' Brocan boomed.

'I was referring to your other children,' Fergus sighed, refusing to be baited into a fight. 'I was talking about Aoife. Have you come to a decision about her future in the holy orders?'

'I have a mind to wed her to the King of the Gaedhals. I

made the decision while I was waiting for you.' The king sighed then he took a mouthful of mead and lay down by the table once more to listen to the views of his trusted confidant. Fergus hardly flinched at the news. He was used to Brocan's abrupt manner.

'It's well known she has no love for the Druid Circle,' his friend shrugged. 'If you can negotiate her withdrawal from the order she would be free to train as a warrior as she wishes. But if, as her guardian, you command her to marry Eber, she will refuse.'

'She only has eyes for that Danaan Mahon,' Brocan shot back. 'Her mother left me for his father. It must be in the blood.'

'Mahon has nothing to do with it,' the veteran retorted. 'She will defy you because you have ordered her to do something she might otherwise have done with or without your approval.'

'I don't understand what you're saying.'

'Tell Aoife about the offer of alliance the King of the Gaedhals has sent. Send Lom and Aoife to Eber's court as your emissaries. And before they go, give them a stern warning about the consequences of misbehaviour.'

'That will only ensure they both cause havoc,' Brocan hissed indignantly.

'That's what you want them to do.'

The king shook his head and sat up again. 'Why?' he asked, confused.

'If Aoife is provoked in the right way she'll marry Eber of her own free will, no need for persuasion of any kind. And that will guarantee your treaty of alliance with the Gaedhals. I agree, there is no other way to secure such an agreement. Marriage into the nobility of the Gaedhals is the only way.'

'My only concern is that she will resent me for bargaining with her life in this manner,' Brocan admitted.

'She'll thank you, in time,' Fergus sighed. 'It's clear she's not content with the life of a Druid in training. Everyone knows it, especially her teacher, Dalan. He's spoken with you about his frustration with her. Let her be what she wishes and do as she pleases with her life. She's too headstrong to follow any other path.'

'Will Dalan agree with you?' the king asked.

'Only Dalan has the authority to reverse his verdict against her. He is the one who set her on this path in penance for her misdeeds. You must ask him.'

'I will,' Brocan decided. 'And then I will ask the Council of Chieftains.'

As he spoke his eyes scanned the Brandubh board again. To his surprise he noticed a gap in his opponent's defences. In a moment he'd moved his warlord down the table to a winning position. And for the first time in a long while Brocan smiled.

Chapter Eight

lumber sang a slow lingering lullaby before spreading its drowsy veil over Dalan the Brehon. And all the while he dimly perceived the menacing presence of the Raven perched high in the rafters.

The intensity of the creature's glare was so threatening Dalan jolted in his sleep several times before exhaustion relaxed him and he rested soundly at last. And when he had been in that state for a long time a dream finally came to him.

A dream unlike any other he had ever experienced.

The Brehon was still conscious of the great black carrion bird looking down into the room. But his perspective of the situation had changed. He wasn't staring up toward the ceiling at the Raven. Rather, he was gazing directly at the bird as if she were seated beside him. This unsettled Dalan's instinctive defences and he teetered between the waking and the sleeping worlds for just a moment. Then, when he realised the Raven wasn't making any threatening moves, the Brehon relaxed again. He felt his shoulders drop as he stretched his neck high and took a deep breath.

Suddenly he felt a sharp pricking sensation on his chest. It soon became an urgent burning sting. It was at that moment Dalan realised he had a beak. But the revelation didn't surprise him at all. It was as if he'd always had this sturdy appendage on the front of his face. In a moment he plunged the point of his beak into the mass of feathers which now covered his chest, scraped the skin underneath and found what he was looking for. With all the deftness of any bird the Brehon plucked the parasite away and in one smooth movement tossed it to the back of his throat. He felt the tiny creature struggle momentarily, then he swallowed hard, cawed with contentment and shook his wings.

In the next instant he scanned the room for vermin with eyes that needed no firelight to spot their prey. It was this keen eyesight which first made the Brehon frown. Suddenly the dreamlike sensations he was experiencing had become vividly real.

His chest rose and fell silently and though he hardly moved at all he was aware of every muscle in this strong body. The feather tips of his wings vibrated gently as he drew in breath. His hard clawed feet gripped the beam with such force he knew the timber would be scratched and splintered where he sat.

The Raven seated on the roof beam nearby slowly cocked her head at him and Dalan stared entranced into the black void of her eyes. The bird narrowed her eyelids, bringing all her skill at scrutiny to bear upon him.

And Dalan's feathers shivered as the bird sized him up.

'You're quite a fellow,' the Raven said in a rich throaty croak.

It was a voice that was utterly feminine. But more like the creaking ropes of a ship at sea it was than the sound any living creature might make.

'My brothers and sisters tell me you are marked for the office of Dagda.'

'I was nominated,' the Brehon replied in a hesitant crow that emanated from the back of his throat. 'I intend to decline the offer,' he added, and realised it was true.

'Decline?' the Raven laughed. 'You'll decline the highest office of your order? You are pushing aside an opportunity to lead your sacred sisters and brothers into the new age which lies before them?'

'I have other work to do.'

'You are so selfless,' the bird retorted bitterly and the sarcasm in her voice was clear.

'You seem to know a lot about me,' the Druid shot back, becoming bolder now.

'Who hasn't heard of the exploits of Dalan, Brehon judge of the highest standing?' the Raven mocked in a childish sing-song voice. 'Saviour of the Fir-Bolg. Slayer of Owls. Mediator, Law-Keeper, Harper, Poet and Hunter of the Watchers. Quite a list of responsibilities. When do you have time to sleep?'

'I thought I was sleeping at this very moment.'

'You are. In a manner of speaking at least. I suppose I could have come to you in some form more appealing to your sensibilities. I could have revealed myself as a beautiful, sensuous young woman, or even as your mother if I'd thought of it. But I have certain standards and I prefer not to lower them unless absolutely necessary. There is, after all, no form so graceful, so strong or so enticing as that of the Raven kind.'

The bird shifted her head as she caught a movement out of the corner of her eye. She stared at the far end of the room for a few breaths then turned back to Dalan.

'You should consider this transformation a great gift,' the creature went on. 'Few of your kind have ever known the ecstatic joy of inhabiting such a body.'

'Who are you? What do you want of me?'

'I am Chief Raven of the Chorus,' she replied. 'It's a very dignified position. When the queen speaks in council to her people it is my duty to lead the assembly in echoing her words. I am her lady-in-waiting, her servant, her messenger, her instrument of justice and her anointed successor. And the queen is coming near to the end of her days.'

The Raven cocked her head toward the end of the room again, taking careful note of the tiniest sounds, scents and scurried shuffles.

'I am the most influential female of my kindred throughout the Isle of Innisfail,' the bird went on, eyes still scanning for prey. 'And I have chosen to speak with you because the queen has charged me with forging a friendship between our peoples.'

'Friendship?' Dalan asked, his voice wary.

'Hard times have come upon my folk,' the Raven sighed, giving the Brehon her full attention. 'Since the Gaedhals came to this land we've witnessed many changes. Not many of them have been for the better. Eber Finn, who calls himself King of the South, has been fortifying Dun Gur by rebuilding the old walls. His people construct dwellings wherever they choose, without consulting their Druids or the spirits which dwell in the land.'

'They are an ignorant folk,' Dalan nodded.

'That is perfectly plain to me,' the Raven snapped back.

'I mean to say that their ancestors have never settled in one place for too long,' the Brehon explained. 'They have lost all knowledge of such matters in their constant wandering.'

'That may well be the reason for their behaviour. But it doesn't make it any easier to bear.'

The bird snuffled her beak against the underside of a wing, shook her head and went on. 'The forests are being cut down faster than they can be replaced. Fields have appeared where once there was only virgin woodland. The green canopy of the forest is shrinking at an alarming rate. Such destruction has never been known. Not even under the rule of the Fomorians who laid some places to waste. So that now nothing grows upon the earth they trod.'

'There are still many forests where the ringing of the axe is unknown,' the Druid noted.

'That is true,' the Raven conceded. 'But your people, who used to be friends of all the woodland folk, have allowed this destruction to go on without a word of protest. What has become of the Brehon law which enshrines the sensible usage of the land? This practice was instituted generations ago. Why has it been so quickly abandoned? And why have the judges of both Danaan and Fir-Bolg turned a blind eye to this unchecked madness?'

'The Fir-Bolg have been busy rebuilding their lives after the destruction of Dun Burren,' Dalan informed him. 'Everyone, man, woman, child, warrior, Druid and king, has been mindful of only one task. The establishment of a new home.' The Brehon shivered, realising this was hardly a valid excuse.

'As for the Danaans, they now dwell beyond the gates to the Otherworld,' he went on. 'They can't be expected to take much interest in the affairs of this Innisfail any longer.'

'They visit now and then,' the bird corrected him. 'They haven't lost their love of this island which was their home. But they come less and less and seem content with their new abode.'

'In time I expect their visits will be very seldom.'

'You're one of them. You drank the Quicken Brew. Will you withdraw to the Otherworld as well?'

'I will one day, that is certain. This world of eternal decay is bearable if one's fate is mortality. But in the Otherworld there is no death, no disease, no suffering. It is the only place for one such as myself.'

The Raven clicked her beak loudly, then spoke again. 'The Gaedhals must be stopped. And there is a reckoning to be paid. The great fire in the western woods destroyed many of the trees in that part of the island.'

'That fire was not the fault of the Gaedhals,' Dalan cut in.

'The spirits of the woods and the gathered owl folk were the cause of that disaster.'

'The fire was started by a feckless Fir-Bolg youth with no respect for the forest folk and their right to seize tribute from all travellers. Sárán, son of Brocan, lit that blaze. I have no love for the owl tribe and in my opinion they deserve every misfortune heaped upon them. But in all conscience I can hardly condone the boy's actions. As chief among the law-keepers of my people I demand recompense for this crime against all the woodland dwellers.'

'I've never heard of such a claim!' Dalan exclaimed. 'I wouldn't know how to adjudge the wrong or tally up the penalty.'

'If I may make a suggestion,' the Raven cut in confidently, as if this speech had been rehearsed. 'The answer is obvious. The price I claim for my kindred and their allies is a deed and promise from your folk.'

'What promise?'

'Your solemn word that you will halt the destruction brought on this land by the wanton excesses of the Gaedhals. Your binding oath that the Brehon laws regarding the cutting of timber and the clearing of land be observed to the letter.'

'That seems a fair price for the loss of the forest,' the Brehon considered. 'The Danaans and the Fir-Bolg negotiated a treaty with the invaders. And no just consultation was sought with your kin.'

'If you can give this assurance,' the Raven went on, 'then I can promise on behalf of our present queen, and our future queen also, that all my kindred will lend your people their strength in time of trouble. They will offer their wings when there is urgent news to be sent and their hearts whenever despair should cast its shadow.'

'I am not able to give you any assurance,' Dalan pointed

out. 'I am merely a judge. Such a treaty would have to be discussed among the chieftains of my people.'

The bird regarded him intently once more. 'Then accept the offer for yourself. Take on the mantle of advocate for my kin and we will offer you alone among your folk the terms I have detailed.'

The Druid turned his head away to consider what the Raven had said.

'I will do as you ask,' he replied finally.

'Do you swear to uphold the rights of all woodland creatures, those of the earth, those of the air and those of the water, to the best of your ability?'

'I do,' Dalan replied.

'Do you promise to uphold the Brehon laws in this regard?'

'I promise.'

'And I in turn pledge the assistance of all my clans.'

'The Queen of the Ravens must be close to death if you can make that promise so securely.'

'She will be dead before dawn,' the Raven hissed in delight. 'At last.'

Dalan drew in a startled breath and the Raven clicked her beak in mockery of his fright.

'You have already quite a task ahead of you,' the bird went on. 'Lough Gur is drying out because of the unusually hot dry summer. If there is no rain soon the waters will be lower than ever before.'

'I have no influence over the weather,' Dalan objected. 'That skill is practised by others of my order.'

'King Eber of the Gaedhals will try to reclaim the land which lies beneath the lough. He'll try to grow more grain and graze his cows upon the fertile pastures there.'

'He has no need of more pastures!' the Brehon retorted. 'Why would he do such a thing?'

'He's planning a war,' the Raven explained. 'He will need

the extra animals and grain to lure adventurers and mercen-
aries to his camp. And he has a hundred horses arriving from
the land of Iber in a week. He needs that ground.'

'Whom does he intend to fight? Would he break his truce
with the Fir-Bolg?'

'No. He wishes the Fir-Bolg to fight beside him.'

Slowly the answer dawned on Dalan. 'Eber is going to
attack his brother in the north?'

The Raven made a gesture the Brehon guessed was a nod.

'I'll do what I can,' Dalan shrugged. 'But if the King of the
Gaedhals really has his heart set on war, how can I convince
him otherwise?'

'It's not for you to do so,' the bird explained. 'I only ask
that you save the lough. My kin have no interest in the affairs
of the Gaedhals, or the Fir-Bolg for that matter. We only care
about the creatures who rely on those waters for their homes
and livelihoods.'

The Brehon was about to speak when a movement caught
his eye at the far end of the room. A small grey-brown shape
flitted out from under the furs to cross the floor in front of the
fire. Dalan watched the little creature as it darted furtively
from one shadow to the next in the hope it would not be seen.
But Ravens use all their senses when they're hunting. The Druid
heard its rapid heartbeat and smelled the aroma of its fear.

The mouse ran round the hearthstone and in seconds was
lost amongst another set of furs. The Brehon looked down,
studying the area in case the tiny animal emerged. He was so
enthralled by the rodent that at first he didn't notice the
larger shape wrapped up in skins and breathing gently.

'He's sleeping peacefully,' the bird noted dryly.

Dalan didn't take the Raven's meaning at first. But then in
a flash of understanding he looked down once more with
fresh eyes. There was a body wrapped in furs on the floor.
And the shape of it was familiar.

'Is that me by the fire?' the Brehon asked in a shocked tone.

'It is. And if you don't mind, I'll have that mouse. They're very tasty, the ones who live in this forest, but I doubt you'd appreciate the subtle flavour of freshly killed rodent that has been fed on the finest grain from Sorcha's storage.'

'You're welcome to it,' Dalan assured the bird. Then he thought of something. 'What's your name?' he blurted.

'What I am called tonight will be forgotten by the morning,' the bird answered. 'For by then the queen will have passed over as all souls must. Then I will be known by the title she bears. I will be called the Morrigán.'

'You'll be Morrigán of all the Ravens?' the Druid gasped.

He had heard the story of the Morrigán many times, though he'd never imagined he would ever meet her.

But before Dalan had even finished his question the Raven had spread her wings and dropped down to the floor. In the next moment the Brehon felt his feathers fall away as his spirit was drawn back to his body. He fell from the high roof beam, gently but surely to the floor.

Dalan felt a rush of air upon his face, opened his eyes and knew he was no longer a bird. He looked up as he heard a cracking sound. And there before him sat the great black Raven with a mouse in her beak.

The cold dark eyes reflected no emotion, betrayed no hint of feeling, yet the Brehon perceived a great intelligence burning deep within. The bird crunched her prey once more then threw back her head and swallowed the tiny broken corpse.

But Dalan found he was no longer fearful of this creature. He closed his eyes again without a thought of danger and was instantly asleep.

Mahon and Aoife lagged behind the others most of the way back to the settlement. Once Iobhar had recovered he was encouraged to walk, but even with his slowed pace he and Lom were soon far ahead of the other two.

An hour's walk from the Aillwee caves Iobhar halted to rest and there he and Lom waited till after sunset. Lom built a fire and began to wonder, as the night dragged on, whether Aoife knew another route.

He was just thinking about moving on when he heard the Danaan's voice reciting a short nonsense poem. The very instant Mahon and Aoife stepped into the firelight Lom knew what they'd been doing all afternoon. Tousled hair, dishevelled clothes and broad smiles told that tale well enough.

Straightaway Lom lifted his pack and helped Iobhar to his feet.

'Let's go,' he said sullenly.

'Is there a hurry?' Aoife begged. 'Couldn't we stay out for the night?'

'Father has ordered us to return by nightfall. There's important news he wishes to share with us.'

'What could possibly be so important?' she moaned. 'Mahon and I don't share much time alone together. There's always someone sticking their nose in on us making sure we're not up to anything.'

'You're an apprentice Druid,' Lom reminded her. 'I understood you were supposed to be practising abstinence for three moons.'

'How did you know that?' she snapped.

'Let's just say a rumour went around that Dalan caught you and Mahon together in bed. And your teacher punished you with three months of self-restraint.'

'It wasn't because we were in bed together,' Aoife blurted. 'It was because I didn't place his harp in her case as soon as

156

I finished playing her. But it wasn't my fault. I was distracted and forgot.'

Mahon looked to the ground, obviously regarding himself as the distraction.

Lom smiled and shook his head. 'Father will burst a seam if we don't get back this evening,' he warned.

It took a little more persuasion to convince Aoife, but when the fire was doused the four of them set out again. They were all tired and their pace was slow so it wasn't until after midnight that they first saw the lights from the settlement's signal torches.

As they approached the timber palisade which marked the outer perimeter of the defensive works Aoife noticed her father at the wall. He was standing in the torchlight with Fergus at his side.

She realised then she was in trouble, but at least her teacher would not be back for two more days. Brocan might be her father but it was Dalan's duty to punish her if she caused offence or brought shame on him through her actions.

Lom saw his father too and rolled his eyes, expecting the worst. Mahon dragged his feet behind the others, hoping he wouldn't be noticed. Iobhar was the only one glad to be back at Aillwee.

The gates swung open at their approach and King Brocan was waiting in the middle of the path. He said nothing as they halted in front of him and made no move toward either of his children.

'We were expecting you earlier,' Fergus said flatly.

'We became lost among the rocky fields,' Aoife stuttered, obviously lying.

'No excuses,' Brocan cut her off. 'I'm well aware the likely reason you're all late. And I'm certain my daughter had something to do with it. Lom lacks the imagination to cause such havoc. Thanks be to Danu who watches us from the heavens, at least one of my children may prove dull enough to be a good leader in a crisis.'

Lom frowned, annoyed as much at the insults as he was at being dragged into yet another fight between father and daughter.

'Wait till your teacher hears about this,' the king snapped. 'He told me of your prohibition in penance for neglect of duty.'

'Is there anyone in Aillwee who doesn't know?' Aoife retorted sharply.

'You will wash,' Brocan commanded, 'then you will attend me in my hall where Fineen has important news for us. I also have an announcement to make which will affect all of you.'

The four of them passed by to their lodgings to do as the king had ordered. When they were out of earshot Fergus addressed his friend.

'So you've decided?'

'What else can I do? If I do not join an alliance with Eber, Éremon will invite me to side with him. Either way the Fir-Bolg will be drawn into a fight which is none of their affair.'

He sighed heavily and closed his eyes. 'If I had not been so proud,' he admitted, 'I would have encouraged the Fir-Bolg to take the Quicken Brew. We could have withdrawn behind the veil of the Otherworld and lived in peace, health and joy forever.'

'I don't imagine the Otherworld to be so perfect a place as it is claimed,' the veteran replied. 'You and Cecht were lifelong enemies, were you not?'

'Indeed we were,' Brocan nodded.

'I would imagine that immortality gives a whole new meaning to the concept of a lifelong enemy.'

Brocan didn't laugh but the thought amused him and he realised it was of no benefit to be talking of 'should have been' and 'might have done'.

'Éremon is already married,' the king stated. 'So Eber will

be our choice for alliance in the coming conflict. Only blood ties will be surety enough for me that the Gaedhals intend no treachery.'

With that he turned around and walked toward his hall with Fergus joining him at his side. In a short while they were seated at the fire again, waiting for the others. The Brandubh table had been put aside and furs spread on the floor for the guests.

When Lom arrived in a fresh tunic and with a clean face, Brocan sent him to fetch Fineen. But the young warrior was gone a long while. He returned after everyone else had assembled to report that the healer was on his way.

Lochie had been just about to search through Fineen's baggage when Lom had found him. The young warrior paused when he first saw the Watcher and for a brief moment Lochie was unsure whether his disguise was imperfect in some way.

But Lom didn't flinch when he saw the healer in the full light of the fire. Lochie promised to come along soon and sent the lad on his way. Then he wrapped Fineen's best green cloak about his shoulders and went to the door.

Just as he was leaving the house Sárán arrived home.

'I've been looking for you everywhere, master,' the young man exclaimed.

For all his skills and mastery of devious crafts Lochie was so distracted by the thought of the performance he was about to give that he almost made a serious mistake. He didn't realise this young student was the twin of the warrior who'd summoned him.

'The king must be impatient to have sent you back after me,' he commented.

Sárán frowned. 'What do you mean?'

'You've barely had time to run to the king's hall and back,' Lochie noted. 'Is Brocan in such a hurry to see me?'

'I haven't been to the king's hall but once today and that was after I returned from Dun Burren.'

'But I spoke with you a short while ago.'

'Not I,' the young man stated. 'It must have been my brother Lom.'

'Are you so alike?'

'You know we're twins,' Sárán replied, puzzled. 'But I wear the copper brown breacan of a Druid healer in training. Lom is a warrior. He dresses in a red patterned breacan. Are you unwell, master?'

Lochie silently berated himself for his error and resolved to be more careful in future. Such a blunder could have easily aroused suspicion. He squinted, leaned forward and confided to the young man, 'I am a little tired. I've had much on my mind.'

'The news you bear must be a burden, master.'

'News?'

'Of the preparations for war at Dun Gur.'

'Yes.' Then the Watcher reached out to touch the lad on the shoulder. 'Which one of the twins are you?' he asked.

'I am Sárán.'

'So you are,' Lochie replied. 'I'm afraid my eyes must be failing me at last. I've been working too hard. I must have myself a rest soon.'

'We've been busy these last three moons,' his student soothed as he took his teacher by the arm. 'You've certainly not been getting enough sleep. You have so much to think about. It's all my fault. I should be more strict with you.'

They started walking in the direction of the king's hall.

'Don't berate yourself,' Lochie insisted. 'I should be looking after my own health and wellbeing.'

'But I'm your apprentice,' Sárán protested. 'It is my duty to serve you. And I owe you a great debt for my crime and your forgiveness of it. You've given me a purpose in life. I only wish to make amends with you and be a good student. One day I would like to be a healer and be held in the same esteem as you are now.'

Lochie tried to take in all this information. There were so many puzzles opening up to him he was beginning to regret his decision to pose as Fineen.

'I'm flattered that you should speak so,' Lochie nodded appreciatively. 'It won't be long before you're a Druid in your own right, if I have anything to do with it.'

'Thank you, master.'

'Tell me,' the Watcher went on, 'what do you think of the coming war?'

'My opinion hardly matters.'

'One day warriors and kings will seek your counsel. It's time you practised expressing your feelings on such matters.'

Sárán stopped walking and turned to face his master. 'I don't trust Eber Finn or the Gaedhals. How can we be certain Eber won't turn against us once victory over his brother in the north is achieved? The only way to ensure he doesn't turn is to demand weapons from his own arsenal. Weapons of iron. As for Aoife wedding the King of the South, I have my reservations.'

'Aoife?' Lochie gasped. 'Married to Eber Finn?'

And he knew immediately that Isleen had had a hand in the Gaedhal's decision.

'To secure the alliance. The king mentioned it to you before we parted.'

'Yes, I remember clearly now,' the Watcher added hastily.

He smiled at Isleen's ingenuity. She would go to any lengths to win a wager.

'It might be the best course of action to take,' Sárán confided. 'She's unruly and not at all interested in her studies. But I object to her wedding a Gaedhal. Surely a suitable husband could be found among our own people?'

Lochie took the lad by the arm again and together they walked on. But the Watcher had already decided Isleen had won this round of their game. To avoid suspicion he would have to play the go-between in the marriage arrangements. The round was lost but the tournament had just begun. 'Tell me more about your sister,' he breathed, mindful of his light-hearted bet with Isleen.

It wasn't more than a few minutes before they arrived at the king's hall but in that short while Lochie learned a great deal that would be of use to him. He resolved to take more care in everything he said. If his strategy were to work it would take his full concentration.

As they entered the hall Brocan stood up to greet the healer.

'We've been waiting for you,' the king stated. 'Would you prefer to repeat for us the news you gave me this afternoon, or would you like me to begin?'

Lochie's eyes widened a little in surprise and he spoke before he'd had a chance to think. 'My news?'

'The information you told me you received from Máel Máedóc, the chief adviser to Eber the Gaedhal,' Brocan frowned.

'Forgive me,' Lochie begged. 'I have been overworking. I am very tired. I beg you tell your news first. I'll wait.'

'As you wish,' the king shrugged. 'Take a seat by the fire till it's your time to speak.'

Lochie made himself comfortable with as little fuss as possible. He didn't want to draw any more attention to himself so outwardly he was very calm. But his mind was racing, trying to elaborate upon the preparations for war which the Gaedhals were undertaking. Sárán sat beside him in the place assigned to students.

Brocan had silenced his visitors and was about to commence speaking when Aoife stood up and interrupted him.

'I wish to withdraw from the Druid Circle,' she blurted. 'I am not suited to life in the orders. I lack discipline and the will to study.'

'You're a fine harper,' Mahon cut in.

She smiled at the young warrior but bit her lip so the king wouldn't notice.

'Father, I am asking that you aid me in my petition to Dalan. I wish to be released so that I can pursue the life of a warrior and train for war.' With that the young woman sat down with eyes averted, waiting for an outpouring of anger from Brocan. But it never came.

The king glanced at Fergus and raised his eyebrows before he answered in a calm voice, 'I'll speak with you about it later. In private.'

Aoife was so surprised at the calmness of his reaction that her mouth dropped open in disbelief. But Brocan went on as if he hadn't noticed.

'I've received an invitation from the King of the Gaedhals to attend his fortress at Dun Gur for a festival to celebrate the harvest and the first blackberries. Fergus and I have discussed the matter and I've decided there is too much to be done here at Aillwee for me to go. So Lom will represent me and accept the hospitality of the foreigners.'

The young man stood up and bowed to his father. 'I will do my best to serve you, Father. Thank you for this honour.'

Brocan waved at him to sit down. 'I will also ask Dalan to go as a representative of the Druid Circle and of the chieftains.'

Lom was immediately deflated — his role would be as a mere symbol, the son of the King of the Fir-Bolg. It would be Dalan who would be conducting any business or negotiations.

'The Council of Chieftains meets here in two days time. The other news I have must wait till then.'

Lochie looked up, expecting to be asked to speak. But Brocan wasn't quite finished.

'I have an announcement to make,' he went on. 'I have decided to appoint Mahon to the task of supervising the building work on Dun Aillil. That is the name I've settled on for the fortress we are constructing at the mouth of the caves.'

Mahon stood up to acknowledge the commission but he didn't get a chance to say anything.

'Of course you will have to stay here when Lom and Dalan travel to Dun Gur,' Brocan went on. 'For we have much work to do and you cannot be spared.'

The king sat down. He'd decided not to tell Aoife of his decision for the moment. And in the event it also silenced any objections Mahon may have had for he assumed his lover would be staying with him.

'Now Fineen has some news which he asked to share with my closest family and advisers.'

Lochie stood up and tried to look confident even though he had only a broad idea of what he was expected to say.

'Go on,' Brocan urged. 'I have a lot of work to do tomorrow. The longer you delay the less sleep I'll have tonight. And Fergus is setting off for his family home after this meeting.'

The Watcher coughed.

'What word do you bring from Máel Máedóc?' the king insisted.

'His greetings,' Lochie stammered. 'The Gaedhals send their good wishes to you in the hope they will have your company for the Lughnasa fires.'

'Is that all?' Brocan asked tersely.

'Yes, my lord.'

The king frowned, realising that Fineen must have a reason for staying silent about the preparations for war going on at Dun Gur. On reflection he understood the wisdom of this silence. He didn't want any rumours circulating about

impending conflict before he'd had a chance to open negotiations with Eber Finn.

'Will you be going past Dun Gur before midsummer?' the
king inquired.

'Quite possibly,' Lochie nodded.

'Then take my message to Eber Finn. Tell him of the work
I'm doing here to fortify the caves. Apologise for me that I
cannot accept his invitation. And inform him my son and a
chief among the Druid kind will come in my place.'

'I will, my lord,' Lochie bowed.

'Now everyone to bed,' Brocan snapped. 'Lom and Aoife,
stay where you are. I wish to see you both after the others
have left.'

Mahon, Sárán and Lochie departed the hall. Fergus waited
by the door to make sure there were no interruptions.

It was Lom who faced his father first as soon as the others
were gone.

'When I issue a command to you, you obey me immediately and without question,' Brocan raged. 'If I can't rely on
you in times of peace, I certainly can't rely on you in battle.
Follow my orders in future. Do you understand?'

'I do.'

'Go to bed.'

'Yes, Father.'

And without another word between them Lom left the
hall.

Then the king turned to Aoife. 'You've been trying to get
Dalan to dismiss you for some time,' he chided. 'Everyone
knows you would rather be a warrior than a Druid. And no
one would want you to do anything against your will. You
would be a bad Brehon judge because your heart isn't in it.'

The king reached for his mead cup and took a sip.

'I don't mind feeding Dalan from our storehouse,' Brocan
went on. 'He's a good judge and a wise counsellor. But I will

not provide for one who cannot match his talent and devotion. We live a precarious existence. One among us who is not worth her dinner is one too many.'

'I'm so glad you've started to see things my way,' the young woman replied. 'Will you help me?'

The king touched his daughter on the top of the head and nodded.

'I will do what I can,' he told her. 'But I want you to think carefully about Mahon. I'm afraid you may have been using him to attract attention to your cause.'

'That's not true!'

'Then how is it you were caught by your teacher in Mahon's bed? Why did you leave a harp by the fire untended? Weren't you meant to be guarding it?'

Aoife looked down in shame.

'It was nothing to do with Mahon. It was all my fault. I wasn't thinking of my duties.'

'This foolishness has to stop. If you are to be accepted into the Warrior Circle you must learn to take your orders from me. If you disobey me you will suffer for it.'

'I will do as you command,' she promised. 'Just release me from this life of study.'

'I'm not sure you understand how serious matters have become,' Brocan pressed. 'You were given over to the Druid Circle to pay a debt for a crime. The debt still has to be paid. Dalan will insist on a fine to buy you out of your obligation.'

'I'll repay you with my loyalty.'

'You'll raise cattle and reimburse me for every cow it costs,' the king told her. 'If you do not strive to be a loyal, obedient warrior, the Brehons will have no choice but to banish you. Do you know what that means?'

'No help from anyone. No word, no sign, no acknowledgment,' she answered grimly.

'You will simply cease to be. No one will dare to so

much as look at you for fear they will be banished too. Think on that before you sleep tonight. That is the path you'll take if you're not careful. And you'll be beyond my intervention then.'

'Will you speak to Dalan for me?' Aoife asked anxiously.

'I will. Now go to bed.'

The young woman stood up, kissed her father on the cheek and wished him goodnight. Then she was out the door past Fergus before the king had a chance to change his mind.

When the veteran stuck his head inside the door the king shrugged.

'I wish I'd thought of that a long time ago,' he sighed.

'A little gentle guidance never hurt anyone,' Fergus replied. 'Now, it's time I was going.'

'Very well then,' the king grunted. 'I have something I'd like you to do for me after you've visited your mother.'

'What's that?'

Brocan stood up and went to a wooden box. He opened it and brought out a length of finely woven yellow cloth with a red, grey and black check design in the weave.

'Go to Dun Gur and present this breacan cloak to Eber. I know I asked Fineen to pass the message on but it's unseemly for a Danaan to be sent on the business of the Fir-Bolg.'

Fergus took the cloak.

'Don't tell anyone I've asked you to do this,' Brocan went on. 'I want you to find out what bride price the Gaedhal would be willing to pay for Aoife.'

'What price are you seeking?'

'The knowledge of iron,' the king whispered. 'So that our people are the equals of their allies.'

Fergus smiled at his friend. They embraced briefly, and then the veteran was gone into the night.

Chapter Nine

I t was still dark outside when Dalan woke with a start. Sorcha was standing by him in the firelight, kicking his foot lightly to stir him. It was a few moments before he sat up and stretched his arms to the ceiling.

Then he was overtaken by a sudden violent fit of coughing that had him gasping for breath.

'Bring up all that silt,' Sorcha soothed as she patted his back. 'A night in a sod house with a peat fire burning does wonders for clearing out the chest.'

Dalan couldn't answer her but if he'd been able to he would have suggested that the thick smoke in the room could hardly be considered good for the health.

It was quite a while before the coughing passed and the Brehon was able to stand. Then he draped his cloak over his shoulders, grabbed his travelling pack and headed outside into the clean air.

'I'll wait for you out there,' he gasped.

The Druid woman grunted assent as she gathered her gear for the journey and piled the furs against one wall. The sky was beginning to brighten at the approach of sunrise by the time she joined Dalan outside.

'We must hurry if I'm to make it to the spring by dawn,' she told him. 'Are you up to it?'

'I've completely recovered,' the Brehon stated confidently.

'You don't travel very much any more, do you?' she asked.

Dalan shook his head. 'I seem to spend most of my time at King Brocan's side, helping him sort out his troubles. When I do go off journeying it's rare I have the opportunity to wander as I please. The joy of travelling seems to have deserted me so that even when I'm off trudging the roads my thoughts are not free to roam as they will.'

'Well this little adventure should change all that,' she slapped his shoulder. 'It's probably time you got yourself fit again.'

She set off along the path to the spring, Dalan following close behind. With the approaching dawn lighting their way and knowing what to expect, the Raven idols were not as disturbing to the Brehon as they had been.

Dalan stayed close behind Sorcha nevertheless. The thought of becoming lost in this wild wood did not appeal to him. There was an ancient menacing spirit about the place, primal, savage and barbarous. And he wasn't ready to encounter it just yet.

By the time they came to the spring the sky was a light grey-blue and cloudless. Sorcha busied herself with preparations for the fire ritual of morning, a rite Dalan had only heard whispered rumours about.

When he was an apprentice Brehon, twenty winters ago, his teacher had warned him about the Ritual of the Sun. It was an arcane practice, it was said, which stirred the power within Sun and Earth. The energy thus raised by the celebrant was immeasurable and unpredictable.

It was this force, so the story goes, that led directly to the destruction of the Islands of the West in days gone by. For the Druids of old used it to their own purposes and the spirit of veneration which lay behind the ritual was neglected and forgotten.

There were some, of course, who always kept the true

169

meaning and purpose of the ritual sacred. But they made their devotions in secret for fear of persecution.

The details of the practice were handed down the generations of Druids as a sacred secret to be shared with only one person, usually a student. So careful had the keepers of the ritual been that even one such as Dalan had never witnessed it. And he had travelled the length and breadth of Innisfail. He'd been nominated to the highest office in the Druid Circle. He'd met most of the travelling Druids of the orders and indulged in endless discussions about the forces of nature and how they might be summoned to a just cause. Yet still he had never seen the Ritual of the Sun.

Sorcha knelt down at the fire pit which had been gouged out of the rocks next to the spring. She carefully placed splinters of wood within, blessing each as she did so. Then she gathered some dry grass and leaves for kindling.

'May I learn from you?' Dalan ventured.

The Druid woman looked down to where he was standing by the spring.

'Come up here then,' she replied after a few moments consideration.

The Brehon was suddenly excited. He felt as though he was about to be initiated into a great mystery.

'Though the details and the practice have long been kept guarded,' Sorcha told him, 'this rite requires no special knowledge or learning. Anyone may take part in it and feel the benefits immediately. But I warn you, it must be performed precisely or the energy which rises may take a dangerous form.'

Dalan made no comment as she began to prepare her sacred fire. Sorcha took a flint and struck it against a smooth river stone. A spark flew out and she deftly caught it in a nest of dry grass and leaves.

Then, as if she were breathing life into it, the Druid woman gently blew on the kindling until the grass began to glow.

Suddenly a flame erupted. She whirled the nest of tinder round her head and it burst into flames. In an instant she had thrown the fiery mass down into the fire pit among the twigs. Then she carefully built the sticks up around the delicate fire until it was burning intensely.

Once Sorcha was certain the fire was well established she opened a wooden box that lay at her side. The box had two compartments. One half was full of butter, the other of what looked to Dalan like a dry compressed herb. Sorcha took a fine copper spoon and sprinkled some of the herb over the flames. Then she picked out a small quantity of butter and placed it in the middle of the fire.

That done, the Druid woman knelt down to stare at the horizon and wait. The Brehon was intrigued by the significance of these items and the meaning behind the ritual. But he was too respectful to ask her anything just now. He resolved to make a full inquiry when the time was right.

Dalan followed her gaze to the horizon and soon understood what she was waiting for. On a hill some four hundred paces away there was a lone standing stone. The top arch of the sun was already outlined behind the monument, its movement clearly visible.

The Brehon was surprised at how quickly the golden orb climbed up into the sky. The stone changed from blue to grey to black in a matter of moments as the sun rose higher above the horizon.

Dalan had watched the dawn on countless occasions. It was his favourite time of day. The beauty of sunrise always touched him to the heart. But this was the first time the deep mystery of the event had struck him so deeply.

Sorcha made no move or sound until the upper rim of the sun just clipped the top of the stone. The monument split the orb in two and light spilled out all around it. The Brehon had to turn away from the intensity of it.

And then he heard the Druid woman chanting. With a musician's ear he listened for words and melody but the language was strange to him. And the tune was just a monotonous repeated phrase.

Yet the Brehon sensed a power within the sounds that reminded him of the song-making of the Druid musicians at the Battle of Sliabh Mis. The warmth of the sunlight bathed his face and the force of it flowed through his body to his feet. His toes tingled no less than his fingertips and he breathed in deeply, savouring the sweetness of the air.

All his troubles faded. He felt refreshed, renewed and ready for whatever challenges lay ahead. So deep was the effect that the Brehon started to hum along with Sorcha under his breath.

The Druid woman paid no heed to the Brehon. All her concentration was focused on the flames of her sacred fire. Her mind's eye was travelling among the embers seeking out the hidden pathways to the Otherworld of the spirit.

The keeping of the ritual had been her duty for the greater part of her life. Her teacher had passed the secrets of its significance to her when she was but nine summers old. And since the old woman had passed away Sorcha had continued to kindle the flames whenever she was certain she would not be disturbed by others. This was the first time for many seasons that a stranger had been present while she was engaged in the Ritual of the Sun. She knew instinctively Dalan would not understand the meaning behind the symbolism and was unlikely to judge her harshly for her dedication to this ancient practice.

As her thoughts became calmer the Druid woman drifted into a peaceful, euphoric state, the natural state of the soul. Singing all the while, she clearly saw in her memories the withered form of her teacher leaning heavily on a staff, speaking of the Oneness of all things, of the great creature composed of everything which drew breath and all that did not.

Sorcha was but a girl in those days and hardly understood the deeper meaning of the old woman's words. It was before her initiation, before she wore the brown robes of the Frith craft and before her head had been shaved across the forehead in the Druid tonsure. Sorcha clearly recalled the fear that had dwelt in her heart at being separated from her mother for the first time.

As the seasons passed Sorcha had grown to love her teacher as a soul-friend and developed a profound understanding of her view of the world. The Oneness her teacher spoke of was not easily discerned at first. It could not be perceived without dedication to the purpose.

Yet once an initiate was opened to an awareness of the Oneness the knowledge became an integral part of their being, affecting every action, thought and word.

As Sorcha watched the flames consuming her kindling she said a silent farewell to the spring and the forest where she had lived since her teacher's death. In her heart she thanked the woods, the waters and the Ravens for the knowledge she had gleaned from them. She wondered how long it would be before she was able to return to this place she called home.

The sun rose higher in the sky, scattering its warm rays across the sparkling stream. Sorcha looked at the ashes one last time and knew that despite taking the Quicken Brew she must one day return to the dust. She had no understanding of how this might come to pass. Then she glanced up at the world around her and was certain that the great living organism of which she was but a small part would guide her to that step when the time was right. Sorcha took a deep breath as the last of the embers died. Abruptly she ended her chant and looked around at Dalon.

'The ritual is done. Now I must wait for the fire to die down. The ashes have a special quality which rejuvenates and heals the sick.'

'I feel like I've never seen the sun rise before,' the Brehon whispered, his voice full of awe.

'I'll teach you all I know, if you've a mind to learn,' she offered.

'I'd like that,' he replied without hesitation. 'I've suffered the Faidh all my life. I would dearly love to learn the skill of the Frith.'

Their eyes met as Sorcha returned his beaming smile.

'We'll be at Aillwee by sunrise,' Dalan told her.

'Go fill our water skins,' she said, turning back to the tiny dying fire. 'By the time you've done that I'll be ready for the road.'

The Brehon climbed down from the rock in the sprightly manner of a younger man. He found the skins by Sorcha's pack and waded into the pool to get close to the spring. All the while the water gurgled cheerfully out from its secret depths within the Earth. And Dalan thought he'd love to live here in the forest far from the cares of the world beyond.

***

Goll woke with a start and sat up. Despite his desperate desire to see he couldn't seem to focus. He was still drowsy and he hated to be in such a state of unreadiness. The warrior shook his head as his hand found a cup full of some liquid. Without thinking he put the cup to his lips and drank the contents.

Almost immediately his vision cleared and he knew the sun had already risen. By his side among the furs was a mass of black matted hair which puzzled him at first. Then he remembered that Mughain had come to his shelter after all the other warriors were asleep.

'The sun's up,' he said, prodding her in the back with his finger. 'This is no time for sleeping. We've work to do.'

Mughain grunted and pulled the furs up over her head so she couldn't hear him. As she did so Goll stood up to get dressed in his fighting gear. He was arranging his breacan cloak when a head poked in through the tent opening.

'Good morning, brother,' Goll said when he recognised Conan's face in the shadows.

'Good morning,' the younger warrior replied. 'I'm sure it will be a wonderful day.'

'Conan, why didn't you wake me?' Goll hissed. 'I told you to make sure I stirred at dawn.'

'The raid is cancelled,' Conan announced flatly. 'I had a dream last night that warned me of your death.'

'Brother, have you been drinking again?' The war-leader stepped forward and sniffed his brother's breath. 'I gave orders there was to be no drinking.'

'I haven't touched a drop,' the younger man protested.

'You're a poor liar.'

'I promise you on the names of the gods our people swear by,' Conan answered solemnly. 'I am not lying to you. Last night I saw your death in my dream.'

'You're mad.'

'If you go down to that settlement this morning with the intention of raiding you will die at the sword of a Fir-Bolg champion,' Conan insisted.

Goll took a few deep breaths, determined not to waste any energy on this foolishness. He would need all his strength for the coming raid.

'Call the Fian together,' he ordered. 'I want to reach the village before the women take the cows out to pasture and the other folk go out in the fields.'

'Didn't you hear what I said?' his younger brother gasped. 'If you go down to that rath you'll forfeit your life.'

'There isn't going to be any fighting,' Goll snapped back. 'We'll be too busy driving cattle and loading grain to have time to draw our blades.'

'But there are four old Fir-Bolg warriors within the walls. They'll surely put up some resistance. And they are a strange race with an uncanny influence over the elements.'

That was enough for Goll. He could bear his brother's prattling about dreams and omens. He'd put up with that since they were children. But now Conan was refusing to obey commands.

The war-leader grabbed his brother's tunic close to the throat and hauled the younger man close. When Goll was certain Conan could see every pore of his skin, every flick of his eye and every twitch of his mouth, he spoke in a low slow menacing tone.

'You'll do as I tell you or I'll give you the beating I should have given you when you were a boy.'

'I'll not see you waste your life on a dozen cattle and a barrel of smoked fish. You could be King of the Gaedhals one day if you're careful. Don't tempt disaster by fighting with the Fir-Bolg.'

'There'll be no fight!' Goll spat back. 'There'll be no need. The Fir-Bolg warriors have nothing better than bronze swords. Those archaic weapons are no match for silvery steel. If those warriors are wise they won't even leave the hearth fires where they slept last night.'

'Brother, I fear for your life,' Conan sobbed, his eyes welling with tears.

Goll frowned. In the past he'd seen his young brother suffer through many delusions, usually related to his overindulgence at the mead barrel. But this was different. There was something in Conan's eyes that spoke of real fear.

The war-leader began to wonder whether he should listen

to the warning. As the first doubts crossed his mind he heard a stirring growl from the bed of furs.

'Come back to bed, Goll. It's cold and I'm sleepy.'

Goll pushed his brother away with a sneer. Then he turned around, grabbed the furs and pulled them from the woman warrior. Mughain curled up to cover her nakedness. Then, suddenly wakened by the cold air, she shook her head to clear it.

'The Fianna are becoming weak,' Goll grunted. 'They have no work to do and so they grow lazy and frightened. Well I'm not going to stand by and watch the Fian bands decline until they're all too afraid or too drowsy to go raiding.'

He turned to his brother. 'Go and fetch the warriors. If you haven't returned with them in the time it takes for me to put on my boots and fasten my cloak, then you'll answer to my blade. Do you understand?'

'Yes, brother,' Conan bowed, shaken by the threat.

In a moment he was gone. Then Goll turned to Mughain. 'You shouldn't encourage him. He's getting worse day by day. I'm certain he's losing his mind.'

'And what if he proves to be right?' the young woman asked. 'Would you throw away all hope of becoming king?'

'I've never aspired to the kingship.'

'But those who have travelled with you and fought under your guidance have considered it for you,' Mughain told him. 'There are those of us who would risk our honour to depose Eber Finn tomorrow if you gave the command.'

'Are all the other warriors of the same mind?' Goll asked, stunned.

'Everyone in our band would stand for you.'

'Even my brother?'

'Especially your brother. You have a loyal and devoted follower there. That's why you should be a little easier on him.'

She wrapped a fur about her body then stood up. 'Don't

throw your life away,' she begged him as she came close. 'Conan may be right in his prediction.'

Goll placed his strong hands on her shoulders. 'Who knows of Conan's prophecy?'

'Every warrior in the band has heard him speak of it,' she replied. 'He told them as soon as he woke.'

'Then I must carry out this raid,' the war-leader decided. 'I must show that I'm not afraid of prophecy. I will prove that nothing can turn me away from my goal once I've set my mind on it. I can't be seen to back down just because of a dream. I want the warriors to follow me to the last.'

He looked into her eyes. 'Don't worry. I intend to be very careful. But if I can survive my brother's prophecy I will ensure the continuing respect of the Fian. I have a feeling I'm going to need that.'

'I can see your heart is set on it,' Mughain sighed. 'At least let Conan and I guard you.'

'Very well,' the war-leader nodded. 'If I'm killed I'll lay the blame on you. You can pay my family the appropriate compensation.'

'Don't joke about such things,' Mughain warned him. 'I don't want to lose you and neither do any of our band.'

'Get dressed,' he told her as he sat down to pull on his boots. 'We've a long walk to the settlement. I don't want the morning to be too far advanced before we get there.'

Fergus looked up at the clear morning sky and found the sun. It was over three hours after the dawn and he judged he would reach his mother's rath within the hour. Up ahead there was a fork in the path which puzzled him.

He hadn't travelled down this northern road for many

seasons because when he lived at the old fortress of Dun Burren he would journey on the southern track. The old veteran stopped when he came to the fork and wondered which path would take him to his mother.

When he couldn't make his mind up he decided to climb a little bare hill that nestled against the path to the left. At the top he looked out to the south trying to spot familiar landmarks. At last he spied a road he recognised winding around some hills to the south-east. This confirmed for him that he should take the left-hand fork.

Taking advantage of these few moments to rest he took out his leather mead bottle and swallowed a mouthful of the honey-golden brew. Just as he was replacing the stopper a flash of reflected sunlight caught his eye and he noticed some movement along the winding road he had observed earlier.

The old veteran put a hand to his beard. There was a large party of warriors running down the track toward his mother's settlement. They were far off so it wasn't easy to discern who they were.

They could not possibly be Fir-Bolg warriors, he reasoned, because every able-bodied person had been employed to the task of building a new fortress at Aillwee. Only lone messengers travelled the roads these days. Then Fergus realised the flashes of light were too bright for bronze weapons.

These warriors were armed with the steel of the foreigners.

'Gaedhals?' Fergus whispered to himself, confused that so many would be abroad at such an early hour.

An overwhelming sense of foreboding descended upon the veteran. His heart jumped a beat. These folk were about to launch an attack on Rath Carriaghe. Visions of Eber's raid on Dun Burren swamped him. The Gaedhals were a vicious and treacherous race. They would not scruple to raid a quiet village without warning.

Before the realisation had a chance to fully form in his mind, Fergus was hurtling down the hillside toward the road as fast as his old legs could carry him. At the fork in the path he veered to the left, his thoughts scattered by fear for the defenceless Fir-Bolg farmers. He knew his mother was already very ill and he worried that any shock might prove fatal. As he sprinted he begged the spirits of the Otherworld to help him reach her in time.

His legs were already tiring by the time he reached that part of the road where he'd first spotted the running Gaedhals. His chest was heaving hard and strained. But Fergus didn't slacken his pace for a second.

A thousand sprinted steps from the settlement he thought he'd have to give up the furious pace. His body was racked with agonising pain; his head was pounding with the rush of blood and the raising of his battle fury.

At the summit of a small rise he glimpsed the rath in the distance. And there he reluctantly stopped for a moment, bent double to catch his breath. After a few deep lungfuls of air he straightened up and looked toward the home of his kindred.

There were strangers in the rath. That was certain. Four men and two women wearing the silvery helms of Gaedhals were driving the cattle out of their hut into the centre of the enclosure. A few others were rounding up the goats and sheep. But Fergus had seen at least a dozen fighters on the road. These accounted for only half that number. His fears renewed, he set off again.

He was slowed by the exertion of his run, his body unable to maintain the pace he demanded of it. Fergus considered dropping his pack by the side of the path to lighten his load, but he remembered that he was carrying Brocan's gift to Eber Finn. If he didn't hide the pack well these raiders would surely find it. And he wasn't willing to waste time doing that. So he ran on until he came to within a hundred paces of the rath.

There he stopped again and found a place under the trees to catch his breath and ready himself for a fight. This took longer than he would have wished but he knew it would be senseless to charge into the fray straight after such a strenuous run. In his urgency he cursed his feeble body that once would have been able to sprint twice that distance, swim a river and still be ready to raise an axe to the enemy.

When Fergus had calmed his breathing he stepped out onto the road. There he had a clear view of the hilltop settlement. And what he saw almost stopped his heart from beating altogether.

Two foreign warriors were dragging an older woman from her house. Fergus knew it could only be his mother. Now his blood rose into a rage that almost blinded him. There was one thought on his mind — to rescue his loved ones from this cowardly attack.

As he redoubled his pace he saw his mother forced to kneel before three Gaedhals, two men and a woman. All three were looking down at her with contemptuous laughter. As the veteran reached the gates of the settlement he drew his sword from the scabbard across his back. He well understood that his bronze blade would be no match for weapons of steel. But he thought that if he could avoid their swords and get a good blow in, he might frighten the Gaedhals into backing off.

It was the woman standing over his mother who saw him first. In a flash she had drawn her sword and stepped up to challenge him. As she came forward the warrior at her side took three paces back and the other man drew his blade also.

'Stand your ground, Fir-Bolg,' she demanded.

Without even hearing her words Fergus raised his weapon and brought it down across her blade with such force he was certain it would shatter into a thousand pieces. But miraculously the bronze sword did not break and the woman warrior was forced to fall back.

'Mughain, come back by my side!' a warrior called out.

Fergus immediately realised this man was the leader of the raid. In the next second he'd managed to get close enough to the woman that he could push her hard. She fell backwards onto the ground with a grunt.

The war-leader stepped up, drew his sword and prepared to meet the challenge.

'What's your name?' Fergus bellowed, his rage getting the better of him. 'I've never killed a warrior who was unknown to me.'

'I'm called Goll mac Morna,' the war-leader replied as he levelled his blade at his enemy. 'I am also known as the king's champion, the Lord of Slaughter and the Guardian of Sliabh Mis.'

'Are you a servant of Eber Finn?'

'My brother's a servant to no man!' spat another warrior.

'Be quiet, Conan,' Goll snapped. 'I'll fight my own battles.'

'You must not fight!' the woman warrior exclaimed, and Goll faltered for the briefest moment.

That was just long enough for Fergus to make his move. In a desperate and dangerous manoeuvre he sent his sword spinning wildly toward Goll, who moved deftly aside to miss it. But even as the champion Gaedhal avoided the weapon, Fergus lunged forward, thumped the war-leader hard in the chest and wrested the steel blade from his hand.

'Now the fight will be fairer,' he declared as he swung the weapon round to get a feel for its balance and weight.

But he barely had the chance to size up the sword before Conan was upon him, roaring a wild battle cry. The ferocity of the attack took Fergus completely by surprise and he immediately retreated a few paces with his weapon raised to parry the Gaedhal's blows.

As soon as Goll recovered he snatched Mughain's blade and joined in the affray. But Conan yelled at him to stay back.

'Two of us will beat him easier than one,' Goll replied.

'You're putting yourself in danger!' Conan insisted. 'Let me deal with this.'

But the king's champion wasn't going to fall back with his tail between his legs. He pushed his brother aside and advanced against Fergus with fire in his eyes. The Fir-Bolg veteran ducked and weaved, avoiding his opponent's blows and launching a few of his own.

'You're a fine fighter for an old man,' Goll complimented his foe, using his sword to block the attack.

'And you aren't bad for a young man,' replied Fergus.

Suddenly the veteran was stirred by a warrior instinct to move quickly in order to save his life. He lunged forward and caught a glimpse of Conan readying to strike at him from behind. In a graceful move the Fir-Bolg raised his weapon high in the air and spun around on one heel. Then, in a magnificent move as well executed as that of any dancer, he swung his sword arm round in a wide arc. He brought the blade close to his chest after it flashed past Goll's head. Then, using the momentum of the move, he struck out at the king's champion with his elbow. Goll fell back, caught completely by surprise.

Conan saw the wide gap in the veteran's defence, raised his weapon and stepped forward to bring the blade down hard on the Fir-Bolg's head. But Fergus had been expecting such an answer to his assault. In an easy sweep he lifted his blade, spun around and lunged down at his enemy with the point of his sword.

The weapon struck home with such force that Conan's leather armour was split at the shoulder. The cold steel ripped the tunic he wore beneath and then it bit into his flesh. The young warrior fell back on his knees, screaming with agony.

As Conan stumbled, Fergus's weapon was torn out of his hands and he was suddenly defenceless. In moments there were Gaedhals all around him and every one of them was armed for war.

They thrust their sword points toward him, threatening and goading. Fergus caught a cut across his arm and another drew a line of blood on his cheek. But he kept a cool head about him, as was his way when all seemed lost.

The foreigners were taunting him now and the veteran knew they were trying to wear him out in readiness for the kill. As another weapon struck him in the back of the leg he teetered forward. In the next moment he was dodging a great long heavy boar-spear that Mughain had dragged out of his mother's house. Fergus had to grab at the shaft of the weapon to fend it off. The young warrior woman was very skilled with the spear, and with half a dozen swift slashes she had his tunic in shreds.

'You've killed my friend Conan!' she screamed in a high-pitched wail of hatred. 'Now I'm going to cut you to pieces and no sorcery will save you.'

Fergus heard his mother crying out for mercy. He smelled the coppery stench of his own blood and felt an aching in his limbs such as he had never known before.

But he wasn't about to surrender and allow these poor farmers to be pillaged. With a final burst of strength and determination he grasped the spear shaft firmly the next time Mughain thrust the point at him. To her horror he twisted the weapon round in her hands until she lost her grip on it. She got clear of him as quickly as she could and he swung the spear over his head to keep the other warriors at bay.

All the Gaedhals retreated to a safe distance and the Fir-Bolg farmers stopped their entreaties. One Gaedhal foolishly leapt forward but the veteran stuck the spear in his arm and he rolled away, crying out for the pain of his injury. Another man came hesitantly forward but a ferocious grunt from Fergus was all it took for him to back down.

Soon the only sound the veteran could hear was the straining of his own breath. He still turned to face the surrounding enemy so they could see the hard resolve in his eyes, but he was feeling weak and unsteady on his feet. He couldn't possibly keep up this defence much longer. The time had come for talking.

'Let these people alone,' he hissed. 'They've done you no harm.'

'Drop your weapon and we'll discuss it,' Goll offered as he strode forward.

Fergus held his spear directly toward the chest of the leader of the Gaedhals. 'Get back or I'll open you up for the crows to feed on.'

Goll mac Morna let a faint smile turn up his lips. He took one step then another toward the Fir-Bolg veteran until the point of the spear rested hard against his leather armour. The two men faced each other eye to eye, faces painted with sweat but neither ready to move so much as a finger width to withdraw.

Then, in a sudden and unexpected move, the war-leader turned his back on Fergus, untied the straps that held his armour in place and let it fall to the ground. In moments he was facing the Fir-Bolg warrior again but now there was nothing but a linen tunic between the spear point and his chest.

'I've faced death a hundred times,' the Gaedhal declared in an emotionless tone. 'Do you think I'm going to show any fear now?'

'Stand back from him, Goll!' Mughain cried out. 'He's already murdered your brother.'

'The boy's not dead,' Fergus scoffed. 'I didn't strike him deep enough to kill him. But he'll think twice before he matches weapons with my folk again.'

The veteran turned his attention back to the Gaedhal who stood before him. 'If I took your life now,' he stated

185

confidently, 'there isn't a Brehon judge who'd find me at fault. You've broken the treaty of Dun Gur. You've brought dishonour on your people and your king. If Eber Finn knew of this he would have you placed under banishment.'

'How do you know my king hasn't sanctioned this action?' Goll shot back.

Fergus let the spear point drop a little before he spoke. 'I know because I'm carrying a message and a gift from my king pledging our alliance with your people. This is in answer to an offer from your king.'

As he heard these words Goll mac Morna's face grew pale and his expression changed from one of arrogant contempt to disbelief. He quickly glanced around the gathering of warriors and saw they were whispering among themselves.

'If Eber made an offer of peace with your people he would have informed the Council of Chieftains,' the war-leader noted. 'I sit on that council and I have heard of no such plan.'

'Perhaps King Eber doesn't trust you,' Fergus snapped, and a murmur of outrage passed around the Gaedhals. Mughain spat at the Fir-Bolg's feet. But Goll knew the old warrior was probably right. This new treaty had been arranged without his knowledge.

The king's champion knew he had to act. Eber had betrayed them. Goll shuddered at all the pretty titles he'd been given. They had been bestowed by a king who had misled his own people. If Goll was going to salvage his pride and the respect of the Fian, it was his duty to remove Eber Finn from office and provide effective leadership to the people of the Southern Gaedhal.

'I did not agree to the treaty of Dun Gur,' he informed the veteran. 'Nor did I have any idea my king was negotiating an alliance with your people.'

Once more he glanced around at his warriors and noticed they had fallen silent and were listening intently to him. Goll looked down at the spear point and decided to deal with this Fir-Bolg quickly and expeditiously. There was work to do and this old man was keeping them from it.

'Throw down your weapon and I guarantee no harm will come to you,' the king's champion soothed. 'You and I have no quarrel. You're obviously a man of honour. If you yield to me I'll see you're well treated.'

'You're raiding my family's home!' Fergus spat. 'If we have no quarrel, why do you have the point of a boar-spear above your heart? Give me an assurance you'll leave my mother's people in peace and I'll hand over my weapon.'

Goll tightened his lips and narrowed his eyes. 'You've injured two of my best warriors, one of whom is my own brother. You're surrounded and outnumbered ten to one. I don't believe you're in a position to press terms.'

'You have a spear pricking at your chest,' Fergus countered. 'I don't believe you're in a position to refuse my terms.'

'What good would it do to murder me?' Goll asked. 'You'd be dead a few seconds after me. And this settlement would be plundered anyway, though I suspect it would be a more thorough sacking if my blood were spilled.'

The war-leader smiled. 'Lay the spear aside and we'll talk.'

'Don't trust him, son,' an old woman's voice called out.

An ancient crone stooped by her ninety winters lifted her staff in the air.

Fergus was strengthened in his spirit to hear such defiance in his mother's frail voice.

'Don't believe a word this ruffian tells you!' she yelled.

Goll smiled when he realised the mother/son relationship and briefly considered using the old woman as a hostage.

'You'd better pray that he does, old woman,' mac Morna advised over his shoulder. 'If he doesn't do as I say, I guarantee this settlement will be scattered stone by stone until there's no trace left of it or its people.'

'Eber Finn would never have sanctioned such a raid,' Fergus noted. 'You savages may all be cast in the same likeness, but your king is wise enough to keep his word.'

'He won't be king much longer,' Mughain cut in.

That confirmed for the old veteran that these folk were renegades who held no respect for King Eber's treaty. For the first time since he was a young warrior, Fergus was stung with an oppressive fear. Every pore of his body shivered with anticipation of an awful blood-letting.

'Order your warriors to leave the rath,' the veteran demanded as he pushed the point of the spear hard against the war-leader's chest.

Goll didn't move. His eyes were fixed on those of his opponent. And the two stood like that for a long while, facing each other down. At last the Gaedhal turned his head slightly and spoke to his warriors over his shoulder.

'I want you all to leave the rath,' he began.

There was an immediate chorus of objections from the Fian.

'You can't give in to him!' Mughain protested.

As she spoke, Fergus nudged forward with the spear and the pressure of the point between his ribs caused Goll to flinch. His eyes caught those of his enemy again. And suddenly his brother's dream came to mind. Perhaps he really was going to die here at the hands of this old man.

'Hear me!' the Gaedhal commanded. 'You will retreat from this rath. But not until this veteran has surrendered his weapon.'

Fergus raised his eyebrows in surprise. 'I won't yield to you.'

'Then we'll stand here until one of us falters,' Goll shrugged. 'I'm a young man. I have a good ten hours in me before I'll need to rest. How long do you think you can last?'

The veteran knew the war-leader was right. He had run a great distance. He was an old man. He was already exhausted. Gently closing his eyes in resignation, he let the deadly spear point drop until it touched the ground at his feet. Then, after a short hesitation, he let go of the shaft.

The weapon fell with a clatter.

Goll smiled and took a step closer to the veteran to put a reassuring hand on his shoulder. 'Thank you,' he whispered.

Then in a flash he drew a long dagger from his belt and, before anyone had a chance to gasp, he drove the weapon hard into the underside of Fergus's ribs.

The veteran's eyes opened wide and his jaw dropped. He threw his head back in inexpressible pain. He reached out a hand to grasp Goll's tunic but the strength was already draining from his body. Fergus leaned forward to support himself against his enemy and the knife bit deeper into him.

Then with his last few breaths he spoke a curse. Part binding spell, part prophecy, such a pronouncement was a powerful declaration that constrained the life of the recipient.

'I lay a Geis on you, Goll, son of Morna,' the veteran whispered hoarsely. 'You'll never sleep in one house more than three nights in a row. You must never show mercy to a stranger as long as you live. If a black pig should come into your possession, not a drop of blood must fall from its body. If your king summons you, you must not tarry but travel to him by the most direct road. No woman may come between you and your next meal. Your brother will be the instrument of your downfall.'

The Fir-Bolg's mother pushed forward but was restrained by a Gaedhal.

Then Fergus slipped to his knees, dead before his body hit the ground. Goll stood grasping his bloody knife but he did not look down. A Geis was an overwhelming burden and the Geis of a dying man was the strongest of all.

As strange as the words sounded to everyone present, every single person knew that Goll mac Morna's fate had been sealed. One by one each of these prohibitions would be broken, there was no doubt of that. And when the last prohibition was concluded it would signal the end of the war-leader's life.

Goll understood now that no matter what happened in the future this raid had changed his life forever. In a sense his brother's prophetic dream had already come true. The warrior threw his knife to the ground and looked around the silent gathering of the Fian.

'Burn it,' he ordered.

'What?' Mughain stammered.

'Burn the whole bloody place down. Burn the houses. Burn the grain store. Set fire to the curraghs. Gather all the cattle, and the goats and sheep. But don't harm a single one of these Fir-Bolg. I want them to live to tell the tale of Goll mac Morna.'

The Fian enthusiastically set about their task while the war-leader stood silently over the body of the Fir-Bolg veteran, the sound of the old woman's keening hollow in his ears. After a long while he glanced down at the bloody corpse and noticed a piece of bright yellow woollen cloth poking out of the pack.

Goll knelt down and pulled it out to take a closer look. It was a finely woven breacan cloak, golden yellow in colour with a pattern of red, black and green checks. Though light-weight, the garment was obviously sturdy and warm.

With the breacan in his hand the war-leader stood up. He knew this must be the gift the King of the Fir-Bolg had sent to Eber Finn. With a smile he wiped the blood off his hands with it. He was about to throw it aside when another thought came to him. This breacan would be the symbol of his kingship. As much as it was a sign of Eber Finn's treachery, it would also be the badge of his own worthiness.

'I have come to save my people from betrayal,' he whispered to himself, wrapping the cloak around his shoulders.

Then the war-leader saw the flames already leaping from the thatch roofs of the low houses. He picked up his sword, helped Conan to his feet and dragged him toward the gate of the rath.

'So much for the premonitions of your dreams,' Goll scoffed as he laid his brother down in the grass outside the walls.

'It would have been better if Fergus had killed you outright,' Conan replied grimly. 'Now there's a Geis laid on you and you cannot avoid your destiny.'

'I make my own fate,' the war-leader replied. 'I always have done. That's how your prophecy was proved wrong. I never believed I would die this day.'

'You'll make a great king,' Conan told him. 'But you're a bloody fool.'

Chapter Ten

A oife sat in the shade of an oak tree, Mahon dozing in her lap. Not far away Iobhar the Gaedhal was also sleeping peacefully, propped up against the gnarled brown trunk. Lom was stretched out on his back in the grass. By the gentle heave of his chest and the occasional snort it was apparent he too was resting deeply.

The young woman stroked her lover's hair as her thoughts drifted off. She was envious of these three lads who were born to the life of a warrior. They were free to follow their chosen vocation without hindrance.

She was not so fortunate. She had committed a terrible crime when she was younger. Her mischievous nature had led Mahon's younger brother to his death. She touched the Danaan's brow tenderly and silently thanked him for his forgiving nature.

If only, she told herself, Dalan could have been so understanding. In judgement for being a party to a young man's death the Brehon had imposed a harsh penalty on her. She was condemned to follow the Druid path.

It was a road she had never wanted to walk. Tedious learning of ancient tales. Endless lessons at the harp. Countless little rituals and observances that drove her to distraction. And all those warm summer days wasted indoors discussing the precedents of law.

She had tolerated the restrictions of this life for three cycles of the seasons because she had really believed she should be punished for her foolishness. But now she was beginning to understand what kind of life lay ahead of her if she continued to honour Dalan's judgement.

And she knew the Druid path was not for her.

Warriors were free to travel the country as they wished and take a spouse whenever they were ready. A Druid might not attain initiation until all their tests and tasks were completed. And as long as she remained a student of Dalan, Aoife knew she would not be allowed to marry Mahon.

The young woman took a strand of her lover's hair and twisted it into a knot. Mahon winced and slapped her hand as the strand tangled.

'Be careful!' he laughed. 'That hurts.'

Aoife let the hair slip through her fingers. 'I'm sorry.' Then she leaned forward to get his attention. 'Have you ever travelled to the north?' she asked in a low voice so the others wouldn't hear.

'Never.'

'It's quite a different country from the west and south,' she told him.

The young Danaan hummed sleepily in acknowledgment.

'I've been there twice with Dalan,' she went on. 'Éremon, the King of the Northern Gaedhals, has built a fort he calls Teamhair. It's a beautiful place. There's a fine house for every chieftain and a great hall where wondrous feasts are held. There are many more Gaedhals in the north than here in the west.'

Mahon opened his eyes to look at her. 'Perhaps Dalan will let me come along the next time you visit the northern king.'

'I'd be very surprised,' the young woman replied, shaking her head. 'He doesn't approve of us spending so much time together. He seems to think I'd be better off with a man of Druid training.'

Mahon closed his eyes again. 'He'll change his mind one day.'

'I'm tired of waiting for him to change his mind!' she growled.

Mahon looked up at her in surprise at the change in her voice. 'We've discussed this many times, Aoife,' he reminded her. 'The only way you'd ever escape your vows and the penalty imposed on you would be to abscond. And where would you run to?'

'Teamhair,' she answered, full of excitement now. 'I'd go to the court of King Éremon.'

'You'd be banished by your own folk!' the young Danaan exclaimed.

'I don't care. I'd be allowed to follow my own destiny. I'd be able to train as a warrior and forget the tedious learning of poems and music.'

'You're a fine musician.'

'I want to live the life of a warrior. It's my true path in life.'

Mahon sat up a little on his elbows, twisted his body round and stared into her eyes. 'We've taken the Quicken Brew,' he reminded her. 'There is no death for us nor sickness. And I'm beginning to believe there's no sense in fighting either. There's no use for warriors in a world without death.'

'The Gaedhals are still a threat to our people.'

'Not as long as you've got one strong knee,' Iobhar quipped bitterly, and betrayed the fact he had been listening in on their conversation all along.

'But you're talking about going to live among them!' Mahon retorted, ignoring the Gaedhal's little joke.

'I'm just saying I don't wish to live any longer under the constraints that have been placed on me.'

'You don't want to be banished,' Mahon told her. 'You can't even imagine what that would mean.'

He lay back down in her lap, closed his eyes and took her hand in his.

'I don't understand why you're not happy,' he continued. 'You're the daughter of a king. You've a respected Brehon for your teacher. You don't have many duties to perform. You have guaranteed good health and a long life ahead of you. You and I are happy together. What more could you want?'

'I'm away with Dalan on his cursed journeys for most of the summer,' she spat. 'I don't really spend that much time with you.'

'I think you'd quickly grow tired of me if you had to put up with me every day,' Mahon sighed. Then he rolled onto his side and put his arm over his head as if to filter out her words.

'Perhaps I'm tired of you already,' she whispered, but he didn't hear her. She was only half glad he hadn't.

She'd always imagined that he'd stay by her side if ever she were banished. Banishment was reserved for the worst of all criminals — oath-breakers and murderers. It was a severe penalty, placing the offender beyond the help and hearth of all kindred and friends. Anyone who assisted a person placed under banishment was themselves banished.

The banished simply ceased to exist. And because they no longer had a place in society, any crime committed against them was ignored by the Brehon judges. They had no claim for recompense nor any hope of appeal against their sentence.

Aoife understood that if she deserted her teacher and went off to Teamhair she would be condemned as an oath-breaker. Banishment would be the immediate result. But she was becoming so desperate it no longer held any fears for her. Her father had promised to speak to Dalan on her behalf but she was growing daily impatient, and there was no guarantee the Druid would free her from her vows.

As she looked down at the handsome Danaan warrior who

lay with his head in her lap she realised something for the first time. She *was* growing tired of Mahon. He was content to waste his days with fishing, mock fights and sleeping. But Aoife knew she needed more excitement. She craved new influences, new ideas, new adventures. Mahon only ever thought about his next meal.

In that instant Aoife realised she was very much like her mother. Riona had tired of King Brocan when they were both still young, but she had remained loyal to him out of a sense of duty. As the seasons had passed, however, Riona had grown more and more bitter at the life she had been given. At last, when she had been unable to bear old Brocan's ways any longer, she had left him for Cecht, the King of the Danaans, who was also Mahon's father. Now, according to all reports, she had found her happiness in the realm of the Otherworld with the Danaan folk.

Aoife briefly wondered whether she could dwell content in the Otherworld. It had been her teacher's decision to remain behind when the Danaans departed, but she had been relieved. There was still too much left to explore in this world and where was the thrill in living in a place that was too perfect, without danger.

Her mind was made up. She had to escape her commitment to the Druid path, even if that meant becoming an outlaw. In the same moment she knew she would have to leave her beloved Mahon who had been her companion, friend and lover for three winters. She felt a twinge of regret for all the laughter they had shared. She frowned when she tried to imagine life without him. He was a good man in his own way, caring, gentle and simple in his tastes.

But the wider world was beckoning to her and Aoife knew she must answer the call. She pushed Mahon's head from her lap, jolting him from his slumber.

'What — ?' the Danaan grumbled. But Aoife ignored him.

'Iobhar!' she cried. 'It's time to teach me something of the bow.'

'Not now, Aoife. I'm tired.'

'Get up off your arse, you lazy Gaedhal, or I'll take to you with my blade.'

'All right, all right,' he groaned. 'Give me a moment to find my arrows.'

Soon they were standing side by side as Iobhar explained the fine points of bowmanship to his new pupil. Aoife took the bow and one arrow which she slotted into the bow-string as she'd been shown. Iobhar stepped closer to her, placing an arm around her shoulder as he pressed his body close to hers.

'Treat the bow like a lover,' he explained. 'Take your time. Let the tension build on the string. Caress the tip of the arrow, and then when you've selected your target, close your eyes for a second and savour the moment. Imagine the arrow flying off to do its work.'

Iobhar felt Aoife's body against his and his one thought was of stealing her away from Mahon for himself. He leaned in closer to whisper directly into her ear. 'I'll take you to the court of the King of the Northern Gaedhals.'

'What?'

'Come with me. We'll run away together.'

Aoife opened her eyes wide and let the arrow fly from the bow. It sailed high into the air in a graceful arc as she shoved her elbow hard into Iobhar's ribs. He stepped back to avoid being winded, but he was certain there was none of the usual violence in her gesture. She hadn't meant to hurt him. She was just being playful.

She turned to look him directly in the eye and they both forgot the lesson in bowmanship for the time being. The arrow sailed off into the distance and was lost. Neither saw it fall.

'Show me again,' Aoife purred. 'I don't quite understand what you mean by treating the bow like a lover.'

Iobhar smiled with half-closed eyes and handed her another arrow. She lined up the notch of the missile with the bowstring and drew back on the bow a little. The Gaedhal moved nearer again and she yielded her body to him, leaning back so they were in close contact.

'The trick is in the way you hold the shaft,' he began, and Aoife let out a deep giggle of delight.

She forgot Mahon was watching everything. In fact she hardly cared. If he didn't want her enough to run away with her, then she'd go north with a man who did.

Then, across the pasture in the line of her bowshot, Aoife caught sight of a thin black-haired young man dressed in the Druid brown of a healer's apprentice. There was no doubt about the identity of the young man. By the loping gait and haughty carriage it could be none other than her brother Sárán.

'A black cloud has just blown in,' she whispered to Iobhar.

'We'll get some rain then?' the young Gaedhal asked, turning to survey the skies.

While he was distracted Aoife let the arrow fly. It sailed off toward Sárán as if rushing to meet him at some predetermined place in the middle of the field. Iobhar grabbed the bow and flung it down when he realised what she'd done.

'Are you mad?' he gasped. 'You'll kill him!'

'I hope it strikes him through the heart,' she hissed. 'I know he hates me for what happened to him. I swear I despise him for leading me to the Druid path.'

'It was none of his doing,' Mahon cut in harshly. 'And well you know it.'

'Get out of the way!' Iobhar screamed.

But Sárán had seen the missile coming toward him and easily avoided it.

'What were you thinking?' Iobhar shouted, grabbing the young woman by the shoulders. 'You could have killed your own brother!'

'You've lived among us long enough to know the Quicken Brew keeps death at a distance from those who supped it,' she sneered. 'Sárán is safe. In any case, the arrow didn't hit him.'

Iobhar stepped back from her, appalled at her lack of concern for her brother's wellbeing. He understood what it meant to have taken the Quicken Brew but was only just beginning to realise how different these people were becoming as they adjusted to the idea of immortality free from injury or sickness.

'I wish he'd leave us alone,' Mahon grumbled.

'Aoife just shot an arrow at Sárán!' Iobhar exclaimed. 'Is that all you can say?'

'She's right,' the Danaan shrugged. 'It might have hit him but it wouldn't have done him much harm. Perhaps he would have suffered some degree of pain for a while, but that would have quickly passed.' With that Mahon rolled over onto the grass and covered his head with his arms to feign sleep.

Sárán leaned heavily on his staff as he made his way toward them, giving the impression of age beyond the span of his seasons. His cloak was impeccably clean, without a wrinkle or loose thread. His long black hair was tied back from his face and the beard which had sprouted on his chin was neatly trimmed.

Aoife thought how much more suited her brother was to the Druid life than she. He seemed to revel in the discipline, the learning and the symbols of his social stature. She could understand how a man such as he so easily accepted the rules, strictures and abstinences required of a student of law and lore.

199

Sárán had always been ambitious for status. And there was no greater status to be earned than that of a Druid adviser. As he came closer Aoife realised her brother could indeed wield a great deal of power if he were set behind the figure of a weak-willed king. The implications of this insight disturbed her greatly and she glanced anxiously at Sárán's twin, Lom, who was lying on his back, breathing slowly.

'Aoife!' her Druid brother called out. 'What do mean by shooting that arrow at me? I'm your brother and a fellow Druid!'

'It's Iobhar's fault,' she explained. 'He's not a very good teacher.'

'You shouldn't be playing with arrows anyway,' Sárán spat. 'It's unseemly for a trainee Brehon to dabble with weapons. Especially the weapons of the Gaedhals.'

Iobhar opened his mouth to protest at being blamed for the whole incident but he was ignored. The apprentice healer went on, speaking as if the Gaedhal were of no consequence at all.

'It's time to come back to Aillwee. Dalan has returned and he has news we all must hear.'

'I'll be along presently,' Aoife replied tersely.

'You must come now. Your father and your teacher have summoned you. Have you forgotten your vows?'

'I remember my promise to both of them only too well!' the young woman yelled back, returning the bow to Iobhar with a growl of frustration.

'What has upset you so?' the Gaedhal asked. 'He's just your brother. You shouldn't let yourself become so worked up by him.'

'This is none of your concern,' Sárán informed him, coming over to shake his twin from his sleep. 'You're not Fir-Bolg. You're just a hostage. You can't expect to be privy

200

to the news and affairs of our kin.'

'Iobhar is our friend,' Lom interjected grumpily, cross at having woken to such petty squabbles. 'He's become part of our family.'

Sárán sneered, casting a hostile eye over Mahon who was still pretending to be asleep. 'If you ask me there are too many foreigners at our father's court. They insinuate themselves into his favour for their own purposes, feed off the bounty of our cattle and steal the hearts of our women.'

'Shut up, Sárán,' Aoife said flatly. 'I'm in no mood to hear any of your bitter speeches today. We've had a fine morning hunting and a relaxing afternoon sitting here under the oak. Don't spoil it all with your hateful words.'

'Dalan has returned,' he answered with icy venom in his voice. 'And at the first opportunity I'll speak with him about your disrespectful ways and the company you keep.'

'Talk with him all you want. Perhaps he'll see the wisdom in letting me change to the warrior path.'

Sárán grunted at her then gave his brother Lom a gentle kick. 'Arise,' he commanded. 'Will you waste your life lying about under the trees? There's work to be done and the treachery of the Gaedhal to be thwarted.'

'Treachery?' Lom repeated in shock. 'What treachery is that?'

'Perhaps if you hadn't been chasing hares across the fields all morning you might have heard what tragedy has befallen our father. Then maybe you wouldn't be so quick to call Iobhar your friend.'

'What are you talking about?' Aoife stormed.

'Fergus mac Roth, our father's friend and champion, has been slain,' Sárán told her, obviously relishing the duty of breaking the news. 'The Gaedhals raided Rath Carriaghe and murdered him in cold blood, contrary to the rules of war.

Then they set his head upon a spear and carried their trophy away. All this was done in full view of his aged and infirm mother.'

At last Mahon rolled over and sat up to speak. 'You're lying.'

'I'm a Druid. I do not lie.'

'Who told you this?'

'A messenger arrived this morning, but Dalan has brought the body back with him for burial.'

'How do you know it was my people who raided Rath Carriaghe?' Iobhar cut in nervously.

'There were many witnesses. And even if there were not, this deed has all the hallmarks of the barbarity for which your folk are known and feared.' A flash of satisfaction passed across Sárán's face. 'I'll see you all back at the fortress,' he stated with a smug smile.

Then he turned sharply on his heel and strode across the field again. He no longer had the gait of an old man but swung his staff beside him with a flourish, obviously well pleased with himself.

Iobhar picked up the bow in one hand and an arrow in the other and for the briefest second he considered using them on Sárán. But Aoife touched him on the shoulder and he turned to face her.

'I wouldn't do that if I were you,' she advised. 'Such a deed would have all the hallmarks of the barbarity for which your folk are known and feared.'

Iobhar laughed. 'I'm beginning to understand why you shot at him,' he admitted.

202

Eber Finn was summoned to the walls of Dun Gur by the sentries an hour before sunset. He climbed the rampart with the captain of the guard and stood while the grim-faced warrior pointed out over the lough to the other side.

The king squinted, unsure why he had been summoned just to witness a boatload of his own Fian crossing the water to the island stronghold. The dying sun reflected off the ripples on the surface of the lough, making it difficult for him to see clearly.

As the little curragh rowed closer, Eber's heart began to fill with dread. Five warriors were seated in the cowhide boat: two at the front, two in the middle and one in the rounded prow. It was this latter warrior, dressed in a bright yellow breacan, who held a great Fir-Bolg boar- spear out before him. Mounted on the end of the weapon was a large dark lump with no discernible shape. The king turned to the warrior beside him with a silent questioning frown.

'It looks to me like a head,' the captain answered gravely.

Eber Finn let out a groan of anguish. Now the boat was closer there was no doubt. It was indeed a head. Long strands of hair hung lankly about the colourless cheeks and the beard was matted with dried blood.

'Who is that in the curragh?' the king asked in a faltering tone.

'Goll mac Morna.'

'As soon as he sets foot on shore,' Eber commanded, 'you will see that he comes to my hall.'

The captain nodded and the king stormed off to await the arrival of the warrior he had so recently honoured. All the way back to his hall he struggled to find some reason in the man's actions.

Eber Finn had a long wait at his fireside before his steward came to the door and coughed to get his attention.

'Goll mac Morna would attend you, my lord,' the man reported.

'Send him in.'

Eber Finn filled a mead cup and drank the contents down quickly, reprimanding himself for not having dealt harshly with this rebellious Fian in the first place. If mac Morna were not so popular with the younger warriors, Eber might have been able to punish him for his misdeeds. It had been Isleen's idea to grant him titles instead in the hope of winning his loyalty. It was obvious now just how grave a mistake that had been.

The king looked up when he heard the cowhide door-flap pulled aside. A tall warrior bent over to enter the hall, carefully placing his helmet, sword, shield and knife on a large stone which was set there for that purpose.

Once that was done the warrior turned to face his king.

'Greetings and blessings to you, my lord,' he began. 'I have returned to your stronghold bearing tidings of war.'

'War!' Eber shouted, barely containing his rage. 'I sent you out with strict instructions. You were commissioned to complete a circuit of the countryside and report to me anything of significance. Didn't I explicitly order you to retreat from conflict if it arose?'

'Yes, my lord.'

'And you've come back with a head on a spear!'

'We were ambushed by a band of renegade Fir-Bolg,' Goll lied.

'I don't care if all the Druid wizards of the north called down the fury of the weather on you!' Eber screamed. 'You were specifically commanded to steer well clear of fighting.'

'By the time they were upon us it was already too late.'

'Too late?'

'There were too many of them. We were overwhelmed.

Would you have me abandon the warriors of my Fian band without a thought for their safety?'

The king narrowed his eyes and gritted his teeth, trying to restrain his temper until he'd heard the full story. 'Where did you get that fine yellow breacan?' he asked.

'The Fir-Bolg war-leader was wearing it. I took it as a trophy.'

'You looted the body of a brave warrior?'

'We were ambushed. There is no honour in such a cowardly attack.'

Eber felt the hairs prickle at the back of his neck. He had the uncanny sense this man was playing with the truth.

'Sit down and tell me the tale,' the king demanded. 'And have a mind not to leave out any detail. We're bound under a treaty with the Fir-Bolg. If they've breached our agreement I'll be seeking recompense from their king.'

'For a people constrained by treaty these folk fought well enough.'

'Where did the ambush take place?'

'At a settlement called Rath Carriaghe,' the champion replied.

'What were you doing near the walls of a Fir-Bolg rath?'

Goll paused, realising he had been foolish to mention this detail.

'I gave you no commission to approach any Fir-Bolg settlement,' the king went on.

The warrior cast his eyes down at the fire and spoke. 'My brother was badly wounded. Another of my Fian band lies in pain on the other side of the lough. The man who attacked us was vicious, well armed and determined to do us injury.'

'One man?'

Goll nodded reluctantly.

'I've heard the Danaans and the Fir-Bolg are masters of

wizardry,' Eber smiled cautiously. 'But tell me, how could a dozen Fian be outnumbered by just one warrior?'

Goll opened his mouth to speak but no sound came out. 'His companions fled before the fury of my men and women,' he managed eventually.

The king sat back as he tried to take in what was being said to him. He understood it was what was being kept from him that was more important than what was actually being said. He knew Goll mac Morna was a dangerous man, a warrior who had the respect of his peers and could raise the Fian against their king if it suited him.

'Would you care for a drink?' Eber Finn asked, trying not to let on that he suspected something was amiss.

He poured out a portion of mead from a wooden jug. Goll took the cup and drank the contents straight down. The champion nodded and the king poured him another measure. While Eber watched the honey-golden liquid swirling into the cup he decided he would have to rid himself of this troublesome warrior.

'Did you bring back any other trophies?' he inquired as he handed the vessel over.

'Cattle, goats, sheep, dried fish, some cheese and a dozen bags of grain.'

'This came from the Fir-Bolg settlement obviously,' Eber stated coolly.

'I only took enough to feed my people. We've been a long time without decent food in our bellies.'

Another piece of the puzzle fell into place. Eber Finn quickly surmised there had been a raid for food which had been interrupted by a Fir-Bolg warrior.

'And were there any other deaths?'

Goll shook his head.

'And you're willing to swear that it was the Fir-Bolg who attacked you first?'

'I am.'

'Then I will stand by you,' Eber assured him. 'But it would be best if you were to leave Dun Gur until this mess is sorted out. You have enough food and cattle to keep your people for a while?'

The champion nodded again. But even as he was doing so the king was frantically trying to think of where he could send this unreliable man. There had to be a place, he reasoned to himself, where Goll mac Morna could not cause any trouble. Yet Eber knew he would have to rely on the champion and his Fian once war broke out with the Gaedhals of the north.

Then the king had a flash of inspiration. A solution came to mind that astounded him with its simplicity and efficiency. If there was to be a war with the north the first battles would have to be fought before the turn of midsummer.

'I've heard that the young warriors are restless,' the king stated as he sipped his mead.

Goll sat up straight on the bench and cleared his throat nervously.

'Máel Máedóc mentioned it to me,' Eber went on.

'The Fian have had no real warrior work for three summers.'

'I thought I sent you out to perform the duties of a warrior.'

The champion turned his head away, obviously unhappy with Eber's definition of what sort of work was suitable for a fighter.

'I wish to confide in you, Goll mac Morna,' Eber Finn whispered. 'There are few folk I can trust these days.'

'What do you mean, my lord?'

Eber smiled, seeing he had the champion's full attention. 'I have a special commission for you, one which must be carried out to the letter. The future of the kingdom may depend on you.'

'I will do whatever is in my power to carry out your

instructions,' Goll replied, sensing something exciting and challenging at last.

'First of all you should know that I am willing to overlook your indiscretion with the Fir-Bolg. I forgive you for failing to obey my instructions on your last errand. But I warn you, you cannot afford to be too free with your interpretation on this occasion. There'll be blood on your conscience if you do, and it will be the blood of your own Fian.'

The king paused to make sure his message was being communicated clearly.

'What I am about to tell you is for your ears only. If the Council of Chieftains got wind of my plans they'd be outraged. If Máel Máedóc found out he might try to have me replaced. You will say nothing to even your most trusted Fian until the last possible moment. Do you understand me?'

'I do.'

'Very well,' Eber sighed, sitting back and reaching for the mead jug again. 'This is your commission.'

As soon as his cup was filled he offered the jug to Goll, who eagerly held out his drinking vessel.

'We are going to make war on Éremon.'

'Your brother?'

'We'll stand against my brother,' Eber Finn confirmed. 'And the whole kingdom of the north. I have information that indicates he is preparing to bring his warriors south to invade our territories with the aim of enforcing his kingship over the whole island.'

'We are too few,' Goll shuddered. 'We can't hope to beat them.'

'If I can mend the damage you've done with your senseless unsanctioned raid,' the king shot back, 'we may be able to count on the support of the Fir-Bolg. If they join us we might have a hope of matching my brother's forces. Then we have some chance of victory.'

'What do you want me to do?'

'Take your band north. Raid the outlying settlements of my brother's people. But mind you don't cross swords with any Danaan or Fir-Bolg. I want you to bring terror to the north. I want you to damage the resolve of Éremon's people before they have the opportunity to attack our folk.'

'This action will harden them against us,' Goll noted.

'Not if you kill as many of their warriors as possible. With every northern fighter who falls to your sword we increase our chance of victory.'

'And so it's your intention to march to Teamhair and take the kingship of this land for yourself?'

'When the time is right.'

The champion fell silent, staring at the fire as a thousand doubts flew through his mind. He considered the dangers of such a venture, though they didn't sway him against the idea. Danger was the trade of all warriors. He guessed Eber was merely trying to rid himself of a threat to his own kingship, but then it struck him that this might present a great opportunity. The commission would be an excellent chance to earn for himself a name more valuable than all the king's titles.

He would fight for Eber Finn until the north was won. Then he would have the leisure to consider whether his loyalty would remain with the king. He still cherished the dream that the Fian bands would one day toast King Goll.

'When would you have me leave to perform this duty?' the champion asked.

'You and your warriors may rest one night in the stronghold of Dun Gur,' Eber answered solemnly. 'Then I forbid you to remain more than three nights in any place until you return to report that victory is within our grasp.'

'Three nights?' Goll repeated in shock

'Are you going deaf?' the king sneered. 'When you come back I'll appoint you to lead the Fianna against the northern

Gaedhals. You'll have the hero's portion of a boar, the finest mead I can find and the gratitude of all the folk of Dun Gur.'

'And what will you give me in thanks?' mac Morna inquired. 'A man who delivers a kingdom should be rewarded by the king.'

'You shall have anything it is within my power to grant,' Eber Finn answered without a thought.

'If I were not a trustworthy man or a loyal servant you might live to regret such a broad promise,' Goll laughed. 'But have no fear, I won't ask for anything beyond my worth.'

With that the king's champion drained his cup, stood up and bowed low. 'If you'll excuse me, I wish to see to my Fian. They've travelled far and need to rest well tonight if we are to leave so soon.'

'Have the stablemen prepare three chariots for me in the morning,' Eber ordered. 'I'll be leaving for Aillwee before the sun is two fingers over the horizon. And report to me before I depart. I've asked Máel Máedóc to prepare a code for the Fian to live by. You will implement those rulings.'

Goll bowed once more and bit his tongue. He told himself his time would come. If only he could be patient, the kingship would surely be his.

'I bid you a good night,' the king nodded. 'And a fair journey. May a sweet breeze carry you to victory.'

In moments the warrior was at the door collecting his gear and then he was gone.

Eber Finn sat staring into the fire for a long time after the champion had left. He wrung his hands, drank cup after cup of honey wine and agonised over the wisdom of his decision. In the end he knew he'd had little choice but to send Goll mac Morna and his miscreant warriors as far from Dun Gur as possible. With luck, the champion would be killed in battle or at least wounded badly enough that he ceased to be a threat.

As these thoughts were coursing through his mind a

familiar voice broke his concentration. It was Máel Máedóc the Druid.

'My lord, I must speak with you at once.'

'If it's about that fool Goll mac Morna,' the king groaned without raising his eyes from the fire, 'I've already dealt with him. I'm sending him away where he can't stir up any further trouble.'

The old Druid frowned. 'I'm heartened to hear that news. But he is just one of the challenges to beset your reign.'

Eber looked up and as he did so he noticed a movement in the shadows on the other side of the hall. A form materialised before him in a breathtaking display of shimmering colour. And from this misty rainbow stepped Isleen.

She put a finger to her lips to silence the king, winked, then smiled. In the next second Máel Máedóc was taking a seat beside him. Isleen squatted down on the opposite side of the fire, her green eyes sparkling like two jade pebbles in the orange light. The old Druid didn't seem to have noticed her sudden appearance, so Eber Finn decided it was best not to express any surprise in front of him.

'The lough is retreating more and more each day,' Máel Máedóc began, leaning forward to press the urgency of the situation. 'I must seek some advice from the Danaans and the Fir-Bolg.'

'I've considered this problem,' the king announced, glancing across at Isleen who'd earlier suggested a course of action. 'If we can find the source of the spring and block it up we'll have fertile grazing ground for our livestock where there is now only water.'

'Under the treaty we must preserve the lough!' Máel Máedóc protested. 'It would be extremely unwise to take such action without the sanction of the Danaan king who once owned this stronghold.'

'Very well,' Eber sighed. 'Tomorrow you'll accompany me

211

to the stronghold of Brocan, King of the Fir-Bolg. I'm sure his advisers will be able to give us some guidance.'

'You're going in person to make amends?'

Eber Finn nodded.

'Is that wise?'

'A great wrong has been done.'

'And we'll need the goodwill of the Fir-Bolg,' Isleen added, though the Druid didn't seem to hear her.

'It's to be war then?' Máel Máedóc inquired with resignation, understanding his king's motives.

'I've already committed myself to that action,' Eber confirmed.

Máel Máedóc stood up slowly and the king noticed his shoulders were hunched over. Old age, Eber realised, was finally showing its effects on the counsellor.

But it wasn't the weight of the seasons that had bent Máel Máedóc's back. It was the burden of his responsibilities. The old Druid knew it was best he accompany the king to Aillwee. The satire would have to wait until their return. But not a moment longer.

'Good night, my lord,' Máel Máedóc offered with a feeble bow.

'Rest well,' Eber replied.

With that the Druid shuffled off to the door and was gone.

'I don't trust him,' the king confided as soon as he had left.

'Nor should you,' Isleen advised. 'He's planning to satirise you and have you removed before the conquest of the north can be undertaken.'

Eber Finn frowned. 'How could you know such a thing? Have you spoken with him?'

'I have not.'

'For that matter, how did you manage to conceal yourself from him?'

Isleen stood up and sauntered over to where the king was

seated. She placed a hand softly on the back of his neck. 'My talents will help install you as High-King of this island,' she whispered. 'All I ask in return is that you ask no questions. It's impolite.'

'What about Goll mac Morna? I fear he's plotting to take the kingship from me.'

'All you need to do is throw a dog a few scraps and he'll gladly follow you afterwards.'

Eber laughed and grasped her hand as she stroked the fine hairs at the back of his neck. 'Sometimes I'm not sure what sort of creature you are,' he told her.

'I'm a woman,' she laughed. 'A woman with grand ambitions for her lover.'

With that she put her lips to his and his doubts were immediately banished.

***

At the cave fortress of Dun Aillil Dalan and Sorcha were being led into the king's hall. Runners had been sent to all the chieftains with news of what had happened to Fergus. And the word that went with the messengers was a call to gather the council, or at least as many as could make the journey.

By sunset several elders of the Fir-Bolg had arrived to take up their seats at King Brocan's side. Two chieftains were seated opposite the king as was the tradition. It was the duty of this pair of elders to face the king down on behalf of their brethren should there be a dispute.

On either side of these two chieftains was a place each for Fineen and Dalan. As the senior members of their order, they were charged with giving advice throughout the meeting and settling minor points of contention as quickly as possible

213

so all important business could be concluded without too much fuss.

When Aoife and her companions arrived, the evening shadows were already deepening. She and Lom went straight to the seats allotted to them. Mahon dragged Iobhar into the hall against his will to sit along the east wall. This was where the hostages were placed when they weren't invited to sit in honour by the king.

Sárán observed their entry with a secret smile. As he took up his position beside Aoife, their father, Brocan, entered the hall. Everyone present stood to bow their heads for his grief. It was well known that Fergus had been like a brother to him.

When the king had stood at his seat for a short while Dalan stepped forward and rapped his ceremonial staff on the floor. Three loud knocks he gave, followed by another three and then another.

Warriors were seldom honoured by the Druid kind other than in poetry and song, so for Dalan to call the assembly to silence with the same ritual knocking that was accorded to the highest Druid in the land was unusual and very moving for those present.

Fergus had been universally respected for his wisdom, fighting skill and, most of all, his good heart. Brocan closed his eyes as they brimmed with salty tears. Even Sárán, who had often differed with the old warrior, bowed his head and sobbed a little.

The hall was still shuddering from the knocks when Dalan began to declaim a poem in his best judge's voice.

'Who watches in the night lest the raiders should come? Which of you stands sentry on the cattle in their pasture? How many of you will take up the weapons of killing and yet be called honourable by all who speak your name?'

The Brehon looked about the hall to catch the eyes of his audience.

'There will be weeping in this fortress tonight. And there will be sorrow for some days yet. But in the Halls of Waiting there will be rejoicing. For this evening there will arrive a warrior who spent his life watching in the night lest the raiders should come. A man who would gladly stand sentry over the cattle and the goats and think it no dishonour that he had been asked to do so.'

He paused for breath and to gather his thoughts. This poem had not been planned. It was flowing out of him fresh and free.

'The ancestors will welcome one of our kindred this night. They will praise him for spending his life with a sword in his hand but no joy in the wielding of it. Together they will sit until the dawn listening to the wisdom of Fergus mac Roth who was a champion, a chancellor and a sturdy soul. Now we salute his spirit as we send his body to the grave and his soul to the Halls of Waiting.'

Dalan went to stand before his seat again. The king waited until the Brehon was beside him once more, then he raised a hand in the air and motioned for everyone present to sit. As one the entire gathering did as he commanded without so much as a whisper among them. Their silence was an expression of respect for Fergus.

'As you have already heard,' Brocan began, his voice cracking with emotion, 'my dear friend and lifelong companion Fergus mac Roth was cruelly slain this morning at Rath Carriaghe.'

Aoife looked up at her father's face and thought she'd never seen him so utterly devastated, so completely lost. Although he had taken the Quicken Brew and usually had an air of youth and health about him, his face seemed to have aged suddenly.

'I'm told by Dalan that a gang of warriors attacked the rath a few hours after dawn. Fergus arrived as the assault was taking place and came to the defence of the folk who lived there. He was outnumbered at least twelve to one yet he chose to stand and fight.'

The king choked back the tears. Dalan lowered his eyes as he recalled the scenes of sorrow when he and Sorcha arrived at the rath on their way to Dun Aillil.

'The barbarians slew him then took off his head. Their gruesome trophy was carried away to Dun Gur, so it is believed. I have sent a runner to Eber Finn demanding an explanation and the immediate return of the stolen article.'

Again Brocan had to stop speaking. He put his hands to his eyes to cover them as everyone kept a steady, unflinching gaze on their king. The silent support he received in that moment must have given him a little strength because he was able to raise his face again and continue.

'Fergus was on his way to give King Eber a gift from me and an assurance I would uphold my treaty with the Gaedhals. I should have listened to my old friend when he warned me not to trust the foreigners. If I had taken his advice we would not be mourning his loss.'

Suddenly the tears began to roll down Brocan's cheeks like a waterfall. His eyes blazed red with weeping and his cheeks sparkled with trails of sorrow.

'I am responsible for my dear brother's death,' he went on unsteadily. 'I killed Fergus mac Roth.'

'The Gaedhals slew him,' Sárán cut in.

Dalan instantly shot a glance at the young Druid that communicated both outrage and warning. But the young man's words reverberated in every heart. The Gaedhals had murdered a champion, contrary to the rules of war. They had broken their treaty. And worst of all, they had treated the body of their slain foe with the greatest disrespect imaginable.

Dalan sensed the anger in the room and decided to focus it

toward something positive, speaking up before any further outrage could be openly expressed.

'It is true that the Gaedhals have violated their bonded promise to us. They have shattered the peace between our peoples. But the only honourable way to deal with this is by imposing penalties according to Brehon law. Nothing will be gained by stirring up anger. We can't hope to defeat them in battle.'

'I will have justice,' Brocan insisted with a determined tone, and for the first time a murmur spread around the room.

Everyone was of the same mind.

'Eber Finn has broken his solemn oath,' the king continued. 'He must be brought to account.'

There was general agreement again.

Dalan put up both his hands to quieten the gathering. 'Clearly a terrible crime has been committed. But it would be unwise to hastily lay all blame on the Gaedhal king. How can we be certain he knew anything about this raid?'

'He's their king,' Sárán called out. 'It's his duty to keep his folk in check.'

The Brehon turned to glare at the young apprentice. Then he cast a questioning eye at the man he believed to be Fineen. Lochie shrugged his shoulders at Dalan's scrutiny, confident that his disguise would not be discovered.

'Your student is a little too vocal,' the Brehon noted under his breath. 'He's forgotten his place.'

Lochie looked around the room before he answered. 'The boy has gauged the mood of the gathering well.'

Dalan frowned at this unexpected reply but he had no opportunity to question the healer. This situation called for firm reasoning and calm consideration. If there was no voice of moderation, this whole meeting could end in another unwanted war.

'A message has been sent to Eber Finn,' the Brehon cut in

217

above the chorus of discontent. 'If he's an honourable man he'll answer the charge brought against him and accept our judgement.'

'The Gaedhals aren't to be trusted,' Brocan bellowed. 'They must be punished.'

Dalan shuddered. The situation was rapidly deteriorating into battle talk.

'There's a Gaedhal among us,' Sárán cried out. 'The hostage should answer for the crimes of his king.'

The crowd stood up together, baying for blood. Lochie rolled his eyes back in his head, delighting in the rising conflict. Then he had an idea.

'Trial of the warrior!' he called out in a commanding voice, and the gathering shouted their approval.

Mahon immediately rose from his seat to stand in front of the terrified young hostage.

'Stop!' Dalan demanded. 'Be quiet, all of you. You don't know what you're saying. This lad had nothing to do with the death of Fergus. How can such thoughts enter your minds?'

He turned to Lochie again, shaking his head. 'Fineen, what's come over you? Have you gone mad? We are supposed to be the guardians of reason.'

It was Brocan who eventually called the assembly to silence. 'Take the Gaedhal to his lodgings,' he told Mahon. 'And see that no harm comes to him. He is in my care and I won't allow him to fall victim to our rage. Dalan is right. The lad had nothing to do with Fergus's death.'

There were muffled protests as Mahon led his friend out of the hall.

'This madness is not the way of the Fir-Bolg,' Brocan went on. 'There will be no war. There'll be no outpouring of anger. I was responsible for the danger my friend encountered. I will challenge Eber to a combat.'

'Wouldn't it be wiser to claim a payment in recompense?' Dalan argued.

'That is for the family of Fergus to decide,' the king shot back. 'For my own satisfaction and that of our people, Eber Finn must be taught a lesson. And I ask you, Dalan, to adjudicate the fight.'

'I won't.'

'You're my adviser. It's your duty.'

'I'm a Brehon judge. My duty is to justice. I will not involve myself in a ritual blood-letting that will achieve nothing but discord and lead to counterclaims of compensation.'

'I'll arrange the contest,' Lochie offered, and for the third time that evening Dalan turned to the healer with a frown.

In that instant the Druid noticed something about Fineen he had never seen before. There was a fire in the healer's eyes that banished his air of humility. His worldly wisdom was still evident. And his features, his stance and his voice were all unchanged. But there was something unfamiliar about his old friend that put the Brehon's instincts on edge.

'I'm a neutral party in this,' the healer went on. 'As a Danaan and a Druid I am best qualified to arrange a challenge.' Lochie paused, seeing he had the attention of everyone and the approval of most. 'But I agree with Dalan. A trial of battle would achieve nothing. It would be more prudent to arrange a test of skill.'

'A test of skill!' Brocan roared. 'What satisfaction will that give? Let me fight him!'

'I have too much respect for you, Brocan,' Lochie stated. 'I will not allow you to dishonour yourself in that manner.'

The king was about to explode in protest but Lochie didn't give him the opportunity.

'Eber Finn has not taken the Quicken Brew as you have. It would not be a fair fight. You're immune to injury.'

Dalan looked at Fineen and relaxed. This was the healer he recognised. Calm, clear-headed and thoughtful.

Brocan breathed out heavily as he realised there would indeed be no honour in such a contest. 'What do you propose?'

'You must give me an opportunity to consider this question carefully,' Lochie replied.

But the Watcher already knew the nature of the test he would set for Brocan and the King of the Gaedhals. These folk were falling into his hands like ripe apples tumbling from a fully laden tree.

'Send another messenger to Dun Gur,' the king commanded. 'Summon Eber to this place to answer for his crime.'

The gathering rose in unison. 'Aye,' they answered together, and then without a word of dismissal the elders began filing out of the hall into the night.

'You have made a wise decision, my lord,' Dalan assured Brocan.

'This brew is proving to be a curse,' the king snapped. 'I should never have allowed it to be administered to me. If I'd had my wits about me I would never have so much as sipped it.'

'Then you'd have gone to the Halls of Waiting,' Lochie observed with a shrug. 'What use would you be to your people then?'

'I've heard enough of that argument. I seek rest. I'm tired of a lifetime of fighting, of dealing with the troubles of my people. My body may be able to go on but my spirit is weary.'

'It's true,' Lochie sighed, and Dalan was surprised at the intensity of his expression.

Sorcha came over and stood by Dalan's shoulder, intending to observe the healer close up. She felt uneasy but couldn't understand what it was about Fineen that disturbed her. As he went on she took careful note of every turn of his eye and of each syllable he spoke.

'We should not mourn Fergus. He has gone to a reward which we will only know in our dreams. We should envy him.'

Brocan reached out to grab the healer's sleeve. 'Sometimes the only thought on my mind is sleep. I close my eyes at night and my body rests but that sort of slumber is unsatisfying. I awake each morning tortured by the knowledge that my soul may never find rest.'

'Think of the good your experience brings to your people,' Dalan cut in. 'It is your destiny to guide them through the future.'

'Wouldn't it be better if they learned to look after themselves? Am I to be here in a hundred generations, still guiding their hands?'

The Brehon opened his mouth to speak but no words of encouragement would come to him. His life was devoted to judging, to preserving all the legal precedents in the old tales and to passing his knowledge to those in need. A life unfettered by death and disease had seemed a marvellous gift to him, a chance to collect knowledge in unprecedented quantity.

'Did the Druids consider the burden they were placing on us all when they concocted the brew?' Brocan went on.

'They had no idea of the consequences of their actions,' Lochie replied.

A part of him was enjoying this immensely. His age-old hatred for these folk meant his twisted spirit revelled in their plight. But another voice spoke deep within the Watcher, a voice he hadn't heard in many generations.

And it was full of compassion.

Lochie chose to ignore it. He was at the helm of this conversation and he wanted to concentrate on steering his own course. The Watcher turned to face the Brehon, who swallowed hard when he caught his old friend's eye. The gold flecks which accentuated Fineen's blue orbs were sparkling with a fire the Brehon had never noticed before.

'When the Quicken berries were presented as a solution to the invasion of the Gaedhals, even the wisest Druids could only see the benefits of such a plan. We were all so enamoured of the idea of long life and perfect health that no one considered the consequences for our souls.' Lochie allowed his voice to exhibit all the bitterness that had attached itself to him through the ages.

Balor of the Evil Eye, his master, had made many promises to the nine Watchers. But the crafty old warlord had never spoken of the loneliness that would be their lot. He had not once hinted at the terrible affliction which would embrace the spirits of each of them or of the hatred that would so easily consume them all.

'Those who drank of the brew have only just begun to understand the awful consequences of our decision,' Lochie went on. 'We now suspect that to stop taking the brew will result in a degeneration of the body, but not in death. Who could have guessed that when the plan was first presented?'

Brocan, Dalan and Sorcha listened intently as the healer continued.

'Some of our companions have chosen to withdraw to the Otherworld and perhaps they will not suffer as greatly as those of us who have remained. But I have a notion even the Otherworld cannot hold back the burden of time forever. For everything travels through cycles of existence.'

Brocan and Sorcha nodded in solemn agreement.

'The trees understand this, so they shed their coats of leafy green in autumn and sleep through the long winter knowing even the mightiest among them cannot hope to fight against the cold. In the Otherworld the trees are said to be evergreen and loaded with fruit. The bite of winter has never been known in that land.'

Sorcha was intrigued. She hadn't ever heard Fineen speak in such a poetic manner. He was a fine healer but he rarely

222

expressed his mastery of words unless it was in riddles.

'I suspect, however, that the cycles of the seasons are merely slower in that place,' Lochie stated. 'For now King Cecht and the Danaan folk are experiencing the glory of spring. All is well for them and they're surrounded by bliss. But for every seedling there must come a snowflake. Each apple must be bartered for a withered leaf upon the branch. And those dry leaves must return to the soil to nourish next season's growth.'

'I don't want to live beyond my span of seasons,' Brocan told him. 'My heart's desire is to embrace the cycles of nature, not to avoid them.'

'I have no answer to your dilemma,' Lochie shrugged. 'But that doesn't mean there isn't one. Perhaps we must all come to some peace within ourselves on this matter. It will certainly affect everyone differently.'

Dalan found he was strangely relieved to hear Fineen make this last statement. He understood that Brocan was deeply unhappy, but he himself was eager to make the most of the great gift the Quicken Brew had granted him.

Lochie coughed to signal he had said enough on this subject for now. 'I will arrange a competition,' he continued after a moment, addressing Brocan. 'If it's a fair contest between you and Eber, I'm sure your honour will be satisfied without the need for warfare.'

'That would put my mind at rest,' the king nodded. 'I know there are some hot-headed warriors on both sides who would eagerly take up the sword again. But that road leads to more heartache. It's taken three winters for us to recover from the last great fight and I fear a far more devastating conflict if we come to blows again.'

Brocan took the healer's hand in his. 'Your people and mine are ancient enemies,' he told Fineen, and for a moment Lochie thought perhaps the king had guessed his true identity. 'Yet I don't consider you a foeman. I would be proud to call you a Fir-Bolg. I am honoured to have you at my council.'

Lochie bowed his head, genuinely moved at the respect shown for the healer. He had not heard such kind sincere words addressed to him for many generations.

'Thank you,' he murmured, touched by the compliments.

Then King Brocan turned to Dalan and Sorcha. 'I trust you are all correct in your assumptions about Eber Finn,' he stated gravely. 'I pray to Danu he knew nothing of the raid against Rath Carriaghe. But the instincts which guide me in my office tell me there is more to all of this than meets the eye.'

'What do you mean?' the Brehon quizzed.

'The southern Gaedhals possess a far larger fighting force than any the Fir-Bolg could field. If Eber has decided to eliminate our folk once and for all, there is little we can do to stop him. I just hope that the death of my friend and champion was not the first blow in a bitter war which will see us all driven from the land of Innisfail forever.'

Then, before anyone could make further comment, Brocan left the hall. And long into the night he wandered the hills in the moonlight, giving over all his thoughts to the loss of his dear friend Fergus.

Chapter Eleven

ochie had so far managed to keep his true identity secret by his sharp wit and instincts. But he knew he wouldn't be able to sustain the ruse forever, especially in front of Dalan, a man who had known Fineen all his life and who had an uncanny sense for anything that might be out of place. It was time to move his plan into action.

When the council dispersed from the king's hall the Druids retreated to their own dwelling where they could be secluded from the rest of the tribespeople. There they'd be free to speak of matters which concerned only the initiated and the novices of their kind.

Dalan and Sorcha were already seated by the central hearth when Lochie came in and sat down with a nod. Sárán followed respectfully after, he and Aoife sitting by the door in the traditional place reserved for Druids in training.

No one spoke for a long while. At last Dalan signalled to Aoife with a wave of his hand and the young woman stood up to fetch his small Brandubh table from where it was hanging on the wall. She carefully laid it between her teacher and his guest, then placed each piece in its position ready to begin.

When she had done that Aoife brought out wooden cups,

giving one to each of the initiated Druids. Then she handed a skinful of mead to Dalan who thanked her with a smile.

As she resumed her seat the Brehon spoke the words of welcome.

'Let us take a cup together to wash the dust of the road from our throats and to bid a welcome to Sorcha of the Spring who will stay a while with us.' He poured out the honey-gold liquid into the three wooden vessels then went on. 'Though we have much to discuss, let us put all the cares of the world away for a while. As is the time-honoured custom I would like to play a round of Brandubh with our guest. She is a woman of great learning, knowledgable in the ways of the forest, the waters and the Ravens of the air.'

Lochie smiled at the Brehon. He enjoyed the quaint customs the Danaans and Fir-Bolg indulged in. It had been a long while since he'd had the opportunity to watch a game played and he was relieved not to be the focus of any attention.

'Fineen is a man of the healing arts,' Dalan went on. 'It was he who was charged with the preparation of the Quicken Brew and he who tends to the daily needs of the people of the Fir-Bolg of the Burren.'

Lochie raised an eyebrow and saw an opportunity to ingratiate himself with Dalan.

'The brew has had an astounding effect,' he commented. 'All sickness and injury have been utterly banished from those who drank it.' He looked at Dalan with a grin. 'Since I administered it to my own people, there has been no illness among them. Now I find my skills are not required. So it is I have come to live among the Fir-Bolg who refused the juice of the Quicken.'

'Indeed,' Dalan laughed, 'your skill is so great you have made your very presence among the Danaan people unnecessary.'

'There will always be a need for wisdom,' Sorcha interjected, raising her cup to toast the idea, 'whether it be the experience you have gained as a healer or the good judgement that has come to you as a result of your hard study and dedication to your craft.'

Lochie nodded, surprised at the complimentary tone of her words. She must know Fineen quite well — he would have to be even more careful. He drank his fill of mead and placed his cup down beside the Brehon for a refill.

'There is none wiser than this man,' Dalan continued when he had drained his own vessel. 'His heart is humble and his words well chosen. There is none among his profession so caring and gentle. There is no one so respected. And there is none like him on this Earth. I would trust him with my life.'

The Watcher regarded the Brehon with suspicion for a moment, wondering whether Dalan might have seen through his façade. He quickly discerned the speech came from the spirit and relaxed again.

'You have already trusted me with your life,' Lochie noted. 'I gave you the Quicken Brew which will make your life easy, long and without pain.'

'I trust Dalan knows it is his responsibility to make his life worthy of the gift,' Sorcha added.

The Brehon laughed, lifted the table around and placed it closer to his guest.

'You will take the white king,' he told her.

'If I take the white pieces the king will be a queen,' she informed him.

'As you wish. The winner will play against Fineen.'

'Then I shall look forward to the contest with the healer,' Sorcha smiled confidently.

'If you can be so sure of beating me,' Dalan laughed, noticing a bright twinkle in her eye, 'then Fineen will not prove much of a challenge.'

'It is not the way of the Brehon judges to practise humility,' Lochie added. 'Perhaps it is something in their training which makes them so. Or maybe they are already boastful and the profession of law is the only one which accepts such behaviour among its advocates.'

'You have a sharp wit,' Sorcha giggled, warming to the conversation.

Dalan's smile dropped from his face and he realised for the first time that he desperately desired this young woman's approval.

'It is a strange thing,' she went on. 'I studied the Brandubh when I was training. I know all about the strategy and tactics of the game. The rules are as much a part of me as my own name. The symbolism of the board and the pieces are clear to me. Yet I know nothing of the origins of the game.'

'There are few who do,' Lochie agreed. 'It is a tale often forgotten and seldom spoken.'

'Do you know it?'

'I do,' he admitted. 'Or at least some small part of it.'

Dalan raised his eyebrows. 'I've never heard the tale of the origins of the game,' he remarked. 'Where would you have heard it?'

'Just because it hasn't come to your ears doesn't mean it has never been told,' the Watcher gently rebuked him.

Now Lochie was fairly confident his trick had not been detected, he was beginning to enjoy his role as the healer. And he could clearly see Dalan was vying for the attention of Sorcha.

The Druid woman picked up one of the white pieces and placed it carefully down upon the board in a new position. As she nodded with satisfaction at the move her eyes caught Dalan's, and Lochie saw the sparkle of interest she flashed at the Brehon. Dalan locked eyes with her for just the briefest of moments but it was enough to confirm Lochie's suspicions.

228

The Watcher smiled to himself. He was pleased the Brehon was preoccupied with Sorcha. It would make his plan easier to implement.

Coughing for his audience's attention, Lochie began the story of the Brandubh. And well he knew this wonderful tale. For though he had been born long after the time when the Ancient Islands of the West were engulfed by the oceans, the story was still widely known in his youth.

He spoke of Manaanan mac Lir, King of the Depths, who brought the game to the Courts of the Four Kings in the Islands of the West. And of the famous sage who had taught its secrets to him. That learned soul was Tuam of the Long Days who outlived all his kinfolk. He who lived alone through the ages, aware of his changing forms and the passing of his soul into one vessel or another. Tuam the Eagle he was also called, for in the time of Manaanan this was the shape he held.

At this part of the story Lochie breathed deeply. It had been a long time since he had been asked to recite a tale. He loved to tell the old legends, though he'd had precious few opportunities in a dozen generations. So he savoured the moment, conjuring the words in his mind carefully before he spoke.

'It was not four seasons before the waves came to wash the Islands of the West away,' he went on. 'It so happened that Manaanan was travelling the coasts of those ancient lands making inquiries about the rising levels of the seas which had been noticed in the previous winter. One day he came to a small fishing settlement where a group of men and women were sitting in a circle listening to the words of a wise speaker.'

Lochie smiled as Dalan made his first move upon the Brandubh board. The Brehon took a dark piece, known as a Raven, and moved it thoughtfully to a new position.

'Manaanan sent his champion to ask the sage his name. The man returned to say it was Tuam of the Long Days whom people had come to hear and that he was speaking on the nature of the world from his own observations. The Lord of the Seas was very interested to hear what the old one had to say so he approached the circle, which parted before him with respect.'

Lochie took a sip of mead as the Druid woman decided her next move.

'Imagine his surprise to learn the speaker was an eagle,' he continued. 'Perched upon a rock the wise old bird was answering the simple inquiries of the fisherfolk and the deeper questions of the older people.'

Lochie clapped his hands suddenly, startling Sorcha so much she dropped the white piece she had been about to reposition. She sighed, retrieved the little queen and placed her down again upon the board, satisfied her play would challenge Dalan.

'Then, before the eyes of all those gathered, Tuam changed his form to that of an old man dressed in white whose face was shrouded in wild white hair and an unruly beard. But Manaanan had seen this done before so he was not impressed. In the Four Courts of the Islands there were many folk whose talents exceeded shape-shifting.'

Lochie knew he had Dalan's attention now for the Brehon was frowning deeply at him. The Watcher did not pause though. He went on to tell of how Manaanan mac Lir laughed at the wise sage called Tuam and called him a simple trickster who had taken these humble folk in with his enchantments.

'But within four seasons,' Lochie went on, 'Manaanan was seeking out the eagle of wisdom to ask his advice on the fate of the islands. Warriors were sent out to look for the sage and they travelled the two halves and the three thirds of the land in search of Tuam.'

Dalan raised an eyebrow. He had never heard Fineen tell such a fine tale. He was impressed with the healer's suddenly acquired skill. Lochie sensed the Brehon's gaze and picked up the pace of his telling a little.

'In time they tracked poor Tuam down but he was nearing the end of his days in that particular form and he refused the summons to come to the Four Courts. So Manaanan went to the sage himself and begged for guidance, for it was obvious the world was changing and the seas had become a great threat.'

Then Lochie explained all that Tuam had told to his noble pupil. The layout of the Brandubh board represented the known world. From around its borders came the Ravens of Death, the black birds who carry upheaval in the points of their beaks. For death was considered nothing more than a change of circumstance in those ancient times and no one feared their own passing but for the sake of their loved ones left behind.

'Tuam of the Long Days explained to Manaanan of the Seas there was nothing he could do to avert the coming disaster which would surely destroy their homeland. The best thing anyone could do was to accept that which they had no power to change and to find some way to salvage something from the wreckage while there still was time.'

The Watcher waited till Dalan had made his move then he finished the tale.

'And Manaanan insisted on knowing what the secret was, the great secret to all the wonders of the Earth and why all things must change with time. Tuam laughed and told the King of the Depths to hold out his hand. And the eagle gave the lord a grain of barley. That was his answer.'

'What does it mean?' Aoife interrupted.

'Hush, child,' the Brehon snapped. 'You know better than to interrupt.'

'It's obvious!' Lochie laughed.

'Is it?' the young woman frowned.

'If you can't see the meaning straightaway, I'm not going to

231

tell you,' the Watcher shrugged. 'It's much better you make such discoveries for yourself. When you think you have the answer, come and ask me. I'll tell you if you've worked it out right.'

'You're making that whole story up out of thin air and mead-brew,' Dalan grunted.

'I told it to you as it was told to me,' the Watcher insisted. 'Are you calling me a liar?'

The Brehon shook his head and looked to the floor, ashamed he had questioned the honesty of his friend. As he did so Sorcha made her final move. In a moment her High-Queen was free from the threat of Dalan's Ravens and she had won the game.

Lochie stood up immediately. 'I find I am exhausted,' he declared. 'If you will excuse me, I must go to rest.'

He turned to Sárán. 'Have you eaten enough?'

The young man nodded.

'Then come along. I'm sure my friend the Brehon has much to discuss with Sorcha and I would not wish to disturb their thoughts any further with my less-than-perfect tales.'

'Your story was fascinating,' the Druid woman assured him. 'I've learned a great deal tonight.'

Her eyes flashed at him in the firelight. But it wasn't a flash of admiration and for just the briefest of moments Lochie felt a twinge of fear. It wasn't the sort of terror that might make a mortal sweat, just enough to add some risk to his adventure.

'Good night, Sorcha,' he bowed. 'May your stay among these folk be enjoyable. And may your quest prove fruitful.'

'My quest?'

'Saving the Watchers from their terrible fate,' Lochie explained. 'I pray to Danu that you find an answer swiftly.'

'Thank you.'

With that he left the House of the Druids and strode off in

the direction of his own little shelter. Sárán followed deferentially behind, always keeping three paces behind his master.

When they arrived at the house of healing the apprentice took his master's shoes and set them on a stone placed just inside the door. Then he went to stir the fire while Lochie settled down amongst his sleeping furs.

'I've never heard that story before,' the young man admitted as he placed a log upon the fire and poked at it with a stick.

'I know many things of which you can have no idea whatsoever,' the Watcher shrugged. 'I understand many others which even Dalan cannot comprehend. He's just a conceited Brehon, after all. Can he change shape at will? Can he know the ways of the clouds and of the night sky? Does he think beyond the petty disputes which arise from time to time in this pathetic encampment?'

Sárán didn't reply, somewhat surprised by his master's immodesty.

'He does not,' the Watcher assured his listener. 'But I do.'

'What's the answer to the question?' Sárán begged.

'What do you think the answer is?'

'The seed is shed from the barley so there will always be more seeds. That way the spirit of the barley will never die.'

'You have the beginnings of wisdom,' Lochie nodded with satisfaction.

'Will you teach me something of what you know?'

The Watcher raised an eyebrow. 'Are you sure you truly wish to learn?'

'I will absorb every scrap of knowledge you have to offer.'

'Then tomorrow we start your education in earnest.'

Two days passed at the fortress of Aillwee before scouts came in to Brocan to report the appearance of three war-chariots approaching from the south-west. It was a hot midmorning which held the promise of a stifling afternoon.

The king took the news with outward calm even though he hadn't slept since he'd presided at the council. He hadn't expected his summons to Eber Finn to be answered with war-chariots. He was determined not to communicate his worst fears to his people lest panic spread through their ranks. So on the pretext of training he called together all his warriors to prepare for a possible challenge.

Since the death of Fergus he'd wondered whether the Gaedhals would challenge him. If Eber Finn wanted to attack, there was little anyone could do to stop him. His warriors were better armed, well trained and they outnumbered Brocan's defenders four to one.

The king knew the fortress could easily be overrun by the Gaedhals but he was determined to defend this last strong-hold of his people to the death if need be. With the canny experience of a war-leader he had gathered food stores together and sent all but the fighting fit to outlying settle-ments to bide their time until the trouble blew over.

The caves had running water in their depths so there would be no shortage of that essential supply even if it didn't rain until the autumn. Where the stone walls remained unfinished the king had erected temporary barriers of timber and rubble.

It was all along this great circular rampart that Brocan's warriors arrayed themselves to await the arrival of the Gaedhals. No one expected a fight so soon. Three chariots posed no threat to Aillwee even if they were loaded down with war-gear and fighters. However, Brocan had ordered this display as a show that he would not give in without a fight. His grim-faced people understood his intentions even if he hadn't shared his thoughts with them.

Fifty spears stood ready on the eastern ramparts where the wall had been completed. This section of the defences was unlikely to be breached. On the western side where the foundations of the stone ramparts had been laid down but not built to the desired height, a further fifty warriors stood with drawn swords. In the centre at the point where a dusty road trailed toward the caves, a hundred of the strongest Fir-Bolg fighters waited. There should have been a gatehouse at this place but work had barely begun.

And in the midst of these strong folk stood the king of that once proud people, staring out toward the south. Brocan quietly surveyed his handiwork, searching for any weaknesses that might be mended before the walls were put to the test.

Stretched out before the circular defences was a field of jagged stones, impassable to horse and foot alike without the expense of precious energy. This had been Dalan's idea, a barren, inhospitable stretch of land that would certainly not inspire the enemy to valorous deeds.

The only way to enter Aillwee easily was down the dusty road. At the end of that track, Brocan's best waited for the coming storm, eyes steady, hands firm and hearts for the most part untroubled.

The Fir-Bolg stayed at their battle-readiness until the three war-carts appeared on the road which led out of the forest to the south. It was at that moment that the more experienced of the fighters began to suspect real trouble. A murmur of unrest spread through the ranks of those who guarded the road. Brocan closed his ears to the mutterings as he signalled for Dalan to come forward.

The Druid had been waiting in the rear for this command. He strode toward the king, dressed in his flowing cloak of Raven feathers and bearing a finely carved staff cut from hazelwood, the universal sign of peace. Even the Gaedhals, who were considered uncouth and undisciplined, would abide by the call for talk before battle.

As Dalan passed through the ranks of the warriors some whispered to him, asking for an explanation; others wished him good fortune, but a few cursed him under their breath. There were some for whom the appearance of a Brehon in his best robes was an indication of trouble on the wind.

Dalan strode out a hundred paces or so, leaned on his staff and rehearsed the speech he'd prepared. But the sight of three chariots charging along at a reckless pace was compelling and he soon fell to wondering what Eber Finn had in store for them all.

The winding road was a long trail of ochre kicked up behind the horse-drawn vehicles. There was no wind so the spiralling dust hugged the track like the tail of some enormous serpent. And this strange dragon had three heads, each as venomous as the next.

Behind him Dalan could hear the deep war drums begin their pounding rhythms. He turned around in dismay, afraid that Brocan had decided to issue a battle challenge after all. He wondered what would become of him if Eber did not respect the signs of his office, and he suddenly felt vulnerable. Sweat gathered at his throat where the Raven feathers wrapped his neck in a soft downy black.

For the first time in his life the Brehon worried that his position and rank might not protect him. If the Gaedhals were determined to crush the Fir-Bolg completely, they certainly wouldn't let a lone Druid stand in their way. Perhaps, he thought, Brocan had been right to be so distrustful of King Eber.

The chariots were much closer now. Dalan could plainly see Eber Finn standing proudly behind his charioteer with a hand on his hip. It was as if it took no effort for him to stay aboard the bucking cart. The King of the Gaedhals was dressed in a black tunic surmounted by a fine breacan cloak of bright red and green checks. The garment flowed out behind him, echoing the way his hair was tossed about in the wind.

Dalan could well understand why his people so eagerly followed him into battle. Eber Finn certainly reminded him of a heroic conqueror. One day the Bards would surely proclaim his story and his name would pass into legend.

Just then Dalan noticed that a strange feature distinguished Eber's chariot from the other two. At the front of the war-cart a spear had been lashed so that it stuck up into the air.

Dalan expected to see a standard flying there but instead there was a strangely shaped object seemingly trimmed with long strands of horsehair. The Brehon frowned in confusion which soon turned to dismay.

As the chariot came ever closer he realised what this decorative object must be and his heart began to pound wildly. He couldn't believe Eber would be so brazen as to taunt King Brocan in this manner.

'He wants a fight,' Dalan whispered to himself in despair, and he knew there was little chance now of avoiding bloodshed.

The Brehon turned around to judge the distance between the walls and where he was standing. In a few breaths he was walking again out toward the Gaedhals, hoping he could put enough distance between the two rival rulers that Brocan would not be able to make out what was mounted on the spear.

He'd gone another two hundred paces before he stopped to give the chariots enough room to safely slow to a halt. Dalan glanced around at the Fir-Bolg stronghold, once more hoping he had acted quickly enough to avoid a dishonourable scene. He had no idea what Brocan might do if he saw the head of his lifelong friend stuck upon the shaft of a boar-spear, but he suspected it would be a hasty and unthinking. And that could only make matters worse.

To the rear the war drums pounded more heavily, then the chariots were upon him and he was caught up in a cloud of swirling choking dust as the creaking war-carts and frothing horses came to a halt all around him.

It was a few moments before the dust settled and Dalan could make out the shape of a man walking briskly toward him. It was the stranger's long red and green cloak that marked him as the King of the Southern Gaedhals.

In the distance the Brehon heard a strident chant taken up by all the Fir-Bolg warriors. And to his great relief he recognised the strains of the welcoming song, a poem which bestowed a greeting rather than a threat.

The pace picked up a little as a group of twenty Fir-Bolg stepped out from the ranks to form a square. Then they proceeded to swing their weapons round in a uniform and beautifully constructed dance which paralleled the rising tempo of the chant.

By that time Eber Finn was standing patiently before Dalan, waiting for the Druid to speak. From a distance the foreigner had appeared older and battle-hardened. But up close his smooth face and bright eyes betrayed his youth.

And there was nothing more dangerous than a young king. Dalan swallowed hard, drew on all his training to calm his voice and demeanour and then he spoke at last.

'King Brocan of the Fir-Bolg sends you greetings,' he began, his eyes straying to the gruesome head set upon the spear. The once rosy cheeks had paled to a sickening grey. The eyes were rolled back to reveal glazed, discoloured whites. The hair was matted with blood and mud, and the mouth hung open as if a scream were issuing forth from the very soul of Fergus mac Roth.

'I am Eber Finn,' the Gaedhal declared. 'I have come to speak with King Brocan.'

The Gaedhal seemed so calm and confident that he

238

appeared almost arrogant. Here he was, dressed in all his finery with just five men to guard him against the host of the Fir-Bolg. Either he was mad, Dalan decided, or determined to present the greatest insult possible under the circumstances.

Before the Brehon had a chance to continue his speech, an old man dressed in the blue Druid robes of a Bard stepped forward.

'My name is Máel Máedóc,' the grey-beard stated in a surprisingly powerful and commanding voice. 'I am chief counsellor to the king.'

Dalan passed a quick glance from one Gaedhal to the other then abandoned the speech he'd prepared. He stepped forward and spoke in a low voice, even though he knew there was no chance King Brocan could hear what was being said.

'Are you seeking war?'

Máel Máedóc raised his eyebrows in surprise and firmly shook his head.

'We have come to make amends,' Eber replied. 'I wish to make peace with the King of the Fir-Bolg.'

'There's little chance of that if you bring the head of his best friend piked on a pole as your peace gift. I suggest you remove it before you bring the wrath of all my people down upon you.'

The king laughed and Dalan breathed in sharply, unable to disguise his disgust and contempt for this brash young man.

'You've misunderstood,' Eber began. 'Among my people it is considered a great honour for an enemy to have his head at the king's spear.'

'Fergus mac Roth was not an enemy of the Gaedhals.'

'He fell in a fight with my warriors,' Eber answered. 'I'm told he fought honourably and well.'

'There was a truce agreed between our peoples,' Dalan snapped in reprimand. 'Or have you no respect for such agreements?'

239

'How dare you speak to me in that manner?' the king shot back, his pride clearly prodded by the Brehon's tone.

'I'll speak to you in whatever manner I see fit. You're nothing but an impudent lad who thinks he can bully his neighbours into submission.'

Dalan knew he was speaking out of turn. Even as he heard the words issuing from his own mouth he understood he was making a terrible mistake. But he simply couldn't stomach the attitude of this disrespectful lout.

'If you imagine Brocan is going to be intimidated by the murder of his friend, you're sorely mistaken. Fergus was a man well loved. His companions won't just stand aside and allow you to treat his death as some sort of game.'

'You'll hold your tongue!' Eber hissed. 'You have no right to address me with such insults.'

'You're a master of insult,' Dalan spat. 'There is no greater slur you could have cast upon my folk than to bring the severed head of such a respected man before us, dressed as you are in your feasting finery. I've heard tell you lack discretion but this provocative act could hardly be considered anything less than a grave affront. If you don't want to find your own head on the point of a Fir-Bolg spear I suggest you conceal your trophy from the eyes of his loved ones.'

'Brocan wouldn't dare touch me.'

'I am the highest-ranking Druid in the western lands,' Dalan informed him coldly. 'I know well enough that the law does not permit the taking of a life for a life. But at this moment I wouldn't dream of stepping in to prevent my king from venting his anger with you in whatever manner he saw fit.'

'I can see I'm wasting my time here,' Eber dismissed, and in the next breath he had turned around to head toward his chariot. But before he had walked more than a few steps Máel Máedóc reached out and grabbed the king by the sleeve.

'What sort of a man are you?' the old Druid demanded. 'Have you no thought of peace? Is war your only concern? What of the good of your people? Do you think they covet the fight as much as you do?'

'Stand out of my way, old man,' the king bellowed. 'You're so dim you've lost sight of the reasons our people came to this land in the first place.'

'We needed land,' Máel Máedóc agreed. 'But our people also sought a place where they could live in peace.'

'There'll be no peace as long as my brother rules the north and covets the country I've conquered. I have no choice but to attack the strongholds of Éremon and remove him from his position. If I fail to do so my own subjects will be usurped from the hard-won fields they till. They'll be replaced by folk who are loyal to my brother.'

'What foolishness it is to foster war in order to nurture peace,' Máel Máedóc scoffed. 'Truly you are but a boy.'

'We'll see what you say when the northerners come knocking at your door, take away your wife, your daughters and your cattle and burn the house of poetry at Dun Gur.'

'And will you serve us any better?' the old Druid asked.

The king did not reply. He dragged himself away from Máel Máedóc's grip, went to his chariot and dislodged the spear. Once he had the weapon in his hand he grabbed a handful of hair and dragged the head from the barbed point. Then he handed the ghastly object to his charioteer.

'Wrap the head in this,' he ordered as he removed his bright breacan cloak.

Then he turned to face Dalan once more.

'It was my intention to show your warrior great honour,' he explained. 'I didn't wish to cause any offence. Renegades murdered him and they have been assigned their punishment as a result. I've brought two chariots as gifts to help pay the man's honour price and smooth the temper of King Brocan.'

241

'You're not bringing war?'

'I wish to strengthen my alliance with the Fir-Bolg.'

Dalan coughed in disbelief. 'Truly you are a strange people.'

'Do you think Brocan will be willing to join with me in my fight against the northern Gaedhals?'

'I can't answer for King Brocan,' the Brehon answered. 'But I'm sure he'll expect more than a couple of war-carts for his trouble.'

'I'll pay him whatever price he asks.'

'You should be more careful with your offers,' Dalan advised. 'There are some folk who might seek to take advantage of such promises.'

'If Brocan doesn't join with me his own people will fall to my brother's warriors,' Eber stated.

'You could pledge all your cattle, gold, weapons and fine cloth but I doubt it would convince my king,' the Brehon sighed. 'You can expect him to ask for something quite different. And I warn you now that to accompany me to Aillwee will be to as good as agree to whatever price he demands.'

'Then let us go.'

'My lord!' Máel Máedóc protested.

'I have no choice,' Eber told his adviser. 'If I don't seek this alliance I may as well fall on my own sword.'

'I hope you don't live to regret this decision,' Dalan added.

And then without another word he strode off toward the waiting Fir-Bolg warriors who stood expectantly behind the walls of their stronghold.

Chapter Twelve

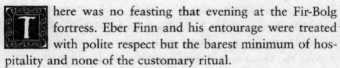 here was no feasting that evening at the Fir-Bolg fortress. Eber Finn and his entourage were treated with polite respect but the barest minimum of hospitality and none of the customary ritual.

The two kings and their advisers lodged at opposite sides of the fortress that night. With the dawning sun they broke their fast together on the eastern battlements, the only part of the fortification to have been completed.

Few words were spoken between the war-leaders, though Dalan, Sorcha and Máel Máedóc launched into a long discussion about the worryingly low level of the waters in Lough Gur. It was Sorcha's opinion that the spring which fed the lough had begun to silt up and that in time the source of that spring would be revealed. Once that happened, she reasoned, it would be relatively easy to clean away the collected debris. Then the lough could fill again.

Dalan was certain that rain would be the saviour of the lough. The west had suffered the longest dry spell in living memory. The fields were turned to golden yellow where usually every shade of green was seen.

Lochie, arrayed in the clothes and appearance of Fineen the Healer, also attended the formal breakfast, though he didn't offer his thoughts on the level of the lough. Indeed he hardly spoke a word to anyone until the Brehon called on Fineen to recount, for the benefit of Máel Máedóc, the history of Dun Gur. Fineen's people had dwelt in that place since the Danaans first arrived in Innisfail, and the healer's knowledge of its history was unsurpassed.

Of course Lochie didn't flinch for a moment. What stories he knew of Dun Gur hadn't been passed down to him in whispers from any teacher. He'd witnessed for himself all the great events of a hundred generations, so it was an easy task for him to speak about them.

He told the gathering about the first of the Tuatha-De-Danaan who had arrived in that part of the country and how they'd fought a terrible battle with the Fir-Bolg on the shores of the lough. Even in those ancient days there were Druids among the Danaan folk who practised the Draoi craft, and it was said that they called a great storm down upon the surface of the lough, which swept waves over the gathered Fir-Bolg force. Then one of the Druids named Dagda stepped into the midst of the fight and sang a beautiful haunting song as he strummed his harp strings.

None among the Fir-Bolg dared lay a hand on the Danaan Druid. A practitioner of the Draoi arts was protected by ancient laws common to both peoples. According to the legends there arose from the lough two enormous worms that churned the waters and put a terror upon the Fir-Bolg.

The defenders threw down their arms and sued for peace; Dagda ceased his song and the creatures from the deep sank beneath the agitated lough again. The victorious Danaans claimed the island in the middle of the lough as their own and set about building a stone fortress there to keep any threat at bay.

As for the Fir-Bolg who were defeated by the use of the Draoi craft, they never forgot the way Dagda had misused his talents. He must have known that no Fir-Bolg would dishonour their name by striking down a Druid. Yet he had drawn on the Draoi to aid the Danaan warriors and so had broken his own vows never to engage in battle. Dagda went on to become the first Danaan to preside over the Druid Assembly and it was after him the office of High-Druid was named.

The Fir-Bolg agreed to throw their swords and war-gear into the lough in pledge of peace. It took two generations for them to rearm and by that time the Danaans were well established in their new home. As for the two worms, no one knew from whence they came nor where they went afterwards. Some folk said they lived on under the waters, appearing now and then to steal a cow or drown a careless boatman. Others claimed they had been merely demons of the mind without substance, conjured up by Dagda's craft. But Dagda always reckoned the worms dwelt in a deep cave in the darkest parts of the lough at the place where the waters emerged from within the Earth.

When Lochie finished this part of the tale Máel Máedóc thanked him. And he inquired whether the two worms he'd referred to were likely to be stirred by the falling level of the waters. The Watcher simply shrugged to indicate that he didn't know.

'Fineen is a trusted adviser,' Brocan assured the old Gaedhal. 'As soon as we have settled matters I'll send him back to Dun Gur to assess the situation.'

Máel Máedóc bowed to show his thanks, but before he could speak another word Eber Finn cut in.

'Let us resolve our differences then,' he offered. 'I'm willing to pay an honour price befitting the rank and status of the warrior who was killed by renegades. And I'll also double the bride price I originally offered you, just to show that I am sympathetic to your loss.'

The king raised an eyebrow. Now he was even more angry.

To use this situation to further negotiations on a marriage arrangement was dishonourable. He steered the Gaedhal back to the point.

'You could treble it and it wouldn't dampen my grief,' Brocan replied tersely. 'Fergus was more than a champion. He was my friend. And he was a messenger sent to you with a gift of good faith, a breacan cloak worthy of a king.'

Eber flinched visibly as he recalled the bright yellow garment Goll mac Morna had been wearing.

'What more can I do to prove my worth to you as an ally and friend?' the Gaedhal asked.

'I challenge you to a test of your valour.'

Máel Máedóc sat forward, the concern clearly visible on his face, but his king didn't hesitate.

'What is to be the nature of this test?'

'I have prepared a journey for you,' Lochie spoke up. 'Accompanied by a Druid of your choosing, you will enter the Aillwee caves, explore the depths and hopefully return unscathed.'

Eber Finn frowned and glanced over at the Fir-Bolg king. He was smiling broadly.

'This would hardly appear to be much of a challenge,' Eber scoffed.

'There is more,' Lochie went on. 'You will take a Druid brew to open your inner eye to the world which exists beneath the Earth. Believe me, there are terrors in that place which will measure the worthiness of your friendship and your hand in battle.'

'How do I know this isn't a trap? How can I trust that your warriors won't be lying in wait for me? Disabled by poison I would never be able to stand against a determined sword.'

'I will undergo the same test,' Brocan replied, hardly able to contain his satisfaction. Here was an opportunity to lay to rest the fears his warriors held for the caves and challenge the Gaedhal at the same time. 'As an act of good faith I will drink the same brew and set off with a Druid in whom I have great trust.'

'I choose Máel Máedóc,' Eber shot back.

'I select Dalan the Brehon,' the Fir-Bolg king smiled.

'Then you shall each take the adviser the other man chose,' the Watcher smiled. 'Dalan will go with Eber Finn and Máel Máedóc will accompany Brocan. If you should encounter one another in the depths of the caves, there is to be no fighting between you. I'll wager there will be enough other challenges placed before you that if you do chance to meet, you'll likely be glad of a face you recognise.'

'How will we find our way out again?' Dalan asked, disturbed by the thought of becoming lost in that underworld.

'I understand that tradition speaks of a river which flows through the Aillwee and emerges closer to the sea. Find that river and you will have discovered a way out of the caves.'

'When is the testing to be?' Eber asked.

'Tomorrow at dawn.'

With that the King of the Southern Gaedhals rose from his seat. 'I shall be ready.'

Then he strode off toward the road, seeking to be by himself for a while. He had no desire to show just how dismayed he was by this turn of events. But he was beginning to wonder if an alliance with the Fir-Bolg was really worth all this trouble.

That evening Lochie took Sárán out on the battlements to view the stars and teach his pupil something of their relationships. The young man had noticed a great change come over his master in the last few days and he liked what he saw. Where

Fineen had once been shy about speaking his mind, he now seemed extremely confident. In place of his reticence to praise he now openly talked of his student's potential to become a greatly respected Druid.

When the lesson was concluded Sárán excused himself to go and prepare his master's fire for the night. But Lochie asked the lad to remain a while.

'I am convinced,' the Watcher told him, 'that you are ready to take your first initiation as a Druid-Healer. I'm very proud of you, my boy.'

'Thank you, master,' Sárán replied, taken aback by such generosity. 'I strive to take your lessons to heart.'

'I believe you do,' Lochie nodded. 'And you will always need to be disciplined if you're to meet the challenges placed before you in the future.'

'Challenges?'

'Within a few days your knowledge and skills are going to be put to the test. I am going to recommend that you continue your training as a counsellor. One day you will advise your brother Lom when he's elected King of the Fir-Bolg.'

'You've spoken of this before,' Sárán ventured. 'But surely I'm too young for such responsibility.'

'Some would say your brother is too young for the kingship. Yet he will be king before long. And your sister Aoife will be a queen.'

'How is that possible?'

'She will wed with Eber Finn,' Lochie told him.

'A Gaedhal?' Lochie nodded sombrely. 'I won't allow it. The Gaedhals are not worthy of wedding into our Fir-Bolg blood.'

'You haven't really considered your words so I'll forgive your hasty disrespectful manner.'

The lad cast his eyes to the ground in remorse and put a hand to his mouth. 'I'm sorry, master,' he mumbled. 'I meant no insult to you.'

Lochie waved a hand in the air to dismiss the incident. 'In time you'll learn that anger, hatred and prejudice are the pastimes of fools. Such thoughts lead to wasteful conflicts. For now you must trust me when I tell you that the Gaedhals will be the saviours of your people.'

'They have invaded our island and brought nothing but war. They murdered Fergus.'

'As I recall,' Lochie smiled, 'you were not all that fond of Fergus. What matter to you if he was killed in a fight with renegades?'

'We only have Eber's word that it was outlaws who attacked Rath Carriaghe,' Sárán pointed out.

'And why shouldn't we believe him?'

The lad looked up to the stars to avoid his master's eyes. It occurred to him that he was merely being stubborn in his distrust of the Gaedhals and their king. And if he was to be a worthy adviser to Lom when he attained to the kingship, he would have to remain unbiased. That was one of the greatest lessons Fineen the Healer had imparted to him.

'You have always said that forgiveness is the most effective healing salve,' Sárán recalled. 'You taught me that it is often difficult to pardon those who have caused offence. I will always be grateful for the way you took me in after the crime I committed against you.'

He turned his attention back to his teacher and noticed an unusual glint in the healer's eye. The lad smiled at his master before he continued.

'I've often thought that if I hadn't lost my temper at the battleground and if my blade hadn't cut open your flesh I would never have been led along this path. I've never been happier than when I've been listening to you speak of all the things you've learned.'

'One day you will speak to your student in the same manner,' Lochie observed. 'And perhaps you'll remember me then. For the moment you must try to understand that Eber Finn will protect your people from destruction.'

Sárán frowned, not comprehending what he was being told.

'I'm speaking of his brother in the north, Éremon,' Lochie went on. 'He is a ruthless cruel man who has continually broken his treaty with the Danaans. He will not baulk at bringing battle to the south or the west if he believes it will benefit his people.'

'But Eber is his brother.'

'And so it is with many brothers,' the Watcher nodded gravely. 'One covets whatever the other holds dear. Éremon cannot be trusted. Eber is your only hope. A strong alliance with him and a swift attack against the north is the only way to secure the future of your people. A marriage with your sister will seal the pact.'

'But Aoife will never consent to such a match.'

'Would you rather see her marry young Mahon?'

Sárán shook his head. 'I've never liked him. He's lazy and he's led her away from the Druid path.'

'She isn't suited to our way,' Lochie replied, placing a consoling hand on his student's shoulder. 'She has no self-discipline or aptitude for the sacred journey. Her path leads elsewhere. And you must set her on that course.'

'Me?'

'If you're to be counsellor to your king you'd best begin to practise now. I've asked your sister to come here to meet with me this evening to discuss her future. But you will speak with her in my place.'

'I can't,' Sárán objected. 'I don't know what to say.'

'Think of your people. Consider that without you the Fir-Bolg could pass into legend and one day may be no more than a frightening tale told to children to keep them indoors after sunset. Is that what you would have happen?'

The lad shook his head. 'I can bring myself to forgive the

Gaedhals if that is what you wish,' he told his master. 'I would do anything you asked of me out of the gratitude and respect I have for you. And if you really believe it is best that Aoife be wed to Eber Finn, then I will accept what you say even if I don't fully understand the reasoning.'

'You'll make a fine counsellor,' Lochie smiled, turning away from the ramparts to walk back to the house of poetry. 'I will speak with you before you sleep,' he said as he disappeared into the darkness. 'I expect a full report of your conversation.'

In the next breath he was gone. Sárán was left to wait the arrival of his sister and to consider carefully all that had been said to him. He understood the need for an alliance and that a marriage was the best way to strengthen such a pact. He could see that if Lom was to be king the chieftains would not accept Fineen, his master, as chief adviser to the war-leader. The healer was a Danaan after all and not of Fir-Bolg lineage. But he couldn't quite understand what events could possibly lead to his father relinquishing the throne. He put that out of his mind for the moment — he had more important matters to resolve.

He considered Aoife and her foolish infatuation with Mahon. Since the treaty and the taking of the Quicken Brew three winters earlier she had all but abandoned her studies to follow her lover like an eager puppy. Dalan was constantly imposing penalties on her to discipline her behaviour. She had become an embarrassment to her family and her vocation. She was just like her mother. Riona left Brocan because of Mahon's father, Cecht. She had since disappeared with him and his folk into the Otherworld. She hadn't visited her children, nor had she expressed any desire to see her kinfolk again.

Their mother was blinded by her lust, Sárán told himself. And in the same way Aoife had so foolishly devoted herself to her beloved, an uncouth, ill-mannered layabout who was content to spend his days hunting for sport or drinking for pleasure.

Eber Finn, on the other hand, was a king in his own right. And if he was victorious against the northern Gaedhals he might be elected king over the entire island. Such a powerful ruler was always in need of advisers. And if his sister were Queen of the Gaedhals it would be natural she'd want her brother to act as counsellor to her husband. There could be no more rewarding, challenging and comfortable position for any Druid.

There was just one problem with this dream, one beesting in the honeycomb. A terrible hostility had developed between himself and Aoife. She had no respect for him and he found her impossible to get along with.

If he was to have any chance of influencing her he would have to win her over. They were both as stubborn as each other, he could concede that. But if compromise would get him what he wanted, that's just what he'd do.

As it happened he didn't have another moment more to think about this problem. Just then he heard soft footsteps on the battlements behind him. Sárán turned around, took a deep breath to ready himself and peered into the night.

'My dear sister,' he began the very second he saw Aoife materialising out of the darkness. 'A very good evening to you.'

'Sárán?'

'It is.'

'What are you doing here?' she snapped. 'I've come to meet with Fineen. We have a private matter to discuss.'

'My master is occupied with preparations for the testing at dawn,' Sárán lied. 'He asked me to meet with you in his place and to pass on your concerns to him.'

The young woman muttered an obscenity under her breath before she spoke again. 'I've nothing to say to you.' Then she turned around to head back to her lodgings.

'Whatever you would say to the healer,' he called after her, 'you may say to me. I am your brother, after all.'

'You've been no brother to me these three winters past,' Aoife shot back. 'You've turned into an arrogant, self-serving fool who has nothing but criticism for me.'

'I've been very harsh, I know,' he offered. 'And I'm truly sorry. It has been just as difficult an adjustment for me as it has for you. I also had ambitions of becoming a warrior.'

His sister turned around and even in the darkness he could plainly see the light of fury in her bright green eyes.

'You haven't had a good word to say to me since we were sentenced to our fates,' she hissed. 'You've snubbed Mahon, insulted me and brought dishonour on your own name. But you're a hypocrite, Sárán. I know you resent the judgement Dalan brought down upon us as much as I do. Yet you pretend to have taken to your enforced vocation.'

'You're right,' he conceded. Though he knew she couldn't have been more wrong. 'I've behaved badly toward you when we both should have sought each other out for support and encouragement.'

Aoife strode up to him until she stood only a few paces away. Then, quite unexpectedly, she slapped him hard across the face. Sárán gritted his teeth as the blow connected. He turned his face away and struggled to restrain himself from returning the slap.

'Do you feel better now?' he winced.

'I'll be in a better mood when I don't have to wear these Druid robes,' she told him. 'I'll be happier when I can wield a sword, make love to Mahon and spend my days in warrior training without having to ask for Dalan's leave.'

'Is that what you came to talk to Fineen about?'

'Your master is a sympathetic man,' Aoife went on. 'I came to ask him for help with my plight.'

'What kind of help?'

'I want to take the test tomorrow.'

'You wish to go into the caves with Eber Finn and our father?'

'It's the only way I can prove to Dalan that I'm worthy of the warrior path. It's my only hope of being freed from the bondage of this vocation.'

Sárán shook his head. 'The healer would never agree to it. He might well understand your motivation but he couldn't allow you to do such a thing without Dalan's consent.'

'And the Brehon would certainly never give that,' she grunted.

And then a thought struck her. She looked intensely into her brother's eyes. 'But you're his apprentice. You could obtain a draught of the Druid brew he's preparing for the morning. And you could be my guide in the underworld of the Aillwee caves.'

Sárán felt a cold shiver of fear spread across his shoulders. He had a terrible feeling his sister was leading him into another disastrous adventure.

'I haven't forgotten what happened to Fearna that night when we tempted him out into the snow. He lost his life because of our negligence and youthful foolishness. Is this to end in another such mishap? And who will be endangered this time?'

'We've both taken the Quicken Brew,' she reminded him. 'No harm will come to either of us as long as we take care not to become lost in the depths. It's fear I wish to conquer. I want to show I'm worthy.'

'And so you shall, surely. But are you certain that taking the test will prove your worthiness? I can imagine Dalan would be outraged if he found out that's what you were planning.'

She leaned in close to him and put a firm hand at his shoulder. 'But he isn't going to find out. Is he?'

Sárán stared back at her, drawn to the vibrant green of her eyes. Her gaze was unflinching and utterly determined. And he knew he had little choice but to agree to help her if he was to have any chance of bringing his own dreams to fruition. Besides, this test might just be as beneficial to his own standing as to that of his sister. If they undertook the challenge successfully they would earn the respect, albeit grudging, of all the Fir-Bolg. And they would need that if they were going to change their lives for the better.

'Do you want to be a humble healer forever?' Aoife asked as if she had been listening in on his thoughts.

Her brother shook his head.

'This is our only chance to free ourselves from bondage. You will move on to greater challenges as a respected member of the Draoi class. And I will be allowed to take up the vocation that has always called to me.'

'Do you know that Father has been negotiating a marriage between yourself and Eber Finn of the Gaedhals?' Sárán asked.

Aoife's expression of surprise showed that she had not heard any such thing, but she wasn't about to admit that to her brother. 'If it buys me my freedom, I'd be a fool not to consider such a proposal.'

Sárán's eyes narrowed as he carefully considered his next words. 'If I help you it might be best for you to no longer live among the Fir-Bolg. A marriage with Eber might be the only alternative left open to you. What will happen to Mahon?'

'A well-trained dog goes out when he knows he's about to be thrown out,' she declared.

'As Queen of the Southern Gaedhals you would wield a great deal of influence,' Sárán went on. 'And Eber Finn may yet rule all the Gaedhals of this island. When he's cold in his grave you'll still be as youthful as ever, and so will Mahon. Would you be prepared to wait for that day?'

His sister smiled. 'I have always admired the ingenious way you approach problems,' she complimented him. 'I could wait. But I'm not so sure that Mahon would be of the same mind. I'm not even sure I'd want to spend the rest of eternity with someone like him.'

'He'll have time enough to cool his injured pride. One day you may thank Danu for his company.'

Aoife smiled and nodded.

'If you should ascend to the throne of the Kingdom of the Gaedhals,' he added, 'you would certainly stand in need of a good adviser.'

'And who better than my own dear brother?' she laughed, but her expression soon turned pensive again. 'There's just one problem. Father will be so enraged that a further penalty is certain to be placed upon us both.'

'I have a strong feeling he won't be King of the Fir-Bolg for much longer. My master has indicated that our father is considering abandoning his office. Lom will likely be elected in his place if I can manage to persuade the chieftains.'

'Why would Father abandon the kingship?' Aoife queried. 'But anyway, Lom is just as hard-nosed as Father.'

'But with myself as his counsellor I have a suspicion he won't be too difficult to handle.'

'Then it's agreed,' Aoife said, taking his hand in hers and squeezing it tightly. 'We'll go together to the depths of the Aillwee and conquer whatever imaginary demons dwell in that place. In that way we'll earn the right to rule and to bring about the changes we desire.'

'If we return,' Sárán sighed. 'Then I imagine there'll be none who can deny us that right.'

With that the two siblings locked in an embrace to seal their pact and made off for the hall of poetry to get as much sleep as possible before sunrise.

Chapter Thirteen

Not long after Sárán and his sister had gone into the hall where the Druids were lodged, two figures emerged from the darkness. They waited in the shadows, whispering for a long while before they moved off toward the house where Eber Finn was lodged.

With infinite patience they watched as each sentry passed them by, then they slipped past the warriors one at a time. At last they were at the door to the guest's hall, breathing hard and shaking with fear.

'I'll wait here,' Mahon hissed to his friend.

'I won't be long,' Iobhar assured him. 'Give me the signal if anyone approaches.'

The Gaedhal opened the door and entered the hall as Mahon slipped back into the shadows.

Once he was inside, Iobhar waited for his eyes to adjust to the gloom. The fire had been allowed to burn down so there wasn't much light. He made his way cautiously to what he thought was the form of a man sleeping. As he got closer he noticed the steady rise and fall of breathing under the furs. With heart beating he reached out a hand to touch the figure, but before he made contact he felt something sharp prodding his back.

'Turn around slowly,' a voice commanded. 'If you make a move to escape I'll skewer you with this blade.'

In the same instant Máel Máedóc rolled over and grabbed the young man by the throat of his tunic and dragged him closer. The old Druid shook his head when he recognised the face before him.

'It's Iobhar, my lord,' he exclaimed.

The king spun the fellow round and with a stern expression demanded to know what the lad was doing trespassing in the guests' house in the middle of the night.

'I've come to ask a favour of you, my lord,' the young man whispered. 'It's not safe for me to remain here. There's a great hatred for the Gaedhals since the death of Fergus.'

'I'm aware of the hostility.'

'I fear for my life,' Iobhar breathed. 'I'm not permitted to carry arms within the walls of Dun Aillil and there are many folk who would think nothing of ending my life in revenge for the death of their champion.'

'You're a hostage,' Eber explained. 'You're under the protection of the treaty.'

'The treaty was broken, my lord. I'm in deadly danger. I beg you to negotiate for my return to Dun Gur.'

Máel Máedóc put a hand on the lad's shoulder to calm him. 'We can't leave him here unprotected while we go off into the caves,' the old Druid argued.

'You may be right,' Eber nodded. 'I'm not at all happy with this testing business.'

He sat back and stirred up the fire with a stick. A little flame soon leapt up and the house was somewhat brighter.

'I'll send you back to Dun Gur,' the king decided. 'You're to report everything that's happened here. Tell the chieftains about the test that's been set for me and command them to march on Dun Aillil in full force if I haven't returned within a week. Do you understand?'

'Yes, my lord.'

As he spoke there was a sound at the door.

'That's Mahon's signal,' Iobhar told the king. 'I have to go now. There are guards approaching.'

'You brought someone with you?'

'He's my friend. Mahon is another hostage, a Danaan.'

'A Danaan?'

'Iobhar!' Mahon hissed through the door. 'We must go.'

'I'll come along presently,' the lad replied. Then he leaned in closer to his king. 'There's one other thing I'd ask of you, my lord,' he breathed, so low that Eber barely heard him speak.

'What is it, lad? Speak up.'

'There's a woman here I've taken a fancy to,' Iobhar blushed. 'I want to take her with me.'

Eber smiled. 'Very well,' the king agreed. 'My guess is that you're planning this elopement without the consent of her father?'

'If he knew he'd probably kill me,' the lad admitted. 'He's well known for his temper.'

'Then be wary of making her your wife,' Máel Máedóc advised. 'Three things are passed down the generations — bad temper, fighting skill and red hair.'

'She has all three,' Iobhar confided.

Eber peered closely at the lad. 'What's her name, this lass of yours?'

'Aoife,' he replied. 'She's the daughter of King Brocan.'

'Who else knows of your intentions?'

'No one.'

'What about that Danaan outside?'

'He also holds Aoife in some affection,' Iobhar revealed with some embarrassment. 'He has no idea I intend to run off with her.'

Eber turned back to the fire so Máel Máedóc wouldn't see the expression on his face.

'Call your comrade in to the fire,' the king ordered after a moment.

Iobhar did as he was commanded and while he was gone Eber whispered a few words to Máel Máedóc. The Druid opened his eyes wide in surprise.

'Why didn't you inform me of your offer of marriage?' Máel Máedóc asked.

'There seemed no need. It's the best course of action. Do you have any objections?'

The old Druid shook his head. 'On the surface it would seem to make perfect sense,' he admitted reluctantly.

'Then you will support me?'

'I will,' Máel Máedóc stated, seeing that he had little choice.

'I'm going to call the guards,' Eber told him. 'If this lad is seen leaving the guesthouse we will be implicated in the abduction of Aoife. That would be extremely damaging to our cause. There's already been enough damage done by young hotheads.'

'I agree.'

'We must get Iobhar out of Dun Aillil as soon as possible before he has a chance to ruin everything I've been working for.'

'How do you propose to do that?'

'I want you to keep the lads by the fire while I go out for a while. When I return say nothing.'

'Very well.'

Just then Mahon and Iobhar came into the house and crouched by the fire.

'This is my friend Mahon,' the young Gaedhal announced. 'He saved me from the wrath of the Fir-Bolg.'

'Did he?' Eber exclaimed. 'Then I'd like to show my gratitude.'

The king pulled out a dagger of shining steel from his belt and handed it to the Danaan.

'This was my father's knife. Show it to any of my people and they will recognise it immediately. Take it as a sign of the peace between our peoples.'

Mahon was humbled by the gift but took it with gratitude, promising to remember the name of King Míl of the Gaedhals and to tell the story of the generosity of his youngest son.

'Now I must go out and arrange for the safe escape of Iobhar,' Eber Finn told them. 'Wait here until I return.'

The two young warriors agreed and the king made his way out into the night.

'How can I ever repay your war-leader for such a gift?' Mahon asked the old Druid.

'You're too grateful,' Máel Máedóc told him. 'Enjoy it while you can.'

With these words the counsellor realised what the king was up to. Eber Finn had gone to call out the sentries, who'd discover Mahon and Iobhar in the guesthouse armed with one of the king's own knives.

Máel Máedóc's conscience wouldn't allow his tongue to stay silent. The result of such a breach of hospitality would surely be banishment. And these two warriors were too young to suffer that fate.

'Go now,' he told them. 'Go and leave this fortress while you still may.'

'But Eber is going to help me escape,' Iobhar replied, puzzled.

'He has his mind set on wedding Aoife himself,' Máel Máedóc countered. 'He's not going to let you stand in his way.'

'Aoife?' Mahon exclaimed in confusion.

'Your friend came here to ask the king's help to get himself and Aoife clear of Dun Aillil tonight.'

The Danaan turned to his friend and shook his head. 'Have you lost your senses?'

'I'm in love with her,' Iobhar declared. 'And she's promised to come with me to the Kingdom of the Northern Gaedhals.'

'I don't believe you!' Mahon countered. 'She holds you in contempt.'

'How dare you speak to me like that,' the young Gaedhal spat.

And the next thing Máel Máedóc knew the two warriors were struggling together, trying to throw each other to the ground. In their frantic efforts they fell back onto the old Druid's bed.

Máel Máedóc tried to tear them apart and talk some sense into them, but to no avail. Mahon still held the king's knife in his hand, though Iobhar was concentrating all his efforts on wrenching it from him.

In the confusion Máel Máedóc gave a cry and withdrew from the fight to sit by the fire. And just then Eber returned with the sentries. Before the lads had a chance to object they were disarmed and laid out on the floor with warriors pinning them down.

Then King Brocan was at the door demanding to know what all this commotion was about in the middle of the night. He took one look at the two lads then turned to Eber Finn for an explanation.

'They broke in here,' the Gaedhal explained. 'Talking some nonsense about stealing your daughter away. I went to fetch the sentries and when I returned I found them struggling with my counsellor.'

Máel Máedóc shook his head as he showed his bloodied hand where the knife had cut him. 'It's nothing. Just a little scratch,' he assured the kings. 'They meant no harm.'

'No harm?' Brocan bellowed. 'They've entered this house uninvited and cut one of my honoured guests. And what's this talk of abducting Aoife?'

'She's promised to run away with me,' Iobhar struggled to say.

'Has she?' Brocan scoffed. 'Well you're not the first young male to fall for her subtle ways. I can forgive you your delusion. But I can't forgive a breach of hospitality. What were you thinking, coming here armed?'

'We weren't armed,' Mahon protested.

'Then how did this cut appear on Máel Máedóc's hand?'

'They used this,' a sentry interrupted, handing the knife to the Fir-Bolg king.

'That's my knife,' Eber announced. 'It belonged to my father.'

Brocan squinted, sensing all was not as it seemed.

'Do you recognise this blade?' he asked the old Druid.

Eber Finn stared hard at his counsellor.

'It was King Míl's knife,' Máel Máedóc confirmed guiltily. It wasn't a lie, it just wasn't the whole truth.

The Fir-Bolg king was satisfied.

'You are hostages in my home,' Brocan told the lads. 'So I don't need to invoke the powers and wisdom of the Brehon judges. You have broken with hospitality, stolen a knife, threatened to abduct my daughter and wounded a Druid in the hand.'

He waited a moment while he caught his breath. He didn't want to appear as if rage had got the better of him.

'I banish you beyond the walls of Dun Aillil. If you come back within the precinct of my home I will command my warriors to kill you.' Then he remembered Mahon had taken the Quicken Brew. 'I'm sure I could devise a suitable punishment for you, Danaan, if I thought hard on the matter.'

Then he ordered his guards to throw them both out the gates with nothing but the clothes they were standing in.

As soon as they were dealt with Brocan offered his apologies to the King of the Southern Gaedhals.

'If I had suspected they had this in mind I would have

thrown them out earlier,' he assured his guest. 'I trust you will find it in your heart to forgive me this terrible imposition?'

'I have already forgiven you,' Eber told his host smoothly. 'This won't be an impediment to our negotiations, will it? I hope to present an attractive offer to you.'

'Do you mean with regard to my daughter?'

Eber nodded.

'Let's conclude the test first and see whether you're worthy of her hand,' Brocan declared. 'Now I must go to my bed. There's much to be done in the morning and I need rest. Goodnight.'

Then he was gone and Eber was left alone with Máel Máedóc.

'I'm sworn to truth!' the old Druid hissed as soon as the king sat down by the fire.

'Then you did a pretty good job of sticking to your vows and serving your king at the same time,' Eber quipped.

'Don't ever ask me to do such a thing again.'

'You are a servant of your people as much as I am,' the king informed Máel Máedóc.

'I'm indentured to the law and to the truth.'

'Then it is certainly time you considered retirement,' Eber finished. With that he rolled himself in his furs and tried to get some sleep.

As the night sky began to retreat before a pale grey morning Brocan rose from his bed and dressed himself in battle array. He pulled on his leggings and strapped them tight. Then he put on his deerskin boots and his shirt of fine linen. Over the top of that he wore a sleeveless leather tunic and a cloak of the finest wool dyed green and black. He had experienced the cold in the deeper parts of the cave and knew he would freeze without adequate protection.

He buckled his belt about him and arranged the breacan cloak so that it was tucked firmly in at his waist. Then he tied his sword sheath to the belt and placed his blade carefully within the leather protector.

In his pack he placed as many dry oatcakes as would fit and half a dozen salted fish. Then he found his leather mead bottle and checked that it was full. In another small pouch that hung from his waist belt he placed two flints, some flax for tinder and a small piece of fire-blackened cloth for starting a fire.

Last of all he took a bundle of twigs and two small pieces of dead oak branch. He intended to take a torch with him as he couldn't be sure how long he'd be wandering within the cave and he wanted to be prepared for any eventuality.

When all was ready he picked up his bronze axe, a small weapon which could easily be carried in one hand or thrust into his belt. It was the symbol of his kingship and a tool with many uses. He wouldn't have left it behind even if he'd been commanded to do so by Fineen.

Then, satisfied he had all he needed, he stepped out of his hall and strode off alone toward the entrance to the caves where a fire had been prepared. A cauldron was bubbling away over the flames. Brocan recognised it as his own; the very vessel which had been gifted to him by the Dagda in a gesture to honour him.

It was known as the Cauldron of Plenty.

As he approached, the king noticed that Eber Finn and his Druid, Máel Máedóc, were already warming their hands in the orange glow. Fineen the Healer was stirring the pot. Dalan and Sorcha were standing nearby.

When the Brehon noticed his king coming down the path

to the caves he picked up a bunch of dried sage and thrust it into the flames. When it caught he blew on it till a thick smoke poured out.

Brocan stopped a short way from the fire and waited till the two Druids approached him, hoping no mention would be made of the events of the previous evening. The king closed his eyes as Dalan bathed him in the sacred herbs in blessing for his journey. Sweet smoke caught in the king's throat but he made no sign of his discomfort.

When the little blessing was done Sorcha whispered in Brocan's ear. 'Have you any experience with the herbs of seeing?'

The king shook his head.

'Fineen is preparing a brew made from redcaps that I have cultivated myself,' she went on. 'They've been guarded by my predecessors for generations, so I can give you some idea of how you might react to them.'

'Go on.'

'You may feel very ill at first. The urge to empty your stomach may be unbearable. But you must try to constrain the urge to retch whatever you do or it may go worse for you later.'

The king nodded. 'What else can I expect?'

'I can't tell you exactly. The experience is different for everyone. The pathways to your inner self may be opened or you may not even pass beyond the gateway of your fears. You may face the elemental demons who inhabit the bowels of the Earth or be confronted with the frightening forms of your nightmares come to life. Indeed, even if you return, you may have lost your senses. Madness lurks in every passage. At the very least you will be changed.'

'I'm ready,' Brocan decided. 'Let this trial begin.'

Sorcha bowed to him as he strode toward the cauldron then she and Dalan followed after. When Lochie looked up from his task he summoned the Druid woman to him with a wave of his hand.

'All is prepared,' he told her.

Sorcha peered into the vessel. The thick brown liquid within bubbled gently and a familiar aroma filled her senses.

'I thought you said you'd never prepared this brew before,' she commented.

'I'm a healer,' he explained, realising she could well be suspicious of his knowledge. 'I have learned all about the redcap broth even if I've never had the correct ingredients at my disposal to make it.'

'But you've never tasted it yourself?'

'No.'

'Have you advised the kings what to expect?'

'I don't know what to expect,' Lochie smiled. 'I told you, I've never tasted the brew myself. And in any case, isn't that the whole point of the exercise, to let them discover for themselves?'

Not for the first time Sorcha's instincts told her Fineen was not being entirely honest. Perhaps it was the unusual air of confidence the healer had somehow acquired lately. She couldn't quite discern what it was about him that put her on edge.

Lochie turned to face the four men who were about to take this challenge.

'Is all made ready?' he asked them.

The two Druids nodded. The kings followed.

'And have you made arrangements for your kingdoms in case you do not return from the caves?'

The Gaedhal looked at the Fir-Bolg and both kings shook their heads.

'What do you mean?' Brocan asked.

'Who will rule in your place should you not come back from this journey?' Lochie insisted.

'Goll mac Morna will have the kingship of the southern Gaedhals,' Eber Finn replied. The king had decided that if he was fated to die then it was likely the destiny of his rival to rule in his place. 'If I am lost then he will make a fine king until the chieftains can decide on my permanent replacement.'

'I can think of no one,' Brocan admitted. 'Since the death of Fergus there isn't any Fir-Bolg I'd trust with the kingship of our people. He was the only warrior experienced enough to do the job.'

'And what of your son?' the Watcher asked.

'Lom?' the king scoffed. 'He's nothing but a foolish boy.'

'Yet he's wise enough to rule until your chieftains have had time to decide on a replacement, as is the custom of your people. He is of your bloodline and so would be the only suitable nominal king of the Fir-Bolg in the interim.'

'I can't leave all I've worked for to a mere slip of a lad who has had so little experience of the world.'

'You must let go one day,' Lochie smiled. 'We've spoken of this before. If you truly wish to sever your ties with this world and find rest, there will come a time when you will have to leave all these matters in the hands of others. Lom will have myself and Dalan to advise him if you're unlucky enough to fall victim to some mishap.'

Brocan considered the healer's words for a few seconds and then nodded his head in agreement.

'You're right. Chances are I'll return without incident so there's really nothing to worry about. Therefore I formally leave the kingship in the keeping of my son Lom. Should I fail to return, he will rule the Fir-Bolg in my place until the Council of Chieftains sees fit to replace him.'

'Let all those present bear witness to these words,' Lochie intoned in the manner of a Druid recording a solemn contract.

Sorcha felt a twinge of disquiet as he spoke the words. Why had Fineen pushed for Lom to be proclaimed Brocan's heir? It didn't make sense.

'Now take a sup of the redcap brew,' the Watcher said, raising a wooden cup high above his head before dipping it into the cauldron. 'If any among you has decided against setting off on this journey, speak now.'

None of them so much as moved a muscle, though Dalan was silently praying one of the two kings would back down. He would rather not go through with this ordeal if it was at all possible. But there was no other Druid of his experience available. And both kings would need the advice of the holy orders. This was one of the duties of his vocation.

'To the kings I say this,' Lochie continued. 'This brew is a gift rarely given to any outside the Druid orders. You have been allowed to take this journey because you are adjudged wise among your people and you have much experience of the world. If you allow your fear free reign you may find yourself trapped and unable to return. This is the only warning I give to you.'

Then he turned to Máel Máedóc and the Brehon.

'To each Druid I give this advice. You will share the experience of the king you've been asked to guide. Don't interfere in his decisions. Don't let your own fears cloud your judgement. And above all don't give anything but advice or you may find yourself sharing the fate of your charge.'

Sorcha stepped forward to speak her piece.

'The brew will not take effect immediately. It may be as much as an hour before you experience any sensations which indicate a change in your consciousness. By that time you should be deep within the caves. You may walk for a while in the Otherworld, or the Underworld. Or you may be overcome with a yearning for sleep. Take care what course you take if you truly wish to return to the mouth of the cave.'

Lochie handed the cup to Máel Máedóc who took a mouthful of the liquid and passed it on to Dalan. The Brehon took his share and then handed the cup to Eber Finn. Brocan was the last to taste the brew and he drained the vessel before handing it back to Lochie.

'Go now,' the Watcher told them. 'And may your gods go with you.'

Máel Máedóc took a lighted torch from the fire and handed it to the Fir-Bolg king. Then he picked up three fresh unlit bundles of rushes and the two of them set out on their journey into the depths of the caves.

When they had been gone for a short while Dalan turned to the King of the Gaedhals.

'I believe we've given them enough of a lead. Shall we go?'

Eber Finn nodded and with a burning rush light in his hand set off. The Brehon followed closely behind carrying spare unlit torches. He waved to Fineen and Sorcha as they departed.

The Druid woman smiled at him and the sparkle in her eyes plainly spoke of her admiration for him. Dalan felt a warm glow in his breast and resolved that when he returned he would spend as much time with Sorcha as his duties would allow.

They were soon within the mouth of the cave and the flickering light from the torch was invisible to any who stood outside. Lochie hardly waited until they were gone before he turned to the Druid woman and made his excuses for leaving. He told her he wished to go and collect rare herbs on the hillsides to the south and that he would have to set out immediately.

'What of the remaining brew?' Sorcha asked. 'You can't simply leave it here where anyone might partake of it.'

'I'll send Sárán to clean it up,' the Watcher told her. Then he picked up his linen herb bag and hurried off toward the main gate to the fortress.

Sorcha watched him as he made his way to the dusty road and she couldn't help but wonder what had come over him in the past few days. She thought she would like to go and eat some breakfast but her sense of duty forced her to stay by the cauldron to await Sárán.

So she stretched out by the fire to warm her hands and await the full glory of the sunrise. And while she lay there she wondered what terrors awaited the two Druids and their kings.

Aoife had woken Sárán half an hour before the dawn and once they'd gathered some provisions they'd gone to observe the proceedings at the entrance to the caves.

Together they'd crouched behind one of the defensive walls and waited until the healer had left Sorcha by the fire.

When the Druid woman had lain by the cauldron a while, they made their way down to her, both shivering with a mixture of excitement and apprehension. Sorcha heard their footsteps and rose to greet them.

'Your master said you'd be along to clean the cauldron.'

'Yes,' the lad replied. 'Aoife came to help me.'

Sárán couldn't believe their luck. Here was a chance to take whatever they needed of the brew without being detected.

The Druid woman never suspected for a moment what they had in mind. Her thoughts were elsewhere. In the short time she had been lying by the fire she had begun to suspect Fineen was not all that he seemed.

'Has your master been ill?' she asked the lad.

'He's never been better,' Sárán replied.

'Have you noticed anything strange about him these last few days?'

'He's been eating better than I can remember, though he hardly seems to sleep at all.'

The Druid woman frowned. 'I'll leave you to your task,' she told them. 'I have a few matters which need my urgent attention. Whatever you do, don't touch so much as a drop of that brew. It will surely be the worse for you if you do.'

'We'll be very careful,' Aoife promised.

With that Sorcha was off as fast as her feet could carry her. Brother and sister pottered about the fire gathering the cooking utensils until she had passed out of sight.

'Now we must hurry,' Sárán told his sister. 'We've no way of knowing when she'll return.'

Aoife already had a bundle of rush lights in her hand. She tied them together with a short thin rope and slung them over her shoulder. Meanwhile Sárán took the cup, filled it to the brim with the thickened brown soup of the redcaps and offered it to Aoife.

'Should I drink the whole thing?' she asked.

'I'm not sure,' he admitted. 'Perhaps we should share this one cupful.'

His sister looked at him sceptically. 'Are you sure this is safe?'

'This was your idea,' he snapped. 'If you're going to change your mind, this would be a good time to do so. But I had the impression you wanted to prove your worth as a warrior. Surely a Druid brew doesn't frighten you.'

Aoife glared at him and snatched the vessel. 'I'm not afraid of it. I'd drink a dozen cups if I thought it would give me what I seek.'

'So be it,' Sárán shrugged.

He watched his sister take a deep draught of the liquid and then he waited to see if any immediate change came over her. When she handed him the cup he carefully observed her eyes and the colour of her skin, but there seemed to be no visible effects.

'How do you feel?'

Aoife took a moment to consider the question. 'It's a satisfying meal,' she began. 'My stomach is surprisingly full. But I can't discern any other effects.'

Sárán decided that the soup probably had to begin digesting before any noticeable changes took place. He put the cup to his mouth and tasted the liquid. To his delight the soup was very tasty. The aroma of fried mushrooms pervaded his senses and his mouth was full of the flavour of winter broth. Without considering that he should probably not drink as much as his sister, he drained the vessel then placed it down beside the fire.

His stomach was bloated as if he'd eaten a huge meal of pork and oatcakes. And a familiar drowsiness descended upon him as it always did after such a meal. He was tempted to lie down by the fire as Sorcha had been doing but Aoife noticed his lethargy.

'Shouldn't we be moving along?' she pressed.

'Yes,' he replied with a yawn. 'I suspect the brew will begin to make itself felt once the broth has started to digest.'

'That doesn't give us long,' Aoife observed and in the next second she was off toward the mouth of the cave, a lighted torch in her hand. Without turning back to her brother she called out, 'Hurry up. I don't want to be separated from you in the darkness. I have a feeling we're going to need to stick close to one another.'

Sárán shook his head to throw off his grogginess, grabbed a rush light and followed after her. And before he knew it they were far enough into the cave that their only light came from those two precious torches.

The first part of their journey was not difficult. In previous generations these caves had been used as homes and for the storage of cheese, mead, ale and butter. The walls had been smoothed and the path between each of the chambers was well worn.

Once or twice they thought they heard voices ahead of them and reasoned that they must be making better time than the other travellers. So at intervals they stopped to rest and give the others a chance to get well ahead of them.

Even at this reduced pace it wasn't long before they reached the place where the single path they'd been following branched off into three passages. This was their first real challenge, to decide which path to take.

It was Aoife who noticed a trail of oat grains leading off down the passage to the left. Obviously someone had dropped them to make it easier to find their way out. Sárán soon discovered white marks etched on the wall of the right-hand passage, and thus their decision was made for them. Without discussing the matter they set off along the middle passage into the inner parts of the Aillwee caves where no living soul had walked in many generations.

They had not gone far when the air suddenly became very chill, like a night in winter without a hearth fire. There was a breeze blowing up the passage into their faces which had a bite to it like a sharp frost.

The passage narrowed within a hundred paces and there above them, set into a niche in the wall, was one of the most frightening sights Sárán had ever seen. And it was at that moment he began to understand the foolishness of what they were doing.

What had at first appeared to be a whitened discolouration of the rock turned out to be a massive skull at least three times the size of any human head. Its vast empty eye sockets stared down on them as they had done for an immeasurable expanse of time.

'What is it?' the lad stammered as he cast a nervous glance all around.

'A dead thing,' his sister replied coldly. 'It cannot harm us.'

'It's a warning not to go any further,' Sárán shot back. 'We've come down the wrong path.'

'Be quiet!' Aoife hissed as she threw down her pack and began to scale the wall toward the strange object.

'What are you doing?' her brother whispered hoarsely in shock.

'I'm taking a trophy. When we return we'll need some proof that we've indeed ventured beyond the outer chambers of the caves. This will be our proof.'

Before he could further object she'd dislodged the skull and tossed it down to him. Sárán caught it with reluctant fingers and immediately placed it on the floor beside him, unwilling to touch it unless absolutely necessary.

When Aoife jumped down beside him she picked it up to get a closer look.

'This was a huge animal,' she gasped, awe-struck by the strange beauty of the lifeless head. 'It must have been four or five times the weight of a man at least.'

Sárán only saw the massive teeth that protruded from its jaws, each one longer and thicker than any of his fingers.

'I don't think we should remove it from the cave,' he said under his breath. 'It may have some sacred significance.'

'Have you ever even heard of the existence of such an animal?' she inquired, ignoring his trepidation.

'No.'

'The people who placed this skull in that niche are long gone and forgotten,' she reasoned. 'They won't challenge us if we take it home.'

She was already emptying her pack of her mead bottle and a joint of smoked boar to make room for it.

'It's certainly not a good idea to abandon our food,' Sárán pointed out. 'We may stand in need of it.'

'I'm not abandoning it. You're going to carry it.'

'My pack is full.'

'Then take a piece of rope and carry the joint over your shoulder. The mead bottle will fit in that pouch at your side.'

Reluctantly he did what he was told, though all his instincts screamed out that they should have left the skull alone. But once they were on their way again he managed to take his mind off his uneasiness by observing the wonders of the caves.

Just past the point where they'd found the skull the roof opened out into a vast rounded canopy that sparkled with innumerable twinkles of light which reflected back from their torches. The air was still cold but the breeze that had frozen their faces had died away. Soon the passage led to a majestic gallery which reached beyond the light of their torches on every side.

At the same time the ground had become rougher, dotted with rounded outcrops of white stone that reflected all light brilliantly. Soon enough they lost all sense of direction in this underground landscape and it was then they had their first strange experience.

Far away, perhaps in the unseen darkness ahead, there was a disturbing sound. It started with a low rumble that built into a roar like that of some unidentifiable wild animal gone on a blood-letting rampage.

Sárán was unable to move for fear. He remained rooted to the spot as firmly as any oak tree. Even Aoife, who outwardly showed no sign of fright, stood perfectly motionless until the sound had passed.

'What was that?' her brother croaked nervously as soon as he'd caught his breath.

She shook her head to indicate she had no idea.

'I hope it wasn't a beast with a skull like the one in your pack,' he stammered.

'Don't be a fool!' she hissed. 'What kind of animal could live in the depths of a cave without sunlight and without any game to hunt?'

Sárán shivered. 'It may not have had any prey for a long while, but whatever made that sound certainly has some now.'

'What are you talking about?'

'Us.'

'Shut up, you coward.'

'If we're set upon, how will we defend ourselves?' he insisted.

'I have a short sword.'

'And an overripe confidence in your ability to use it,' he quipped, but there was no humour in his voice.

'We'd best move on,' Aoife noted. 'Perhaps you're right. There may be some creature dwelling here in the depths. And should that be the case, it will find us all too quickly if we stand still too long.'

She strode out, stepping carefully over the stones as she went. Her brother followed but he was already considering the possibility of turning back. It was only then he realised the hopelessness of their situation. Unlike the two kings, they'd not laid a trail to guide them back to the surface.

Here in this immeasurable chamber they had already lost all sense of direction. He had no idea how they were going to find their way out of this maze. All they could do was press on into the dark and hope they found a passage which led home.

Within a hundred hard-slogged steps they came to a blank wall which Aoife decided to follow around to their right. After a further hundred or so paces a small opening just big enough for them both to crawl through appeared in this wall.

There was no discussion. They simply got down on their hands and knees and, pushing their packs ahead of them, squeezed their way through the tiny tunnel to the other side. Their torches scorched the ceiling of the passage but they were careful not to let them go out.

So it was they came to another opening at the end of the

tunnel. But what appeared before them was no damp and roughly hewn chamber weathered by the ancient forces of water or the upheavals of the Earth. This was a square-shaped room cut from the stone to form a near perfect box. At the far end was a doorway shaped with an elegant arch above it. And this led off into a further passage.

'What is this place?' Sárán gasped. 'Who could have built it?'

'It doesn't matter,' Aoife told him. 'It's dry here and we can rest with some degree of safety. No creature can enter this chamber save through the passage we've just traversed or through that doorway over there.'

She pointed to the arch. 'I'll guard that door. You rest here. From the rate at which our torches have burned down I'd guess we've been walking almost an hour.'

Sárán needed no further prompting. He was used to travelling on foot across the countryside, following his master on their journeys. But this expedition was another matter. He found himself to be almost completely exhausted and he couldn't believe they'd only been walking an hour.

When he'd lain down on the smooth floor for a short while he remembered they had taken the seeing brew.

'Are you feeling ill at all?' he asked his sister.

She didn't have a chance to answer. Right at that moment Aoife began retching violently. The acrid stench of her bile soon filled the little chamber and Sárán felt his own gut begin to tighten. Before he knew what was happening he was spewing out the small amount of broth he'd consumed just an hour earlier. The instant his stomach was empty, however, he felt completely well again.

The two of them sat for a short while on opposite sides of the room while the colour returned to their faces.

'I didn't expect that,' Aoife admitted. 'It's a long while since I was so violently ill.'

Her brother was about to express a similar sentiment when they heard another sound which seemed to come from somewhere along the passage Aoife was guarding. But it wasn't any animal crying, nor was it the noise of falling rocks. It was a human voice, that of a young boy, screaming out to them, so chilling and unexpected that both of them were on their feet in a flash, their sickness forgotten and all strength returned to their limbs.

'Aoife!' came the call echoing down the passage. 'Aoife, help me!'

Then the voice faded away sharply and was gone.

Through the arch and down the passage they rushed at a frantic pace, driven on by a primal fear. And before they were aware what was happening they had passed into a new part of the cavern system and the effects of the seeing brew had come upon them.

Chapter Fourteen

Eber Finn walked tirelessly for more than an hour when the Brehon called him to a halt to rest. They had long since passed into a part of the caves that was breathtakingly beautiful but very strange.

Dalan's keen instincts were calling out a warning of danger if they didn't slow their pace and take better note of their surroundings. He hadn't understood the reasoning behind this journey from the beginning.

All he knew was that out of pride two otherwise sensible rulers had decided to endanger their own lives in an ill-conceived attempt to prove their worthiness. The Brehon had never understood the ways of the warrior class. Sometimes they seemed like children playing at some silly game.

The King of the Gaedhals conceded a short rest break but just as he was sitting himself down he felt an unaccustomed rumbling in his stomach. At the same instant Dalan felt his own guts contract and he remembered the warning he had been given to try and control the urge to vomit.

The two men looked at each other as an unspoken acknowledgment passed between them. And both managed to keep themselves from becoming violently ill. But it was a long struggle which left the pair of them exhausted.

At length, when they'd rested and the spasms had passed,

Dalan got to his knees, found his mead bottle and took a sip. The Gaedhal watched, unwilling to chance a drop of the liquor lest it make him ill again.

'Why did you accept this challenge?' the Brehon asked him as he put away the bottle.

'To win the respect of Brocan.'

'He's a hard man to win over.'

'I need the aid of the Fir-Bolg,' Eber explained. 'Without more warriors my reign will end soon enough. My brother Éremon is a greedy man. He's amassing a force to bring south after the winter. If I don't strike first I'll lose my kingdom and very likely my life.'

'He's your brother. Surely you could sit down together and talk this through. Why must it come to war between you?'

'Because from the very beginning it was his plan to let me conquer the south with my followers while he concentrated on the north. Now that the conquest is done and he holds his part of the country securely, he has his sights set on the south.'

'And why should my people care which of you rules?'

'Éremon may be my brother but he and I are very different. He takes after our father, Míl, who was a renowned warrior but a poor king. War is a tool he uses to distract the chieftains and the people from his lack of skill at peaceful kingship.'

'So once Éremon has defeated you,' Dalan cut in, taking the Gaedhal's story to its logical conclusion, 'there'll come a day when he needs to find someone else to fight.'

'And the Fir-Bolg will be his next victims,' Eber nodded. 'Unless we unite against him.'

'Brocan is concerned for his sovereignty.'

'I have no wish to deprive him of that. I am only concerned with the survival of my own kingship and all I have worked for these three winters past.'

The Gaedhal reached into his pack and took out an

oatcake. 'I wish I could see the future,' he laughed before he bit into the hard biscuit.

'Then there would be no challenge to your life at all,' the Brehon noted. 'I haven't been cursed with such vision except in tiny glimpses, but I don't live with as much uncertainty as you do.'

'What do you mean?'

'Have you heard of the Quicken Brew?'

Eber shrugged his shoulders. 'I've heard rumours of a potion that grants eternal life and health, if that's what you mean.'

'You face death every day of your life,' the Brehon sighed. 'I'm just beginning to understand what a gift that may be. It spurs you on to achieve your goals because you know you have but a short time in which to make your dreams come true. It's but three winters since I drank the Quicken Brew and I'm already growing indolent.'

'If you truly have been granted eternal life, there is no need for hasty decisions. You can approach your objectives without the necessity of hurting other folk along the way.'

'That is a very simple way of looking at the problem,' Dalan told him. 'But it shows that you perhaps have a good heart beneath that warlike exterior.'

'Do you think I would be a warrior or a king if I had a choice in the matter? Don't you think I'd devote my life to music and pleasure if I was given the opportunity? It seems to me you've overlooked the finest aspects of your gift.'

'Aoife shares that gift. I'm told you have made an offer of marriage.'

Eber nodded.

'Has she taken the brew also?'

'If you marry her she will certainly outlive you,' the Brehon said. 'Are you willing to risk a Fir-Bolg Queen of the Gaedhals who is undying?'

282

'Will our children possess the attributes granted by the Quicken potion?'

'Possibly, but I cannot say for certain.'

'I'll be content if the match secures an alliance between our two peoples. In time we shall be one folk with common blood ties and traditions. If that is the cost of my ambitions, then so be it.'

Dalan stood up, grabbed his pack and shouldered it. 'Your ambitions won't be served by sitting here on your backside. Let's get this journey over with. I have a yearning to be seated at my own hearth with my friends.'

Eber Finn was up in an instant. He took his torch from the ground where he had planted it and they set off down the long corridor of stone once again. They had not travelled far when they came to a low wide passageway that had to be traversed on hands and knees.

'Dalan!' Eber exclaimed suddenly, breathless with excitement. 'What's this?'

The Brehon edged forward to where the king was now lying on his back under a smooth section of the roof. Eber was running his fingers gently over the stone and under his hands there was a beautiful drawing etched in black.

Such was the workmanship of the drawing that Dalan was breathless for several seconds, awed by its intricacy. Someone had depicted in charcoal tones two large animals standing on either side of what looked to be a diminutive human figure. The animals were completely covered in hair and they sported massive paws. Their mouths gaped open viciously and they were rearing up on their hind legs menacingly.

But despite their fury and incredible size the human who sat cross-legged between them seemed calm and unafraid.

'Bears,' the Brehon stated with confidence. 'That's what they are.'

'I had no idea there were bears on Innisfail,' Eber gasped.

'There aren't any these days. They were hunted out generations ago. There is no one living in this land who has seen such an animal in the flesh.'

But the drawing was so incredibly lifelike and seemed so fresh that Eber Finn was not convinced. 'Well I've seen a bear,' he told the Brehon. 'In the Iberian lands they still roam wild. They are formidable beasts and I wouldn't like to come across one without a dozen warriors by my side.'

Dalan smiled. 'You won't. As I said, they haven't lived here for generations. The last of their kind was hunted down ages ago.'

But just as he finished speaking a ferocious roar met their ears, distant and faint but certainly real.

'What was that?' the Gaedhal stammered once the sound had faded.

'I don't know. But I'm sure it wasn't a bear. Let's go on and find out.'

They edged their way to the end of the passage until they were once again able to stand, and it was then that the king's torch caught a strange sight in its light.

Where the passage twisted around to the right there was an unusual shape outlined against the stone. A huge dark creature was lying down across their path.

'That's a bear,' Eber whispered. 'And there is no way past it but over the top.'

Dalan frowned, unable to believe his eyes. Certainly it looked like an enormous hairy animal lying fast asleep on its side, but something about its appearance was not quite right.

He observed the creature for a few minutes before snatching the torch from Eber's hand and striding confidently forward. When he came to where the bear was sleeping he suddenly kicked the animal hard in the stomach.

The Gaedhal could hardly believe his eyes. In a flash he'd

drawn his sword and rushed forward with a battle cry to slash at the creature's head.

'I'll save you!' he bellowed as the blade fell neatly across the bear's neck.

The great hairy head lolled forward and rolled across the floor. As Eber watched, the entire animal seemed to collapse into the floor in a cloud of dust. Fur flew in all directions, making both of them sneeze uncontrollably.

But the Gaedhal wanted to be certain he'd finished this monster off. As he struggled to wipe the tears from his eyes he struck out again and again at the vanquished beast until he felt Dalan's hand restraining him.

'It's been dead longer than either of us have been alive,' the Brehon coughed. 'Now stop stirring up the dust and stand back.'

It was true enough. Though the fur had more or less survived the ages, there was no flesh whatsoever on the animal's body. The head was nothing more than an empty skull. Massive and frightening it might have been, but it was also lifeless.

Eber Finn waited while the dust settled. Then he collected a large piece of the bearskin and rolled it up. He tied rope to either end and fastened the trophy to his body.

'This will make a fine cloak to present to Brocan as a marriage gift.'

Dalan nodded and wiped the sweat from his forehead. 'I haven't felt so frightened since Isleen led us into a battle with the owls in the Fomor Forest.'

'Isleen?' Eber shot back.

'The Watcher.'

'What is a Watcher?'

'An ancient force conjured in the days of our forefathers by the enemies of the Danaan and Fir-Bolg,' Dalan explained. 'Isleen is one of only two remaining Watchers. Their sole purpose is to spread havoc among mortal kind.'

Eber was shocked. Surely the Brehon wasn't referring to *his* Isleen. But he could hardly ask — if he revealed that he'd been consorting with this Watcher, it could spell the end of any hope of alliance with the Fir-Bolg.

'Are they really all that dangerous?' he inquired, all the suspicions he'd held about Isleen starting to make sense.

'More deadly, more treacherous and more pitiful than any creature that ever walked. They're shape-shifters. They influence the world around them, the thoughts of men, the desires of women. Bless the Goddess Danu you know nothing of them.'

The Brehon sighed deeply, realising they were wasting precious time. 'Now you have your trophy, perhaps we can consider returning to the cave mouth,' Dalan begged. 'I'd rather return home before the seeing herbs take their full effect.'

'Nonsense!'

And with a laugh Eber Finn was off down the passage once again, searching for more adventure. But the Brehon, following close behind, shared none of the king's joy at roaming this underworld kingdom full of long-dead monsters. For Dalan was beginning to experience an overwhelming sense of foreboding such as he hadn't known since before the coming of the Gaedhals.

Máel Máedóc had just sat down when the first effects of the seeing potion came upon him. He'd had some experience of similar brews when he was a young Druid in training, but it had been many seasons since he'd consented to partake of them. This was mainly because he had never felt entirely comfortable with the way his mind behaved under the influence of such herbs. Máel Máedóc was a man who liked his life to remain ordered and simple. If there were to be challenges to his way of thinking he preferred them to be easily recognised and quickly dealt with. But the seeing potions opened his mind to often frightening visions.

The old Druid had seen but twenty summers when he'd had his first experience with a potion made from a flowering plant known as the gloves of the goat-headed god. The effect on him was unusually prolonged and profound, so much so that his teacher forbade him to take the potion ever again.

His next experience was ten autumns later, as part of the Samháin rituals, when he was fed a small amount of dried mushroom similar in many ways to the redcaps Sorcha had provided. His teacher had passed on by that time so his guide was a good friend who was a herbalist and well versed in the ways of seeing. He still couldn't recall much of that experience other than the long period of recovery that followed. His guide had misjudged the dose and poisoned them both. Máel Máedóc had survived, but his friend had not been so lucky.

Such were the dangers of these preparations. Anyone who took these seeing brews was changed forever; some for the better and some for the worse. Máel Máedóc's own limited experience had led to him being extremely cautious in every aspect of his life.

Yet here he was in his old age taking part in a strange journey which could end in his own death. He'd only agreed to take part because it was his duty to stand beside his king. Only a few days ago he'd been busily composing a satire against Eber Finn. Now he was risking his life in order to honour his duty to the man.

His senses were reeling from the dank air in the cave and the unfamiliar ground they had covered. But he was not yet so groggy that he felt the need to stop. It was Brocan who had called them to a halt.

'I'm ill,' the Fir-Bolg king stated.

These were the first words he'd spoken to the Druid since they'd entered the darkness.

'Shall we rest?' Máel Máedóc inquired.

'You're the old man,' Brocan dismissed. 'I'll rest when you're ready.'

'I would like to move on.'

'Very well.'

The king ignored the trembling in his guts and continued on, though his legs were unsteady and his pace had slowed. The old Druid observed the difficulty Brocan was having and was surprised that he himself was only suffering from a mild giddiness.

'I would like to stop for a while,' Máel Máedóc said finally.

He'd barely finished speaking when Brocan collapsed on the ground and curled up in a tight ball of pain. The Druid offered him a taste of water from his bottle but the king refused it and it was a long while before Brocan stretched out again and grunted in relief.

'I thought my guts were going to explode,' he gasped when he could speak again. Then the king noticed that Máel Máedóc wasn't showing any ill effects.

'I have much experience of the seeing herbs,' the old Druid declared, though this experience was obviously unlike any other he had been exposed to.

'Have you ever seen anything like that?' Brocan asked, pointing to the ceiling.

Máel Máedóc looked where the king was pointing but couldn't at first understand what he meant. All he could see was a plain, rocky grey roof, damp in places but otherwise unremarkable.

'What have you seen?' the old man demanded, but as he spoke his eyes were opened in a way he'd never known before.

Hundreds of tiny lights of red and green and the brightest yellow began to dance around the wall to the accompaniment of the most wonderful melody that had ever met his ears. The tune was light and merry and in no time Máel Máedóc's toes were tapping in rhythm to the music. Then, as if he had no control over himself, he was on his feet, discarding his staff to step out a lively jig such as he'd hadn't danced since he was a lad. The lights grew brighter by the moment until the entire passage seemed to be alive with their vibrant presence.

And something else happened to Máel Máedóc. He experienced a great opening of his heart, a precious joy that entered his soul and rejuvenated his very being. He threw his arms out in ecstatic thanks to whatever unseen power had granted him this wondrous gift. And as he offered up his gratitude enlightenment struck him.

His own life, everything he had ever said and done, even his eventual death, meant nothing to the greater cycle of the universe. He was just one small part of an unimaginably immense organism that followed its own patterns, rhythms and rules. But as insignificant as he was, he was still a part of that unknowable being and as such would always remain a part of it, even beyond death. After his passing his body would break down into dust and return to the Earth. But his soul would move on and change into something completely new yet positively alive.

This concept had been taught to him by various teachers all his life. He had discussed it with his learned friends and students alike, and yet he had never really been convinced of the truth of it until now.

And with this realisation all the cares of his office, all the concerns of his vocation and all the accumulated regrets of his lifetime were released into the air and blew away like as much ash scattered on a dungheap.

The music was growing richer by the moment. Drums, pipes and whistles joined in the chorus with the delicate notes of the harp picked out above the other instruments. There were voices joining in also but Máel Máedóc didn't listen for the words they were singing. His entire being was lost to the melody and the ecstatic dance. Even Brocan was no longer of any concern to him. The old Druid didn't give a thought for his duties or his responsibility as a guide to the Fir-Bolg king.

This uplifting sensation of Oneness with all things was what he'd been searching for all his life. Through long seclusion and meditation he'd tried to achieve this state. When that path had proved fruitless he'd turned to music and poetry. He'd glimpsed the ecstasy of being, certainly, but he'd never been immersed in it, never been swept up in the joy of living as he was now.

As all these thoughts flowed through the mind of Máel Máedóc, the Druid's body began to twirl in a dance such as he'd never attempted before. With arms still outstretched he turned round and round until everything about him, stone walls, rocks and the flames of Brocan's torch all blurred into a weird mix of colour and light.

But despite this constant spinning, Máel Máedóc didn't feel at all dizzy or disoriented. In fact, if anything, the more he twirled the sharper his awareness became until he began to sense the presence of other folk milling about in the chamber.

Once or twice these strangers were so compelling in their silent observation that Máel Máedóc very nearly ceased his dance altogether to ask them who they were.

But his feet would not do his bidding.

'I don't care if I die now!' he cried out for the sheer joy of expressing an end to all sorrow. 'I'll never be unhappy again. I'll cling to this feeling for the rest of my life.'

As he spun round again he caught sight of Brocan, who had a look of genuine concern on his face. Before he'd come round once more, Brocan had his arms about Máel Máedóc.

The old Druid fought him off for a short while, then his knees began to buckle under him. Before he knew what was happening the old man had lost all sensation in his legs. If it had not been for the king's strong arms about him he would have surely fallen face first onto the rocky floor. As it was, Brocan was sufficiently affected by the seeing brew himself that he struggled to hold the old man up.

The next thing Máel Máedóc was aware of was the ceiling of the cave. This and this alone filled his consciousness, though at times he glimpsed Brocan's face. The entire chamber seemed to be spinning as if he hadn't stopped dancing.

The old man knew his body was being twirled around by the ever-moving floor beneath him. But he was not in the least sickened by the sensation. If anything he was thoroughly enjoying it.

Brocan, on the other hand, was struggling to fight off the effects of the brew, for his instincts told him there was some-thing terribly wrong with the old Druid. The king searched around in Máel Máedóc's pack for his water bottle. His hands seemed unwilling to do as they were bid and the search went on for an interminable period. It was all Brocan could do to concentrate on this simple task. At last he found the bottle but his fingers refused to grasp it.

It took an incredible force of will for the king to lift the bottle and remove the stopper. He placed the vessel at the old man's mouth with trembling hands that spilled the precious liquid all around. But Máel Máedóc drank deeply and for a few moments his eyes focused and cleared.

To his intense frustration Brocan could not keep his atten-tion on anything for more than a split second at a time. Once Máel Máedóc had taken a drink the king was so exhausted from the effort of finding the bottle that he slumped back against the wall. Then his entire body began to grow numb.

All his senses were dulled. Sounds were muffled. Colours brightened. Odours strengthened. His mouth tasted salty and dry but he didn't have the energy to take a sip from his companion's water bottle. And the mere thought of taking a draught from his own mead bottle turned his stomach.

It was then that Brocan noticed his rush light was flickering. Somehow he'd managed to drop it on the ground where it spluttered dangerously close to extinction. If the light went out they would certainly be in trouble. If it was difficult to find a water bottle it would be impossible to locate a flint and tinder in the pitch blackness.

With all his strength Brocan sharpened his resolve and moved toward the torch. Though he couldn't manage anything better than a slow crawl across the floor he soon had his hands on the shaft of the rush light. With the greatest care he propped it up against the wall so that at least it would continue burning. When he was certain the light was safe he rolled over on his back and became conscious of the sweat running down his face like a mountain stream.

And as he lay on his back he began to feel an unfamiliar and disturbing coldness spread across his body. It started in his feet then engulfed his ankles and calf muscles. Wherever it went it left behind a paralysis so devastating that Brocan could not so much as twitch a muscle.

By the time panic set in, it was already too late. His hands and arms were lumps of cold immovable stone; his heart was slowing and his breathing had become strained and irregular. Only two parts of him seemed immune to this affliction: his mind, which raced on, fuelled by fear; and his eyes which, though they would not move in their sockets, remained open and aware of every subtle movement in the chamber.

This was how, after a long while lying on his back unable to move, Brocan first noticed a small group of strange folk standing at one end of the passage, quietly observing him.

They were dressed entirely in the skins of animals. Their hair was long, brown and filthy. They were shorter than average, with large eyes and hands. And none of them spoke a single word, though Brocan sensed they wanted to communicate with him.

At length a woman came to sit beside him. Gently she propped his head up under his pack and he felt a few drops of water pour into his mouth. The king tried to thank her but his lips and tongue would not answer the call to speak.

The strange woman stroked his hair and stared intently at his helpless face. Her eyes were like those of a seal — large, black and wet. After a short while she motioned to her companions and there was a flurry of movement. But Brocan had exhausted his reserves of energy.

His eyelids would not remain open, no matter how he struggled against them. At last the woman closed them for him and he fell into the deepest sleep he'd ever experienced.

For all the noise of folk scurrying about him, for all the concern he held for Máel Máedóc's wellbeing, Brocan let himself be transported to the realm of sleep. And once his soul was floating at peace, he allowed the ship of his spirit to float aimlessly on a flat featureless sea of restfulness.

Sorcha went directly to the hall of poetry, hoping to find Fineen. But by the time she got there he was nowhere to be seen. Her suspicions were definitely aroused now. It would have been almost impossible for him to have reached the hall, collected his things and gone off in search of herbs as he had intended.

To be certain she went down to the main gates of the fortress and inquired of the sentries whether the healer had passed that way. They told her no one had entered or departed the gates since sunset the previous evening.

To make certain her instincts weren't playing tricks with

her, the Druid woman began a systematic search of the entire fortification, beginning with the king's hall, then the house of the chieftains and any place it was likely Fineen might have gone before setting out on his expedition.

She asked everyone she met along the way but no one had seen the healer all morning, which was strange since he was such a popular figure. Everywhere he went folk looked out for him either to thank him for some cure or to ask his advice with a health problem.

In the end Sorcha decided to return to the hall of poetry once more to see if he'd returned there. But there was no sign of him. His bed had not been slept in. His travelling pack had not been touched. And his clothes were still laid out for the day as if he'd not yet awoken.

In the course of her curiosity Sorcha opened Fineen's box of herbs. And there she saw something which made her blood run chill. A thin grey film of mould covered every leaf, twig and seed within the box. Nothing had been touched for days.

This was not just unusually careless of the healer. It was highly unlikely. And it convinced the Druid woman she had stumbled across the reason why Fineen had been making her feel so uneasy.

She thought back to the conversation she'd had with him a few nights before and her mind began to race with possibilities. How did he know so many tales that hadn't been told in generations? Where had he gained his knowledge of the Watchers? He'd certainly not known so much when they'd first met.

Her heart racing furiously, Sorcha made her way back down to the cave entrance to speak with Sárán. To her surprise she found the cauldron still propped over the fireplace and the contents settling into a solid mass within.

'Where are the two trainee Druids who were sent to clean

this vessel?' she asked the guards who had just been posted to ensure no one entered the caves.

The two men looked at each other and shrugged.

Now Sorcha was beginning to feel more than uneasy. She grabbed a torch from beside the fire, lit it and prepared to venture into the Aillwee by herself. She knew this was perhaps a foolish act but her concern for Dalan and the others was overwhelming.

She suspected that she had discovered one of the Watchers going about his mischief in the guise of the healer, but she hardly dared admit this even to herself, for the idea was simply too disturbing.

She intended to go as far into the caves as was safe and no further. But the sentries had been given strict instructions to stop her from entering and no amount of arguing or begging had any influence over them. At last she simply tried to push past the two warriors but they easily picked her up between them and carried her back to the cauldron. When they set her down by the fire the larger of the two issued her a stern warning that she would not pass them as long as they had any strength.

Downcast but desperate to do something, Sorcha threw down the torch, turned on her heel and headed off toward the main gate of the fortress. Then, without so much as a water bottle or a cloak in case the night turned cold, she set off down the dusty road toward her home in the forest.

She had just entered the woods which lay directly to the south of Aillwee when a familiar voice called out to her. The Druid woman stopped in her tracks when she heard the call and waited until the huge black bird descended from the trees to stand beside her on the path.

'I've been waiting for you,' the Raven cawed in her gravelly tones. 'There's terrible news on the wind.'

'Why didn't you come to the Aillwee and speak with me?'

'Not all the Fir-Bolg are friends of the Raven kind,' came the reply. 'King Brocan fought a battle against my cousins the owl folk and many of them died. I won't easily forget that.'

'What's your news, my friend?' Sorcha pleaded. 'I must hurry home if I'm to have any chance of saving Dalan from terrible danger.'

'Dalan is safe for the moment,' the bird assured her. 'It's Brocan and the old Gaedhal Druid who are in trouble.'

'What do you mean?'

'The Watcher lured them into the caves to do away with them.'

'I don't understand.'

'The one who has been posing as Fineen to influence the King of the Fir-Bolg and his people.'

'And what of Fineen himself?'

'The healer has been sleeping in the hidden depths of the cave for several days. He likely won't awake again for many generations.'

'So that wasn't Fineen who stirred the brew this morning and sent the kings out on their quest?'

'It was the Watcher who calls himself Lochie.'

'I suspected something was awry. How do you know this?'

'My people speak to all the kindred of the sky, the waters and the Earth,' the Raven replied. 'The tale passed quickly from the cave-dwellers to the bird folk.'

'And what of Aoife and Sárán? Have they gone into the caves too?'

'I haven't heard anything about them,' the bird shrugged. 'But I expect they'll be safe for the time being. The Watcher has plans for them. He wants that pair kept safe.'

'Will you do something for me?' Sorcha asked.

'I'll do what I can to help.'

'Gather your kindred and search the fields all around. There must be many small and hidden entrances to the

Aillwee caves. I know there are streams which disappear underground and others which emerge from the depths. Scout them out in case there should be any sign of anyone making their way out.'

'And I will pass the word to the underground dwellers that they may keep a watch also.'

'Without your aid Brocan may be lost to us and the tide will turn in favour of the Watchers and their meddling schemes.'

'Brocan's fate was sealed when he set foot under the cave's stone roof. The Gaedhal Druid is also beyond any aid. Alas, I fear no one now living shall see either of them again.'

'Hurry off on your task,' she pressed. 'I must go back to my house and I'll await your word there. I have a good store of dried herbs which may stem the terrible effects of the seeing herbs and I suspect there will be those in need of my healing.'

'I will do as you ask,' the Raven nodded as she clicked her beak. 'But don't put too much hope in the herbs you've gathered. Dalan set off on this journey willingly. He may not appreciate it if you try to bring him back too soon.'

'I have much to do and little time in which to do it. I can see no other course open to me but to prepare for the worst.'

The Raven cocked her head to one side and clicked her beak again.

'I'll send out the word to all my kindred,' the bird assured her. 'But don't hold too high a hope of helping them. You are but a Druid woman. You're not as wily as the Watchers.'

The bird spread her wings and took off, soaring to the south-east in the direction of the caves. The Druid woman watched after until the Raven was nothing more than a black speck in the far distance.

Then Sorcha said a little prayer to the Goddess Danu and turned away from Aillwee toward her forest home, a plan to rescue her friends formulating in her mind.

Chapter Fifteen

Eber Finn must have rushed on at a frantic pace for another hour when he suddenly stopped in his tracks and without a word to Dalan lay down. By the time the Brehon caught up with him the Gaedhal was fast asleep once again, curled in a tight ball.

Dalan, however, wasn't the least bit tired. His senses had begun to awaken and he resented having to stop their journey on the whim of his companion. It crossed his mind that it would do no harm to go on a short way and scout the passage ahead, but his sense of duty restrained him. So he sat down, bundled some twigs out of his pack and prepared a little fire to keep himself warm while he watched over the sleeping king.

A long while passed. The only sound to be heard was the crackling of the flames. Dalan began to wonder why he hadn't been affected by the seeing brew. True, he had suffered some discomfort in the stomach, but his other senses had remained largely free of any hallucinations.

The Gaedhal was breathing deeply now and so it seemed Eber had also escaped without having his consciousness disrupted too much. Dalan sat back against the hard stone wall and relaxed. His thoughts bounded from one subject to another as he began to drift off. Every once in a while Eber would twitch in his sleep and the Brehon would stir to check the fire or listen to the silence beyond their little camp.

Knowing the king would want to press on as soon as he awoke, Dalan closed his eyes to rest.

When Eber Finn finally stirred he was instantly awake. He had been engulfed in one of the deepest sleeps it had ever been his pleasure to experience. His dreams had been so pleasant and peaceful that they'd added to the sense of contentment that flooded his consciousness. Every fibre of his being was now tingling with anticipation and excitement. And his mind raced ahead to the future where he would rule as king of all the Gaedhals of Eirinn.

He resolved to do it all without Isleen. She had seduced him and drawn him into this current course of events. But if she truly was the Watcher Dalan was seeking, then she was a dangerous person to have about.

He sat up before the dying fire, noted that the Brehon was sleeping soundly, and placed a few more kindling twigs around the coals. Then he gently blew into the fire to stir up the heat and get the flames going again. As he did so he thought he glimpsed a familiar face. The king shook his head. Surely he couldn't have seen Goll mac Morna's eyes staring back at him from the fire.

But when he looked again there was the warrior's arrogant grin and his confident nod. Eber Finn was fascinated. He stared deeper into the flames until his eyes began to lose focus.

It was then he saw a wider scene laid out before him. And it was the aftermath of a terrible bloody battlefield. All around the muddy field there were strewn hacked and mauled bodies. Most were dead but some still writhed about in agony, the looters moving through their ranks with clubs to silence their screams. Old women vied with young brigands for the best boots and clothes. Young girls sang sweetly as they rifled the pouches of the slain, their hands caked in blood.

Eber's face paled in horror at the sight. This was a side of battle he'd never witnessed. There was no honour for the dead. They'd been left where they lay without so much as a word spoken over their bodies or a relative come to claim the corpses.

Without warning the King of the South suddenly found himself walking through this horrific scene. And the stench of spilled blood was everywhere. He covered his face with his sleeve as he picked his way through the carnage until at last he came to an open space where there were fewer bodies.

In stunned silence he sat down cross-legged to look back over the field and wonder what kind of battle had gone on here and where this place might be. Just then he heard a movement behind him. He turned around and there were three horsemen astride enormous animals, larger than any he had ever seen.

'What's your name?' one of the men demanded.

'Eber Finn,' the stunned dreamer replied.

All three of the horsemen laughed loudly, and one of them dismounted, striding over toward him.

'I suppose you're going to tell us you're the High-King of Eirinn?' the warrior scoffed as he drew his sword from its sheath.

'I'm the King of the Southern Gaedhals,' Eber snapped, not taking kindly to this fellow's tone.

Once again all three warriors laughed heartily.

'Which side were you on?' the warrior demanded to know.

Eber shook his head. 'I don't know what you mean?'

'In the battle. Which side did you fight with? Lom of the Dark Glen or the Fianna of Dun Éremon?'

'Éremon is my brother,' the king stuttered.

The warrior stepped forward and grabbed Eber by the throat. In a second he'd tossed the king to the ground.

'Stop playing games with me,' he bellowed. 'Which side did you fight on? I haven't got all day.'

'I told you, my name is Eber Finn. I'm King of the Southern Gaedhals.'

'King Eber is at Teamhair,' the warrior replied coldly. 'And you're too shabby to even be admitted to his court. Now tell me who you sided with if you don't want a beating for your insolence.'

One of the other warriors rode forward. 'Slit his throat,' he suggested. 'I wouldn't like to risk letting any of those buggers get away. Lom would skin us alive.'

'It's his brother I fear,' added the third man.

Suddenly Eber understood what he was witnessing. This was a glimpse of the future. He quickly decided to glean as much information as possible from these men.

'I fought with Lom,' he chirped up. 'I'm sorry, my head is still spinning from the fight. I must have been struck from behind.'

The three warriors looked at him with suspicion but the dismounted man seemed convinced.

'I know how he feels. I was knocked on the head myself and thought I'd never get my senses back.'

'A thick skull usually protects a small wit,' the first warrior laughed. 'Get up on my horse and we'll take you to our commander.'

'I'd rather be left here to rest a short while first.'

'You'll come to Goll mac Morna and let him decide what to do with you,' the warrior told him. 'I don't care if you're the High-King himself, I can't let you roam the battlefield in case you're one of Éremon's men. They're under banishment all of them, though they've ignored the orders for the most part.'

'Eber Finn's the High-King?'

'You poor fool. You've really lost yourself, haven't you?

Come back with us. Have a meal, sit by the fire with a jug of mead and before you know it you'll recall your name.'

Eber was about to protest further when he heard the unmistakable sound of a chariot being driven hard. He turned around in time to see Goll mac Morna at the reins and then his heart began to pound that he might be recognised.

Goll stopped the war-cart and dismounted. Then he strode over to where Eber was struggling to his feet.

'What's going on?' the Fian leader demanded.

'We found this straggler crawling among the dead,' the first warrior reported. 'We were about to bring him to you.'

'What's your name?' Goll asked.

'He reckons he's King Eber Finn,' the warrior laughed.

Goll squinted as he examined Eber's face. All expression left his eyes. And then he turned to the warrior who had pushed the king to the ground.

'Poor bloody fool!' Goll scoffed. 'Even in the state he's in with his brains knocked about he'd be a better king than the one we're stuck with.'

He leaned over Eber again.

'I wish you were King Eber Finn,' he told him. 'I'd slit your throat now and save myself the trouble of chasing old Éremon's people round the countryside.'

Then the Fian leader frowned. 'I know your face from somewhere,' he declared. 'Are you one of Lom's people?'

Eber nodded.

'And what do you think of our High-King?'

'I always think highly of kings,' Eber answered. 'It's the polite thing to do.'

'But kings are meant to be the guardians of the people,' mac Morna argued. 'Surely you wouldn't say the High-King has been on the side of the common folk.'

'I'm just a humble warrior. I know nothing of such matters.'

'Are you with me?' Goll whispered.

Eber shook his head and threw up his hands to show he didn't understand.

The war-leader laughed. 'Perhaps you're not as witless as you seem. When I go to Teamhair I'll need some loyal warriors behind me. If I'm going to rid this country of Eber Finn I'll want reliable men to do my bidding. You look like a strong fellow who doesn't answer back when he's given an order. How would you like to serve the new High-King of Eirinn?'

Eber Finn felt the blood drain from his face. He wanted to scream out that this man was a traitor to his king and an oath-breaker. He was tempted to make a grab for a sword and stab the treacherous son of Morna between the shoulders. But he knew this was merely a dream vision.

'I am Eber Finn,' he declared. 'I am King of the Southern Gaedhals.'

The large warrior who had thrown him to the ground stepped forward to whisper in Goll's ear. 'He must be mad after all, my lord.'

'Let him be,' Goll decided. 'He's no use to us like that. Poor fool.'

With that the Fian leader returned to his chariot, took the reins and drove off, followed at a discreet distance by the three mounted warriors.

Eber Finn was left there in the mud to consider all that he had witnessed. He took one more look at the battlefield before his head began to swim. He closed his eyes to wipe his brow and when he opened them again he was staring into the dying flames of the tiny fire and Dalan was wide awake, watching him intently.

Sárán ran on through a wide low opening until he realised he'd entered another chamber. His torch was still burning fierce and bright, but it might as well have been a candle for all it revealed to him. Aoife had lagged behind him for a while and when she caught up she was breathless. The two of them leaned against each other and listened for any further cries.

'I could have sworn I heard someone calling your name,' Sárán told his sister.

'I heard a call for help,' she gasped. 'Who would be calling out to me? No one knows we're here.'

As she spoke the cry was repeated, and without any hesitation they were off again in search of the disembodied voice. Before they had gone another two hundred paces their feet were suddenly wet and they had to stop in their tracks.

When Sárán held his torch aloft they were both shocked to find that a great dark lake extended out into the blackness before them. They were standing on a sandy shore lapped by tiny waves. A slight breeze caressed their faces, which surprised them, for they were deep underground.

The calls had ceased but they were both led on by a desire to track down their source. So they edged their way around the waterline until they came to a rocky outcrop that jutted into the water and blocked their access to the next part of the beach.

Neither of them hesitated to climb up over these rocks, though the going was tough and Aoife was beginning to tire. She had moved around from the landward side of the rock to get a better footing when her exhaustion finally got the better of her and she slipped.

Sárán managed to grab her before she tumbled into the icy waters but within seconds he'd overbalanced and the pair of them slid over the loose stones into the lake. The water was deadly cold. It instantly sucked the breath from Aoife's lungs. She couldn't even scream out in shock.

Her brother hardly fared any better. And what was worse, they lost their lighted torches and were plunged into total blackness. By the time they managed to struggle back to shore their clothes were soaking wet and they were exhausted and near to half drowned.

On the sand at the water's edge Sárán went through his pack by touch until he found the leather pouch he kept his flints in. The tiny firestones were dry and so was the small amount of tinder he'd stuffed inside the pouch. But everything else they possessed was wet through.

The spare torches were well coated with pine resin so he decided to try to build a small fire. Aoife was shivering from the cold and huddling close to him for warmth. In the total darkness it was difficult to make a spark let alone build a fire. But somehow, with luck and perseverance, he soon had a small blaze going, not enough to dry their clothes but certainly enough for a little light and some warmth.

They held each other close to preserve body heat while the fire took hold, and for a long time neither of them could speak for shivering. When Aoife finally managed to say something it was just a stuttered expression of her extreme discomfort.

'Stay still,' her brother advised. 'We'll rest before we move on. If we sleep we'll conserve energy.'

He pulled a wet oatcake from his pack and found his knife. Then he cut a piece of meat from the smoked pork and handed it to his sister. But her stomach was still strained from the after-effects of the seeing brew so she refused the meat.

Sárán forced himself to eat a few morsels then lay down and snuggled into Aoife's back.

'I'm freezing,' she cried.

'Be quiet.'

'I'm cold.'

'I told you to be quiet,' her brother snapped. 'We wouldn't be in this situation if it hadn't been for your foolish desire to prove yourself. Now it's up to me to find a way out of this cave before we die of cold. You will rest and when you awake be ready to move on under my direction. I'll not be following you any longer. Do you understand?'

Aoife didn't reply. She was already asleep. And considering the unbearable cold, Sárán was quite surprised. But then he began to feel his own body slowing into sleep. At first he wondered if this was what it was like when death came and he panicked for a second. The he recalled the Quicken Brew. Confident he would wake again after a short rest, he closed his eyes and surrendered to his exhaustion.

It may have been hours later that they woke, or it may have been no more than minutes, for time means nothing in the deep uninhabited parts of the Earth. But they had certainly not rested enough when a noise stirred them both from sleep.

It was a surprising sound to be hearing far underground. It was the music of a harp picking out a delicate melody in a lively tempo.

Chapter Sixteen

When Brocan awoke he spent a long while staring at the ceiling. He hadn't slept so deeply nor so peacefully since he'd been a little child lying in his mother's arms. Stretching his limbs as his body returned to wakefulness, he told himself he would rise after just a little more rest.

His attention was drawn to the high arching roof of the cavern above him where the flickering firelight caught the shadows on the rough surface and made them dance wildly. For a long time he lay like that, his thoughts drifting until at last a vivid picture came to his mind.

In his reminiscences he travelled to the place where he'd been born and raised, the fortress of Dun Burren. Many happy memories flooded over him and a wide smile illuminated his face.

As clearly as if he had been standing on the walls of his old home he looked out and saw a woman running up the path to the main gate. Her hair was a long coppery-red river that flowed over her shoulders, down her back and touched her thighs. Even at fifty paces her eyes were the brightest green he'd ever seen, except for those of his daughter. She was slender, gentle, mischievous and merry. She was a beautiful spirit with a passionate heart. She could dance through the night even after the musicians had gone to their rest. And she was the most wonderful, loving, difficult, contrary, tempestuous, sensuous woman he'd ever known.

Her name was Riona. She had been his wife and his queen. And when she'd left him for King Cecht of the Danaans a light had been extinguished in his life. Brocan had lost the joy of living and the passion he'd had for fighting.

His heart was sick for the loss of her. His spirit had shut itself away from joy. And nothing, not even the Quicken Brew, had been able to heal the wound he had suffered at their parting.

All food was bland, all mead was bitter. His duties had become empty and meaningless, though he struggled to continue to serve his people. The only thing he'd desired since she'd gone away was sleep. Sound restful eternal slumber.

Brocan's heart had had a tiny crack in it since she'd gone. Like a cooking pot that slowly leaks, the joy had been seeping out season after season until now his spirit was a dry, withered thing. And death would not be any comfort to him. His soul could not go off to the Halls of Waiting to renew itself in the waters of the Well of Forgetfulness. Although his body was strengthened by the Quicken Brew, his spirit was trapped. No Druid potion could heal the ailment from which he suffered.

It was sadness that finally stirred Brocan from his rest. He couldn't bear to think about Riona any longer, nor could he face the pain he was suffering deep within himself. So he rolled over on his side, ready to get up.

It was then he noticed the roaring fire that lay between himself and Máel Máedóc. He must have been sleeping very soundly not to have noticed the old Druid building up the flames. But where could all this kindling have come from? There was surely more stacked up in the flames than he'd been carrying in his pack. And what of those two logs? They defied explanation altogether, for there were no trees growing underground.

'Máel Máedóc,' he whispered. 'Are you awake?'

'Did you see them?' the Druid replied as he turned his head to face the king. 'They are the most beautiful folk I've ever seen in my life.'

'Who?'

'The folk who came to help us.'

A sudden rush of remembrance came to Brocan; a glimpse of a strange woman's face. 'I thought I was dreaming,' the king replied.

'I thought that at first too. But I've never had a dream so wondrous, so calming and so filled with the power of healing.'

'Are you feeling better?'

'I am,' Máel Máedóc smiled. 'But this cave will be my last resting place. My time has come.'

'Don't speak so. You're suffering from the brew. You mustn't think that you're going to die yet.'

'Not quite yet,' the old Druid replied. 'First I must deliver a satire. Then I will bathe in the sacred river. And after that my soul will be set free.'

Brocan was puzzled by these words but he convinced himself the old man was simply suffering from a strange vision that would soon pass.

Máel Máedóc's eyes sparkled and a smile spread across his face as if he'd heard the king's thoughts. 'I've found my peace,' he nodded, tears welling up in his eyes. 'I'm going to sup with my ancestors. But the longer I delay the more I will suffer the pains of my aged body.'

The king felt the emotion welling up in his throat and he couldn't speak.

'Help me,' the Druid asked calmly.

Brocan looked away, refusing to believe that Máel Máedóc

was about to breathe his last in this hidden cave far from his kindred and in the company of a stranger. But when he could bring himself to turn back and look at the Druid's face he knew immediately the old man was speaking the truth.

There was a peaceful serenity in his moist grey eyes that had not been evident before. And his skin had begun to drain of all its colour. This was the touch of death, nothing was more certain.

'How can I be of assistance?' Brocan asked, choking back the tears.

It wasn't that he felt any particular attachment to this Gaedhal. But he considered it a great privilege to be in the presence of one who was about to embark on the mysterious voyage to the lands beyond life. It was a journey Brocan expected he would never experience for himself.

'Bring Eber Finn to me.'

'What hope do I have of finding him in this vast cavern?' the king countered. 'You could be gone long before I returned.'

'You'll find him not far away,' Máel Máedóc assured him. 'I've been told he's just beyond that passage.'

'Who told you?'

'The shining people.'

Brocan looked over his shoulder and down the passage in the direction the old man was pointing. He was not convinced. It was very likely the Druid had imagined these folk.

'I didn't invent them,' Máel Máedóc snapped. 'You saw them too but you'd rather forget about them. They make you uneasy. Well I've got nothing to be uneasy about. I'm dying.'

'Who are they?'

'They didn't tell me.'

'I'll go and take a look,' Brocan promised. 'But I'm not going to wander too far. I don't want you to be alone for too long.'

'I'll still be here when you get back,' the old Druid scoffed.

'I'm not in a hurry. I still have one duty to perform. I should have put it behind me before I parted with Eber Finn but I was weak-willed and lacked the resolve. It's an unpleasant task but I must have done with it before I go.'

The king stood up, grabbed a torch and headed off down the passage. As his light disappeared in the infinite blackness, Máel Máedóc remembered something important.

'Take care of the shining ones!' the old Druid called out. 'They're not as friendly as they might appear.'

If the king heard, he did not answer. And Máel Máedóc could only hope Brocan would be wise enough to face any threat alone.

Dalan gathered his pack and lit a new torch as soon as he realised the Gaedhal was wide awake.

'Shall we go on?' the Brehon asked.

'Yes,' Eber nodded, anxious now to return to his people and defend himself against the machinations of Goll mac Morna. 'I think it's time we put an end to this foolishness and found our way out of the caves. Fineen spoke of a river that runs out from the caverns to the south. Perhaps if we can locate its source here in the depths we'll have a chance of finding our way back to the Fir-Bolg fortress.'

'I believe you may be right,' Dalan agreed. 'If you listen carefully you'll hear the sound of what may be river.'

Both men fell silent, concentrating on the noise. It was faint but unmistakable and it was emanating from a spot further down the long passage they'd been following.

'Your heart is still set on war?' the Brehon asked.

'It matters little what I think or desire,' the king replied.

'My brother is readying himself for conflict and my most trusted champion sees an opportunity to seize the kingship for himself. I must stand for my people and protect them from two enemies who would enslave them.'

'But the Druids of your people would surely not allow Éremon to conduct a war against you?'

'The chief Druid of the Gaedhals in this land is my eldest brother, Amergin. He and Éremon have always been close. When we first landed they sent me to the south in the hope that I'd be defeated or possibly killed in battle. They didn't imagine that our mother would choose to accompany me or that I'd be victorious. Now I'm a thorn in the foot of their intentions. Éremon rules the north because Amergin supports him. The chieftains accept this situation because they revere the memory of our father, Míl.'

Eber picked up a torch and held it in the flames until it caught. Then he went on.

'I am the youngest surviving son of Míl and Scota. According to the traditions of my ancestors I should never have had the opportunity to rule in my own right. But my chieftains have expressed their confidence in me as a war-leader and it is my duty to perform that task to the best of my ability.'

'And why hasn't an older, more experienced chieftain stepped forward to be considered for the kingship?'

'The influence of my father should not be underestimated. The mere mention of his name is enough for many. He was a legend even in his own time. It is too often assumed that his sons were cast in the same metal.'

'So Éremon is not his father's son?'

Eber ignored the question and continued. 'It's true there were many good reasons for our journey to these islands. Invaders from the south were harassing outlying settlements and our cattle herds had grown to the point where the land could not feed them.'

Eber breathed deeply as he thought fondly on his homeland.

'Life was different there. My father's kingship was strictly regulated by the Druid orders. Éremon could not accept many of the rulings the wise ones passed down on him. He saw this new land as a means to escape their strictures.'

The king looked away in shame as he went on. 'I must admit I agreed with him then. But now I understand that he is greedy. He seeks to change the whole weave in the fabric of our society. I believe the king should be the servant of his people. In the same way the Druids preserve tradition and law, the war-leader should tend to the defence and physical needs of his kinfolk.'

'But your brother would turn this way of life upside down?'

'He was always enamoured of gold,' Eber Finn sighed, and knew he was also speaking about an aspect of himself. 'Wealth should be a reflection of a chieftain's success at feeding his people. If they have the leisure to produce luxuries then he deserves to benefit. But Éremon would have the people pay him a price for his skill that is beyond their means, for not every harvest is a good one.'

'That is slavery!' the Brehon stated in horror.

The King of the Gaedhals nodded. Eber closed his eyes for a moment, realising he too had once believed such methods were acceptable. Now he was changing his opinion. A king should be the servant of his people.

'When I set out for the new land I held many beliefs in common with my brother. But I've witnessed the struggle for survival that has been thrust upon my loyal supporters. I understand now that every decision I take affects the lives of everyone in my clan. There has been enough suffering. I don't wish to see any more.'

A transformation of heart struck the Gaedhal as he spoke and was clearly reflected in his eyes.

Dalan raised his eyebrows and clapped a hand across the king's back.

'I believe I may have misjudged you,' the Brehon admitted. 'You have a way to go, but I would say you're on the path to wisdom. You'll be a good king one day.'

'That is my only ambition.'

'If you will accept my advice along the way, I'd be honoured to help you in whatever way I can.'

The two men shared a smile and without any further discussion headed off down the passage that led toward the sound of water falling. The going was hard but both of them had lightened their hearts.

The further they walked the damper the air became, and before long the stones seeped water and the path became slippery. This slowed their progress but they were obviously nearing their goal so neither man gave expression to his frustration.

At length they rounded a sharp bend in the passage and a blast of cool air hit their faces. And carried on the breeze was a merry song — the music of a river rushing along its course. Eber Finn ran forward to where the path passed into a wide entrance. The Brehon followed him step for step. At that point the floor disappeared unexpectedly and the king lost his footing. In a flash Dalan was at his side and had hauled him up onto safe ground again.

The pair lay back with heaving chests until the excitement of the moment had passed, then the Brehon sat up and looked down at the foot of the cliff. There far below was a wide torrent with sandy banks and mossy rocks.

The whole scene was lit from above by sunlight which filtered in through openings in the cavern wall on the opposite side of the river. The nearest opening was at least a thousand paces away, Dalan reckoned. To reach it they would have to climb down the cliff, cross the torrent and scale the other side. Such a journey could easily take two days. It was out of the question.

'What shall we do?' the Brehon mumbled under his breath.

'There must be another way down,' the king suggested.

But they hadn't passed any forks in the tunnel. This seemed to be the only opening to the river on this side. Eber dangled his legs over the edge and sat with his chin resting in his hands while he considered their situation.

The cliff was almost sheer to the bottom. There were footholds but he couldn't be certain how secure they might be. He had a length of rope in his pack but he was sure it wouldn't be long enough. It was as he was pondering the problem that he caught a strange glimmer out of the corner of his eye. The king squinted, concentrating on the area where he thought he'd seen the little light.

Suddenly his hand was on Dalan's arm and his fingers were squeezing tight.

'Look!' he gasped. 'Down there. It's a fire.'

The Brehon shielded his eyes from the sunlight and looked carefully. But he couldn't locate any fire.

'Are you sure?'

Just as the words left his mouth the Brehon caught sight of the flames. The fire was far off in the depths of darkness at the lower end of the river, but there was no mistaking the flickering reflection against the surface of the water.

'That's the direction we're headed in,' the king said. 'Perhaps Brocan and my adviser have made better time than we have.'

'They've taken a different path, that's all,' Dalan corrected him. 'What shall we do? Scramble down or retrace our steps and seek out another passage to the river?'

'We could wander these stone corridors for the rest of eternity and not find our way back to the river,' Eber judged. 'In my opinion we should try to climb down the cliff face.'

Dalan edged closer to the brink. His heart raced at the thought of making that descent.

'Look,' he began nervously, 'the truth is, I'm not very comfortable with heights.'

'What have you got to be worried about? You've taken the Quicken Brew. What possible harm could come to you if you fell?'

The Brehon looked over the cliff again and laughed at himself a little.

'I'm the one who's risking his life,' Eber went on.

With that the Gaedhal found the rope in his pack and fastened it around an outcrop of rock. He tied a sailor's knot that would allow him to slip the rope away when they had climbed down to the full extent of the line. Then he tested that it would hold his weight.

'Shall I go first?'

'Is this a good idea?' Dalan stuttered, terrified at the thought of plunging down the cliff face suspended on such a flimsy-looking cord.

'You have nothing to fear,' the Gaedhal reminded him. 'Even if you fall, no harm will come to you.'

'I've never really put the brew to the test before,' the Druid admitted. 'It has only been three winters since I drank of it.'

Eber smiled. 'You Druids are all the same. You steer clear of danger. You spend your whole lives learning rules and laws. You love to tell tales of the heroes of the past. But when it comes down to it you're all just hiding from life. You're afraid of what might happen to you if all your rules fell apart.'

'I'm not frightened of death,' Dalan snapped back indignantly.

'It's life that scares you,' the Gaedhal cut in.

And with that he wrapped the rope around his waist and prepared to start his descent to the river.

'There's a ledge just above where this rope runs out. It's wide enough for both of us to stand on. I'll meet you there.'

In the next second he was off, carefully finding a foothold here and there and letting out the line gently as he went.

Dalan watched from above and tried to tell himself Eber was right. He had nothing to fear. Even if he slipped and fell he was unlikely to be killed. Yet all his instincts told him this was foolishness. Eber Finn's rebuke, however, stung his pride, and as the king reached the first ledge Dalan decided to fight off the fear that was overwhelming him.

He wrapped the line about his waist in the same manner the Gaedhal had done and, his eyes fixed firmly on the placement of his feet, lowered himself over the edge of the cliff.

The first thing he noticed when he stepped off the ledge was not fear. It was a confidence he had never known before. This wasn't nearly as frightening as he'd imagined and now that he was committed to this course of action it seemed almost enjoyable.

But then Dalan made a terrible mistake. In his new-found self-assurance he ventured to look down to see how far it was to where the Gaedhal was waiting for him. It was just a glance, no more than a glimpse, but it was enough to turn his stomach. Suddenly his heart was beating in his mouth and his hands were sweating around the rope. His fingers seemed incredibly weak and his knees were shaking as a cold dread began to engulf him.

All his former confidence was swept away on a rising tide of panic. And it was the kind of terror that would have seen him running as fast as he could in the opposite direction if he hadn't been halfway down the cliff.

'Take it easy, Druid,' the king called up to him. 'Don't rush yourself. Keep your eyes on your boots and choose your next foothold carefully. Don't think about how frightened you are. You have a job to do, so concentrate on it.'

'My hands won't support my weight.'

'I don't understand you folk of the Draoi path,' Eber Finn scoffed. 'You can stand up to kings. You can talk with confidence in front of hundreds of your kinfolk. You pronounce the law and judge transgressors as if it were the easiest thing in the world. You can even compose and play the most beautiful music without a second thought.'

The Brehon closed his eyes as he listened to the king's words. Then he pushed his forehead into the back of his hand as he desperately gripped the line.

'Yet give you a simple task and you lose your nerve,' the Gaedhal concluded. 'How do you expect a warrior to respect your words if you haven't the heart to suffer the same risks and the same trials as the rest of us?'

'I'm not a warrior!' Dalan hissed. 'I didn't choose to walk the same path as you. How could you know what I've suffered in order to gain my education and the respect of my peers?'

'Show me your worth, Druid,' Eber countered. 'Keep your mind on the journey and drive away all thoughts of your destination. If you think too much about where you're headed, you'll be distracted and then you'll surely falter.'

Dalan heard these words and knew the king was right. He took three deep breaths to steel his nerve and then looked down at his feet. The next outcrop of rock that appeared as though it could hold him was just a short step away.

He lowered his left foot onto the stone and transferred his weight. He took another breath before he spotted a place for his right foot. His toe found a solid support and he let out a little of the line about his waist.

In this manner he slowly made his way down to where Eber Finn was waiting for him. The king was obviously impatient. When the Brehon was finally standing at his side on the narrow ledge the Gaedhal sighed heavily and snatched the rope from him.

Then, in a practised manoeuvre, Eber flicked the line with one hand and it fell down on top of them. Dalan pressed his back to the wall, his palms flat against the rock. He tried to steady his breathing, to ease the deafening pounding of blood through his body. But before the Druid had settled himself, the Gaedhal had secured the rope again and was back down the cliff face. The Brehon could only wonder at the man's determination. Little by little he felt respect blossoming for this foreigner.

In this way the two of them inched their way down the sheer rock face, relying on the rope when there was no footing to be had. Nevertheless the descent took longer than even Eber had imagined for it was difficult to judge the distance from the top of the cliff.

When at last the Brehon dropped down onto the soft sand at the very base of the rock wall he fell on his face and stayed that way for a long time, clutching at the grains with his fingers. Eber Finn coiled the rope and calmly placed it in his pack in case they should stand in need of it again.

'I'm ashamed of myself,' Dalan finally admitted when he lifted himself up off the ground onto his knees. His face and clothes were covered in sand. 'I was so frightened I thought my heart was going to stop.'

The Gaedhal leaned over, grasped him by the hand and helped him to his feet.

'So was I,' he admitted. 'There's nothing like a challenge to get the heart pumping. And when my blood is up I know I'm really alive.'

The Brehon looked into Eber's eyes and saw he was speaking the truth. Then the two of them fell into each other's arms and laughed.

But their relief was short-lived. As they broke from their

embrace the two men realised they were not alone on the narrow sandy beach at the bend of the underground river. Dalan swallowed hard and the Gaedhal drew his sword. But before they fully understood what was happening the whole area was lit by the flames of a hundred torches.

***

It was Aoife who dragged herself to her feet when the sound of the harp met her ears. Her brother looked up from where he lay but wasn't keen to go off searching in the dark for the mysterious musician.

'We haven't any torches left,' he reasoned. 'We'll just get hopelessly lost.'

But his sister didn't take any notice of him. The melody was compelling and familiar and it called to her like the voice of a dear friend. She took a dozen steps away from the fire while Sárán struggled to rise on his elbow.

'I'm too tired to go off searching the cave,' he told her. 'Let the harper come to us.'

When she offered no answer the young man looked up. His sister was gone.

'Aoife!' he cried, panic lending a tremble to his voice. 'Where are you?'

'There's a light up here,' she answered. 'I think I've found a way out of the cave.'

In a flash Sárán was on his feet, running toward the rocks behind the little beach. But the shadows concealed many hidden pitfalls and he tripped on a sharp jutting stone. He was just getting to his feet again, rubbing his shin where his breeches had been torn open, when Aoife appeared at his side.

'I've found an exit,' she informed him, grabbing his hand and dragging him along between two huge boulders. Within ten steps they'd rounded one of the massive stones. There before them was a hole in the rocks worn smooth by water over thousands of seasons.

The passage beyond was lit by an eerie blue glow and a freezing wind issued forth from it. Sárán recoiled as soon as he set eyes on the entrance to this new corridor. An inexplicable terror shook him and he knew without a doubt that it would be a mistake to enter this part of the cave system.

But Aoife was keen to explore beyond the doorway. She made a few tentative steps toward the passage, though her brother stayed where he was, frozen to the spot. As she turned to check whether he was following her, a shadow appeared behind her, and Sárán's eyes widened.

The sound of the harp met their ears again as Aoife dashed back to stand by her brother. The shadow grew as a hooded figure made its way down the passage toward them. At last the stranger stood silhouetted against the faint bluish light behind him. He was nothing more than a dark outline but he inspired such fear in Sárán that the young man could have fled there and then. And if it hadn't been for his sister's tight grip on his arm, that's exactly what he would have done.

As they watched, the stranger turned around and headed back in the direction he'd come. Aoife was off after him before her brother had a chance to object. Reluctantly he followed her, calling her name to no avail.

The passage was incredibly cold. Ice clung to the rocks, making the floor dangerously slippery. Several times Sárán fell over hard against the wall or slid along as the corridor descended. Aoife, however, had always been more sure-footed than her brother and she was soon far ahead of him. Sárán struggled along as best he could but it wasn't long before he was out of breath, too exhausted to call out.

A wailing wind greeted him as he entered a new chamber and flakes of snow began swirling all about him as he walked. The young man was very concerned now. There was no sign of Aoife anywhere.

Just as he was wondering whether she had been set upon by the hooded stranger, his sister appeared. She ran into him on her way back down the passage, nearly knocking him over in her haste.

'You won't believe what lies beyond that stretch of corridor!' she told him. 'I can scarcely believe it myself.'

Sárán frowned. 'I don't want to know!' he stormed. 'Do you have any idea how dangerous it is to be running around in these caves? We don't know what dwells down here beneath the ground. We're going back to the lake right now.'

'But that passage leads to the outside world. We're free!'

She grabbed his arm to drag him on along the corridor. Before they'd travelled far a bright light filled the cave and the wind built in intensity. There was snow all around and the ice was treacherously thick on the ground.

Moments later they were standing at the cave mouth looking out over a wintry landscape.

'It was midsummer when we entered the Aillwee,' Sárán protested. 'How could it have come to winter so quickly?'

'I have no idea,' his sister replied. She pointed to a spot on the other side of the field which lay in front of them. 'But I recognise that wood over there. It's not far from our old home at Dun Burren.'

'I don't understand,' Sárán breathed. 'There's something terribly wrong. There can't be snow on the ground.'

'I don't understand it myself,' Aoife admitted. 'But I see we're safely out of the caves and that's the most important thing. Over there is the road to Aillwee. If we run we'll make it to shelter before nightfall.'

The next thing he knew Sárán was running as fast as his legs could carry him through the heavy snow toward the woods at the other side of the field. He'd completely forgotten about the stranger they'd seen in the cave. He was overjoyed to be free of the eternal darkness.

They had almost come to the line of oak trees that marked the woods when his instincts called to him again. Out of breath he dropped back behind his sister. He'd taken her word that this was a place not far from the old fortress of Dun Burren, but now that he looked about him he wasn't entirely convinced. Stunned that he could have failed to question Aoife's judgement, he stopped in his tracks to search for familiar landmarks.

Sure enough, the grove of trees directly ahead of them was a familiar sight. It certainly reminded him of the woods near Dun Burren. But the slope of the hill behind the trees wasn't exactly as he remembered it and the fields had been turned under the plough where nothing had ever been planted.

Then he spotted a small building not far to the left of the woods. It was an unusual shape for a dwelling — squarish rather than round. Indeed he'd never seen any building constructed in that shape before.

'Aoife!' he called.

She pulled up and squinted to try and make out what he was pointing at. Then she signalled that they should make toward this strange building. Their paths met when they were less than twenty paces from the door.

The wind whipped up into a gale that tore at their clothes so they had to lean into it to make progress. As they trudged on, the snow deepened and the sunlight faded. By the time they came to the door of the unusual building it was night.

Sárán yelled to his sister to be careful but his words were swept away by the tempest. Her hand went to the door and pushed it open and Aoife was inside in a second. Her brother followed after and slammed the door behind him, leaning on it to keep the snow out.

Aoife went straight to the window to pull the curtain across but she was astounded to find that the opening was covered by a solid sheet of semitransparent glass. It was similar to the beads her mother had often worn but it had no colour at all so that she could see the world outside with surprising clarity. She shook her head as she ran her hand over the smooth surface. It was the most beautiful thing she'd ever seen. But it was icy cold.

It was then she noticed a roaring fire set in a hearth built into one wall of the house. Neither of them had ever seen anything like it. They were used to houses built around a central hearthstone. This was certainly a peculiar house.

But the unfamiliarity of their surroundings didn't stop them from huddling together in front of the dancing flames. Before their fingers were warm they'd helped themselves to spoonfuls of a thick barley broth that was bubbling away in a pot over the fire.

A black cat appeared and rubbed itself against their legs with a welcoming purr. It jumped onto Sárán's lap and began a long discourse in the language of its breed, with many enthusiastic mewls and the occasional nip to keep the young man's attention. He stroked the animal across the back and it arched its body in response.

While her brother was engaged with the cat, Aoife took time to observe the interior of the house. There was a bed of straw raised slightly off the floor with room enough for one. Next to this there was a little table on which were carefully placed several unidentifiable articles.

Her curiosity aroused, Aoife got up to inspect these items more closely. There was a candle made of wax so smooth and fine that it looked as if it had been carved from bone. Beside this was a silver ornament as long as her forearm. She lifted it up to take a closer look. It seemed to be a simple cross with many knotted designs woven over its surface. As she couldn't discern any possible purpose for the item, she placed it back on the table.

Then she noticed a cloak laid out on the bed as a cover. She brushed the palm of her hand over the garment and gasped.

'It's the softest wool I've ever known!'

The words were no sooner out of her mouth than the door swung open and a short man dressed all in dark brown entered the house. He shook the snow off his boots, drew the hood from his head and turned to the fire.

And when he did he nearly jumped out of his skin with fright.

'Who are you?' he demanded tremulously, his voice filled with apprehension. 'You're not robbers, are you? If you are, I've nothing of any value.'

His eyes strayed to where Aoife was leaning over his bed, her hand still resting on the cloak.

'I'll give you warm clothes if you need them, but I beg you to leave that cloak. It was a gift from a dear friend who has long since departed these shores.'

The man was not much shorter than Sárán but he was very thin. His clothes hung off him as they might if they'd been hung over a tree. And his head was shaved in a most peculiar fashion. All the hair had been cleanly shaved from his crown in a circle.

Aoife frowned to understand what the stranger was saying through his thick accent.

'We haven't come to steal from you,' her brother assured him. 'We're seeking shelter from the storm.'

The man scrutinised them both carefully when he heard their speech.

'You're from the north then?' he asked. 'I can tell by the way you frame your words.'

'We were born in Dun Burren,' Aoife informed him.

'Dun Burren? Can't say I've ever heard of that place. Is it near Emain Macha and the seat of the UiNiall?'

Brother and sister looked at each other with puzzled expressions.

The stranger noticed this so he decided to introduce himself. 'My name is Caoimhan.'

'I'm called Aoife and this is my brother Sárán,' the young woman replied, edging away from the bed to stand by the fire.

'You're welcome in my humble home,' Caoimhan told them. 'I trust you've had something to eat?'

The two travellers nodded.

'How came you to this part of the Burren?' he inquired as he took off his cloak and hung it on a peg at the door.

'We were lost in the Aillwee caves,' Sárán replied.

Caoimhan turned around sharply and looked at the young man with such intensity that Sárán took a step toward his sister.

'You can't be serious!' he laughed. 'For a moment there I thought you were telling the truth. No one's been within those caves in living memory.'

Suddenly his face paled as he realised the young man was very serious.

'Your name is quite unique,' the stranger stammered, changing the subject. 'I don't think I've ever heard it before.'

'I am Sárán, son of Brocan, who is King of the Fir-Bolg of the Burren.'

Caoimhan's eyes bulged out of his head and he made a simple gesture with his right hand, touching the top of his forehead, his chest and each shoulder in turn. Then he fell to his knees with his hands clasped tightly before him.

Neither Aoife nor her brother could understand the language that now poured out of his mouth so they waited patiently for this fit to pass. It was considered impolite to ask too many questions of a host.

'This is not our country,' Sárán whispered to his sister. 'We have to go back to the caves. We've crossed over into the Otherworld.'

'The Otherworld!' Caoimhan cried catching the word. 'By Brigit's holy gown I'm surrounded by Faerie folk. First there was the ghost at the woods, then the Raven and now these two.'

He stood up.

'I beg you to leave me in peace. I'm but a humble collector of tales. Whatever your quest I cannot help you. God knows I've spent months trying to aid that poor lost soul who haunts the oak grove, and all to no avail.'

'We'll go,' Sárán assured him. 'We'll return to the caves and bother you no more.'

Aoife grabbed the sleeve of her brother's tunic. 'If we go back into the caves we might never find our way out again,' she hissed under her breath.

'We're going!' her brother insisted as he shook off her hold.

Then he made for the door. Aoife followed him reluctantly but she didn't forget to thank their host for the meal and his fire before she departed. Outside the snow was falling lightly now and so the near-full moon lit the landscape a pale blue.

'I know exactly where we are,' Sárán told her when she stood beside him. And then he set off down toward the woods with his sister trailing behind.

They hadn't gone far when a terrible recognition hit her. 'I won't follow you!' she cried. 'I know where you're taking me.'

'Come along,' he ordered. 'I've a feeling that many things have changed in this countryside, but that wood is known to me.'

Grudgingly she continued on behind him, putting her feet in his prints in the snow so that the going would be easier. Then a stone's throw from the trees, Sárán stopped to squint at the grove.

'That tree was a sapling when we were last here,' he asserted. 'And the younger ones were not even acorns in the kernel.'

Aoife caught up with him and leaned heavily against his shoulder, panting.

Her brother sniffed the air. 'He's still here,' Sárán told her. 'I can feel his presence as clearly as if he were touching my arm.'

'Don't speak so!' she stuttered.

But as she spoke her worst fears materialised before her eyes. In the shadow of the trees there was a movement and then a rustling of branches high in the ancient oaks. A figure clad in white like the mist of midnight took form at the edge of the grove.

'Who comes to my abode?' the figure whispered, and both of them knew the voice immediately.

'Sárán, son of Brocan,' the young man answered. 'And Aoife, the daughter of the same king.'

Like a clap of thunder Aoife heard her name repeated as the wind suddenly blew into a violent gale. Branches were ripped from the treetops, twigs scattered in their faces and snow whipped up into whirlpools of white hate.

'How dare you trespass in my woodland without leave?' the spirit screamed.

And then as abruptly as the tempest rose it dropped.

'Is it really you, Aoife?' he asked.

She nodded.

'Why did you leave me here for so long? I've been waiting and waiting. I'm cold and tired. Where's the horse? Now we must be getting back to your father's fireside at Dun Burren. He'll be worried about us.'

'We were frightened,' she answered with shame in her voice. 'I'm sorry that we deserted you, Fearna.'

The spirit floated toward them over the snow, coming close

328

enough that they could recognise his face without any question.

'It's strange,' he confided. 'The mead has worn off almost entirely. I'm quite sober. It must be the cold that cleared my mind.'

'He doesn't know what's happened,' Sárán whispered to his sister. 'He doesn't realise he's dead.'

Aoife's breath caught in her throat. She was so terrified by the ghostly vision that bobbed before them that she could hardly breathe.

'I know you don't belong here any more than I do,' the spirit replied sharply. 'A thousand summers have passed since you murdered me.'

The wind tore at Aoife's clothes and hair and she was forced to cover her head with her hands.

'Look at me!' Fearna screamed.

The young woman forced herself to look up into the wild blue-violet eyes of the lost soul.

'May you never find peace,' the spirit whispered, his voice venomous and full of vengeance. 'May love elude you till the last. May you know my agony every day until you cease to live.'

'I'm sorry!' she bellowed, crying tears that turned to ice as they rolled down her cheeks. 'I've already paid the price. I've been forced to pay for the terrible wrong I did to you.'

The ghost rushed closer and the wind dropped away again as he hovered before her. 'Your brother has paid for his part in my death. But you led me to this wood. I've been imprisoned here since then. I loved you and you toyed with me. You'll suffer for your crime. I promise you.'

The ghost stared silently at the sobbing woman and then smiled.

'The next man you meet who is not of your bloodline will change your life,' he stated, pronouncing his Geis slowly so

329

as to savour every moment. 'You'll fall in love with him. You'll know what it is to have true feelings for another human being. You'll treasure his every utterance; each private word shared alone will be worth more than a mountain of gold to you.'

Fearna's eyes shone with hatred.

'But the one who truly loves you will wander Innisfail searching for you until the world changes and the bellringers come to this land. The mumbling folk will be your saviours. Until the ones who follow the one god help him, you will be under this Geis. And then I'll have no further quarrel with you.'

When he had finished speaking the ghost drew back toward the trees and vanished into the shadows. The snow began to fall again and Aoife turned to make her way slowly back to the cave.

Sárán followed after her, unmoved by all that had been said. No fear had touched his heart while the spirit issued his Geis. He'd stood ready for his own punishment to be announced and yet none had come.

As Aoife trudged away her brother stopped and turned to face the trees.

'What of me?' he called out. 'Don't I deserve to carry some burden for what I've done?'

Instantly the ghost appeared before his eyes, surprising Sárán so much that he started back.

'I don't know how you crossed the gulf of a thousand summers so easily,' Fearna stated. 'Perhaps there is some lesson for you here. Did you meet anyone?'

'We met a man called Caoimhan,' the young man answered.

The ghostly figure laughed. 'You'll always be known as the Raven. That's what they called you when you were a boy. And that's how you'll be known forever more.'

Sárán was about to ask what sort of punishment that was

when Fearna faded once again before his eyes. He knew instinctively he would not be able to summon him up again so he spun round to follow after his sister.

Aoife found the cave entrance easily. She waited for her brother to catch up and as soon as he arrived she plunged back into the passage. But Sárán understood they had never really left the cave at all. The place they'd visited was just a vision of the future.

This was his first real experience of the dreaming state that older Druids taught their students about. And though he often convinced himself of his worthiness, this was the first time he'd truly felt as though he was suited to his vocation. There were realms within his mind to be explored. The seed of excitement had germinated in his soul. The real adventure was only just beginning for him.

Once inside the cave they soon found their way back to their fire. It was burning brightly, tended by unseen hands while they were gone. Beside the little blaze was stacked a small pile of dry driftwood, gathered perhaps from the shores of the lake.

Neither of them commented on this. It occasioned no more than a questioning glance between them. Aoife and Sárán each had other thoughts to occupy their minds.

Chapter Seventeen

Brocan ran on down the passage until he thought it imprudent to continue. He didn't want to stray too far from the chamber where he'd left Máel Máedóc. The old man was frail and the journey into this dark damp place was obviously more than his body could take. The redcap brew must have strained the Druid's stamina to breaking point.

Brocan stopped in the middle of the passage and held his torch high to light the way ahead. But there was no sign that the corridor might lead him to Eber Finn. In the distance he plainly heard the roaring of water, which he decided must be a massive underground river. Máel Máedóc had mentioned that he intended to bathe in a sacred river before he passed over.

Brocan scratched his head and gave up. It was better to be at the old man's side, he told himself. There was nothing to be gained by rushing around alone in the dark.

He turned sharply on his heel and suddenly glimpsed a flash of brilliant golden light. He shook his head in disbelief and wondered if the seeing brew was affecting his judgement. Just when he had convinced himself his eyes were playing tricks on him he saw another flicker of brilliant light. This was rapidly followed by a shot of red that momentarily illuminated the entire passage as far as he could see.

His first thought was that Máel Máedóc was in danger. He drew his sword and, torch held out before him, retreated back up the corridor to where he'd left the old Druid. At last he caught the faint flicker of firelight which marked the entrance to the chamber where Máel Máedóc would be waiting.

Brocan's pack was still there and the small blaze he'd kindled for the Druid was still alight. But to his horror the old man was nowhere to be seen.

'Máel Máedóc!' he called, and his voice echoed back to him many times before he realised it was probably a mistake to make so much noise. He didn't want to draw the attention of the folk who'd taken his companion. His instincts told him their intentions weren't good.

It was then he noticed many footprints in the mud. Two sets were deeper than the others, which could only mean this pair were bearing a weight, very likely the body of the old Druid.

Brocan tightened his grip on his sword and followed the tracks back up the corridor until he came at length to a low entrance he hadn't noticed as they'd passed by earlier. He bent double and poked his torch through. Then he stuck his head in to see what lay beyond.

It was another passage, though much narrower and lower than any he'd experienced so far. But he pressed on, unwilling to desert the Druid in what might prove to be the last hours of his life.

This passage led into a chamber which was a crossroads where five corridors met. The floor was flat stone so when he tried to find footprints it was in vain. He ran to each opening and listened carefully. But none of the passages was willing to divulge its secrets. In frustration he returned to the centre of the room and held his torch low, waiting in silence. It was only a short while before his patience was rewarded.

From the stone corridor to his left he caught the tiniest reflected glimmer of a far-off red flash. His heart pounded in his chest in relief and he was off as fast as he dared on the uneven ground. This passage was wide and the ceiling high, so he held his torch aloft with his blade thrust forward in case he should suddenly stumble upon the owners of the footprints. An unfamiliar incense caught in his nostrils as he passed under a low arch and soon the cave was filled with thick sweet smoke.

The pounding in his heart was immediately eased by the heady blend of fragrances that washed over him. But his warrior instincts were aroused and he was not about to let his guard down for a moment.

Brocan's progress slowed almost to a halt because the smoke became so thick he couldn't see but a few paces in front of him. He cursed the incense under his breath as he waved his sword about in an attempt to clear the air. At last he had to stop. The smoke had filled his lungs and he was having severe difficulty breathing. He placed the point of his blade on the floor to rest on the weapon and the soft ground gave way a little.

As the king looked down and noticed the mud beneath his boots, a hand fell upon his shoulder from behind. The king nearly jumped out of his skin with fright.

He spun around, attempting to raise his sword to defend himself. But before he could bring the blade to bear he felt hands upon the weapon twisting it in his grip until he had to let go. It was suddenly whipped away out of his reach and he uttered a cry of despair.

Before he knew what was happening, something thumped him just below his rib cage. The blow knocked the wind out of him and he dropped his torch, which seemed to extinguish itself before it even hit the ground.

The cave was plunged into utter darkness and Brocan sank

to his knees in pain, trying to regain his precious breath. The air was not so smoky close to the floor, so he was soon breathing more easily, but there was a thick sweat on his brow that dripped down his cheeks in rivulets.

Blinded by the subterranean night he was at a distinct disadvantage. Whoever had attacked him obviously didn't need much light to navigate by. These strange folk, whoever they were, probably had highly sensitive eyes from generations of dwelling in the dark.

Mustering all his concentration, Brocan sat still to listen. And as he did so his whole body began to shiver. All around him he could hear little whispers, some light-hearted, some deeply malevolent.

'Who's there?' the king gasped.

An abrupt silence fell over the room. Then there was a groan which he thought was very likely the old Druid slipping in and out of consciousness.

'My friend is dying,' Brocan pleaded. 'If you have any compassion at all, please let me comfort him in his last moments.'

He hadn't finished the final syllable of his entreaty when the chamber filled with a blinding red light that stung his eyes. He shaded his face from the brightness as a hundred voices spoke to him at once in a language he'd never heard before.

Brocan curled up on the floor in the mud. Every time he tried to look up a great pain struck at his eyes like spear points prodding at a boar. Even through the cover of his hands the light was painfully bright.

Hands searched his tunic, relieving him of his short black meat-knife and the ceremonial bronze axe he'd tucked into his belt.

'Let me see your faces!' he cried, and instantly the light died away.

Cautiously Brocan raised his head. There was but one

lamp burning in the cave now. It was held by a tall woman with a misshapen head who grinned like a demented child. All around her were gathered the most peculiar faces Brocan could ever have imagined. Some were scarred; others sported boils or hideous sores that oozed pus. Yet others were incredibly beautiful, with long features that seemed unnaturally distorted but nonetheless extremely appealing.

Their dress was all of one colour — a dark green that blended remarkably with their surroundings. The cloth was unevenly dyed so it resembled the rough texture of the rocks in this part of the cave.

None bore any weapons that he could see. That eased his mind a little. But there was a threat implied in the way they leaned forward at him with their drooling lips and wild eyes.

'Who are you?' the king managed to stammer at last.

Every one of the strangers took a frightened step back when he spoke. Then the chamber was full of their unrecognisable speech as they all tried to talk at once. It was the woman with the torch who finally silenced this cacophony with a high-pitched screech. Everyone lowered their heads in deference to her words and several touched the hem of her clothes or kissed her hands in reassurance. Clearly this woman was highly respected, perhaps even feared, by most of these strangers.

The woman moved forward, her gait twisting her body awkwardly. Her left leg was shorter than the other so her mass was thrown off centre as she moved. Four paces from the crouching king she stopped and drew a deep strained breath into her lungs. When this hissing ceased she raised her right hand and with her three flat fingers spread wide tapped her chest lightly. Then she spoke a word in her guttural language.

Brocan frowned as he tried to repeat the two syllables. A distant memory stirred in him as he pronounced the foreign word over and over. And then at last recognition swept over him and he spoke the word in shock.

'Fomor?' he muttered, disbelieving.

The woman turned the corners of her lips up as saliva dripped from her mouth. Then she stood to her full height, placed her deformed hand on her chest again and cried out in triumph.

'Fomor!'

Dalan's hands were so tightly bound behind his back that his fingers had turned numb. He was exhausted after having walked so far along the slippery river bank. He glanced across at Eber Finn, who struggled to smile reassuringly at his companion through a bloodied lip.

Neither dared speak lest their captors dish out another brutal beating. The Gaedhal had taken the brunt of the assault at the foot of the cliff. Eber didn't have the Quicken Brew flowing in his veins so he was looking the worse for his resistance. Dalan had also been given a good thrashing but he'd quickly healed. There was no outward sign he'd been punched senseless to the ground while the king leapt to his aid. After their capture they had trudged for what seemed hours with few rest stops, many beatings and no water to moisten their tongues.

They didn't understand a word that had been said to them by the warriors who'd taken them into custody. And if they'd been disoriented before the fight at the foot of the cliff, they were now totally lost.

At last the party of twelve guards and two prisoners rounded a bend in the river. Immediately they climbed a steep stairway cut into the rocks and then stepped onto a wide flat platform chiselled from the dark grey stone.

Dalan stopped, frozen by shock at the scene laid out before him. He shook his head, believing this was a hallucination brought on by the seeing herbs.

Eber Finn was struck speechless at the spectacle. His feet continued to march on but his mouth was wide open and his eyes round with amazement.

On a cliff face not unlike the one they'd descended a thousand tiny yellow lights shone out in the half-darkness. Each one was a dwelling carved into the rock with a narrow path outside the door. The paths all converged along the bottom of the cliff to form a wide road. And this was the route they were following toward the city that hung over the underground lake.

'By the breath of Danu!' Dalan gasped in awe, and he felt a hand across the back of his head.

'Who are these people?' Eber whispered, but the Brehon nodded sharply to silence him.

A big brute of a man with a massive jaw and a skull that swept back almost to a point at his crown grabbed the king by the shoulder. He grunted a few unintelligible but obviously threatening words and Eber turned away to avoid the foul stench of his rotten teeth. The warrior pushed the Gaedhal on toward the underground citadel. Eber stumbled for a few steps but soon regained his feet, glaring in fury at the guard.

All about them now were hundreds of figures silhouetted against the doors and windows of their homes. The entire city was turning out to get a glimpse of the two prisoners. Before they'd come to the main crossroads which led to the town the guards halted and Eber and Dalan were led down a side road into a small cave. As soon as they were inside, a massive wooden portcullis descended from the ceiling on a rope and pulley.

They were trapped.

The Brehon and his companion were left to stare out through gaps in the gate at their captors who now busied themselves kindling a fire and keeping onlookers at bay. Eber slid down to his knees and sighed in defeat.

'Why are they keeping us here?' Dalan asked under his breath.

Then a man spoke up from the rear of the cave. 'Because the Fomor never allow strangers within their settlements.'

The Brehon spun around and a familiar warrior arrayed in the manner of the Fir-Bolg stepped from the shadows.

'Brocan?'

'It is,' the king confirmed.

'How long have you been here?' Dalan pressed.

'An hour or two. They set upon Máel Máedóc as he was resting and dragged him away.'

'Why weren't you at his side to protect him?' Eber snapped.

'The old Druid sent me off in search of you,' Brocan replied sharply. 'If it hadn't been for that I might have been able to hold them off. But I would have been forced to yield before long — there were simply too many of them.'

'What was that you said about the Fomor?' the Brehon cut in.

'These folk who dwell in this underground town are Fomorians. Perhaps the last remnants of that people on this Earth.'

Dalan put a hand to his chin and shook his head. 'There haven't been any Fomor in these parts since the time of Balor of the Evil Eye,' he scoffed. 'How can you be sure?'

'That's what they call themselves,' Brocan shot back. 'Their queen told me so. And I seem to remember a great tribe of owls who attacked my people in a forest not so many winters ago. They were Fomorians, weren't they?'

'I suppose you could say the owls were, in essence,

Fomorians, but I would class them rather as spirits of the woods summoned up by the Watchers.'

'Well these folk aren't ghosts,' the Fir-Bolg king replied. 'They're real enough. And they're as ugly as any description I've ever heard of the Fomor.'

'Who are the Fomor?' Eber Finn interrupted.

'Ancient enemies of the Danaan and Fir-Bolg peoples,' Dalan explained quickly. 'Their armies were destroyed generations ago and their tribes scattered to the four winds.'

'Except for these folk,' Brocan added.

The Brehon shook his head. 'It's not possible that they could have lived here in this place all this time without anyone suspecting,' he reasoned. 'The Fomor are a bitter folk who would not have willingly deserted the land of Innisfail. They would have made their presence felt, I'm sure. There's more to this than meets the eye. If we stay calm we'll find a way out. I suspect this whole experience has some connection with the Watchers and the seeing brew we each drank.'

'You'd better see to Máel Máedóc,' the Fir-Bolg king said dismissively. 'I believe he is in need of a fellow Druid.'

'What do you mean?' the Brehon frowned.

Brocan turned and pointed to the rear of the cave where the old Druid lay propped against the wall.

Dalan was at the old man's side in an instant. He quickly checked Máel Máedóc's heartbeat, breathing and the colour of his eyes. Then he examined the Druid's tongue.

'I'm dying, brother,' Máel Máedóc struggled to say. 'I must conserve my energy for King Eber.'

'The king is here,' Dalan soothed. 'Would you speak with him?'

Máel Máedóc's eyes widened and some colour returned to his cheeks for just a second. Then he nodded as he grasped the Brehon's hand. 'But I fear I'm too late to sail home with

340

you,' he gasped. 'You must promise me you'll bathe me in the sacred river.'

'I don't know what you mean,' Dalan replied, a frown of confusion across his brow.

'Fetch the King of the Gaedhals,' Brocan cut in. 'I'll make sure the old man has his last wish fulfilled.'

The Brehon shrugged and with a wave of his hand summoned Eber Finn to his side. The Gaedhal knelt down and gently took the hand of his counsellor.

'How are you feeling, Máel Máedóc?' he asked with genuine concern.

'Is that Eber Finn who calls himself King of the Southern Gaedhals?'

'He's holding your hand,' Dalan confirmed.

The old man sat up and stared directly at his king. And Eber was surprised at the rage burning in the grey of those aged eyes. 'Are you in pain?' he whispered.

'I am.'

'What can I do to help you?'

'Listen.'

'Listen?'

'I have a poem for you.'

'Save your strength, my loyal friend,' Eber urged. 'This is no time for a song.'

'This is no ordinary song.'

'Rest quietly.'

'This is my satire on you.'

The King of the Gaedhals sat back and let the Druid's hand drop from his. 'You're weary. You don't know what you're saying.'

'I am tired. But I should have spoken my mind a long time ago. A curse upon my gentle tongue that did not have the will to condemn you. But if you go on to conquer the whole land you will have earned this disgrace a hundred times over.'

'I beg you to lie back and rest.'

'Your father, Míl, would not have let matters come to this. Your mother, Scota of the Flaming Sword, would have scolded you ceaselessly had she been alive. I am the only one who remains. I'm the only one who remembers the days when kings were honourable.'

'Hush now,' Eber insisted. 'You're upsetting yourself unnecessarily. We'll talk when we return to Dun Gur.'

'He's not going back to the fortress,' Brocan cut in. 'Can't you see he's dying?'

Eber shot an angry glance at the Fir-Bolg king which clearly suggested he should not be interfering in this matter.

'Let him have his dignity,' Brocan pressed. 'He is a learned Druid and he has a few words to speak before he passes.'

'Very well,' Eber conceded, making no attempt to conceal his displeasure.

Máel Máedóc stared directly into the king's eyes, ran the tip of his tongue over his lips to moisten them and began his poem.

'I saw a child playing at being a warrior. In the field he trampled down the oat stalks, leaving a terrible trail of their dead and wounded in his wake.'

Eber Finn looked away but the old Druid grasped his hand so tightly the king was compelled to turn back to him.

'For now it's only oats that fall before his weapons. But soon enough, if he has his way, there'll be warriors wallowing in blood upon the battlefield. And to what purpose?'

The King of the Gaedhals opened his mouth to protest but Máel Máedóc gripped his hand with his last reserves of strength and would not give him the opportunity to speak.

'This war-leader comes of solid stock. His brothers are renowned, a poet and a king. He learned his craft well from his kinfolk. So why does he behave like a little boy with a new amusement? By what right does he bring war to the land of peace?'

'I won't listen to this!' Eber fumed.

'Be quiet,' Dalan advised him firmly. 'There is no greater insult you could offer than to interrupt a poet during the recital of his work. If you have any decency you'll shut your mouth and take his criticism in good spirit.'

Thus reprimanded, the king bit his tongue and resolved to sit out this humiliating tirade. It would be ended soon enough and then Máel Máedóc would no longer be able to interfere in the affairs of the kingdom.

'Walk carefully along the road to conflict, my son. With each step remember that every king must surrender his throne one day. When you're gone they will sing about your deeds. Let the songs be joyful ones and your soul will live forever. If your father were here, wise Míl whose memory is sacred, what would he choose to do?'

Dalan nodded encouragingly. The poem was not a fine composition, it lacked subtlety and metre, but the message was clear. The Brehon noticed the colour drain away from the old man's face and he forgave the inadequacies of the poem. Here was a Druid at the end of his life. This was a counsellor who had spent his strength in dedication to his duties. At the last his gifts had failed him but his honour was assured.

Máel Máedóc lay back to close his eyes. 'There has been enough war,' he whispered. 'I place a Geis on you.'

'No!' Eber hissed.

'If your brother should come with the blade of battle lust you will not draw a weapon against him. If your brother should denounce you to your kinfolk you will make a gift of two portions of your land to him. No black pig shall perish within the borders of the country which you rule. No bird will feast within your hall. No woman shall have cause to call you miserly. No rival will ever suffer hunger while he dwells on your land.'

Máel Máedóc smiled.

'You, not I, will devise the Code of the Fianna, so that folk in future will remember you for your wisdom.'

The old Druid let his mouth drop open and for a moment the king thought there would be more. But Máel Máedóc was dead. His heart had stopped beating and his breath was gone.

They all watched as the life drained his frail body. But only Dalan saw something strange rise up from the corpse. It looked like a golden butterfly, exquisitely formed and as bright as the sun, but the Brehon knew it was the Dealan Dé, the departure of Máel Máedóc's spirit.

Eber Finn felt the gnarled fingers relax in his hand but it was a short while before he realised what had happened. When he saw Máel Máedóc had passed over, the king stood up and moved slowly away to the gate.

Dalan covered the face of his brother Druid with a cloak while Brocan went to stand with the Gaedhal. The two kings spent a long time in silence, staring out at the guards, until Eber Finn finally spoke.

'He was a good man.'

'Most of their kind are,' Brocan whispered, not wishing the Brehon to hear his words. 'They have chosen a life in which it is difficult to be otherwise.'

Then he placed a hand on Eber's shoulder in reassurance.

'Kings may be called good in their time but our path is not so clear. We must be ready to risk condemnation to ensure the safety and security of our kinfolk. A Druid may understand this and advise us wisely. But in the end no one blames a catastrophe on poor advice.'

Brocan's eyes now spoke of the change that had come upon him. He was overwhelmed by compassion and a sense that he would never be the same again.

Eber hummed in recognition of the wisdom of these words. And he recognised some transformation had taken place for the other king. Perhaps in much the same way as was happening to him. The Gaedhal now regretted his harsh words to Máel Máedóc.

'Will you help me?' he asked the Fir-Bolg king.

'If it is within my power to aid you, then I shall,' Brocan confirmed. 'But I too would avoid a war as long as possible. Perhaps we should send a delegation to your brother's court before he has the chance to raise his army. The longer we stave off any conflict the better it will be for everyone.'

'I know Éremon's mind,' the Gaedhal sighed. 'He may politely listen to our assurances of peace, but if his heart is set on war no force on Earth will stop him. We must be ready.'

Brocan shrugged. 'For now you need not worry too much. There's nothing you can do while you're imprisoned by the Fomor.'

'Then I'll escape,' Eber Finn told him through gritted teeth. 'I have a duty to my people and I will not be swayed from that for another instant. Are you with me?'

Brocan looked out at the half-dozen guards who loitered around the cave mouth. Then he turned and glanced at the lifeless form of Máel Máedóc lying beside the wall.

'I'll help you in whatever way I can,' the Fir-Bolg king replied. 'But I promised the old Druid I would bathe him in the sacred river. I intend to keep that promise.'

'Are you mad?' Eber sneered. 'He's dead! There's nothing you can do for him now.'

'The body may be cold but I sense that his spirit is not yet at rest. I will do as he asked and then I'll find my way out of the caves.'

Brocan turned to the Gaedhal and leaned close. 'The lake must run off into a river. And the river surely feeds out into the open ground to the south. I'm certain it emerges somewhere on the Burren. If you can but find your way to the lake you may have a chance of escape.'

'The waters are icy. Anyone stupid enough to try swimming the lake would be dead within a very short while.'

'Then find yourself a boat,' Brocan recommended, not bothering to hide his frustration. 'I imagined you to be a resourceful man who could easily adapt to any situation.'

'Where will I find a boat?'

'These folk live by the shores of the lake. Don't you think they'd have some use for water transport?'

'Come with me.'

Brocan shook his head. 'You must take Dalan. I'll remain with Máel Máedóc's body and see he receives the funerary rites to which he's entitled. Perhaps I can create some confusion and give you a chance to slip away.'

As he spoke a thronging crowd of Fomor appeared on the path which led to the cave. All were carrying torches and most were chanting a rhythmic song full of malice.

As the Brehon came to the gate to see what the commotion was all about a tall figure dressed in a long thick black fur stepped out from the crowd. The garment draped over his shoulders and dragged behind him. On his head he wore a massive skull which concealed his face completely.

The bear-man raised his torch in the air and gave an order in his own language. The gathered Fomor were instantly silent. Then the stranger strode to the gate and stood just three paces away from the captives. If it hadn't been for the heavy portcullis he could have reached out and grabbed any one of them.

'Why you come here?' the figure demanded in a thick accent.

'You speak our language!' Dalan exclaimed.

The skull mask turned as the bear-man scrutinised the

Brehon. 'I am Druid,' the stranger declared. 'I have much knowing.'

'I am also a Druid,' Dalan replied, seeing a hope of reasoning with these people through their holy man.

'You Fir-Bolg,' the bear-man spat, pronouncing the name of Dalan's folk with obvious disgust. 'Why you come to the home of the Fomor?'

'Fomor?' the Brehon repeated, scarcely believing his ears. 'I was taught that all the Fomorian people were scattered after the death of Balor.'

'Your teacher not very wise,' the Fomorian Druid smiled. 'Why you come here?'

'It's difficult to explain,' Dalan began.

'I listen carefully.'

The Brehon glanced at Eber and Brocan as he tried to summon the right words. 'The Fir-Bolg have a fortress at the mouth of this cave,' he ventured.

The bear-man shrugged. 'They should stay there. This Fomor ground.'

'These two kings came into the caves to complete a test.'

The skull turned briefly to regard Brocan and Eber. 'Very foolish.'

'My brother Druid and myself accompanied them to offer advice along the way.'

'Not wise.'

Dalan shut his eyes for a moment as he tried to gather his thoughts. He couldn't help agreeing with the stranger. It was, in his opinion, an extremely stupid risk they'd taken in penetrating the caves so deeply.

'We must find our way home,' the Brehon sighed.

The bear-man immediately turned to his people and spoke at length to them in their exotic tongue. There were raised voices from the crowd and angry outbursts until finally the Fomorian Druid turned to the captives again.

'You may not leave.'

'What are you going to do with us?' Eber bellowed.

'You stay here. You find road to Fomor place. You must not go tell Fir-Bolg or Danaan.'

'We were lost,' Dalan explained. 'None of us would ever be able to find our way back here again.'

The bear-man made no reply. Clearly he was unmoved by this plea.

'We'll swear an oath of secrecy,' the Brehon offered.

The Fomorian turned around again to face his own folk. He spoke to them briefly and there was cautious assent from the gathering. Dalan's suggestion did not seem to have been met with much opposition.

'Fir-Bolg evil folk,' he told the Brehon when he had concluded his explanation to the gathered Fomor. 'Not welcome here. You go down river far away. Not come back. Not speak kinfolk this place.'

'I promise,' Dalan assured him. 'If you help us, no word of your settlement will ever pass our lips.'

The bear-man raised his torch in the air as he spoke a few Fomorian words. The portcullis lifted with a groaning of ropes and pulleys. And suddenly they appeared to be free.

But the crowd edged closer, snarling and spitting at the prisoners. Some waved their torches; others wielded clubs of heavy timber. At another word from the bear-man the crowd parted to allow them to leave, but the Fomor were still threatening their captives.

'May we depart?' Dalan called out to the Fomorian Druid.

'You go,' he nodded. 'We chase you out. River that way. Run fast or we kill you.'

The three men looked at each other in alarm. Brocan glanced back at the body of Máel Máedóc.

'I'm staying,' the Fir-Bolg king announced.

'You must come with us!' Eber urged.

'I'm in no danger,' Brocan replied calmly. 'The Quicken Brew will preserve me. Indeed it is you, Eber Finn, who should be worried. You're a mortal. Death comes very easily to your kind.'

The Gaedhal's face turned white. 'They'll kill me!' he hissed.

'Count to one hundred before you follow after me,' Brocan smiled.

In a flash the King of the Fir-Bolg was off down the path, running the gauntlet of countless Fomorian fists and clubs.

Dalan held the Gaedhal by the sleeve to restrain him. 'Do as he says,' he advised. 'He's drawing them off so we can get away.'

Together they watched the crowd disperse to chase Brocan. Soon there were only a few children and old folk milling around them.

The bear-man walked up to Dalan and stood close enough that the Brehon could hear the man breathing.

'You a little wise,' he nodded, and then he stood aside to observe what happened next.

Chapter Eighteen

Dalan counted to a hundred as Brocan had commanded. Then he dragged Eber down the path toward the river as fast as they could run. All the strongest Fomor had chased after the Fir-Bolg king so the going was easy.

A few well-aimed blows fell across their backs as they started out but it was nothing compared to what Brocan must have been suffering. Not far along the track they lost all their pursuers, save for a few young children who continued to throw stones all along the way.

The Brehon tried to place himself between any blows aimed at the Gaedhal. He knew that no matter how vicious the assault the Quicken Brew would heal him.

At length they came to a crossroads. Further down the path which curled to the right they saw a great crowd of folk. Dalan realised these Fomor must have been chasing the Fir-Bolg king. So he led Eber Finn along the path which forked to the left.

In a very short while they had come to the water's edge and, blessing their good fortune, they found a leather curragh upturned on the shore. There were two poles lying alongside the little vessel which would serve for oars. The two men quickly had the craft in the water and were well out on the lake before the Fomorian mob noticed them. By now they were out of reach but they still pushed their poles vigorously through the icy blackness to ensure there was no chance of being recaptured.

It was a long time after, when the lights of the settlement were distant and faint, that Eber finally sat back in the boat with his oar beside him.

'That's enough!' he sighed. 'Now we must rest.'

Dalan looked over his shoulder at the shimmering yellow lights. Then he gave in to exhaustion and sat down facing the Gaedhal.

'What will become of Brocan?' Eber said after they'd both lain there in silence for a long time.

At that moment he saw a light on the shore not far off but he didn't have the will to stand up and begin paddling again. The boat drifted silently on and he reasoned that the folk on shore probably wouldn't notice their passing if they made as little noise as possible. But the shifting current of the river that fed through the lake was unpredictable and it was not long before the curragh ran into a submerged rock. The vessel lay caught, barely fifty paces from the shore.

Dalan peeped over the rim of the boat but couldn't see anybody near the fire, which struck him as very strange. But there was no time to question their luck. He whispered instructions to Eber and the two of them slipped over the side of their vessel to free it from the rock.

As soon as they did this, the light curragh was whipped up out of their hands by the current. The boat was swept toward the shore, leaving the pair of them splashing about in the freezing lake. In moments the chill waters began to sap their strength, but the pair managed to make it to the sandy bank. Dalan helped the king out of the water and over to the fire.

There they sat trying to warm themselves. It was the Brehon who recovered first, the Quicken Brew working its magic. He went to the shore and dragged the curragh up to where the current wouldn't be able to reach it.

Then he made his way back to where Eber lay.

'We mustn't tarry here long,' he told the Gaedhal. 'The Fomor will be upon us if we don't get a move on.'

'I'm so cold,' the king stuttered.

'Whoever lit this fire can't be far away,' Dalan insisted as he dragged the king by the sleeve.

But Eber wouldn't budge. 'Let me warm myself!'

In the end the Brehon relented. He let the Gaedhal curl up close to the little blaze for a while but kept a watch on the rocks nearby, ready to run if the Fomor appeared.

The fire died down to almost nothing in a very short while and there was no other light. So Dalan persuaded the king to get back into the boat. Just as Eber stood up there was a noise behind them which made both men jolt in surprise.

In nervous haste the Brehon grabbed Eber by the back of the tunic and forced him to the shore. But along the way the Gaedhal fell hard and the wind was knocked out of him. He lay on the sand trying to catch his breath while Dalan prepared to meet the enemy with his fists.

Two figures loomed out of the darkness carrying a meagre little light between them. The Brehon couldn't make out their features but he feared the worst. In an attempt to frighten them he stood up to his full height and raised his arms in the air.

'Halt!' he cried, realising too late that the Fomor wouldn't understand him. 'Come no closer or you'll meet with your deaths.'

His words seemed to have the desired effect. The two strangers stopped in their tracks and seemed to be whispering excitedly to each other. Then all of a sudden they strode confidently forward.

'I told you to stay where you are!' Dalan bellowed, summoning his most commanding voice.

But the strangers ignored him and in a few seconds were within a stone's throw of him.

The Brehon looked around for some weapon to defend himself. He grabbed one of the poles they'd used to paddle the curragh. With this makeshift weapon levelled in front of him Dalan prepared for the worst.

'Get up, Eber!' he hissed. 'You're supposed to be the warrior, not me. I can't hold off two of them.'

'It's no good, they've caught us,' the Gaedhal replied in resignation. 'I can do nothing.'

But even as he spoke the king's eyes widened with curiosity. The two figures walked upright with no sign of any serious deformity, unlike the Fomorians they'd already encountered.

Just then Dalan dropped his pole in shock.

'Aoife?' the Brehon gasped. 'Sárán? What are you two doing here?'

'Thank the Goddess Danu you've come!' the young man shouted. 'We were sure we'd never find our way out of this maze.'

Eber Finn forgot his pain, astounded at their sudden appearance. 'Where did you come from?' he asked incredulously.

'We were hiding behind the rocks,' Aoife admitted. 'We saw the boat but thought it best to conceal ourselves until we could be certain you were not hostile. In the end we thought it best to take a risk and ask your help.'

'You've saved us from walking around lost in these caves for the rest of eternity,' Sárán cried as he threw his arms about the Brehon.

'We've barely escaped the same fate ourselves,' Dalan told him, gently disengaging himself from the young man's embrace. 'And we've no guarantee that we're travelling in the right direction. But there's room for you both in the curragh, though I can't say you deserve it after such defiance.'

'I'm sorry,' Aoife offered. 'I know we shouldn't have

entered the caves but I had to prove myself.'

'I won't speak of this with you now,' the Brehon replied sharply. 'I'm angry and deeply disappointed in you. Your behaviour is unfitting of an aspiring Druid.'

'I'm not an aspiring Druid!' she snapped. 'Can't you get it through your thick tangled locks of hair that I don't belong in your world. I was meant for the warrior path.'

'That's enough!' Dalan bellowed, losing his temper. He instantly regretted his harsh tone but he was appalled at his student's attitude.

'We'll have plenty of time to discuss this if we ever find a way out of the caves,' he added in a somewhat gentler voice. 'For now we'd better be moving along. There are creatures dwelling on this shore who bear us great malice and I wouldn't like to be captured by them again.'

Sárán wanted to ask what kind of creatures could possibly live so deep underground. Then he remembered the skull his sister had in her pack and his curiosity took second place to fright. He ran to the boat to steady it, eager to be out on the water where the subterranean monsters would not be able to reach them.

With that the four of them boarded the leather vessel and pushed off into the current. Soon they were being swept along ever faster, and in the distance they could hear an ominous roar that grew with each breath and thundered across the vast cavern.

Brocan led the Fomor a merry chase down the narrow paths that led to the lake and then back again in a huge arc. By the time he returned to the cave where they'd been held prisoner he was tired but not yet exhausted. And he was gratified to find only the Fomorian Druid waiting for him.

His bruises and cuts were already healing. And he was glad he'd found the courage to press on through the melee.

The bear-man bowed to the king when he arrived and Brocan returned the gesture.

'I would like to carry the body of the Druid, Máel Máedóc, down to the lake,' the king told the Fomorian. 'He is a man of honour who deserves to have his last wishes fulfilled.'

'You may do so,' the bear-man answered in a clear tone without any of his former accent.

'Are you the same man who spoke with us earlier?' Brocan asked in surprise.

'I am.'

'You don't have a Fomorian accent.'

'I'm not of the Fomor,' the bear-man shrugged. 'Though I have a knowledge of their tongue. I am a Fir-Bolg like yourself.'

'How came you to live among them?'

The stranger laughed. 'I don't live among them. I haven't even spoken with any of the Fomor for longer than I can remember.'

Brocan frowned in confusion. 'I don't understand.'

'The Fomor were scattered to the four winds long ago. Certainly there are none now living in Innisfail.'

'But ...' the king began.

'You saw a vast host of them,' the bear-man stated with a nod. At that he slipped off the skull that covered his face to reveal a bald head and a pair of bright green eyes.

'Who are you?' Brocan gasped, feeling as though he should recognise this fellow.

'I have had many names. But you may call me Lochie.'

'Lochie the Bard?'

'You remember me!'

'Dalan told me you were one of the Watchers.'

'I have that honour,' Lochie nodded.

Brocan felt a cold shiver grip his body. He half turned to scout out a path to escape.

'You won't get far,' the Watcher warned him. 'And in any case I have a feeling you'll be happier here.'

'What are you taking about? Why would I want to live among the Fomor? They are the enemies of my people.'

'Didn't you hear me?' Lochie laughed. 'There are no Fomorians. I created them. They were an illusion helped along by the seeing herbs I administered to you before you started out on this foolish journey.'

Brocan shook his head, struggling to understand what was being revealed to him.

'I've been posing as Fineen,' the Watcher admitted. 'I was very convincing, wasn't I?'

The king numbly nodded his agreement. 'Why did you do such a thing?'

'It suited my purposes,' Lochie explained. His voice was soothing, like that of a doting parent indulging a child. 'Don't worry about Fineen. He's safe. No harm will come to him.'

'Dalan told me you are an enemy of my folk,' Brocan ventured. 'He told me you would do everything in your power to bring havoc and misery to the Fir-Bolg.'

'Dalan is a fine storyteller with an impressive imagination,' the Watcher noted with a gleam of mischief in his eye. 'But he hasn't quite got a grasp of what I'm up to yet. Let me assure you, I have no intention of bringing misery to your people. They are quite capable of doing that without my help. I'm merely pushing events along to their conclusion.'

'To what end?'

'I'm attempting to inspire Dalan to help me on a certain matter. And I want him to act quickly.'

'Why don't you simply ask him?'

'This way is much more interesting,' Lochie shrugged. 'And in any case I have made approaches to the learned Brehon. His progress is a little too slow for my liking.'

'I don't understand why you would have wanted us to venture down into the caves,' Brocan said. 'Why did you go to all this trouble?'

'To teach Dalan a lesson. And to offer you freedom from your affliction.'

'Affliction?'

'The Quicken Brew. I happen to know how you feel about the whole business. You told me. Remember?'

'I talked with Fineen about it,' the king recalled. 'So that was you?'

'Indeed. I understand how you feel because I'm under the same sentence. However, I and my companion do have hope of escaping our bonds. With Dalan's assistance I believe we might be free before the end of winter.'

Lochie came and put a hand on Brocan's shoulder, but the king recoiled from his touch.

'You, on the other hand,' the Watcher went on, 'have no hope of freedom. You will never know death. I cannot help but feel sympathetic toward you.'

'How do you know the Quicken Brew is so powerful? Not even the Danaan Druids can predict whether its effects will last indefinitely.'

'The truth is,' Lochie admitted, 'I inspired the Druids to concoct the brew. I know what effect it will have because when I was of the Fir-Bolg, before I served Balor, I was among those who were instructed in the secret of its properties. That was long ago when I was a Druid myself.'

Brocan swallowed hard. 'Why did you do such a thing? Why bring so much misery into the world?'

'I often ask myself the same question,' the Watcher answered. 'I suppose it is because I was offered this task and took it

357

on willingly. I could have refused but I chose to accept. It is in my nature to bring heartache to the folk I swore to hate. Just as you must act in the manner of a king, so I must be true to my vocation.'

Lochie threw up his hands in a gesture of helplessness. 'Of course I had no idea I'd be doing this for more than a hundred generations,' he sighed.

Then his eyes brightened again. 'The Quicken Brew was one of my finest tricks. On the surface it would appear to be a wonderful gift which fulfils the wish of every mortal. But of course, as you and I know, the price of immortality is a high one.'

'My soul will never find rest,' Brocan stated bitterly. 'Without any chance of death, my spirit will be trapped in this body for all eternity.'

'That may be true,' Lochie agreed. 'But there is an alternative to death. And I am willing to offer it to you.'

'Why should I trust you?'

'You have no reason to,' the Watcher laughed. 'But let's say I have a compassionate streak in me even after all I've been through. Indeed, as it becomes clear that I may soon find the release of death, I've softened my attitude a little to your people.'

Lochie turned to face the Fomorian settlement where hundreds of tiny lights were still sparkling in the windows of the houses.

'Let me show you something,' he said, waving a hand across the scene.

The view changed before Brocan's disbelieving eyes. Suddenly, all the lights went out, the pathways disappeared and there was only the black icy lake with its blue reflections shimmering across the roof of the cavern.

As Lochie turned to face the king again a familiar form appeared at his side. The figure stretched and yawned as if waking from a deep restful sleep. Brocan recognised the man immediately but he was not convinced of his identity.

'Fineen?' he whispered. 'Is that you?'

'Brocan? Where are we?'

'You are in the depths of the Aillwee caves,' Lochie informed him. 'Don't you remember?'

The healer shook his head to clear it. 'Have I been asleep?'

'You have.'

'For how long?'

'A week, no more.'

'Why have you brought Brocan to this place?'

The Watcher looked into the eyes of the Fir-Bolg king. 'Brocan is seeking sleep. He wants to be free of the Quicken curse.'

Fineen thought carefully about Lochie's words before he asked another question. 'Are you going to imprison him also?'

'I have a feeling the king will come here of his own free will. And I will return you to Aillwee if you wish, though I regret that I cannot allow any recollection of this adventure to remain with you.'

'I'm not sure I wish to return,' Fineen cut in quickly. 'I had the most wonderful dreams. And I've never rested so well. I don't want to go on living forever, watching the world change, witnessing the suffering of others and unable to make any real difference to their lives.'

The Watcher was beaming with joy. 'Now perhaps you understand a little of what I've been subjected to all this time. I was a good man once, before I took on the duties of my vocation. I assure you that in time you will learn to free your soul from your dreams for a while and live other lives. You may never know death but the sleep I offer you will be sweet.'

'I will sleep, Lochie,' the healer decided without any further thought on the matter. 'I was frightened of you before I knew any better. Now I'm grateful for your compassionate gift.'

'How can you trust him?' Brocan snarled. 'He brought the Quicken Brew upon us. He drew the Gaedhals to our island. He has probably been behind every petty conflict that's beset Danaan and Fir-Bolg since the days of Balor.'

'It's true,' Lochie agreed pleasantly. 'You shouldn't make any rushed decisions. You can't possibly be sure you can trust me. How do you know I'm not leading you into a trap from which there is no escape?'

'I certainly thought that at first,' Fineen conceded. 'After you lured me down into the caves and left me, it was a while before sleep came upon me, and so I had time to think carefully about my future. I have no desire to live forever. And since that is likely to be my lot, I would rather sleep and dream, far from the harsh world of war and want.'

Brocan strode up to the healer and threw his arms around him. He was solid. He smelled of dried herbs and physician's powders. And something in his eyes hinted that this truly was Fineen the Danaan.

The king turned to Lochie. 'How can I be certain that all you say is true?'

'What is the alternative?' the Watcher shrugged. 'Would you be happy with everlasting life? Could you learn to quiet your restless soul? How would you keep boredom at bay?'

Brocan dropped his chin to his chest and considered these questions. Eventually he looked up and asked, 'Can I be certain my people will be well governed in my absence?'

Lochie laughed raucously. 'You've already left the kingship in the hands of your son Lom. Nothing is certain in life.'

'You tricked me.'

'I admit it. But is there anyone else who could do the job better? Will Lom be such a disastrous leader? Don't you think he'll learn as he goes along? Isn't that what you did? Come now, if you really want to let go of life you must cut all your ties. Abandon all attachments to the world and your former ways. Then you'll be free to move on to new challenges.'

'That's what death is,' Fineen agreed. 'All of those things.'

'And more,' Brocan pointed out.

'But for the time being my offer is all you can expect.'

The King of the Fir-Bolg looked once more into the healer's eyes. Then he turned and glanced at Máel Máedóc's corpse covered in his cloak at the back of the cave.

'Help me give this mortal the rites of passage,' the king asked. 'When that is done I'll try this sleep of which you speak.'

'You have promised to renounce your kingship over the Fir-Bolg?' Lochie pressed. 'And pass the title to your son?'

'And so I will.'

'Then I have a little surprise for you once we've dealt with the Gaedhal's burial,' the Watcher smiled. 'I'm sure you'll be very happy with it.'

At that Brocan went to where Máel Máedóc's body lay, lifted the corpse in his arms and carried it down toward the lake. Lochie followed in silence with Fineen until they reached the water's edge.

Then, with great solemnity, they set about farewelling the spirit of Máel Máedóc, one-time counsellor to the King of the Southern Gaedhals.

Chapter Nineteen

Dalan began to feel very concerned for their safety almost as soon as they entered the narrow channel which poured out of the lake. As they paddled on they passed many half-submerged boulders, some bigger than the king's hall and all surrounded by vicious eddies that could spin the boat as easily as a leaf. Thanks to Eber standing in the stern with one oar to steer, they managed to avoid the worst obstacles. But the going wasn't easy.

The curragh was sturdy but it wasn't strong enough to carry four adults under these conditions. Eber Finn often had to stop paddling so they could scoop out water with their hands just to prevent the vessel from sinking.

The thundering rumble of a rushing rapid was building in intensity, though they had no inkling how far ahead it might be. Dalan told them to be ready for a rough ride and to cling to each other if the boat tipped over.

Aoife was shivering with the cold. Sárán was shaking with apprehension. Eber Finn was proud and resolute. He showed no emotion whatsoever, no fear, no feeling. It was only when his gaze strayed to the young woman who sat opposite him that any glimmer was reflected in his eyes at all.

Once or twice she caught him glancing at her and at last they exchanged a smile. After that Aoife stole many glances at the strong confident warrior who stood at the stern guiding the little craft on its way. Here, she told herself, was a man who embodied all the values she held dear in life. He was no untried boy like Mahon. He had sailed with his clanfolk across the seas from their homeland and carved out a kingdom for himself in this land. Even though she'd once thought of him as the enemy and held his people in contempt, she couldn't help but admire his calm resolve in the face of danger.

If Sárán was right and their father was planning to marry her to Eber, it would free her from the Druid path once and for all. Besides, she thought with a glint in her eye, marriage to such a man might satisfy more than just her ambitions. She would speak with her father at the first opportunity.

Until that moment she hadn't missed Brocan but now she suddenly wondered where he could be. 'What became of my father?' she asked.

Dalan was about to answer her when Eber cut him off.

'I owe my life to your father,' he declared. 'If it hadn't been for his sacrifice I would most certainly have been killed. I am in debt to him and to his kinfolk.'

'It is by no means certain that Brocan is lost!' the Brehon protested.

'What chance does he have?' the Gaedhal reasoned. 'Even if he manages to escape danger he will likely be hopelessly lost among the twisting passages of the deeper caves.'

Then he turned to Aoife and as his eyes met hers she felt her cheeks blushing.

'Do not fear. You will never want for anything while I am alive. You are the daughter of Brocan and I will do whatever I can to make your life comfortable. I can't replace your father but I'll be your protector.'

Aoife bridled at this last comment. She didn't need a protector. But her pride cooled almost immediately and she felt flattered, even a little excited at the prospect of this fine young warrior taking care of her.

'Thank you,' she answered. 'You're an honourable man.'

At that instant the boat was spun around violently and they were all soaked in a spray of freezing water. Aoife lost her grip on the side of the craft and was flung face first onto the soft leather floor.

Before she knew what was happening she felt a strong hand grab her arm and pull her back to her seat. She spat out a mouthful of water and looked into Eber's eyes again. He smiled and sat her down beside him. Then, seemingly unflustered, he picked up his oar and steadied the curragh as best he could.

He didn't say anything for a long while after that but her attention never left him for a moment. Aoife could still feel a burning sensation on her arm where he'd touched her. She'd never experienced anything like it before.

When Eber did speak again it was a sombre warning.

'There is white foam on the river ahead,' he declared.

The noise of tumbling water grew louder and louder. Dalan gripped his seat in terror. He'd never mastered the art of swimming. Though he could keep his head dry in a calm lake, he'd always avoided the sea for fear of being overpowered. Now he was about to be tested in white water.

At length they could all feel a fine spray on their faces and this made Dalan's heart beat faster than ever. It was a sure sign that the rapids ahead would be particularly rough, but as he didn't want to frighten the others he kept this fact to himself.

It was Eber who broke the tension among them by holding out his oar so that everyone could grasp it.

'Hold onto this tightly as the boat starts down the rapids,' he advised. 'If you keep a firm grip we won't be separated.'

The others did exactly as he told them, and just as their

fingers touched the pole the boat jolted from its first encounter with the raging torrent. Suddenly the vessel spun around in a circle, and when it stopped Dalan could see sunlight streaming into the caves from somewhere in the distance.

'We'll soon be out of this mess!' he cried, taking his hand off the oar to point.

Just as he did so the curragh was shaken again, this time across its bow. The Brehon made an attempt to grasp the oar once more but his hand missed and he was thrown backwards out of the boat with such fury that he had no chance to resist.

Suddenly his head was dragged under. His nose, eyes and ears filled with water, dulling all sound and blotting out all light. In desperation he reached out for the curragh, but his hands only found sharp rocks.

It was then he knew he was in real trouble. Instinctively he curled himself into a tiny ball, tucking his head against his chest and covering the back of his neck as he tumbled onward, battered by the fierce torrent.

He caught the cries of his companions now and then but their voices seemed to grow fainter each time his head surfaced. He managed to take one last breath before his body was dragged down into a deep hollow. Above him he could see foaming bubbles where the rapids poured into this depression and he realised he must have been thrown over a waterfall. His lungs were bursting and for the first time since he'd taken the Quicken Brew he despaired of losing his life.

The leather strap that held his matted locks in place was gone, torn off by the fury of the river, so his hair was thrashing all about him. The Brehon was terrified. He'd never felt so helpless, so completely engulfed by the forces of nature. He briefly considered giving in. It would be so easy to surrender to the will of this unstoppable force. But some inner strength took hold of him and he struggled to the surface.

It was Aoife who saw his head pop up out of the depths but by then the curragh was downstream and out of reach.

'We're not far from the mouth of the cave!' she cried. 'We'll wait outside for you.'

Then the little boat disappeared behind a rise of water. Dalan was swept along until at last he did give up the fight. Instead of curling up to protect his head, he lay out flat on his back and tried to float with the current.

This proved to be the worst thing he could have done. Before he travelled the length of a curragh his neck was jolted and he felt a pain along his spine such as he'd never known before. He didn't have a chance to give voice to his agony before the world was veiled in blackness and he knew no more.

Aoife clung to the oar with all her might, refusing to surrender to the power of the river. But despite her best efforts the raging water tore at her hands until she couldn't hold on any longer and she was thrown overboard.

As she struggled to the surface for air she caught glimpses of the sunlight pouring in through the cave opening where the river spilled out of the darkness. But she had no idea how far it was or whether the going would be any easier once they were out in the open air again.

As her head was forced under the water once more her hands were dragged along a rock and torn to shreds by the sharp edge of stone. Aoife would have screamed in agony but to do so would have filled her mouth and made it impossible to breathe.

So she let go of her hold on the oar and on the pack which contained her bear skull trophy. In seconds she'd rolled out of the curragh.

Then the river took her, smashing her head against its hidden teeth until at last she gave up the fight and let the water have its way with her. Before she lost consciousness a poem came to her mind. Dalan had taught it to her. It was an invocation of Danu.

Goddess of the Flowing Waters, hear my words. Lift me up on the tide of your being. Carry me safely to your harbour. Queen of the Tempest, quench my thirst. On the journey of life you are my guide. On the voyage to far horizons you will be my oar and my rudder. May your star light my way. May your moon moisten my eye. And when I come to the other shore, hold me to your breast before I sail on.

That prayer was still echoing in her mind when her heart lost hope and she let go her senses. The river carried her swiftly through the worst it had to offer, as if it had some personal malice toward her. And when it was done, the torrent threw her up onto a sunlit beach formed by the first bend it travelled under the sky. There she lay for a long while on her back, barely breathing, until at length she was found.

The sand was stained red all around her from the injuries she'd taken. Her clothes were ripped and bloody, her hair all tangled with weeds, bracken and dirt. For all the world she might have been a newborn child with the river's afterbirth still clinging to her skin.

When Eber first set eyes upon her silent form his soul cried out for the loss of one so proud and so beautiful. He stood over her for a long while, silently mourning the loss of this jewel he'd never held. And he dreamed of what his life might have been like if the river hadn't snatched her away just at the very instant he'd discovered her.

They would have made a formidable alliance, he told himself. She of the flaming red locks, a young wild warrior woman, and he the High-King of all Eirinn. With this one as his queen he would have had real inspiration.

But she was beyond his reach now, a corpse without a glimmer of the fire that had burned in her spirit. Eber bowed his head, struggling to understand his cruel destiny.

Isleen had once held this place in his affections, but he saw now that she was old and cynical and had gradually poisoned him until he could no longer see the good in anyone. Aoife had granted him a glimpse of another possibility. A life full of joyous passion; each day an adventure, every breath a taste of ecstatic laughter. What bitter fate it was that he'd seen his future in her eyes just before her body was shattered and her life wrenched away.

Suddenly he was overcome with emotion. All his selfish plans had come to nothing. He'd watched his mother perish on the battlefield of Sliabh Mis. He'd earned the contemptuous satire of a wise Druid. And soon he would have to fight a terrible war with his own brother.

Aoife's cold body, lying face up in the sand, seemed to symbolise the futility of all his hopes. He'd lost the heart to wage war since entering the caves. He'd glimpsed a peaceful prosperous future for his kinfolk once the Danaans had been defeated but the fighting wasn't ended. Indeed he despaired as to whether he'd ever know peace in his lifetime.

The King of the Southern Gaedhals was still standing over Aoife's body when Sárán found him. The young man saw Eber's bowed head and the slump of his shoulders but he was unprepared for the sight that greeted him when he touched the warrior on the shoulder.

The Gaedhal looked up and his face was awash with tears. He'd been crying like a little child. His eyes were red, his nose was a stream of shiny mucus, and he drew his breath in great sobbing gasps.

'I've been a bloody fool,' he wept. 'I've only ever thought

of what I could gain from life. I've never considered what I could give to my people.'

The king wiped his nostrils with the back of his sleeve. The change that had come over him was strengthening its hold.

'Máel Máedóc was right. I've never thought of anyone but myself. I've been preparing for war in the same way another king might prepare for a feast. Now I understand what the old Druid was trying to say to me. I can perceive it in the unseeing eyes of this young woman who was just another playing piece on my gaming board.'

The young Druid was so moved by this display that he put his arms around the king and hugged him tightly until he'd squeezed the sadness out Eber. When the Gaedhal was breathing softly once again, the young man released his hold.

'It's my fault Máel Máedóc is dead,' Eber said quietly. 'I caused the death of Fergus and the loss of Brocan. My own mother fell in battle because of my ambition. How many other lives have been destroyed through my stupidity?'

'Anyone may have faults and most of us do,' Sárán soothed, and for the first time he considered himself worthy of the title Druid. 'But it's true that a king must learn to curb his lest he bring his people to ruin. Everything you've done was likely through foolishness, not stupidity.'

Sárán lowered his face so the king wouldn't see his own pain.

'You may not believe it but I know how you feel,' he admitted. 'You're not an idiot. You're taking the first steps in learning from your mistakes.'

Eber wiped a hand across his eyes.

'You'll be a fine king one day,' Sárán went on. 'I can see you have a good heart. It's just that you've been misguided. That's why kings must have wise and reliable counsellors. Without someone well versed in tradition and law there would be constant chaos in the land.'

369

With a nod the king acknowledged the words.

'It's not too late to change your life for the better.'

'She's dead,' Eber sobbed. 'Aoife died because of me.'

'Whatever happens to my sister is of her own making,' Sárán rebuked him. 'She's headstrong and wilful, and she's not exactly sinless either. And as for your assumption that she's dead, I suggest you take a closer look at her body.'

Eber glanced into the young man's eyes and then stared down at where Aoife lay. To his utter astonishment her chest was heaving gently and the cuts upon her hands were already beginning to fester.

'The Quicken Brew is very powerful,' Sárán explained. 'My sister is not dead, though she may have appeared so. She was injured very badly. We'll start a fire to dry our clothes and by the time that's done she should be wide awake and hungry.'

Eber Finn knelt down at Aoife's side and took her bruised hand in his. And there he sat murmuring a private prayer until the young woman opened her eyes. Then he smiled broadly and kissed her gently on the forehead.

'I dreamt I was waiting by the spring at the Well of Forgetfulness,' she told him. 'But no one would pass me the cup. The guardians turned me away. Then I tried to follow the light into the heavens but my wings would not do their work and I fell back down to Earth.'

'You've come back to me,' Eber stammered. 'Now my path is clear.'

'I've come back,' she assured him, still groggy. 'It's not my time yet.'

'Nor will it ever be,' her brother cut in sombrely. 'We will never taste the water of that well. It is forbidden to those who have chosen the water of life.'

Sárán left them there while he went to look for the Brehon. He had not been gone long when he returned with Lom. His brother had been out with a large party of Fir-Bolg warriors searching the countryside for the place where the river emerged from the depths of the caves.

Sorcha travelled home as quickly as she could, collecting various fresh summer herbs along the way to use in focusing herself on the Draoi skill of the Frith. In her heart she sensed that Dalan was about to face some grave danger.

She rebuked herself for allowing him to venture off into the caves under the influence of the redcaps. Even a trained Fritheoir such as herself rarely undertook such vision journeys, for the pitfalls were many and the perils incalculable.

Many vision travellers had been seduced by the sensual delights of the dreamworld and been lost forever in that place.

When she reached her home in the woods Sorcha set about sealing the house so she would not be disturbed. Just as she was closing the door for the last time the Raven came to her to give a report.

The underground-dwellers, the Sen Erainn, had passed word to the Raven kind that there were intruders in their territory. And they were much aggrieved by the coming of the strangers. But they'd agreed not to approach or interfere with any folk from the world above. As long as their presence was not a threat to the kinfolk of Sen Erainn.

Sorcha told the Raven she intended to bring on the Frith to augur Dalan's whereabouts.

'Once I know where to look for him I intend to summon the shape-shift,' she informed the bird.

The Raven cocked her head, as if only half believing what she heard. 'You'd take such a risk for that Brehon?' the bird quizzed. 'You don't have enough experience to know the signs of danger. Yet you would place yourself in danger for this Druid? Willingly?'

Sorcha nodded determinedly.

'If you're to serve my people in future days you can't afford to foster any such attachments,' the Raven advised. 'Remember you chose to come to us of your own free will. None among my kindred cajoled you or threatened you. It was your own decision. And you've always known the cost.'

'I understand,' Sorcha breathed. 'Don't worry. I won't allow myself to become too attached to the Brehon.'

'You already have,' the bird mocked, clicking her beak to emphasise the point. 'I warned you it would be difficult to follow this path, but you wouldn't listen to me. Now you're going to use the skills I've taught you for your own selfish purposes. I can't say I'm impressed with this turn of events.'

'I'm not doing this for myself. I can't solve the mystery of the Watchers alone. I need Dalan's help. And you never told me I wasn't to practise the skills I'd learned. What's the point of studying the art of the shape-shifter if I'm not permitted to put it to good use?'

The Raven clicked her beak again and raised her wings so they spread wide.

'Very well,' the bird decided. 'I'll allow you to undertake this foolish venture. But I'm coming with you. And if I tell you to leave, you will obey me. Do you understand?'

'I do.'

'Then go about your preparations while I try to take a rest in the rafters. You won't be ready to start your journey till long after sunset so I'll have a chance to get some sleep. I've been on the wing all day at your behest. I think I deserve a little sleep.'

It was long afterwards that the bird awoke to find Sorcha deep in a trance of the Frith. The Raven stretched her wings, yawned loudly and prepared to come to the Druid's aid.

Dalan lay on the rocks with his clothes wet through for what seemed many hours. While the Quicken Brew worked healing wonder on his hurts he struggled to concentrate his thoughts on the journey he'd just undertaken.

It was almost completely dark in this part of the cave. The only light was reflected from the arch where the river poured out into the sunshine of a bright day. But the Druid could not bring himself to leave the gloom yet.

The darkness was unusually comforting. The Brehon felt safe here in this part of the subterranean world. Besides, he knew that the only way for him to leave the cave was to plunge into the freezing river again. He wasn't ready to do that just yet.

As his body mended itself he stared at the cavern roof where a scattering of bright crystal sparkles were laid out like the stars. But his mind would not be reined in. It was overflowing with snippets of vivid recollections of his life and what he assumed were tantalising flashes of the future.

He recalled what Sorcha had said before they'd set out on this expedition. She'd called this cave the Womb of Danu. The Goddess of the Flowing Waters was certainly present in this place. Her voice was the roar of the rapids and her breath was the unexplained breeze that wafted through the deepest caves.

Dalan felt about for his pouch and found the mead bottle. As he pulled out the stopper it struck him that to emerge from this cavern ejected by the river was like a rebirth, a new beginning. Certainly he would never be the same again. He'd discovered qualities in himself which he'd never recognised before. He'd been forced to admit that, despite his training, his discipline and decorum, he was capable of fear, anger and bouts of bitter temper.

As he made this admission to himself he sensed a presence nearby. His first thought was that the Fomor had come upon him again. But then he realised he sensed no hint of malevolence.

Indeed, as he let himself relax, the only sensation he experienced was of a pure nurturing love that enfolded him in the same way a mother's love enfolds her child. Danu was his mother now, he understood. She had guided him throughout his life. She had dusted him off when he'd taken a fall and clothed him in her finest garments as he progressed through the many stages of his Druid training.

He was glad he'd left the Raven-feather cloak with Sorcha. When he emerged from the cave he would be naked as a newborn baby, ready to begin his next incarnation. Perhaps he would even feel capable of accepting the highest honour his order could bestow.

Dalan shook his head. There were more pressing concerns. The Watchers had to be dealt with. They were a danger that could not be allowed to roam freely in the land. He would wait until they were laid to rest before he took the title of Dagda.

He sipped from the mead bottle. The sweet liquor tingled his tongue and brought a fire to his throat. And as it passed into his belly the Brehon understood that even the Watchers were nurtured by the hand of Danu. All things were in her care, whether they seemed good or evil.

'Thanks be to thee, Danu,' he whispered. 'You who brought me from yesterday to today. I will bathe my face in the light of the sun as you've bathed me in your birth waters. Grant sweetness to my mouth, wisdom to my speech. Fill my eyes with love and my thoughts with benevolence. I would travel the land in the likeness of a deer or a horse or in a suit of black feathers if you but desired it.'

He took a deep breath and savoured the taste of the air. Suddenly and unexpectedly the Brehon was overcome by an immeasurable sense of guilt. He was ashamed that he'd lost Eber Finn, Sárán and Aoife in the depths of the cave and failed them in his duty of care. Danu would never have deserted him in his need, he told himself. Yet he'd abandoned his charges to an unknown fate, giving in to the torrent when he could have fought it. When put to the test, his resolve had failed him.

Dalan had always been a hard judge of himself. That was why he excelled at his vocation. Most of the time his self-criticism was healthy and pushed him to greater achievements. But when coupled with a feeling of guilt it could turn him to the darkest thoughts and cripple him with cold lethargy. He was surely wise enough to recognise this trait in himself but he wasn't perfect. There were times when he preferred to indulge himself in feelings of worthlessness.

This was one of those times.

The events of the last few weeks had worn him out. The daily tasks which marked the duties of his profession and the constant worry over the Watchers had taken a heavy toll on his body.

In the half-light of the cave he sighed to release his pain and he was surprised at how comfortable the stone floor felt beneath his back. He vowed to himself that in future he would strive to be more like his guide, the Goddess of the Flowing Waters, Holy Danu, the Mother of the Moon.

The Brehon's eyes remained open, though the lids were heavy; his ears were pricked for the tiniest noise. Long afterwards, when his mind had slowed, it struck him that he should still have been experiencing the effects of the sacred meal. The seeing brew was reputed to be quite powerful. Yet apart from some discomfort and a few minor delusions, he'd not really noticed any significant change in his perceptions.

His mind seemed clear enough, even after the damage he had suffered to his body. He was not ready for such an experience, he concluded; Danu had protected him and kept him from harm.

Filled with shame that he had proved unworthy of the gift, Dalan sat up to listen more intently to the sounds of the eternal underground night. He soon began to feel a chill all through his body so he wrapped Sorcha's cloak around his head and huddled in a ball underneath, his knees under his chin. The damp air had developed a bite as strong as the depths of winter and he was soon shivering uncontrollably.

His feet began to numb just as they might if he'd been foolish enough to go walking in the snow at midnight. Then he realised he was about to succumb to the effects of Sorcha's sacred feast.

At first he was grateful that he'd proved worthy. But then his heart began to race as he worried about being alone on this journey. He had no experience of this induced madness, though he had known a few Druids who had set out on a similar journey of the senses, arrogantly believing they were wise enough to find their own road unaided. Precious few had returned to the land of living consciousness with more than a fraction of their mind intact.

Dalan's senses were as sharp as ever and he wasn't sleepy. He thanked the Goddess his thoughts were relatively calm. If panic set in he knew he could lose his bearings and be lost forever in the realm of delusion.

It was usual for him to become drowsy before he entered the trance state of vision dreaming so Dalan was quite unprepared for what happened next. Just as he beginning to consider starting a small fire to light the area and keep himself warm, a low, ominous boom shook the ground beneath him.

He immediately threw the woollen cloak away from his

head so he could hear each sound in the cave. But the rumbling had already passed like the low growl of far-off thunder. Long minutes passed before another roar shook the floor. It was far more intense and went on for much longer. The final shivers of this boom had just died away when a massive explosion filled the air. Dalan covered his ears, instinctively cowering to protect his head in case the roof should fall in on him.

Every part of the cave shook violently with the shock of the blast. Stones fell from above and splashed into the lake. The Brehon felt the vibrations shaking his stomach until he thought he would surely lose control of his bowels.

Then, without considering the wisdom of his actions, he got up and ran like the wind along a passage that led away from the lake edge. Another roll of booming thunder rattled the cavern floor and Dalan fell against the wall, burying his head in his arms. He wrapped the cloak about his head as if it could protect him from the heavy falling debris.

Rocks fell from the roof and crashed to the ground all around the Brehon. He flinched as small stones hit his head and shoulders, but all the while he kept his face hidden. Slowly the shower of rocks subsided and the thunderclap passed, leaving in its wake a profound silence. Tentatively Dalan took his cloak from over his head but almost immediately he had to shield his eyes from a blinding light.

When he could manage to look around him the Brehon was surprised to see that a large hole had been blasted in the wall opposite. Miraculously all the rock had collapsed around him instead of on top of him.

He stood up and kicked away the debris, relieved that he had found what might be a path back to the settlement of Aillwee. But when he saw what lay beyond the ruined wall, his relief quickly turned to amazement.

There were trees and flowers of every kind and the

babbling of a little stream in the background. The air was bright, dry and full of every insect imaginable. Dragonflies of iridescent green and sparkling gold hummed in tune with the largest bees Dalan had ever seen. There were tiny flies whose bodies shone in every shade of blue and red. Butterflies danced around between the branches and crickets gave their merriment a rhythmic rise and fall.

The Brehon was awe-struck. A few minutes earlier he could have sworn he was far beneath the ground and yet here was honey-golden sunlight and all the living creatures of the world above. Entranced by the glimpse of this garden he slipped through the hole in the wall.

Immediately Dalan's mood changed completely. His heart was filled with such joy that he thought it would surely burst. There was no fear in this place, and he felt an overwhelming urge to throw his arms wide and dance in delight.

As he twirled about the garden all cares dropped away until his head began to swim and he had to stop himself. His stomach was turning but it wasn't the unpleasant retching urge he'd experienced with Eber. This was a drunken heady illness that might well be followed by a headache in the morning.

He forced himself to stand perfectly still so he could observe his surroundings and slow the spinning sensation that threatened to throw him off his feet. Presented to his unbelieving senses was a garden of dreams set among the most luxuriant well-trimmed lawns. There were trees of every variety the Druid knew, and many he did not.

The reddest roses vied for position with tall foxgloves of vibrant magenta, and all the fragrances melded together in an intoxicating mix.

Then he noticed a great gathering of golden butterflies exactly the same as the one he'd seen escaping Máel Máedóc's corpse. It had never occurred to him that the Dealan Dé might delight in flocking together in this manner, hundreds of souls fluttering through the air in a wild frolic.

As Dalan struggled to take all this in, a thick cloud of minute orange beetles swarmed around his head so that he was completely disoriented in the midst of their thronging dance.

When he had managed to brush them away and pick the stragglers out of his ears, the Brehon caught the scent of lavender on the breeze. So enticing was this heady aroma that he had no choice but to follow it to its source.

Soon Dalan was making his way along a narrow, well-worn path that wove its way between apple, birch and oak. Nightshade bordered the path and violets were set behind them, but it was the scent of lavender that lured him on.

At length he stopped to catch his breath and take in all the beauty which surrounded him. As he was about to step out again a green apple fell from a nearby branch and to his amazement it ripened as it plummeted earthward. When he picked it up it was as red as any rose, though its brothers on the tree were still quite green. With that it finally struck Dalan that he must have strayed into the land of dream visions.

He knew it was wrong to eat or drink in that place but he was suddenly shaking with hunger and the apple was too tempting to lay aside. He held the fruit up to observe it and the apple seemed to him to be the most gorgeous thing he'd ever seen. Its skin was smooth, the red shot with traces of green and yellow in the grain. The fruit beckoned to him to take a bite and Dalan couldn't fight against the urge to sink his teeth into its flesh. He lifted the apple to his mouth. His lips parted and his tongue prepared for the sensuous delights of its juices.

The Brehon breathed deeply just as the skin met his lips, and in the next instant his teeth were closing round the precious treasure. The skin crunched under the strength of his jaws and a succulent liquid poured into his mouth, more satisfying than a draught of cold water on a hot day, more sweet than any honey, more intoxicating than the finest mead.

In the same instant the juices touched his tongue, Dalan's head began to spin and a flash of bright white light blinded him. It was so intense he covered his eyes and fell to his knees, dropping the apple as he curled up in pain.

But as suddenly as it had struck him the agony passed and he ventured to look around him once more. The garden was as tranquil as it had been a few moments earlier but the Brehon felt a renewed sense of wonder.

Where the colours had been merely beautiful before he had bitten the apple, they now had profoundly deeper shades. And every flower, every leaf and all the countless buzzing insects were surrounded by halos of pale light. Dalan held up his hand before his face and saw to his amazement that he was bathed in a golden illumination that shimmered through red, brown and violet. Sorcha's cloak was no longer merely deep blue but painted in all the shades of the rainbow.

He searched around him for the apple, determined to take it home with him. But all he found was a brown soggy lump that fell apart when he tried to pick it up. The disgusting mess retained the aroma of the strange fruit but Dalan knew instinctively that it had lost all its magical properties once he'd taken a bite.

Despite the terrifying pain he'd suffered when he tasted the apple, he was completely refreshed and ready to continue his journey. The Brehon got to his feet and looked around him, struggling to understand what he saw.

The scent of lavender came to his nostrils again. Dalan shook his head, hoping to clear his mind, but instead the colours all around him blurred and a dizziness came over him that forced him to lean against the apple tree.

He recalled his childhood teacher talking of the subtle

energies that emanated from all plants and creatures. A few individuals were sensitive to these energies and some were said to be able to see them. Dalan knew then that he'd been granted the gift of such sight, though it made him feel quite ill. He could only hope the talent would soon pass. He blinked his eyes but the colours intensified. He waited a moment, breathing deeply to balance himself.

As soon as he was feeling better he pushed away from the tree, ready to go on. It was then the Brehon caught a glimpse of a huge black shape among the branches. The figure was so dark that it seemed to swallow all light around it. Startled, Dalan took two steps back.

And then for the first time since he'd entered this garden a sensation akin to fear came over him. The black shape shook itself, spreading its wings to reveal its true nature.

It was a Raven.

There are some folk who believe all these birds look the same. Indeed it's difficult for one not born of the Raven kind to tell each creature apart. But Dalan recognised the bird immediately. It had the same menacing presence as the Raven that had perched in the roof timbers of Sorcha's house.

In unspoken acknowledgment the bird turned her head to one side so she could get a better look at the Brehon. Then she shook her feathers again, clicked her beak three times and, to Dalan's initial relief, flew off.

But she wasn't yet out of sight before he regretted her departure. She was the only creature he'd recognised in the illuminated garden. And she had spoken to him once in a dream. The thought struck him that the Raven might be able to answer the innumerable questions that had bubbled up in his brain.

Without another thought he forgot the sweet scent of lavender and took to his heels to try and catch up with the black bird. But the faster he ran the further on the Raven flew, until the Brehon almost lost sight of her among the higher branches of a great yew tree.

By now he had very foolishly strayed from the path and he became entangled in a huge, sprawling blackberry bush. Little thorns tore at his skin and cloak and the more he struggled the worse his situation became.

At last, with the Raven sitting in the yew tree watching him, he gave up the fight and let the blackberry bush hold him up. Dalan's chest heaved from exertion, his head was spinning again and his throat was parched.

Before his eyes were half a dozen berries, sparkling dark buds of moisture. It didn't cross his mind that it was the wrong season for these fruit or that he should be more careful. For the second time that day the Druid, who should have known better, reached out, plucked a fruit and stuffed it into his mouth.

The juice quenched his thirst immediately but a disturbing change occurred. The glow that had surrounded everything abruptly took second place in the Brehon's senses because his ears were alive with sounds such as he'd never heard before.

He was suddenly aware that all the beetles sang a similar song. The butterflies, too, had their own particular chant, and every ant was merrily engaged in a common chorus as it worked. The flowers had the sweetest voices, high-pitched and delicate. The bees serenaded them but their humming was not what Dalan was accustomed to. To his utter surprise the honey-makers seemed to be composing poems in their own language. He could almost pick out the words, though he couldn't understand them.

It was then the Brehon noticed a thrumming melody that underpinned all these various choirs. As he looked about him he realised this was emanating from the trees. And all the different clans, from the oak to the birch and elm, had their own intricate part to play in this symphony of the garden.

The blackberry bush had its own melody too, a sweet lilting refrain that lifted the Brehon's heart so that he couldn't help but hum along. He joined in with the bush and they chanted their tune together. As he became more confident Dalan put a few words to the air and he sensed the blackberry bush wasn't holding him any longer.

It was hugging him close.

As this realisation struck him he tried to stand up by himself and found he wasn't restrained at all. High above in the mighty yew tree the Raven gave a joyous if slightly mocking laugh.

In less time than it takes to draw twenty breaths the Brehon was making his way forward again. His mind was reeling from the intensity of light and sound that bombarded him. Like a drunkard who has lost his way he stumbled over a low stone wall and fell onto a close-clipped lawn bed, the softest bed ever known. The grass was fragrant, moist and refreshing, so much so that Dalan was overcome by the urge to slip into a powerful sleep.

He stood up and noticed the yew tree just ahead of him on the other side of the lawn. He was about to step out toward it when he realised how well tended this garden was. The grass was cut short and there were no weeds anywhere to be seen.

'There must be a gardener!' Dalan exclaimed.

The words were barely out of his mouth when two things happened. First, the Raven spread her wings wide and dived out of the tree directly toward him, and second, the Brehon felt unseen hands tugging at his cloak.

The garment fell to the ground behind him but he was too concerned by the unexpected attack to see to it. In the next breath he was cowering on the grass expecting to feel a biting beak at the back of his neck.

But nothing happened. There was no flurry of wings or

screech of anger. Nevertheless, it was a long while before the Brehon dared look up to find out what had happened.

There was no sign of the bird high in the yew branches, just the ever-present symphony of creation and the illumination which bathed the spirits of all he saw. Dalan breathed more easily and lay back on Sorcha's cloak to take stock of all that had happened.

He closed his eyes to rest them and wished he could have shut his ears in the same manner. It was then he noticed the warmth of the sunlight on his skin and remembered that he was deep within the secret places of the cave. Surely, he told himself, there could be no sunshine in this place.

He opened his eyes again and stared skywards into a deep blue void that was unlike anything he'd ever seen before. The sun was there in the western sky but the stars were also visible as tiny points of light.

The Brehon sat up to admire this new spectacle and as he did so he noticed a movement underneath the yew tree at the far side of the lawn. Intrigued, he got to his knees ready to stand, but before he could get up the figure moved from the shadows into view.

And Dalan gasped in amazement when he recognised the woman's face.

Chapter Twenty

Brocan stayed by the funeral pyre until the last embers were glowing orange and there was nothing left of the old Druid's corpse. Fineen went to where the river flowed into the lake to fetch some fresh water.

When he returned Lochie was waiting, head bowed, behind the king. The Watcher looked up as Brocan stirred and got to his feet.

'You've done your duty to him,' Lochie declared. 'We should envy him. He has set out on his voyage back into the light. May we all be granted passage for that journey one day.'

The king didn't reply. He had spent the long while in contemplation of Lochie's offer of sleep.

'My soul is tired,' Brocan whispered finally. 'I haven't the stomach for living among my own kin. I am the only immortal among them except for my children. Perhaps after I've had some rest I'll have the strength to go on again.'

Lochie hummed a little under his breath to indicate he understood what the king was saying.

'I'm just not sure whether I should trust you. You're a Watcher, a sworn enemy of my people and a Fomorian.'

'I may have lived among the Fomor,' Lochie protested, 'but I was born a Fir-Bolg. I was banished because I disagreed with my king and the High-Druid. All of us were Danaans or Fir-Bolg.'

Brocan raised his eyebrows. 'Dalan told me you were servants of Balor, the warrior king of the Fomor.'

'We were never servants,' the Watcher snapped. 'We were misled.' Lochie moved closer. 'That's all long ago,' he told Brocan smoothly. 'What happened a hundred generations or more ago has no bearing on you.'

He placed himself directly in front of the king to press home his next point. 'What you must understand is that my companion and I are very powerful. We're determined to find a way to break the enchantment that binds us to this world. Whether you decide to accept my offer of rest or not is up to you. But you can't prevent us from carrying out our plan.'

Lochie opened up his palms to indicate he had nothing to hide.

'I'll be honest with you, we've created the perfect conditions for a war. And we've made it obvious that we are to blame for the coming conflict. In this way Dalan will work harder to rid the land of our presence forever.'

'Why would you work for your own destruction?' Brocan asked.

'You'll understand when a hundred generations have passed you by and your yearning for peace has become an agony of regret. I'm offering you some respite from that pain. In return you'll be doing me a great service.'

'What service?'

'If you're out of the way and your son is left to rule, it will be easier to manipulate the situation to my advantage.'

'I don't want my kinfolk to suffer.'

'The world is full of suffering,' Lochie scoffed. 'Even the Quicken Brew has not put an end to that. Even though you may never know ill health or death, there are other kinds of discomfort. Folk will suffer whether I have a hand in it or not. And some will greatly benefit.'

'How?'

'Your children will learn some valuable lessons,' the Watcher replied. 'And from what I've seen of them, a few hard experiences won't do them any harm. But most important of all, the end result will be that the land is rid of my kind. That can't be a bad conclusion.'

'I will have to think more carefully and discuss this with Fineen.'

'He's already made up his mind,' the Watcher said, and Fineen nodded gravely in acknowledgment.

'But don't just take his advice,' Lochie added. 'There are others who decided to take the long sleep.'

As he spoke a woman appeared from out of the shadows behind him. She was dressed in a long green gown of shimmering velvet and about her shoulders was a cloak of fine crimson. Her hair was copper red and it cascaded over her shoulders like a waterfall of fire.

Brocan recognised her immediately.

'Riona?' he gasped, only half believing what he saw.

'Greetings, husband,' she answered and there was such emotion in her voice as he'd never heard before. 'I've come to beg you to come with me to the land of sleep.'

'This is a trick!' the king raged as all the bitterness of separation rose in him and none of the sense of loss he genuinely felt. 'My wife would never return to me.' Brocan shut his eyes so she wouldn't see his rising pain or the tears that threatened to blur his vision. Despite the pain Riona had caused him, he knew he still loved her. And his heart ached to be with her again. But he knew her to be a defiant woman, too stubborn and proud to come begging for anything from him.

'I am your queen,' she retorted. 'I've lived with Cecht these last three winters in the realm of the Otherworld. But for all the gifts I found there, for all the joy I experienced, my life was empty without you. Despite your faults, despite your arrogance and stubbornness, I miss you.'

'Lochie, you've gone too far!' Brocan shouted as he turned on the Watcher. 'I might have considered your offer if you hadn't tried this foolish deception. Riona would never speak like that to me. This is another of your illusions meant to convince me to make a favourable decision.'

He glared at the queen. Then he frowned as the bitterness passed away to be replaced by hope. His unspeakable sorrow at her loss began to well up once more. Brocan was a stubborn man, however. And through all else that he was experiencing it was his only armour against possible disappointment.

He wanted to see Riona but he feared the wounding that would result if this proved to be an illusion.

'Well it won't work. I wouldn't have that woman back if she were the last living soul in my kingdom. She betrayed me and her children. And she deserted her people in their hour of need. She's a cruel, heartless, selfish creature who thinks of nothing but her own pleasure. She can rot in the Otherworld for all I care.'

With these words he turned to storm off up the sandy beach. But he hadn't gone ten paces when he heard a bitter wail that gripped his heart and froze his feet to the spot.

It was Riona.

A great tearing of his spirit threatened to bring Brocan to his knees. He steeled himself and swung round to face the woman he had once called his queen. For a moment he didn't care if this was nothing more than an illusion. An image of her might be the closest he'd ever come to being with her again.

'It's too late for that,' he stated coldly. 'Go back to Cecht. You made your decision and I've made my peace with it.'

Riona spun around and ran off into the darkness. The king

lowered his eyes and stared fixedly at the rocky floor of the cave as tears began to well in the corners of his eyes.

At last he lifted his face to Lochie and spoke. 'I've made up my mind.'

The Watcher waited to hear what he had to say.

'Sixty summers have passed by since my mother bore me. I've already lived longer than any of my clan has ever managed before. I've seen war, death, famine, betrayal and the murder of my dearest friend. It's unnatural to go on indefinitely without rest. My soul yearns for peace.'

'And you shall have it.'

'Will I dream?'

'You will dwell in the land of dreams until such time as you are ready to take up a life in the outside world again. And whenever you wish you may return to the realm of slumber. All you need do is return to these caves and lie down to sleep.'

'Can you guarantee my son will reign as King of the Fir-Bolg in my place?'

'Lom will rule your people. You have my solemn promise on it.'

Brocan smiled grimly, his expression one of relief rather than happiness.

'I will be monarch in the country of rest.'

Lochie nodded. Brocan shrugged at the title which now described his state of being. But he claimed it with pride.

'Then let me be known as the King of Sleep.'

The Brehon stayed on his knees as the woman crossed the lawn and stood in front of him. She held out her slender hand and he thought it was the most beautiful sight he'd ever beheld.

The fingers glowed with a golden light that emanated from the tips and coloured her flesh a deep yellow. Her eyes were bright jewels set in a halo that shone with all the brilliance of a sunset moon in summer.

'I've been searching for you,' she whispered. 'Did you lose your way?'

Dalan couldn't find the words to answer her so he nodded. The woman grasped his hand and helped him to his feet. He was surprised to find that his legs were numb and that it was difficult to keep his balance.

'Can you walk?' she asked.

Again he nodded silently. With her hand still tightly gripping his, the woman led him down to the yew tree. Once he was walking the Brehon began to feel the life come back into his legs.

They skirted the huge tree and came to the crest of a grassy ridge that rolled down onto a verdant plain. There at the foot of the rise stood another tree. It was the same one Dalan had seen the last time he'd wandered in the spirit with his guide Cuimhne.

They stood there for a little while enjoying the fresh breeze against their faces. Dalan closed his eyes, overwhelmed by a sense that he was perfectly safe with this woman. Then he noticed the intoxicating scent of lavender once again. It drowned his senses with its warm cleansing fragrance.

As he opened his eyes he realised the scent originated from the mighty tree which grew at the foot of the ridge. There were many different fruits hanging from its branches, some familiar, some utterly foreign. Its leaves were those of a rowan, painted in countless subtle shades of green. The fine branches intertwined as if woven together by some skilled craftsman. Under and over, under and over, each knotted twist of vines or branches had its own symmetry.

'Shall we go down and sit under the tree?' the woman

offered. 'You've come at a marvellous time. The rowan is bearing its summer crop. There's fruit upon the ground and a carpet of lawn on which to rest your head.'

'Are you my guide?' he managed to say.

The woman laughed. 'No one can guide you but yourself. I'm just a companion on the road.'

'But you've guided me before,' Dalan protested.

'Your own spirit spurs you on.'

As she spoke she took his hand again and began the long walk down a winding path to where the shade of the tree darkened the grass. The closer they came to the rowan the more Dalan was intrigued by the magnificent tree.

'I've never seen anything like it!' he gasped when he realised it was even larger than he'd remembered.

'You've never seen this tree before,' his companion assured him gently. 'You may have encountered her sisters who are scattered round this country. But few folk come here more than once.'

The Brehon sighed to indicate he understood, then, with eyes ever upward, he followed on. With each step his sense of awe deepened until they were very nearly at the bottom of the hill and his heart was beating with excitement.

If he'd stood on the woman's shoulders he wouldn't have been able to reach up and pluck a leaf from the lower branches. Brocan's hall could have been carved out of the rowan's trunk and there would have been room for sleeping quarters as well. What had appeared to be a ring of shade beneath the tree proved to be something else entirely. The grass all around was littered with thousands of tiny rowan berries laid out in a thick, tightly woven carpet of regal red.

'Lay your head down here,' she motioned to him and the Brehon cautiously put a foot on the berries.

The rowan fruit was remarkably soft underfoot.

'Is this the Quicken Tree?' he gasped, eyes raised to the treetop.

'This is the tree which grows in the Land of Promise,' she affirmed. 'All the other Quicken Trees are her children. She is the queen of her breed.'

Dalan looked up into the branches again and a movement caught his attention. In amongst all the magnificently interwoven boughs was an ominous black shape.

The Raven gave a tiny cry no louder than he might have expected a robin to give. But the voice was unmistakably of the carrion kind. He took a step back as the huge bird spread its wings to dive earthwards.

It seemed to Dalan that the Raven never took its eyes from him as it swooped down, and he briefly wondered if it was going to misjudge the distance and hit the ground. But he should have known that a dive from the treetops was a simple matter for one of this kind. The Raven pulled out of the dive suddenly and began instead a circuit of the tree. As it came around for the second time a remarkable transformation took place. The Brehon watched transfixed, hardly daring to breathe.

The air sparkled as if the sky were spewing specks of silver snow. And the Raven grew legs, arms and a human body. All its feathers disappeared the instant it set foot upon the ground.

And Dalan recognised the form it had taken. His heart missed a beat for joy and he ran to embrace his friend, feeling a sense of immense relief that she'd come to him.

'Sorcha!' he sang as he grabbed her in a little dance of jubilation. 'I'm so happy to see you.'

'Who is that woman?' she asked him sternly. 'The one who brought you here.'

'This is Cuimhne,' Dalan informed her.

But even as he spoke the name he understood he had been tricked.

'That's not my name,' the other woman protested. 'I'm called Isleen.'

As he heard the Watcher's voice the Brehon felt a faintness descend upon him. And if it hadn't been for Sorcha he would have fallen down where he stood. She wrapped her arms about him to hold him up and he hugged her as tightly as he could.

'You're a Watcher,' he groaned when the power of speech returned to him.

'You're an Ollamh Brehon,' she teased.

'Why did you bring me here?'

'I don't want you to forget me,' she shrugged. 'I'm hoping you've found an answer to our little dilemma.'

'I believe I've found a song that may release you both from your enchantment,' Sorcha cut in.

The Watcher's eyes lit with excitement but it was an unnatural brightness that made Dalan and Sorcha turn their faces away.

'I'm happy to hear this news,' Isleen nodded. 'I've come to let you know that you have until Samhain Eve to effect your remedy. If on that night Lochie and I are still abroad in the land, you and all the people of this island will know what real havoc is. Hear me well, Ollamh Dalan the Brehon. Our patience is wearing thin.'

'Why can't you give us a little more time?' Sorcha pleaded. 'We want to help you. You must believe that. But this pressure is unnecessary.'

'Is it?' Isleen scoffed. 'One day perhaps you'll understand how I feel. Until then you can take my word for it. Every moment has become an unbearable agony. Every breath is an eternity of waiting. My soul is wasting away. My spirit is hungry for rest. And I will do everything in my power to gain that rest. Even if it means the destruction of the Gaedhals.'

'How are the Gaedhals involved in this plan of yours?'

Dalan demanded. 'They have no quarrel with you nor you with them.'

'Don't I?' she spat. 'I have a grudge against all those who possess the gift of death and do not value it. The Gaedhals will not escape my wrath.'

'Why can't you simply wait until we've discovered the cure for your malady?' Sorcha cried. 'Why must you continue to spread such misery?'

'It's my nature,' the Watcher replied with a shrug. 'I may show compassion now and then when the mood takes me, but I was commissioned to bring chaos and disorder. It's all I've ever known. You can't really expect me to change, can you?'

'What compassion have you ever shown?' Dalan retorted.

'I admit it is rare,' Isleen shot back. 'Lochie is guilty of that trait more than myself. He's already offered the long sleep to the Danaans who have not gone into the Otherworld and to the Fir-Bolg.'

'The long sleep?' the Brehon repeated.

'When death cannot touch you, sleep may comfort you. Brocan and Fineen are resting deeply now in a secret place beneath the earth. And there they'll remain.'

'You've made them prisoners?'

'One day when the weariness strikes you, Dalan, you'll understand. But I suppose by that time I'll be long gone. I won't be able to help you to find the Land of Slumber.'

As she spoke, her form shimmered and she rose into the air until she could reach out to pluck a branch from the tree. Three thick interlinked vines broke off together in the shape of a staff. Once she had this in her hand she dropped back down to the ground and held it out for Dalan to take.

'Accept this gift,' the Watcher told him. 'I'm unaccustomed to granting such indulgences but I want to thank you in advance for all your good endeavours.'

'I don't want a reward,' the Brehon replied, shaking his head.

'Take it, you ungrateful little nobody! Who do you think you are? To refuse a gift from one who has supped with heroes, danced among immortals and shared the beds of kings. Take it!'

'I don't need a staff.'

'That's where you're wrong,' she declared, and with a mighty swing of the branch she struck Dalan just below the knee. The knee dislocated and he fell over in agony clutching at his leg.

Sorcha was by his side in a second. Her skill in the healing arts was insignificant compared to Fineen's but she knew how to comfort such an injury. Dalan fought her off at first but then he succumbed to her insistent ministrations.

He lay down on his back in the rowan berries and it was then he noticed Isleen had disappeared.

'How did you come to be here?' the Brehon asked Sorcha as she put her hands to the collar of his tunic and untied the bindings that held it tight about his neck.

'I come here often at the command of the Queen of the Raven kind,' she answered in a formal tone.

She lifted the tunic up over his head and wrapped it into a tight ball. It was a simple pillow but Dalan was grateful of it.

'We'll be home soon,' she soothed as he struggled to keep his eyes open. 'Don't let yourself fall asleep. Stay awake with me until the healing is done.'

Under the influence of the Quicken Brew it wasn't long before the pain had ceased to burn at Dalan's knee. Then he stretched out properly upon the carpet of berries, thinking that it was the finest he could remember.

He placed his hands behind his head and lay on his back, drinking in the heady fragrance of lavender as Sorcha gently stroked his hair. Now he could discern other scents mixed in with it and he struggled to identify them all. Apple was the strongest. There was a hint of rose too, but he couldn't name all the other spicy aromas. When he opened his eyes to ask his companion she was kneeling beside him, slowly untying the binding of her own tunic.

Fascinated by the delicacy of her hands he watched her nimble fingers at their work. When the cords were free she slipped the garment over her head and Dalan felt a sudden urge to reach out to her and hold her close.

The mystical glow that had enveloped the garden was gone. Sorcha's flesh was a healthy pale pink, but he was too shy to look anywhere other than directly into her face. When she'd rolled her tunic up she laid it down beside his head and for the first time his eyes strayed down across the smooth skin of her shoulders.

Her arms were crossed self-consciously over her breasts as she stared down at him with eyes full of loving tenderness. The Brehon lifted his trembling hand to touch her lips with the tip of his finger.

She closed her eyes and gently kissed his hand. And before Dalan was fully aware of what had happened they were locked in a passionate embrace there under the Quicken Tree on a carpet of red berries in the Land of Promise.

Chapter Twenty-One

Lochie sat himself down at the gaming table, a flat slab of rock lying on its side by a tall tooth-shaped standing-stone in the cleared circle at the heart of a wood. His opponent spread out the Brandubh cloth and set the pieces in their starting positions. Her eyes sparkled with merriment as she watched him fill two cups with mead. When all was ready she handed him the white king.

'You may begin when you're ready,' she told him.

He placed the piece in the central square where the High-King always commenced the game. Then he moved one of the four lesser kings into a strategic position to initiate play.

Isleen didn't hesitate. In a moment, seemingly without thought, she'd moved one of the twelve dark Raven pieces. Lochie gave a breathy snigger but didn't respond immediately. He took careful note of all the possibilities, thoughtfully determining the best course of action.

Then he picked up a piece opposite the central square and shifted it along to a new position where it could easily be taken. In a flash Isleen had surrounded this lonely white sacrifice and it was removed from the game.

Lochie was anything but disappointed.

'You're too hasty,' he told her. 'You don't look at all the possibilities.' As he spoke he shuffled his High-King out from its sanctuary and moved it to the edge of the cloth. 'Some-times it's better to concede a little ground in order to achieve a long-term ambition.'

Isleen brushed the wild red hair from her eyes and stared him down.

'That was one of the quickest games I've ever played with you,' he chortled victoriously. 'You slip your guard too often. You should take more care.'

'And you're just upset because I won our little wager,' Isleen countered. 'Aoife will marry Eber Finn. I knew it from the start. Mahon was never right for her.'

Lochie gathered the pieces together and began setting them out for another round. 'I wasn't aware our wager was settled,' he remarked casually. 'Eber and Aoife haven't wed yet, have they?'

'They will do so soon enough,' she promised. 'I've seen to it that Eber understands the value of such a match.'

'Have you indeed? And is he a man ruled entirely by duty or obligation to his position?'

'He will do as I advise.'

'And what of his heart?'

'Men like Eber Finn have no heart,' Isleen asserted. 'Their ambitions are solely focused on kingdoms, wealth and prestige. No woman could ever give him that.'

'So there's no chance he might fall in love if the right woman came along?'

Isleen looked at her companion with suspicion.

'What are you up to?' she asked.

'Nothing! I was just asking a question. Surely he's as vul-nerable to a beautiful female form as any other man.'

Isleen picked up the High-King to take her turn with the white pieces.

'The wager isn't settled until Eber marries Aoife,' Lochie added. 'So I wouldn't be so confident of victory if I were you.'

'The war will start before winter. On the feast of Samhain Eve they'll be wed with great ceremony and celebration.'

'The war!' her companion exclaimed. 'I'd almost forgotten about the coming conflict. We've done well, haven't we?'

'Let's wait and see.'

'What of the Brehon?' Lochie asked.

'He's enlisted the help of a young woman Druid who knows something of the song-maker craft. With her Draoi skill at the Frith and his determination I'm certain we'll be free before midwinter's day. That is, if the war doesn't distract them.'

'It will stir them to more diligent researches,' Lochie assured her. 'Have faith.'

'What, in mortals?' Isleen scoffed, making the first move of the new game.

'But the Brehon has partaken of the Quicken Brew,' he reminded her. 'He's no longer mortal. He'll live forever if he so chooses.'

'Will you tell him there is a way to avoid that fate?'

Lochie shook his head. 'No one ever helped us,' he reasoned. 'Why shouldn't the Danaans and the Fir-Bolg find their own solution? It's enough that there is a way to end the imprisonment of the Quicken. In time they'll discover it.'

Isleen raised he eyebrows sceptically, then said, 'It's your move.'

Lochie picked up a piece seemingly at random and moved it across the board to a position where it was vulnerable to attack. Then he confidently sat back with his hands behind his head.

Isleen took a long while to make her next move. When she did Lochie's piece was still on the board.

'You're too suspicious,' he told her.

With an exaggerated sweep of his hand he moved another dark Raven into line with his first one. A single white playing piece was wedged between them. This he lifted up and placed down at his feet.

'You open yourself up to capture,' he dismissed. 'You should try to see the world for what it is.'

'Aoife is in love with Eber Finn,' Isleen grunted, put out by the capture of her piece. 'No force on Earth could stop her wedding him.'

'She'll bed him, that's certain,' Lochie quipped. 'But a wedding takes much more finesse, forethought and foolishness. And she lacks the first two.'

'What becomes of our wager if it isn't settled by Samhain Eve? Or if we are freed of our enchantment before Aoife makes up her mind?' Isleen asked.

'I hadn't considered that possibility,' Lochie admitted. Then an idea struck him. 'If she hasn't married Eber by Samhain, you should concede the wager to me.'

Isleen laughed. 'But if her mind isn't set on Mahon either,' she hummed, 'then I have won.'

'Very well!' Lochie agreed. 'You may consider the challenge laid down afresh.'

Dalan lay on his back for a long while, staring at the ceiling and trying to recall how he came to be in Sorcha's house in the middle of the woods. The fire was burning brightly in the central hearth and the Raven which usually perched in the rafters was nowhere to be seen.

He was still drowsy and rather confused. His last memory was of entering the strange underworld garden through a gap in the cave wall. The Brehon found himself wondering what had become of Brocan. He prayed silently that the king had found his way out of the Aillwee without being captured by the Fomor.

Suddenly he began to question his whole experience among the Fomorians. He was certain none of that race lived anywhere within the borders of Innisfail. He asked himself if it could have been the legendary people known as the Sen Erainn who'd accosted them. But his mind was too weary for such thoughts and he soon drifted into a hazy observation of the rafters where many varieties of herbs hung slowly curing in the smoky atmosphere.

At length he realised his throat was parched dry. He lifted himself up a little in the bed and to his surprise discovered that he was completely naked under the furs. He blushed at the thought of Sorcha undressing him while he was still unconscious.

At his side on the floor he found a jug of water which he snatched up and put to his mouth. When he'd had enough he placed the vessel down again and brought up a belch of air.

Suddenly there was a movement beside him and the furs were thrown back. Dalan nearly jumped out of the bed in fright.

'Can you pass me the jug?' Sorcha asked as she rolled over.

Underneath the furs she wasn't wearing a stitch of clothing. The Brehon's jaw dropped open in surprise but he made no move to lift the water jug.

'What's the matter?' she laughed. 'Haven't you ever woken to find a naked woman beside you in bed before?'

'I usually recall getting into bed with her,' Dalan stuttered.

'You were in no state to remember anything. It was all I could do to bring you back from the garden in the Land of Promise.'

'The Land of Promise?'

She sat up and ran a hand through his hair to soothe him. 'You really don't remember anything do you, you poor dear?'

Dalan was speechless, embarrassed that he had no recollection whatsoever of what must have been a remarkable experience.

'Water?' Sorcha sang.

The Brehon sprang into action, handing her the water jug and watching in wonder as she drank her fill.

When she'd finished she leaned over him to place the empty vessel back on the floor. Dalan shuddered to feel her warm flesh pressed hard against his own.

'You really don't remember anything of our little adventure, do you?' she laughed softly.

'I can't say that I do.'

'Can you bring to mind the tree? The carpet of rowan berries?'

Dalan shook his head.

'Then let me refresh your memory,' she whispered.

With that she snuggled in close to the Brehon, took his hand in hers and kissed his fingers one by one.

The long column of Fir-Bolg warriors and chieftains came to a halt at the edge of Lough Gur the day before the midsummer feast. A hundred folk gathered from across the Burren gazed in stunned silence at the view presented to them. Such a spectacle had not been witnessed since before the days of their grandsires.

The shimmering waters had retreated. The once mighty lake had withdrawn. And the waters that remained lapped against muddy banks. Dun Gur was no longer an island. A causeway, laid with stones to form a road, now linked the fortress to the shore.

Dalan, Sorcha and Lom stood together on the grassy slope

that led down to the stone path. No words passed between them but their eyes spoke of their dismay. The Brehon recalled his promise to the Raven that he would protect the lough. Clearly he would have to bring all his influence to bear on Eber if he was to keep his vow.

Sárán pushed forward through the crowd, dragging his sister Aoife behind him until they were shoulder to shoulder with their brother.

'What are you waiting for, Lom?' he asked. 'We should be getting on. There's much to be done before sunset.'

His brother woke from his half-dream and stared into Sárán's eyes with deep concern. 'What has happened to the waters?'

'The Goddess Danu is angry with the Gaedhals,' Sárán explained.

'Don't be ridiculous!' Dalan laughed. 'The Lady of the Flowing Waters doesn't punish her own children. She is our Mother. The lough is drying up because there has been no rain for three moons.'

Sárán tightened his lips. He knew there was no point in arguing with the Brehon, whose opinions were highly regarded by Lom. But Dalan would not always be around to advise his brother, the new king of the Fir-Bolg. So Sárán kept quiet. For now.

'The waters will return when the skies open up again,' the Brehon assured everyone. 'There is no omen in this.'

'Dalan is right,' Sárán agreed cannily. 'Today we enter into an alliance with the Gaedhals which will ensure the survival of our people and our lands. Lough Gur is welcoming us. See, the road before us is passable. We'll be the first warrior band ever to march up to the gates of this fortress. This is a clear sign that the future is bright for our kindred.'

Dalan grunted indignantly and rolled his eyes at the opportunism of this young fellow. But Sorcha grabbed the

Brehon by the elbow and squeezed it tightly to indicate he should not be so open with his criticism.

Sárán went down to the mud bank with Aoife still in tow. He dipped his hand into the dwindled lough and tasted the waters.

'Lough Gur is as sweet as ever,' he declared.

Dalan clenched a fist and turned away, ready to address the crowd. But he didn't get the chance.

'Let him be,' Sorcha whispered. 'We have more important matters to be concerned about. Don't be worrying about what that lad has to say. He's quite capable of making a fool of himself without any help from you.'

'He hasn't even been properly welcomed into the Druid orders yet,' Dalan hissed under his breath. 'Who does he think he is?'

'Lom chose him as his adviser,' Sorcha reminded him. 'And Brocan endorsed Lom's leadership of the Fir-Bolg. The chieftains will soon choose a better king and a worthier Druid to the task. In the meantime they can do no real harm.'

'Bring forward the weapons!' Lom commanded.

His voice cracked with nervous tension but no one seemed to notice. Soon everyone in his retinue had a sword or spear and a great bronze shield. Only the Druids refrained from taking up the weapons.

When Lom saw that all was ready he called out to his brother. 'Are you ready, Sárán?'

'I am.'

'Then lead us into the fortress.'

Aoife and Sárán climbed back up the bank, their feet caked in mud to the ankles. They quickly cleaned their boots on the grass then made their way to the head of the column. After a few whispered words between them they set off over the stone causeway toward the waiting watchmen on the other side.

The Gaedhals had gathered on the bank to watch the

spectacle of the approaching force and sentries ran this way and that sounding the alarm. Before Sárán and his sister were halfway over, a hundred warriors of the Fian were waiting in three close-knit ranks to block their way.

The Gaedhals lowered their spear points as the two came closer and halted. Sárán turned to his brother and waved. Then Lom set out across the causeway followed by all his warriors in their battle array. Only Dalan and Sorcha stayed put.

As the Fir-Bolg marched in four broadly spaced lines they hummed a stirring chant that was proud and threatening. The Fian closed their ranks, lifted their shields and gave an answering call that sounded like a pack of hounds howling in unison.

'This is foolishness!' Dalan sneered, but Sorcha hushed him.

'They're warriors. They have their way and we should respect it.'

'I wish I knew what those two lads had in mind. To come to this fortress armed for a fight is worse than stupid. Even with the causeway laid down the Gaedhals would easily hold the gates. They haven't got a chance of defeating them.'

The gathered Fir-Bolg halted half a dozen paces from where Aoife and her brother were standing in front of the spears of the Fianna. The song abruptly ceased as they lowered their weapons ready to make a charge.

'Who comes here to Dun Gur, armed for war?' a voice challenged from behind the ranks of battle-ready Gaedhals.

A warrior stepped out through the forest of spears. His sword swung in his hand and his shield was at his shoulder. On his head he wore a helm fashioned from bright gold and across his body he wore a yellow breacan cloak.

Every Fir-Bolg warrior recognised Eber Finn, but tradition demanded that he identify himself. Sárán bowed and threw open his cloak so the Fian could see he was a Druid and unarmed.

'Who would stand in the way of the kindred of Lom mac Brocan, King of the Fir-Bolg of the Burren?'

'I am Eber Finn. I rule the people of the Kingdom of the Southern Gaedhals.'

He took his time to observe the grim warriors who faced him down.

'There is peace between our peoples. A naked blade is not a sign of friendship.'

At those words Lom stepped up past Sárán and Aoife with his sword pointed to the ground.

'I am the king of these folk,' he declared. 'I've come to bless the hand of my sister who has chosen to wed with Eber Finn of the Gaedhals.'

'It's unwise to whip a willing horse,' Eber quipped.

'I'm not here to fight you,' Lom smiled.

As he spoke he lifted his weapon high in the air. Then he swung it around his head and tossed it as far as he could into that part of the lough where a deep pool remained. The bronze sword skipped across the water with a mighty splash and then it was gone.

Before Eber understood what was happening, all the Fir-Bolg followed their king's lead. Swords, spears, shields and harness fittings all flew into the water on each side. So astonishing was this sight that the Fian let their spear points drop to the ground and looked at each other in confusion.

'As you see,' Lom declared, 'we are unarmed.'

Then Eber understood exactly what the young Fir-Bolg king had done and he gazed admiringly on the lad.

Dalan laughed. Now he could plainly see Lom's plan. With one stroke he had put himself on equal standing with Eber. If the Gaedhal was so desperately in need of a Fir-Bolg alliance, he would have to arm the warriors of the Burren himself. And that meant the Fir-Bolg would no longer bear the weak bronze in battle. They would carry iron. Perhaps Lom would not be such a foolish king after all.

'I see a hint of your father in those eyes, King Lom,' Eber noted. 'Your people are welcome. But first I have a gift for you.'

The ranks of the Fian parted and a man struggled forward bearing another on his back.

'I present to you Tuargain the wheelwright and Méaraigh the blacksmith,' the Gaedhal announced. 'The one is blind and the other is lame but they are the finest craftsmen my people have to offer. They will live among your folk and teach you the mysteries of iron-making.'

'And if you'll arm us with your weapons we'll fight faithfully by your side,' Lom added.

'I will do so,' Eber promised. 'Now come into my home and feast with your friends. Let's talk not of war but sing songs of love. Tomorrow I'll wed Aoife of the Sparkling Eyes and our alliance will be as solid as stone forever more.'

A cheer went up from the Fir-Bolg ranks and that was closely echoed by another from the Gaedhals. Then the two opposing groups of warriors ran toward each other to embrace. Eber waited until Lom, Sárán and Aoife approached him. He took each brother by the hand and welcomed them heartily, then he noticed Lom was still carrying the bronze axe of kingship.

'Will you throw that into the lough also?' Eber asked.

'I have another fate in mind for this,' Lom answered enigmatically.

Aoife caught the Gaedhal's eye at that moment and Eber's face lit with admiration.

'You'll be Queen of the Gaedhals by Samhain if you wish. Or earlier if you desire it,' he told her.

'I don't care,' she told him with a shrug. 'As long as you are my husband I'll be content.'

The two of them shone like bright torches, each trying to outdo the other with the light of their joy. A piper struck up a dance then, a strange melody such as only the Gaedhals knew how to play, and everyone began an impromptu celebration there in the middle of the new causeway.

Sorcha and Dalan watched the proceedings from the bank, happy enough to stand by and not take any part.

'Will you take up the position of adviser to Eber Finn?' Sorcha asked.

'I am honoured that he asked me,' Dalan replied. 'But I'm not sure I'll have the time to perform my duties to the full satisfaction of the king.'

'He'll be looking for a steady guiding hand. Before Samhain Eve I'm convinced he'll be sorely tested. And I don't doubt that Sárán and Lom will also need some reining in.'

'Have you seen this in your augury?' the Brehon laughed.

'I have divined this through the Frith craft and by my intuition.'

'And what can you tell me of the Watchers?'

Sorcha shrugged and looked down at the muddy ground.

'It is beyond my skill to see such things,' she admitted. 'Perhaps the Watchers are preventing me from seeing too much.'

'I wish I knew what has become of Brocan,' Dalan sighed. 'If he were here I'd feel a little more at ease about what is yet to come.'

'I've searched for him with all my skill. And the only vision which came to me was of Brocan sleeping peacefully by the shores of a huge black underground sea.'

'I believe I know the place you're speaking of,' the Brehon told her. 'I hope he rests well in his dark kingdom under the earth. I'm sure he wouldn't have been happy living among us. The Quicken Brew was such a heavy burden to him.'

'Perhaps in time we'll begin to understand how he felt,' Sorcha offered. 'I pray we don't turn out as bitter as the

Watchers have.'

'I'll not be bitter as long as I can stand with you,' Dalan blurted.

Sorcha smiled at his clumsy manner and took his hand gently in hers.

'Then let's wait here a while longer and let the others have their celebration. For we should make the most of our time together. Who knows where the road will lead us tomorrow.'

Epilogue

F all in love with the dunghill and you won't mind the stink. A traveller told me that. He was searching the world for his long-lost love and not doing a very good job of finding her. So I told him that honey is sweet but only a fool would try to lick it off a thornbush.

My argument didn't sway him at all. When we parted he went off trudging the roads again, full of hope, high ideals and sickening optimism. Poor ignorant fool, so typical of your folk. But I'll tell you more of him another time.

If I sound like a scornful old bugger, remember you've only heard part of my tale. So I'll forgive you for misjudging me.

Here's another good saying. You must have heard it. The eye of a friend is the best mirror. I don't know about you but I've never mastered the art of looking at myself. No one really does, do they? We're here to be mirrors for one another. We've all got stories to tell. In my tales you'll likely find something of yourself. We all walk the same road, it's just some of us get lost along the way or choose to be waylaid or set ourselves down to sleep too long.

I've met travellers aplenty who've abandoned themselves in the Forests of Greed. I've seen the haunted eyes of those who glimpsed the burning bridges which span the River of Fear.

I've heard the anguished cries of those who've tarried too long in the Valley of Doubt.

There are countless diversions to distract you from the road. Keep a watch on yourself. Don't forget who you are or where you're going. Your ancestors forgot once. So foolish of your kind.

It would have been better if they'd stayed beyond the Ninth Wave. I've told you all about the Ninth Wave, haven't I? It was not so much a warning as a reminder to those who lived on the island of Innisfail not to stray too far from home. To cross the Ninth Wave was to go beyond the help or hope of their kinfolk who dwelt on shore.

The world beyond the Ninth Wave is wild and unpredictable. Only storms or invaders ever came from there. And sometimes both.

When the Gaedhals sailed into their waters the Danaans used arcane songs and music to conjure a mighty storm. Waves and breakers the height of ten ships bore down upon the invading fleet, scattering boats in every direction. The initial rage of the storm dispersed the main body of sea craft, sending many straight to the bottom of the ocean.

In the midst of this turmoil, Amergin the Bard stood up on the steerage deck of his Gaedhal ship and raised his hands to the sky. Then he spoke a poem over the ocean spray which calmed the furious gale and settled the surface of the sea. You may have heard about it. They say he was the greatest Bard who ever lived. He wasn't a Bard's belch compared to one fellow I used to know.

But that's a different story. As I was saying, with all those wild winds blowing and waves crashing down, you'd expect the Gaedhals to have turned around and sailed back to the lands of Iber, made the best of things there and told everyone to steer clear of the Danaans. But your folk are renowned for their stubbornness. A goat is always just getting into mischief or just getting out of it, as my father would have said.

Iobhar imparted his foolishness to Mahon after their banishment. I'll tell you what became of them another time.

So now you know two-thirds of my tale, and if you're patient I'll return when my belly is empty and relate the rest of it to you. A Raven will happily dance until he's fed. Then he'll fly off again, only to return when scarcity prompts him to beg.

That's the Raven game.